HRJC

The Great Pencil Quest

another WALLACE the BRAVE adventure

Will Henry

Andrews McMeel
PUBLISHING®

NOV 2023

Complete Your Wallace the Brave Collection

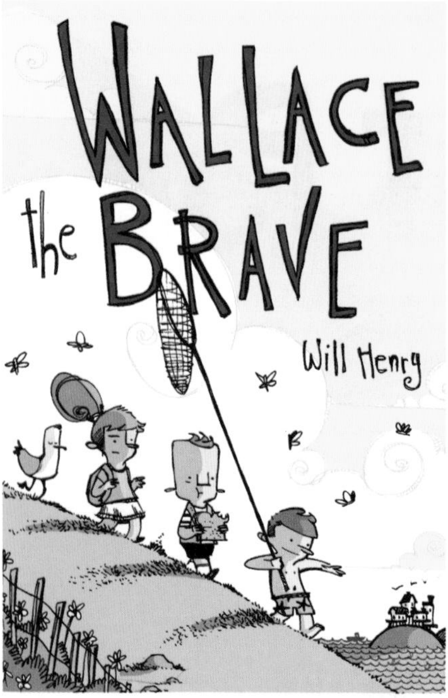
WALLACE the BRAVE
Will Henry

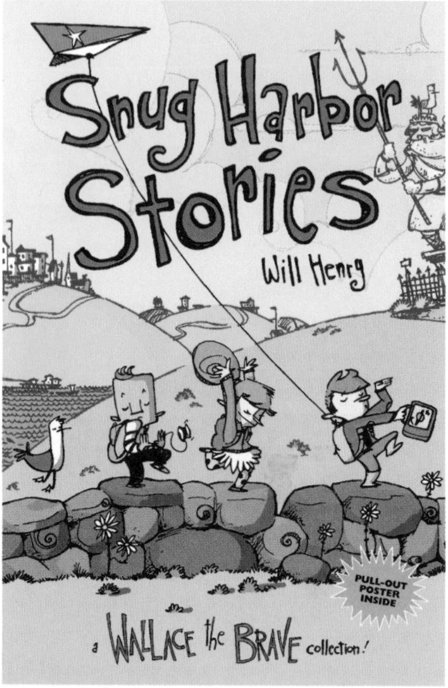
Snug Harbor Stories
Will Henry
PULL-OUT POSTER INSIDE
a WALLACE the BRAVE collection!

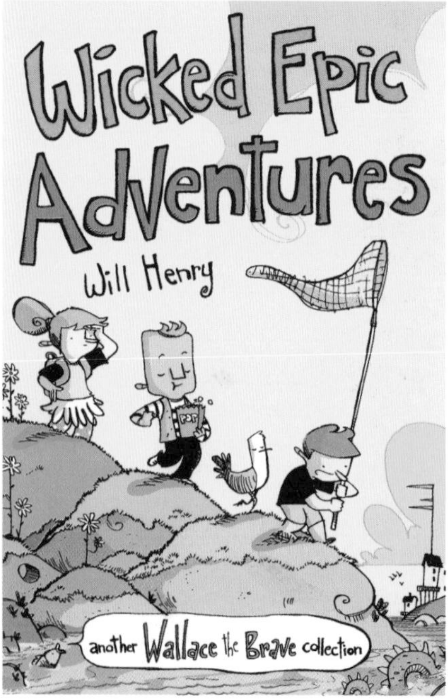
Wicked Epic Adventures
Will Henry
another Wallace the Brave collection

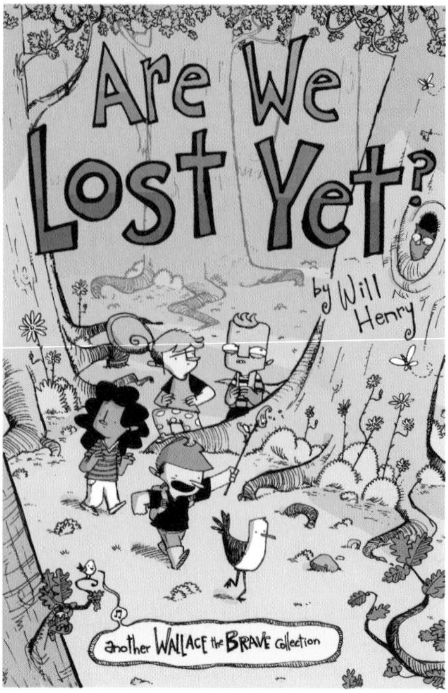
Are We Lost Yet?
by Will Henry
another WALLACE the BRAVE collection

to my mother

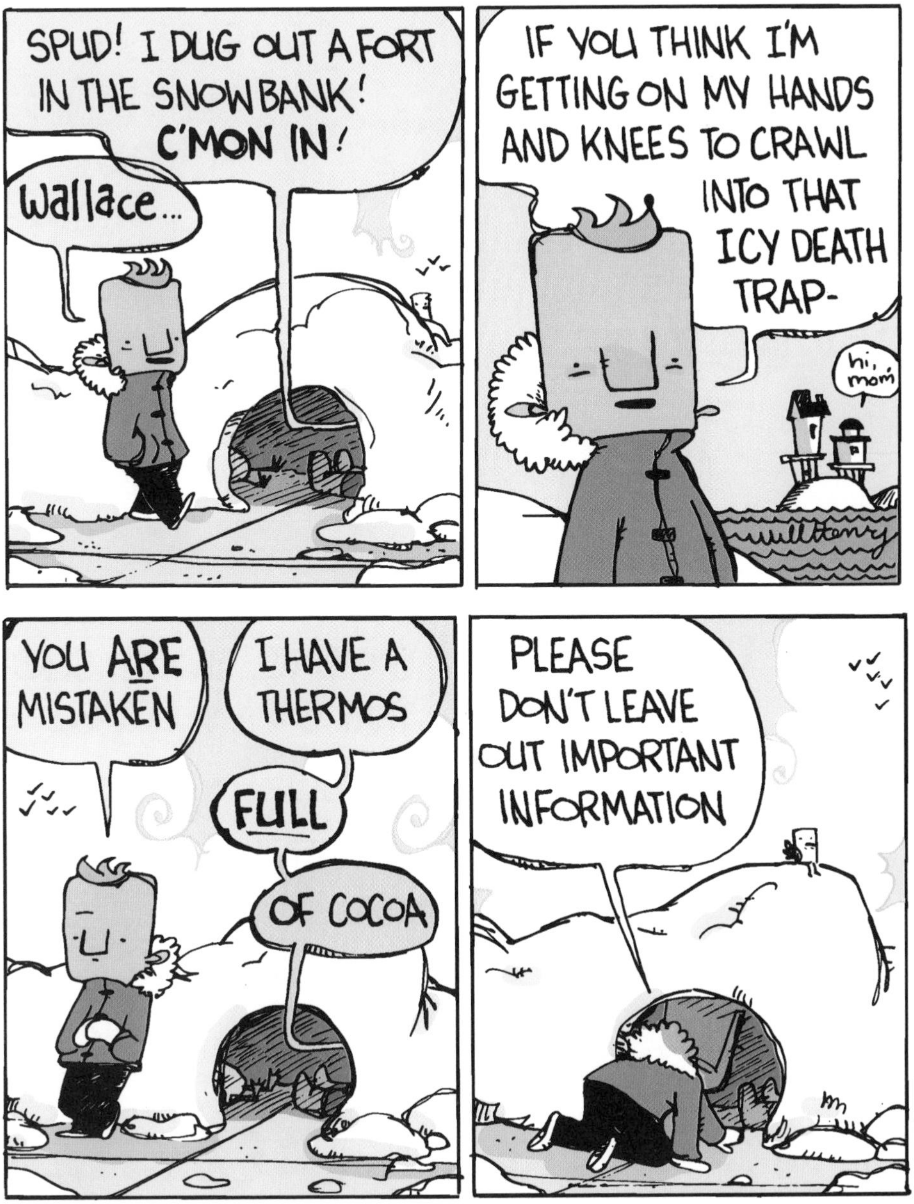
SPUD! I DUG OUT A FORT IN THE SNOWBANK! C'MON IN!
wallace...
IF YOU THINK I'M GETTING ON MY HANDS AND KNEES TO CRAWL INTO THAT ICY DEATH TRAP-
hi, mom
YOU ARE MISTAKEN
I HAVE A THERMOS
FULL
OF COCOA
PLEASE DON'T LEAVE OUT IMPORTANT INFORMATION

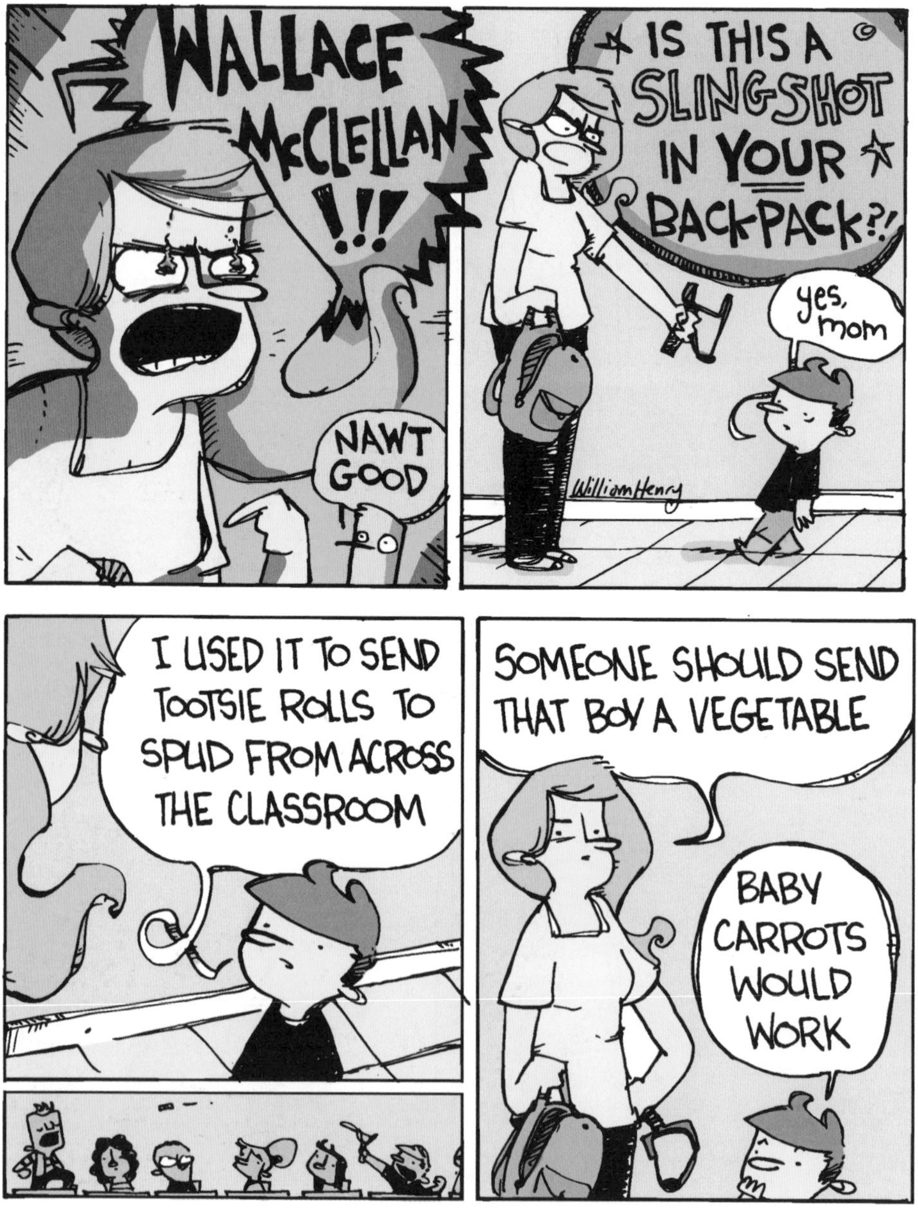
WALLACE McCLELLAN !!!
NAWT GOOD
IS THIS A SLINGSHOT IN YOUR BACKPACK?!
yes, mom
William Henry
I USED IT TO SEND TOOTSIE ROLLS TO SPUD FROM ACROSS THE CLASSROOM
SOMEONE SHOULD SEND THAT BOY A VEGETABLE
BABY CARROTS WOULD WORK

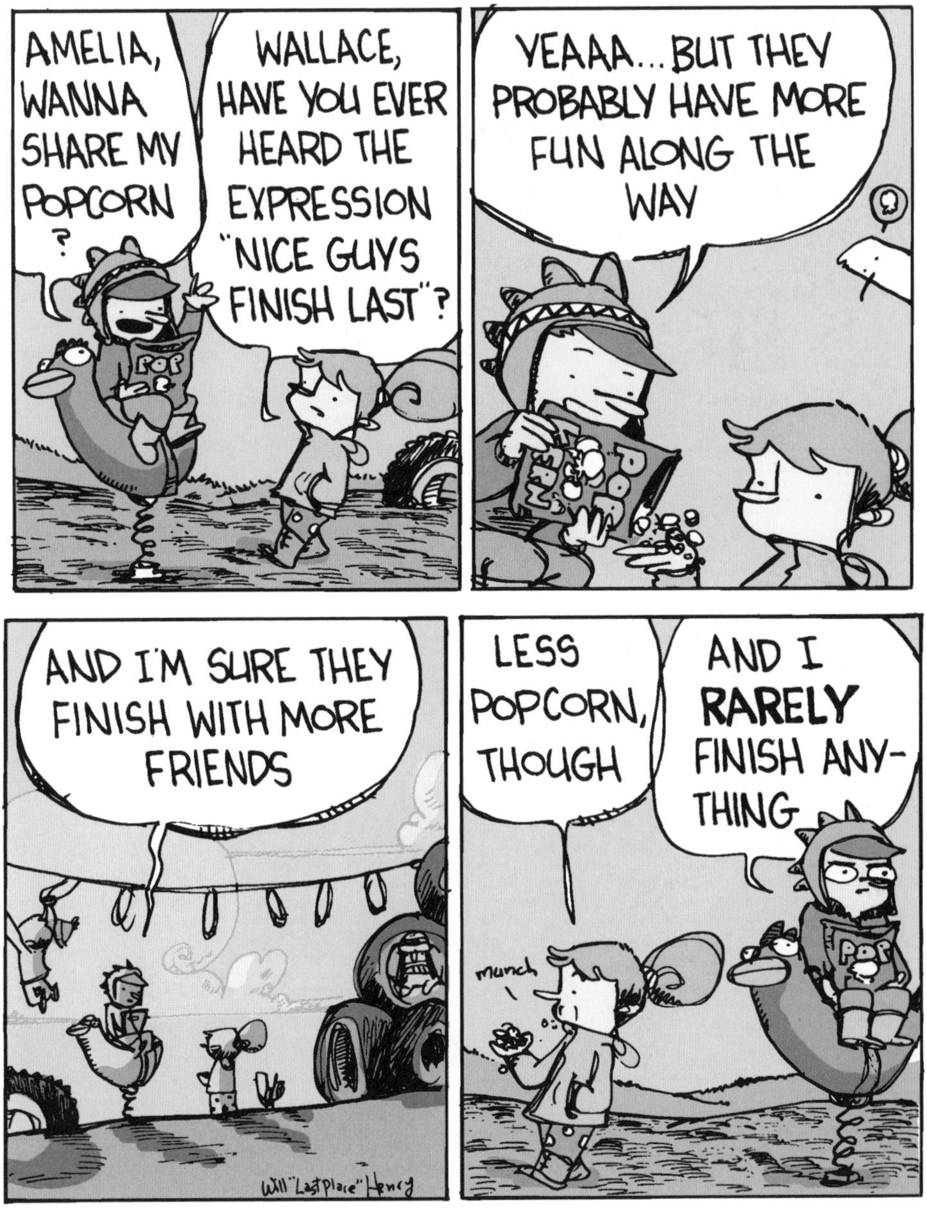
AMELIA, WANNA SHARE MY POPCORN?
WALLACE, HAVE YOU EVER HEARD THE EXPRESSION "NICE GUYS FINISH LAST"?
YEAAA... BUT THEY PROBABLY HAVE MORE FUN ALONG THE WAY
AND I'M SURE THEY FINISH WITH MORE FRIENDS
LESS POPCORN, THOUGH
AND I **RARELY** FINISH ANY-THING
munch
Will "Lastplace" Henry

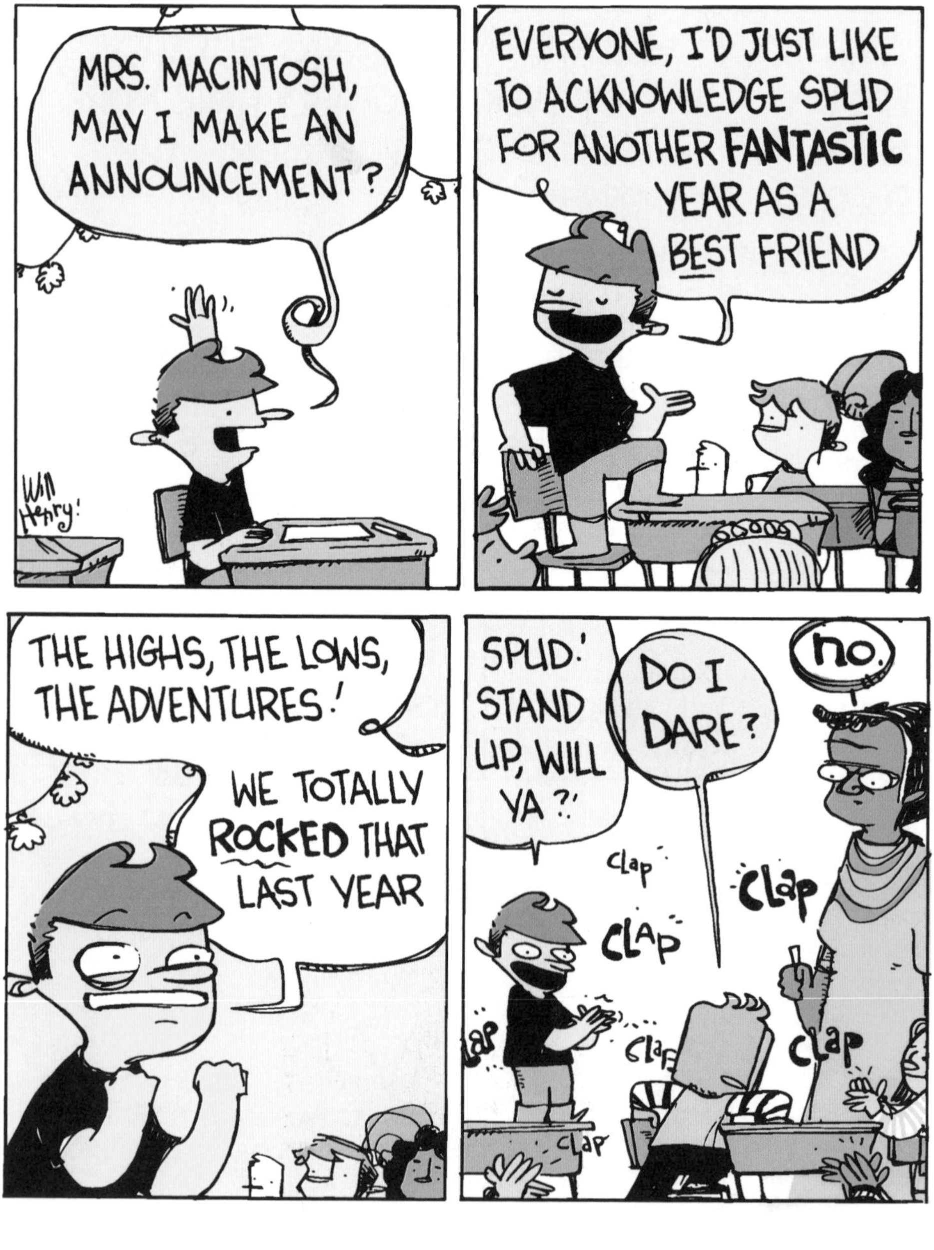

MRS. MACINTOSH, MAY I MAKE AN ANNOUNCEMENT?
Will Henry!
EVERYONE, I'D JUST LIKE TO ACKNOWLEDGE SPUD FOR ANOTHER FANTASTIC YEAR AS A BEST FRIEND
THE HIGHS, THE LOWS, THE ADVENTURES!
WE TOTALLY ROCKED THAT LAST YEAR
SPUD! STAND UP, WILL YA?!
DO I DARE?
no.
CLAP
CLAP
CLAP
CLAP
CLAP
CLAP

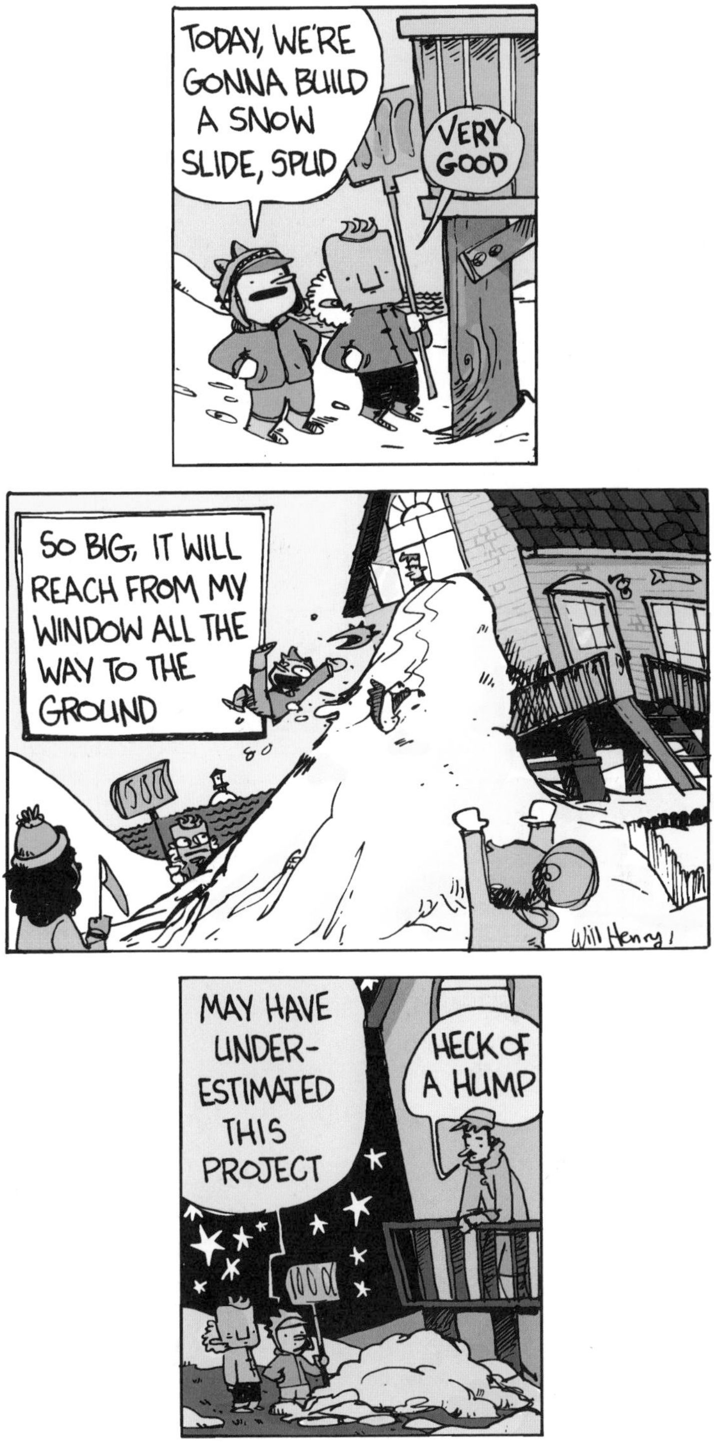
TODAY, WE'RE GONNA BUILD A SNOW SLIDE, SPUD
VERY GOOD
SO BIG, IT WILL REACH FROM MY WINDOW ALL THE WAY TO THE GROUND
Will Henry!
MAY HAVE UNDER-ESTIMATED THIS PROJECT
HECK OF A HUMP

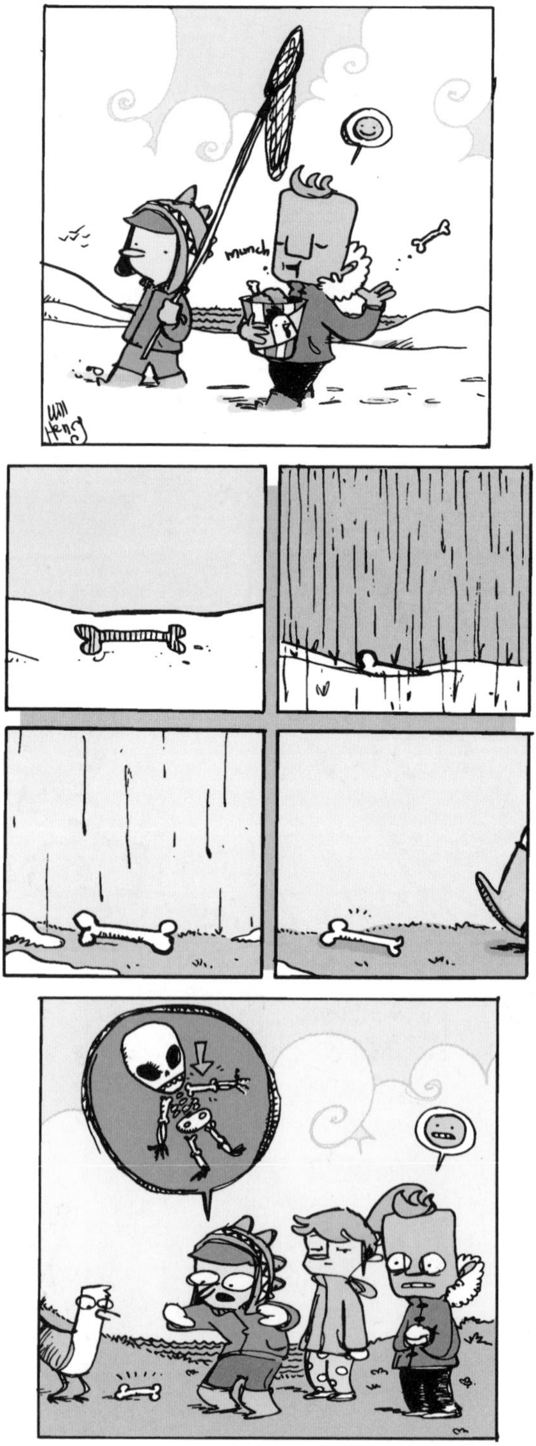
munch

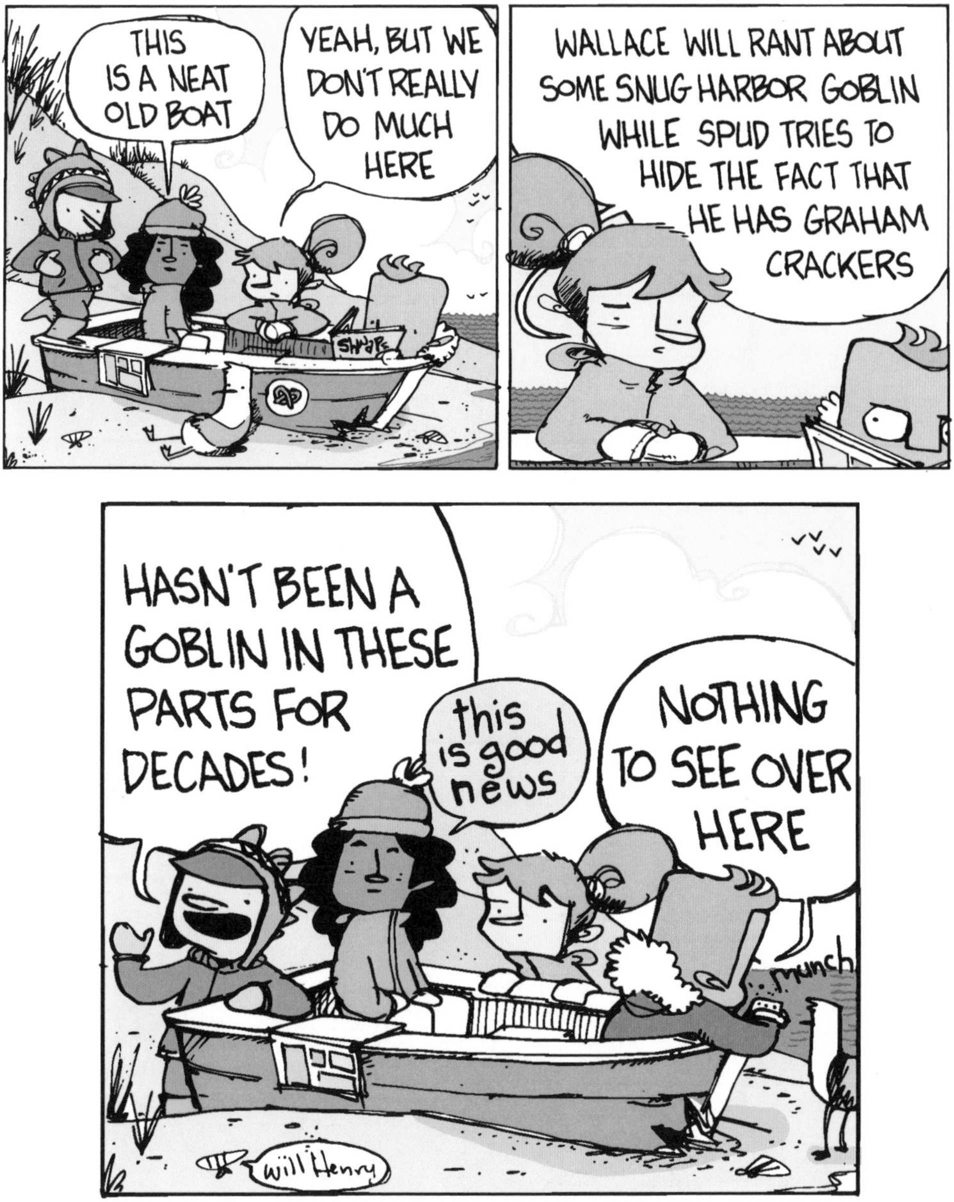
THIS IS A NEAT OLD BOAT
YEAH, BUT WE DON'T REALLY DO MUCH HERE
SWAPS
WALLACE WILL RANT ABOUT SOME SNUG HARBOR GOBLIN WHILE SPUD TRIES TO HIDE THE FACT THAT HE HAS GRAHAM CRACKERS
HASN'T BEEN A GOBLIN IN THESE PARTS FOR DECADES!
this is good news
NOTHING TO SEE OVER HERE
munch
will Henry

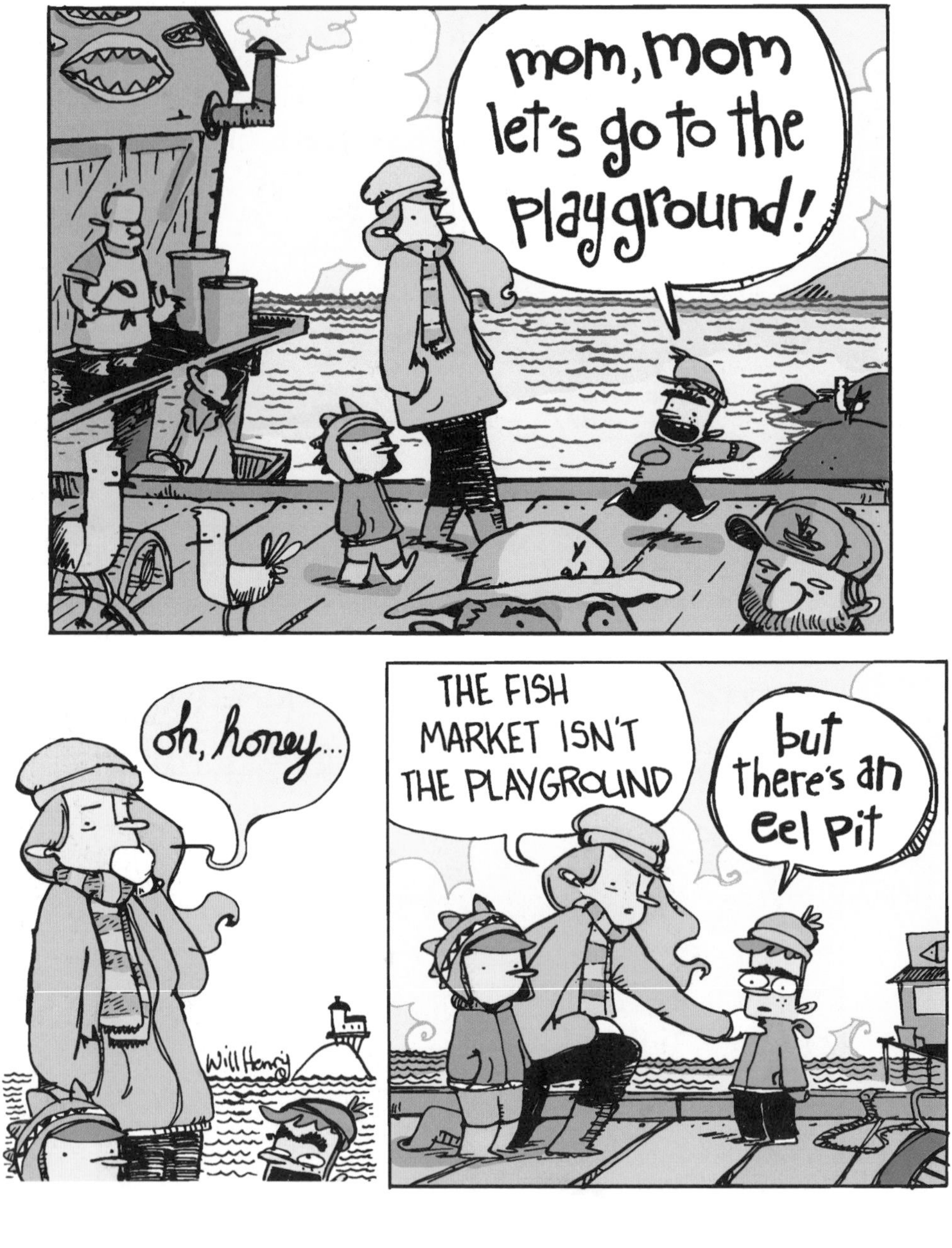
mom, mom let's go to the playground!
oh, honey...
Will Henry
THE FISH MARKET ISN'T THE PLAYGROUND
but there's an eel pit

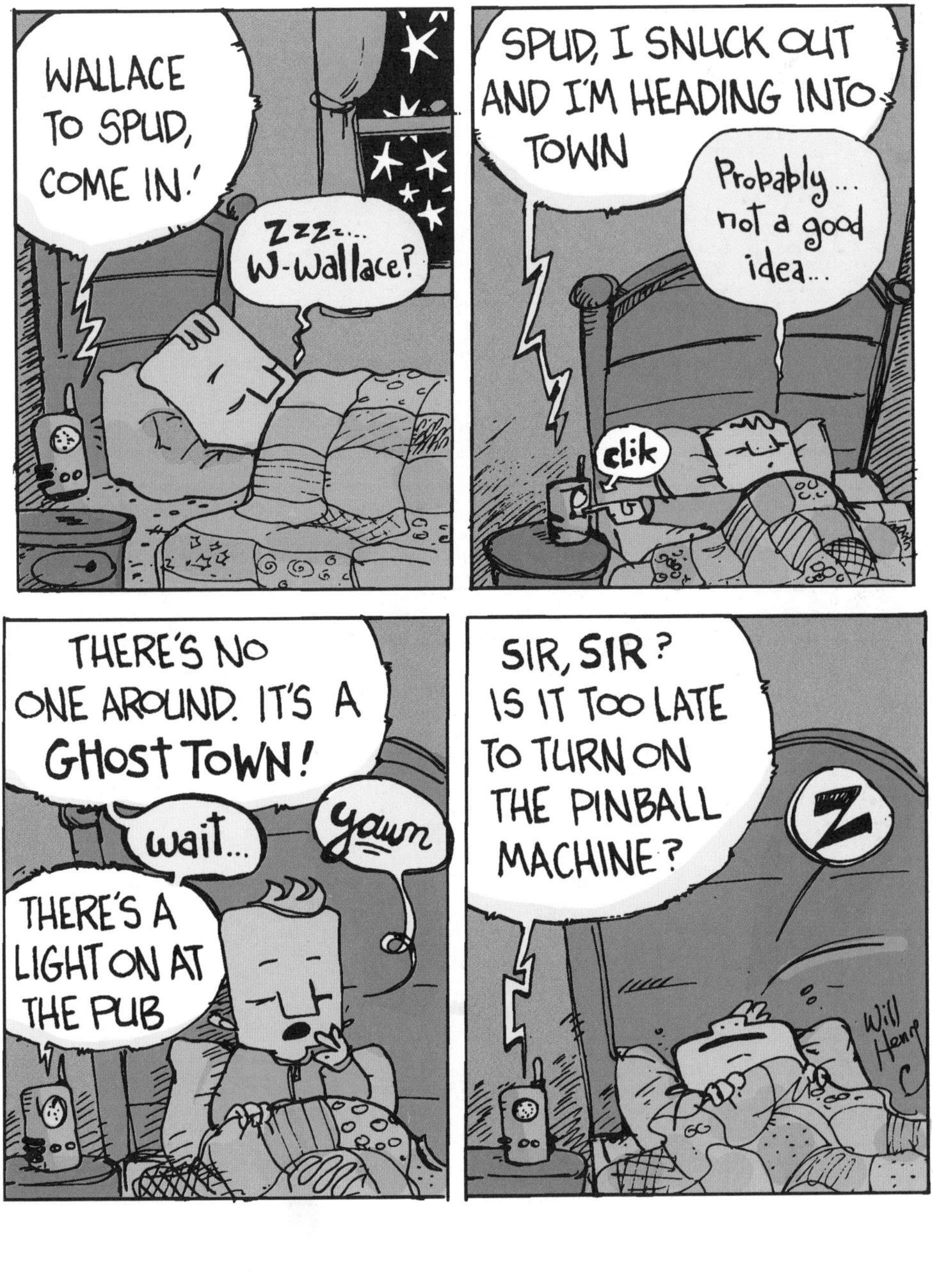
WALLACE TO SPUD, COME IN!
ZZZz... W-Wallace?
SPUD, I SNUCK OUT AND I'M HEADING INTO TOWN
Probably... not a good idea...
clik
THERE'S NO ONE AROUND. IT'S A GHOST TOWN!
wait...
yawn
THERE'S A LIGHT ON AT THE PUB
SIR, SIR? IS IT TOO LATE TO TURN ON THE PINBALL MACHINE?
Z
Will Henry

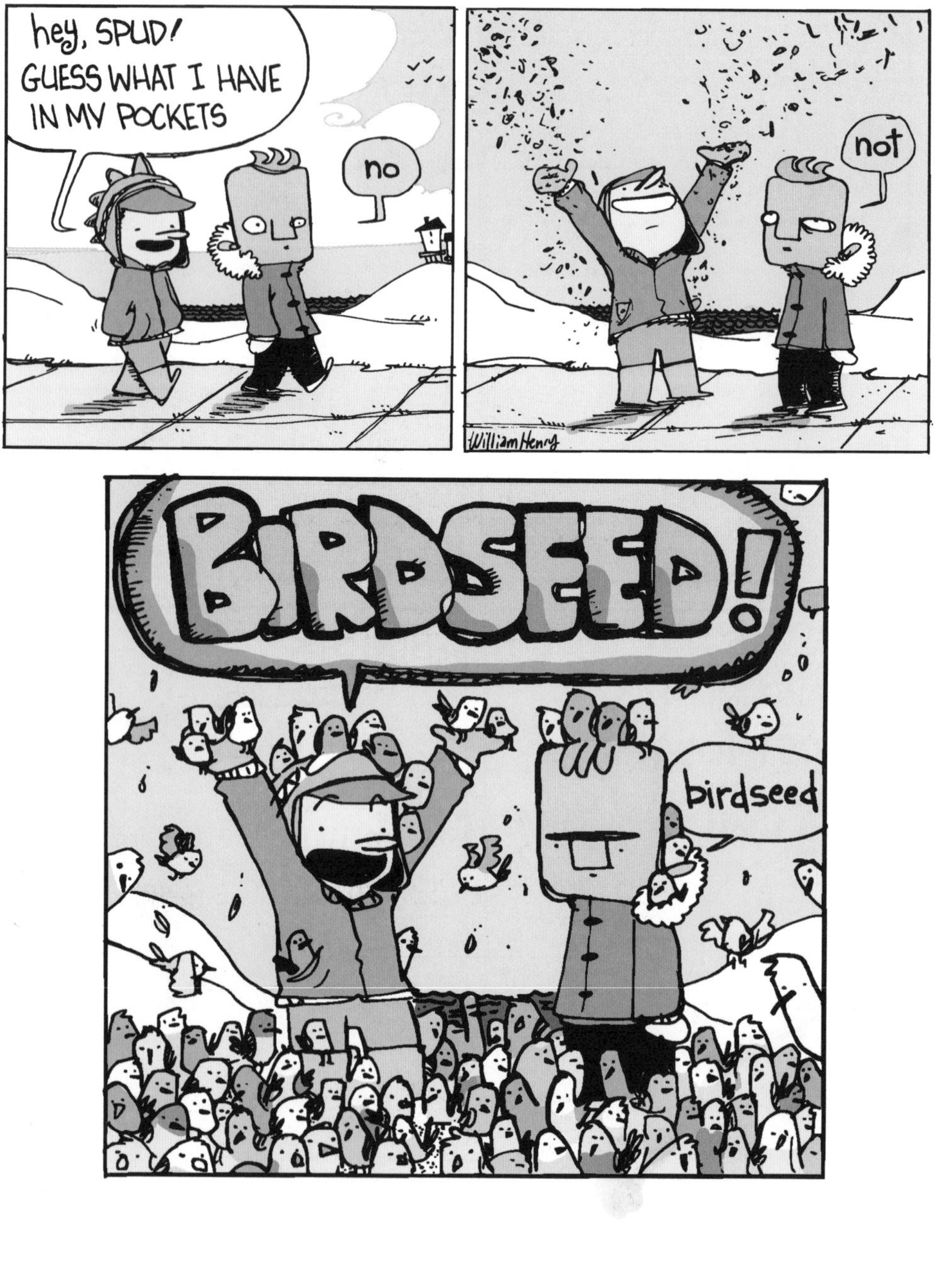
hey, SPUD!
GUESS WHAT I HAVE IN MY POCKETS
no
not
William Henry
BIRDSEED!
birdseed

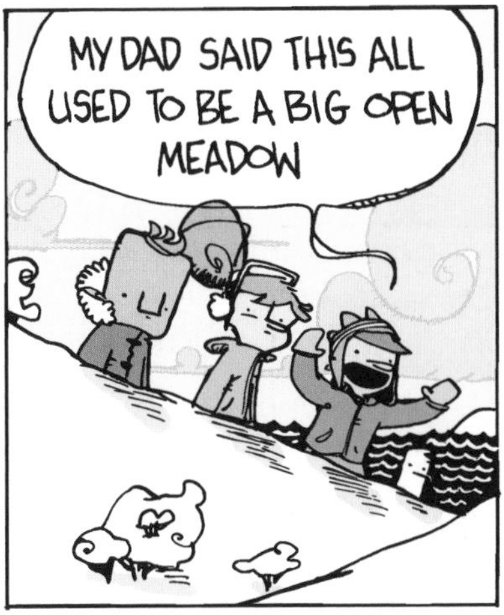
MY DAD SAID THIS ALL USED TO BE A BIG OPEN MEADOW

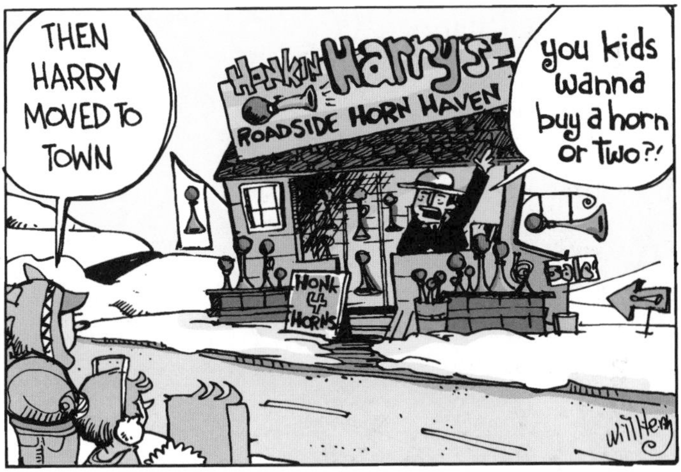
THEN HARRY MOVED TO TOWN
HONKIN' HARRY'S
ROADSIDE HORN HAVEN
you kids wanna buy a horn or two?!
HONK 4 HORNS
SALE

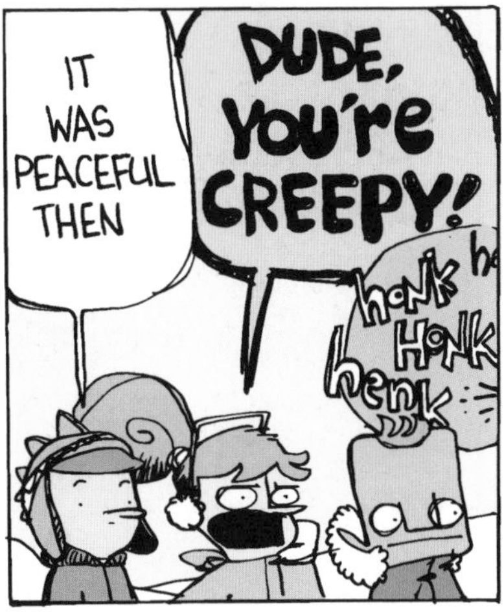
IT WAS PEACEFUL THEN
DUDE, YOU'RE CREEPY!
honk HONK henk

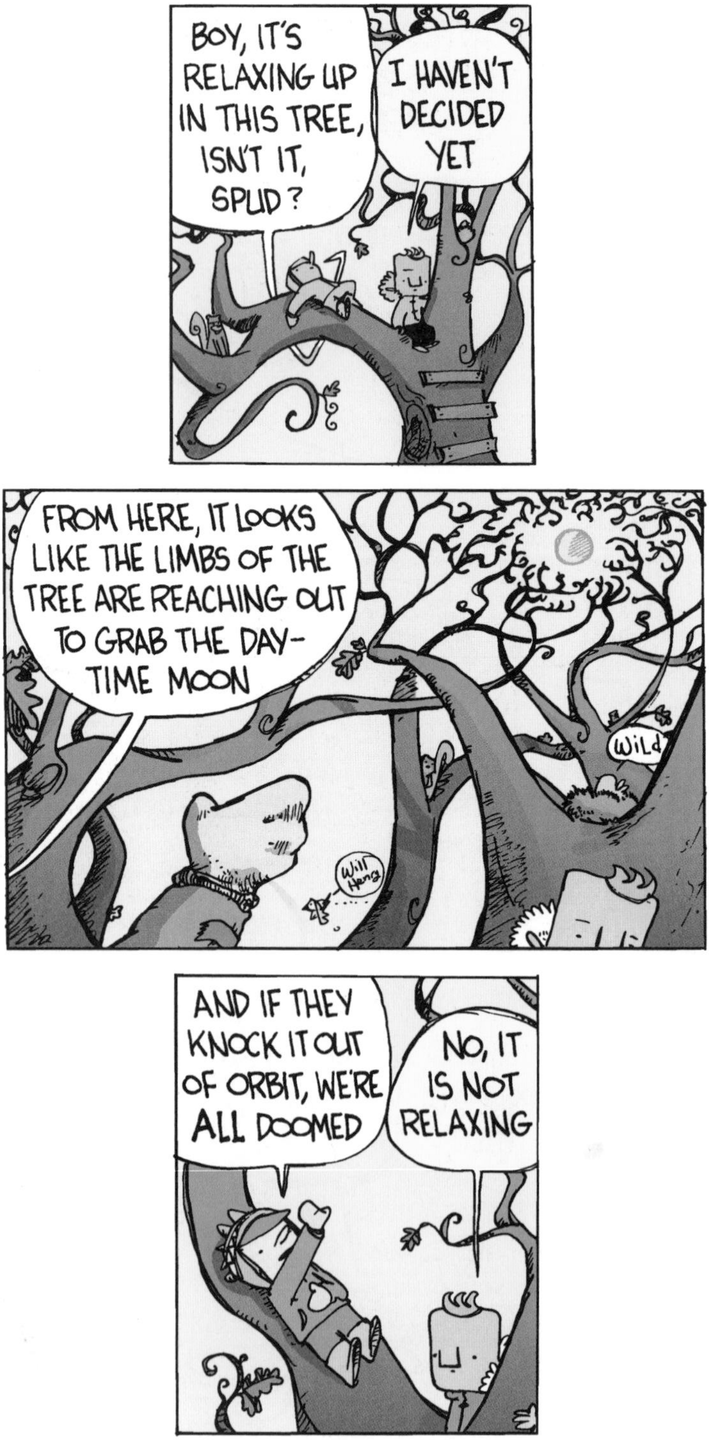
BOY, IT'S RELAXING UP IN THIS TREE, ISN'T IT, SPUD?
I HAVEN'T DECIDED YET
FROM HERE, IT LOOKS LIKE THE LIMBS OF THE TREE ARE REACHING OUT TO GRAB THE DAY-TIME MOON
WILD
AND IF THEY KNOCK IT OUT OF ORBIT, WE'RE ALL DOOMED
NO, IT IS NOT RELAXING

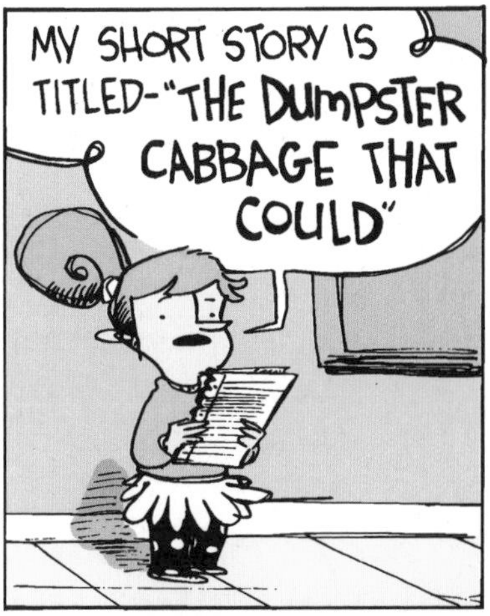
MY SHORT STORY IS TITLED-"THE DUMPSTER CABBAGE THAT COULD"

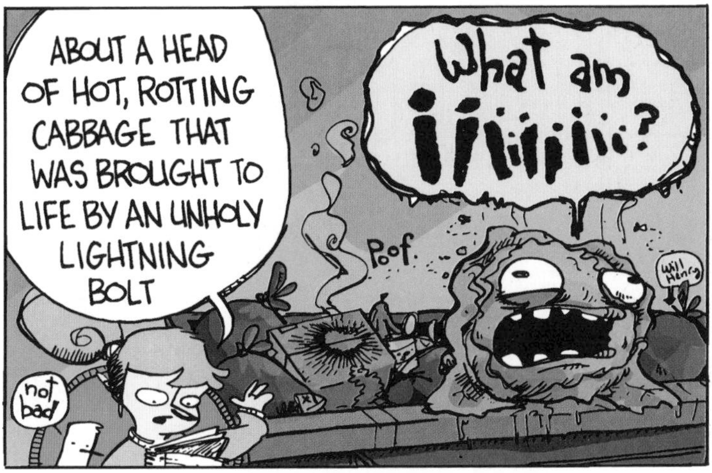
ABOUT A HEAD OF HOT, ROTTING CABBAGE THAT WAS BROUGHT TO LIFE BY AN UNHOLY LIGHTNING BOLT
What am iiiiiiiiiii?
Poof.
Will Henry
not bad

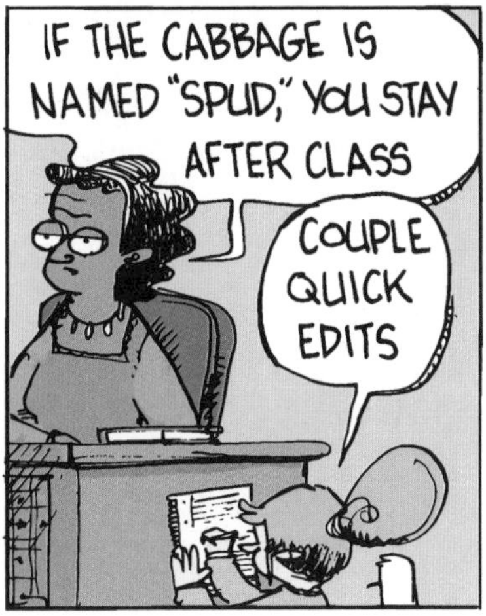
IF THE CABBAGE IS NAMED "SPUD," YOU STAY AFTER CLASS
COUPLE QUICK EDITS

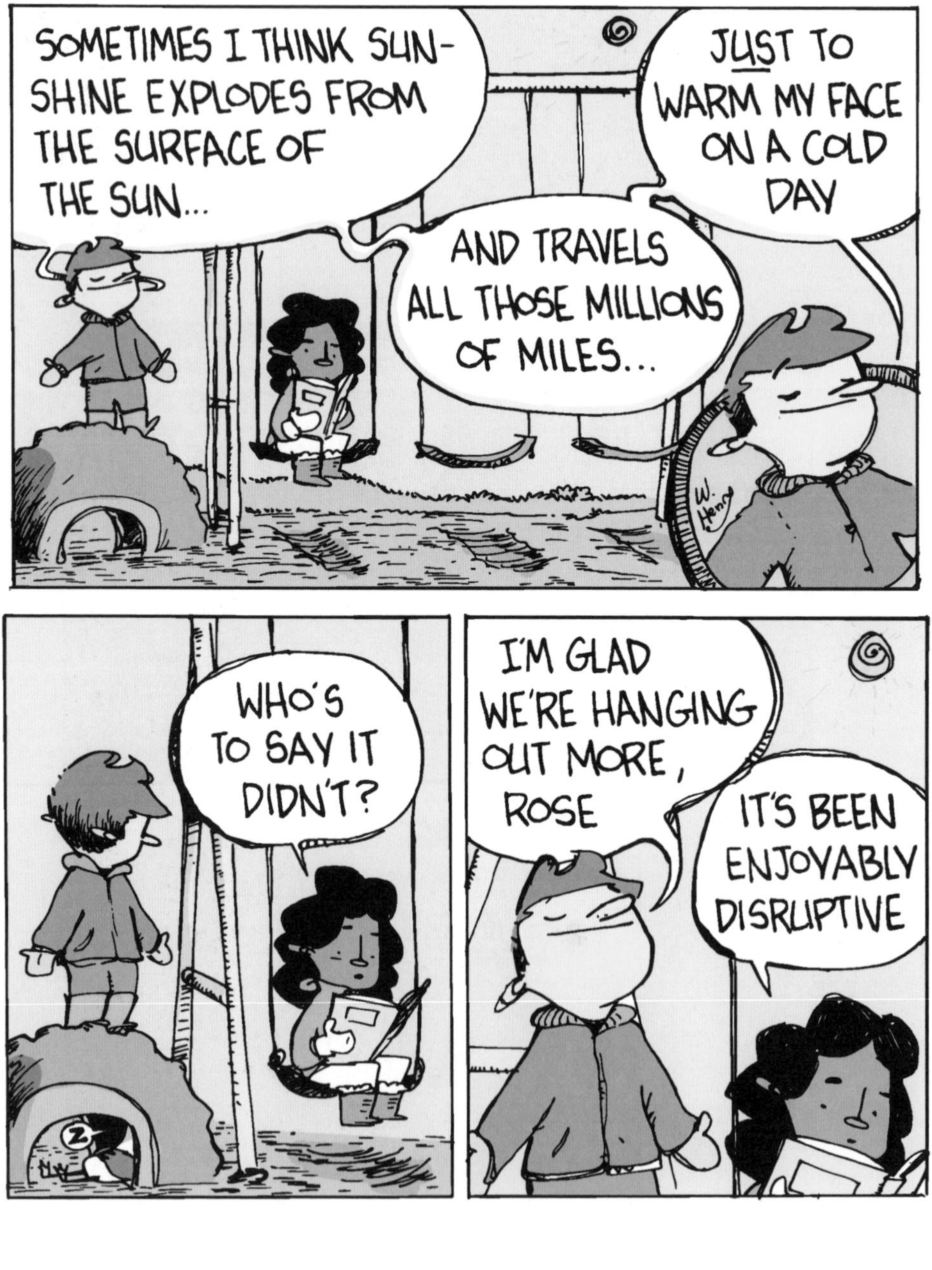
SOMETIMES I THINK SUN-SHINE EXPLODES FROM THE SURFACE OF THE SUN...
AND TRAVELS ALL THOSE MILLIONS OF MILES...
JUST TO WARM MY FACE ON A COLD DAY
W. Henry
WHO'S TO SAY IT DIDN'T?
I'M GLAD WE'RE HANGING OUT MORE, ROSE
IT'S BEEN ENJOYABLY DISRUPTIVE

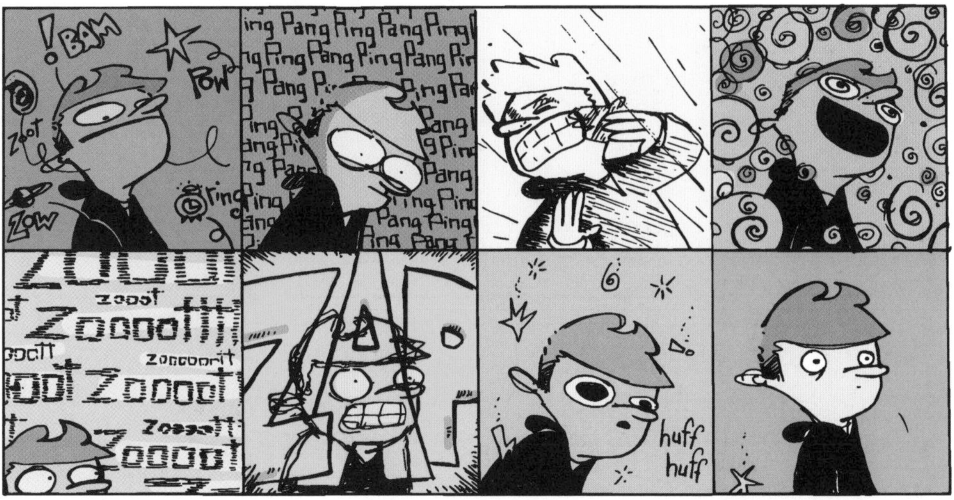
BAM
POW
Zoot
Ring
ZOW
Ping Pang Ping Pang Ping
Ping Pang Ping Pang
Zooot
Zooooott
huff
huff

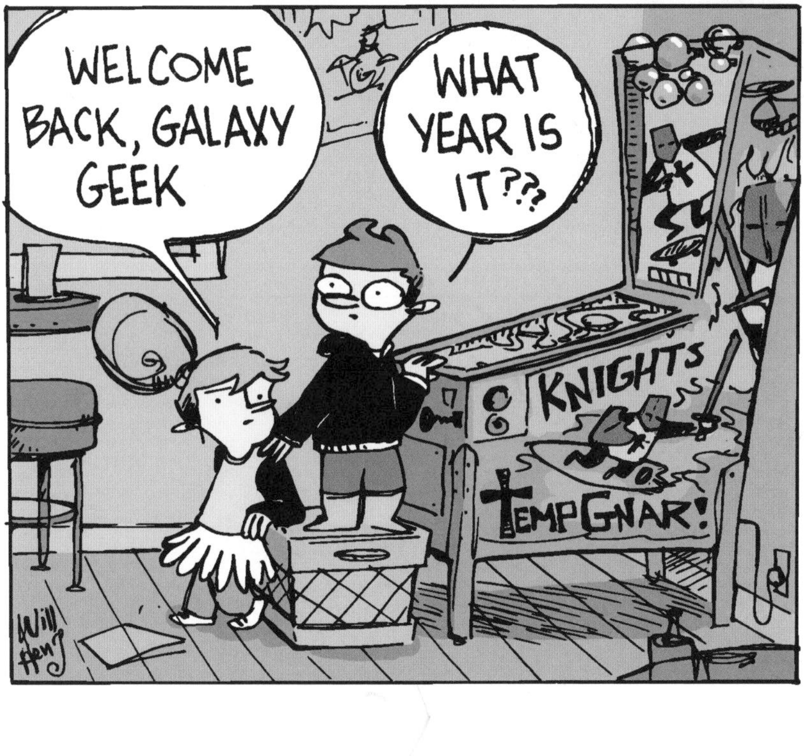
WELCOME BACK, GALAXY GEEK
WHAT YEAR IS IT???
KNIGHTS
TEMPGNAR!

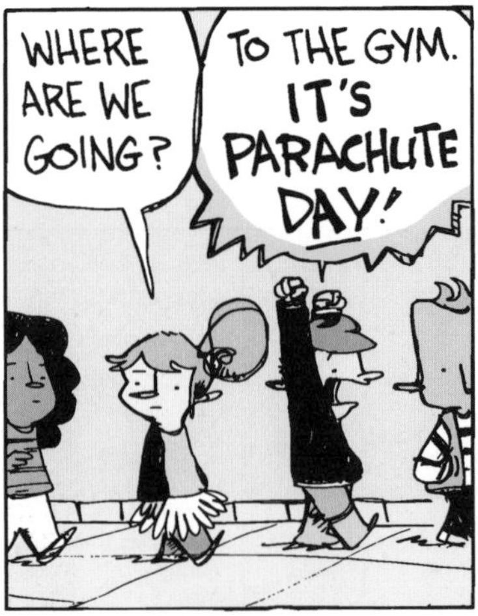
WHERE ARE WE GOING?
TO THE GYM. IT'S PARACHUTE DAY!

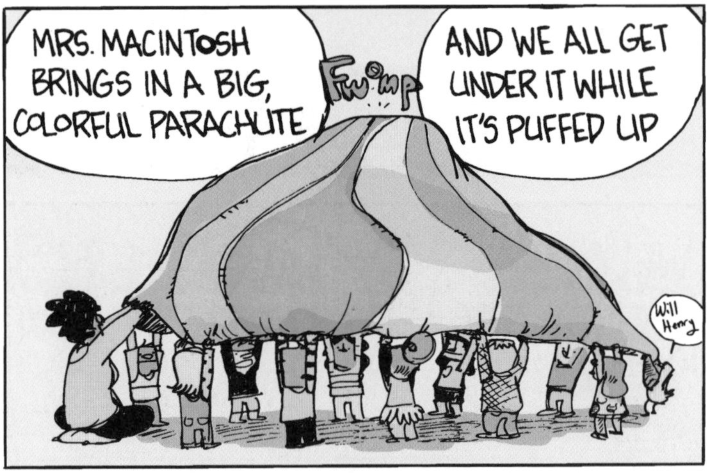
MRS. MACINTOSH BRINGS IN A BIG, COLORFUL PARACHUTE
FWOMP
AND WE ALL GET UNDER IT WHILE IT'S PUFFED UP
Will Henry

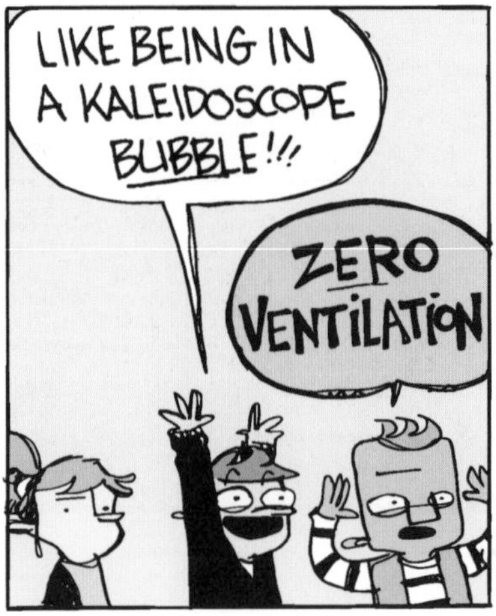
LIKE BEING IN A KALEIDOSCOPE BUBBLE!!!
ZERO VENTILATION

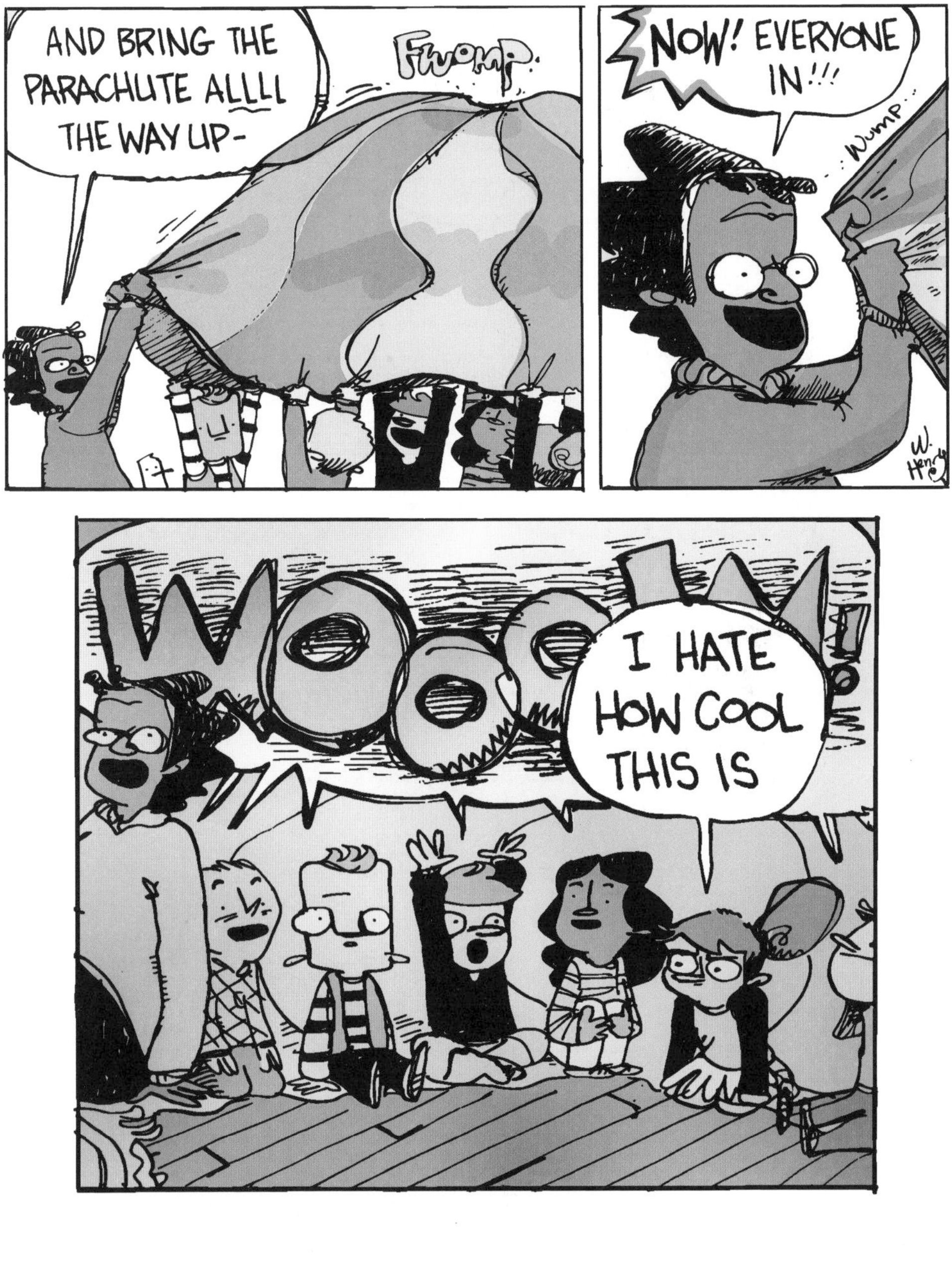
AND BRING THE PARACHUTE ALLLL THE WAY UP-
FWOMP
NOW! EVERYONE IN!!!
WUMP
I HATE HOW COOL THIS IS

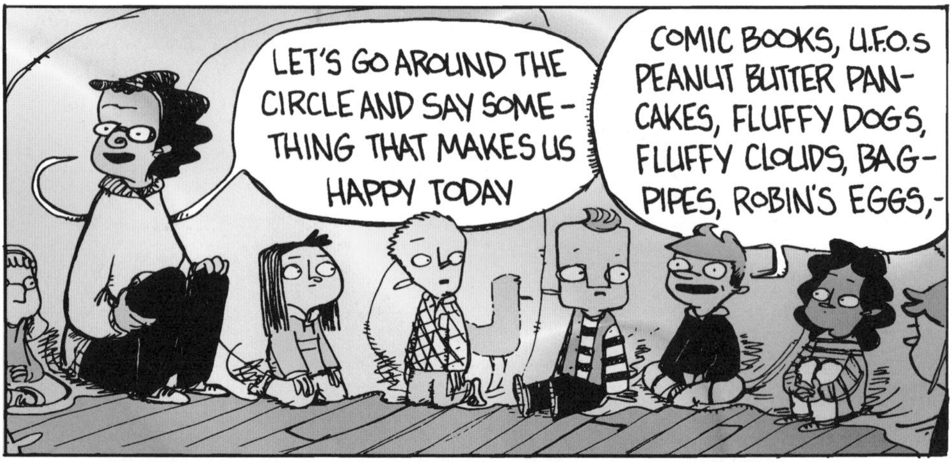
LET'S GO AROUND THE CIRCLE AND SAY SOME-THING THAT MAKES US HAPPY TODAY
COMIC BOOKS, U.F.O.s PEANUT BUTTER PAN-CAKES, FLUFFY DOGS, FLUFFY CLOUDS, BAG-PIPES, ROBIN'S EGGS,-

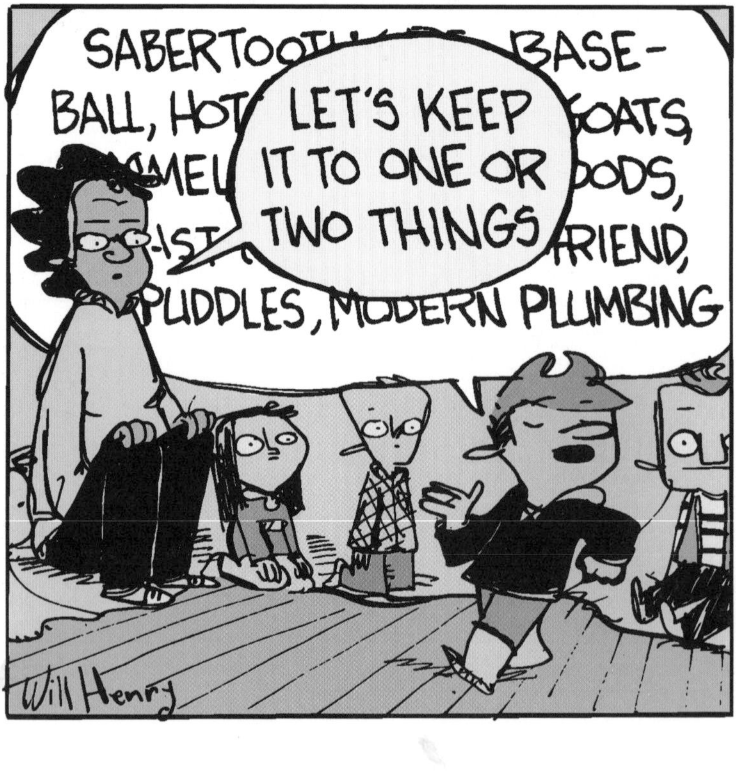
SABERTOO BASE-BALL, HOT GOATS, FRIEND, PUDDLES, MODERN PLUMBING
LET'S KEEP IT TO ONE OR TWO THINGS
Will Henry

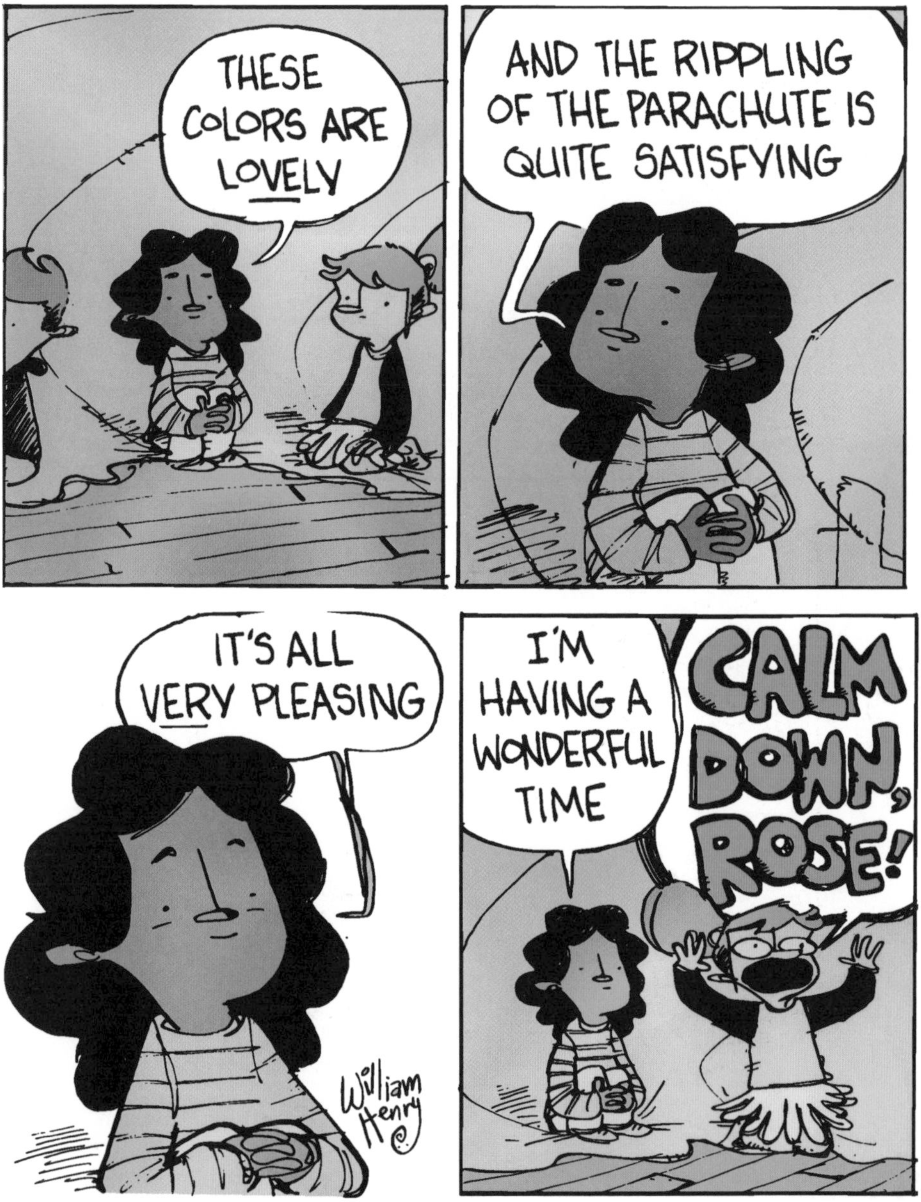
THESE COLORS ARE LOVELY
AND THE RIPPLING OF THE PARACHUTE IS QUITE SATISFYING
IT'S ALL VERY PLEASING
I'M HAVING A WONDERFUL TIME
CALM DOWN, ROSE!
William Henry

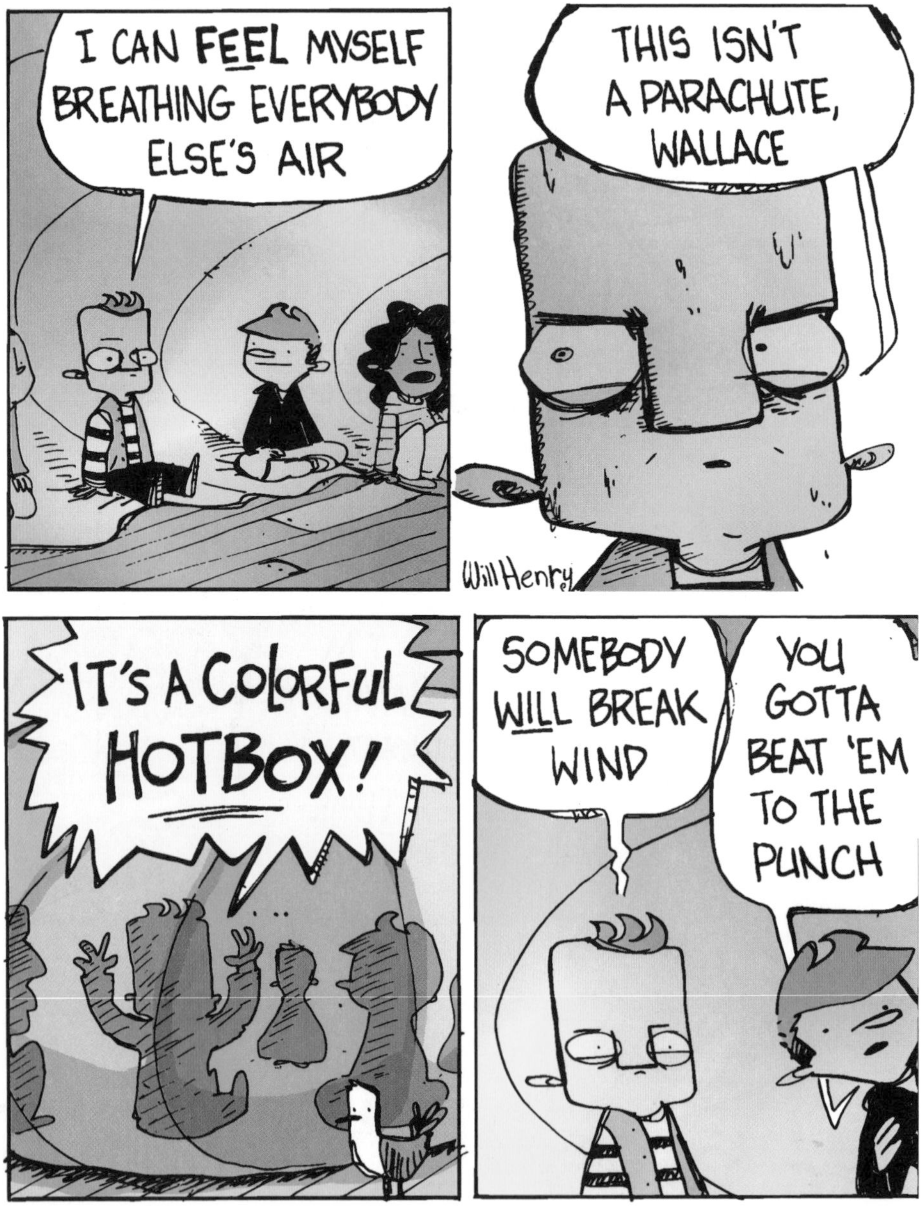
I CAN FEEL MYSELF BREATHING EVERYBODY ELSE'S AIR
THIS ISN'T A PARACHUTE, WALLACE
Will Henry
IT'S A COLORFUL HOTBOX!
...
SOMEBODY WILL BREAK WIND
YOU GOTTA BEAT 'EM TO THE PUNCH

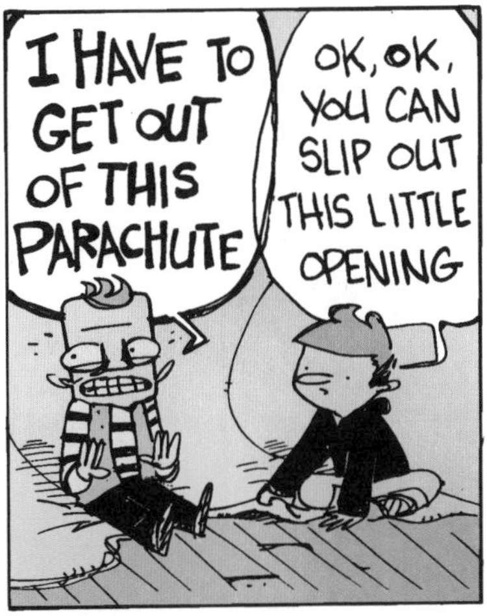
I HAVE TO GET OUT OF THIS PARACHUTE
OK, OK, YOU CAN SLIP OUT THIS LITTLE OPENING

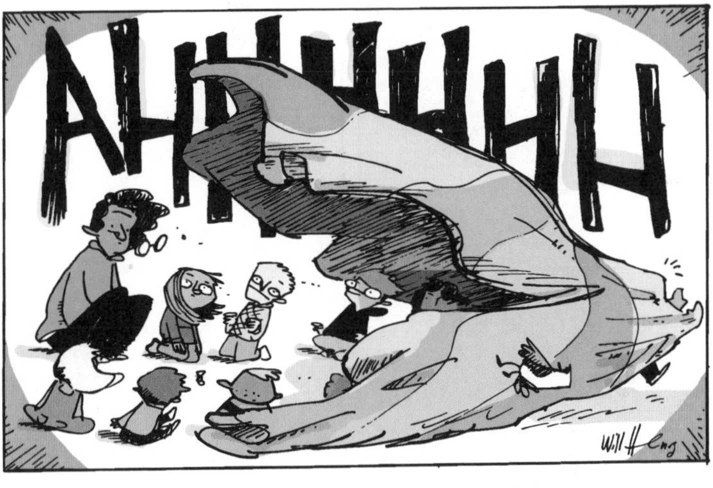
AHHHHHH

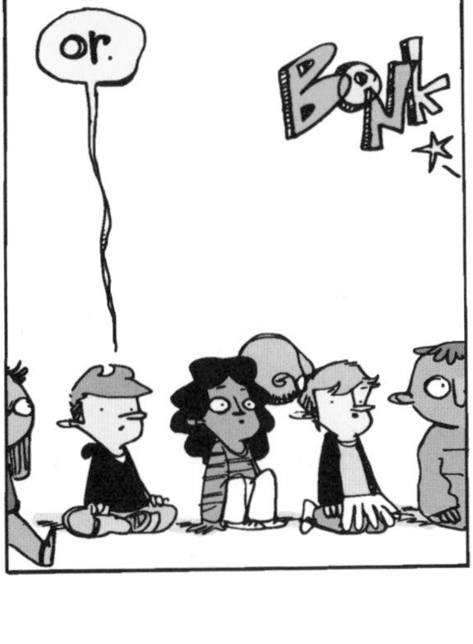
or.
BONK

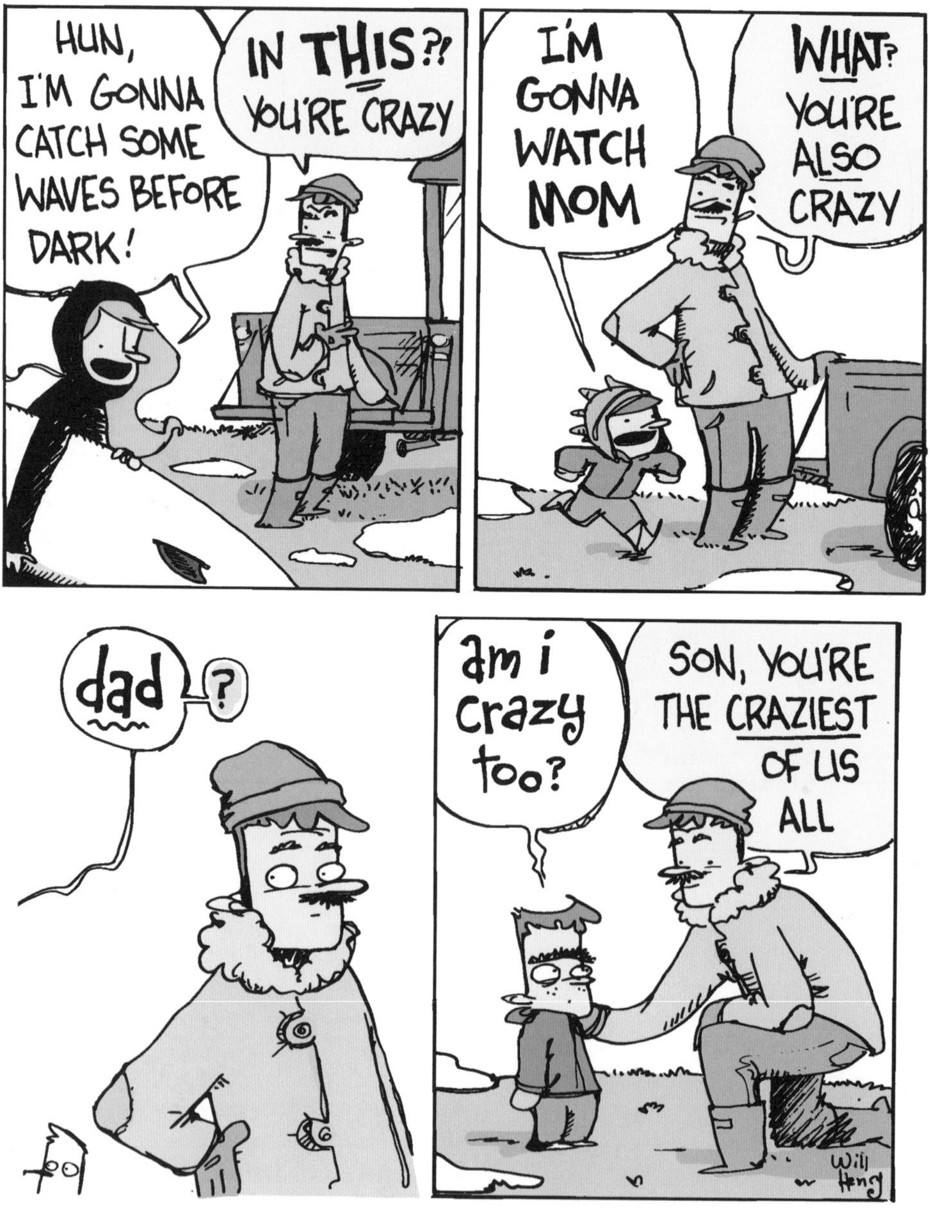
HUN, I'M GONNA CATCH SOME WAVES BEFORE DARK!
IN THIS?! YOU'RE CRAZY
I'M GONNA WATCH MOM
WHAT? YOU'RE ALSO CRAZY
dad ?
am i crazy too?
SON, YOU'RE THE CRAZIEST OF US ALL
Will Heng

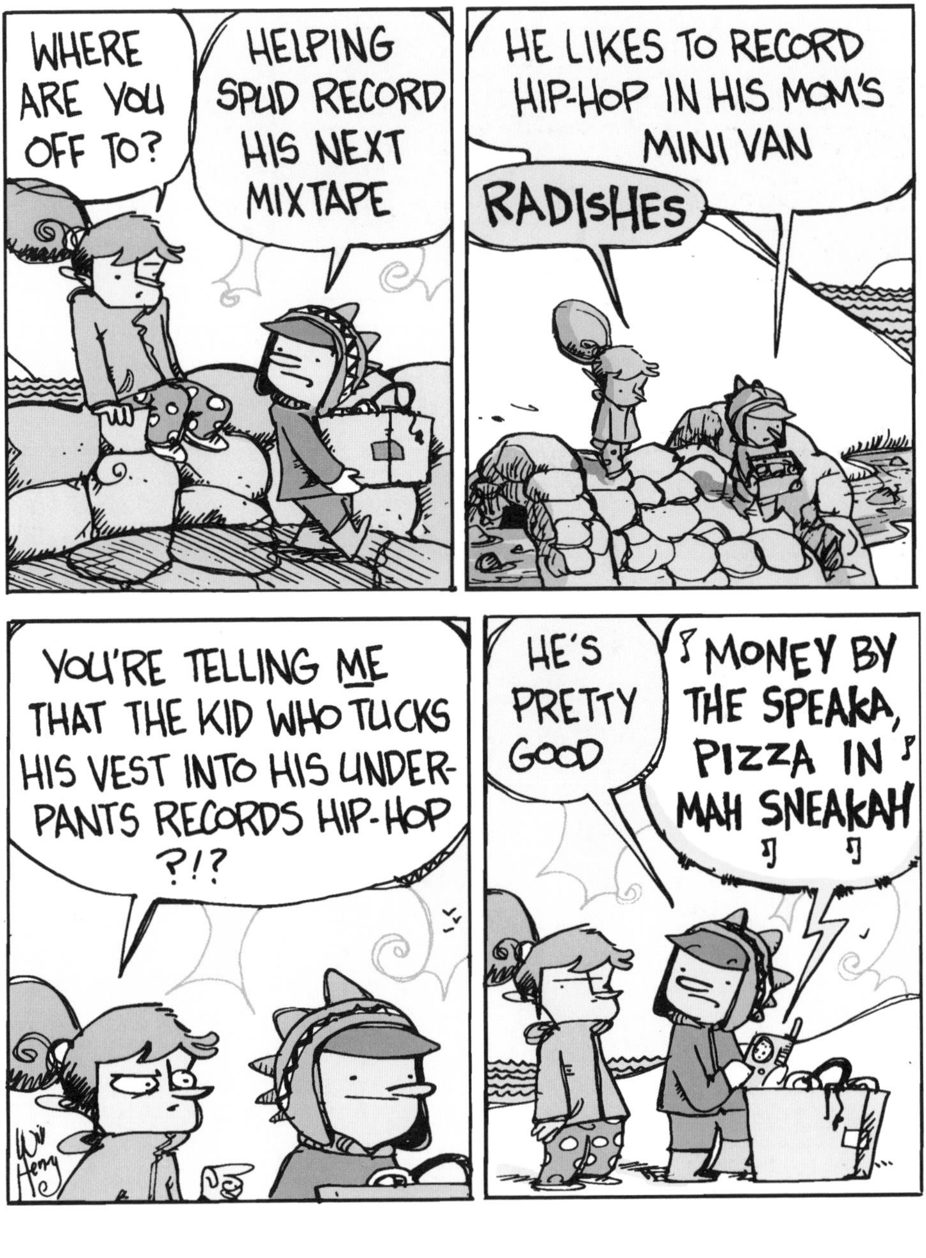
WHERE ARE YOU OFF TO?
HELPING SPUD RECORD HIS NEXT MIXTAPE
HE LIKES TO RECORD HIP-HOP IN HIS MOM'S MINI VAN
RADISHES
YOU'RE TELLING ME THAT THE KID WHO TUCKS HIS VEST INTO HIS UNDER-PANTS RECORDS HIP-HOP ?!?
HE'S PRETTY GOOD
MONEY BY THE SPEAKA, PIZZA IN MAH SNEAKAH

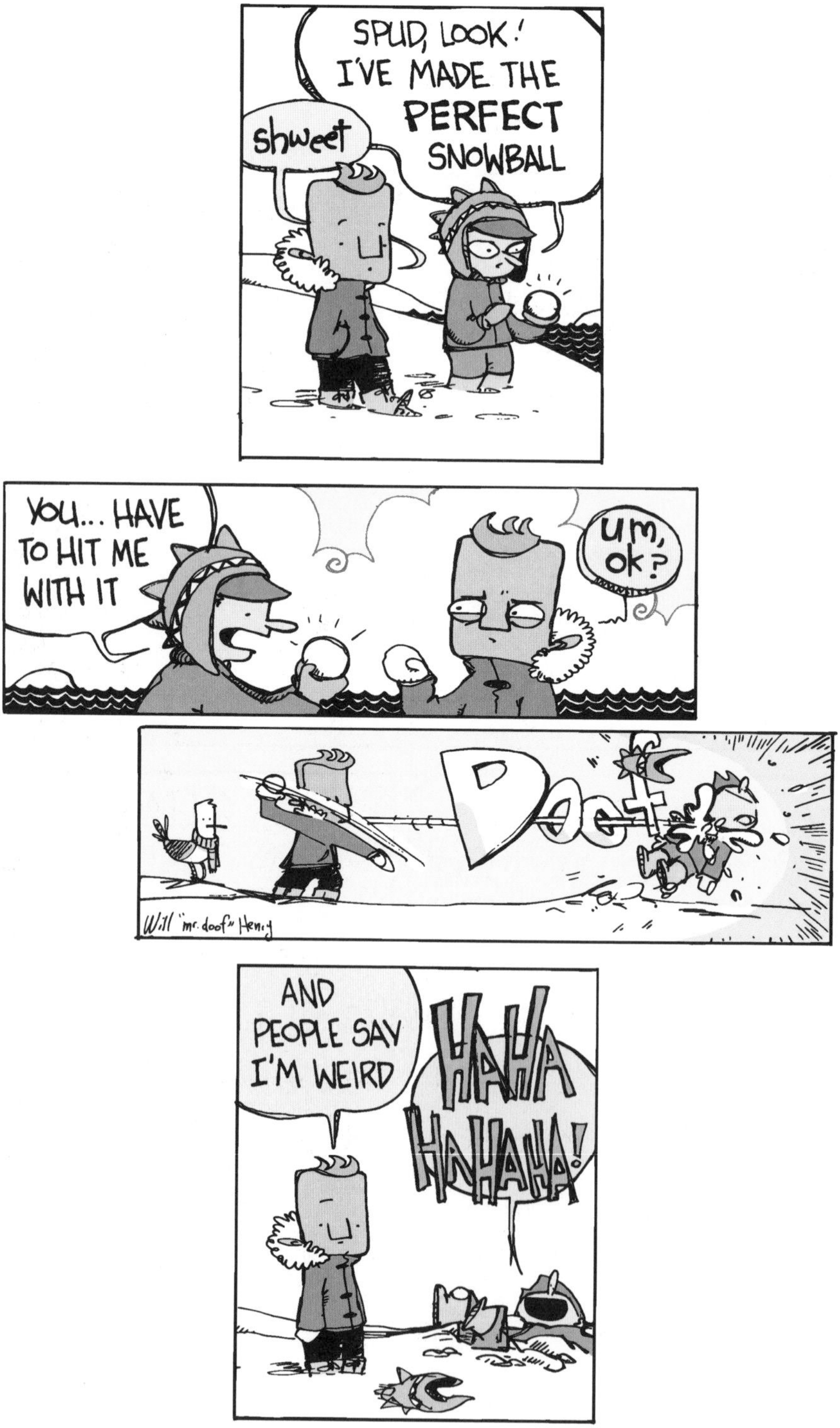
SPUD, LOOK! I'VE MADE THE PERFECT SNOWBALL
shweet
YOU... HAVE TO HIT ME WITH IT
um, ok?
Doof
Will "mr. doof" Henry
AND PEOPLE SAY I'M WEIRD
HAHA HAHAHA!

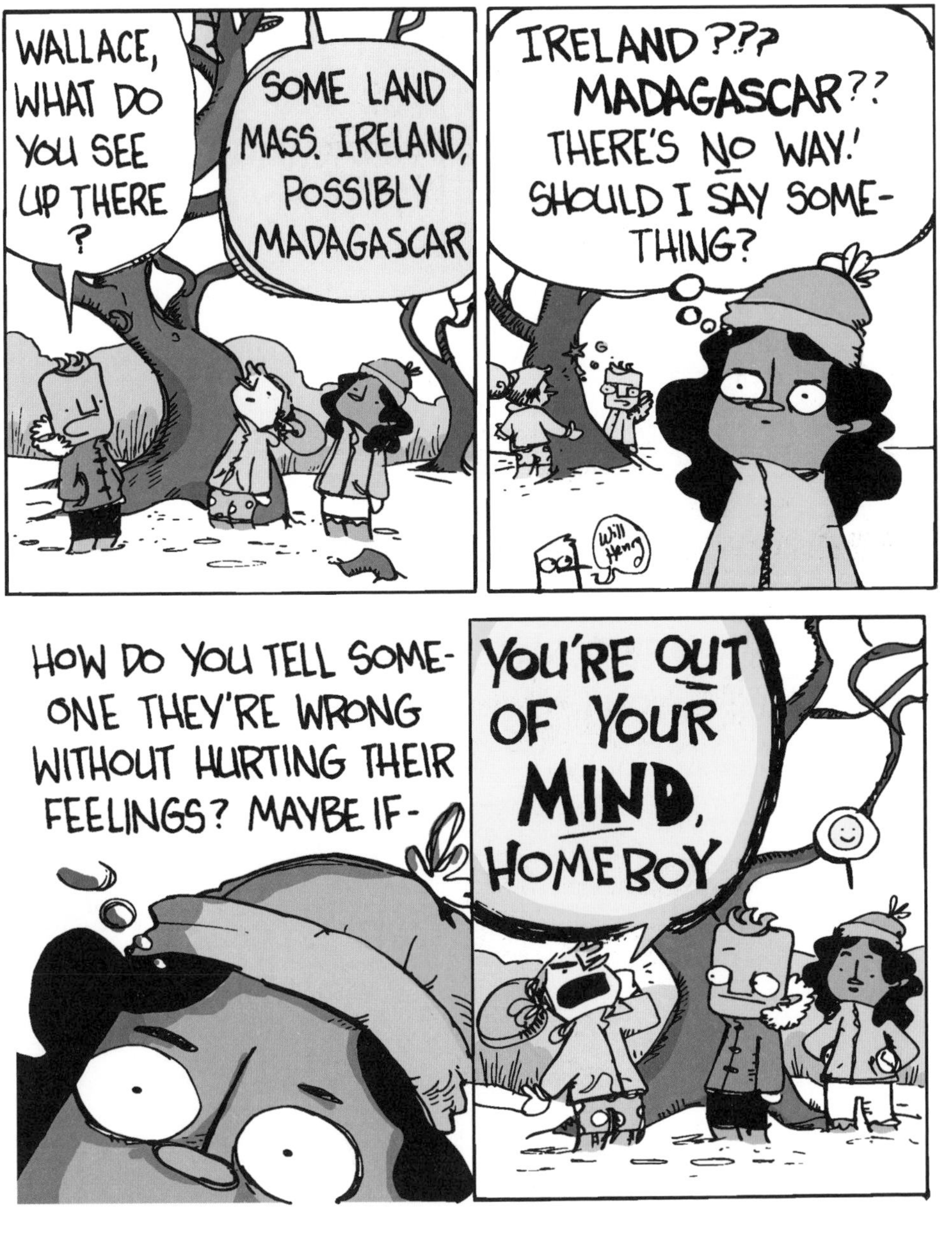
WALLACE, WHAT DO YOU SEE UP THERE ?
SOME LAND MASS. IRELAND, POSSIBLY MADAGASCAR
IRELAND ??? MADAGASCAR?? THERE'S NO WAY! SHOULD I SAY SOME-THING?
Will Heng
HOW DO YOU TELL SOME-ONE THEY'RE WRONG WITHOUT HURTING THEIR FEELINGS? MAYBE IF-
YOU'RE OUT OF YOUR MIND, HOMEBOY

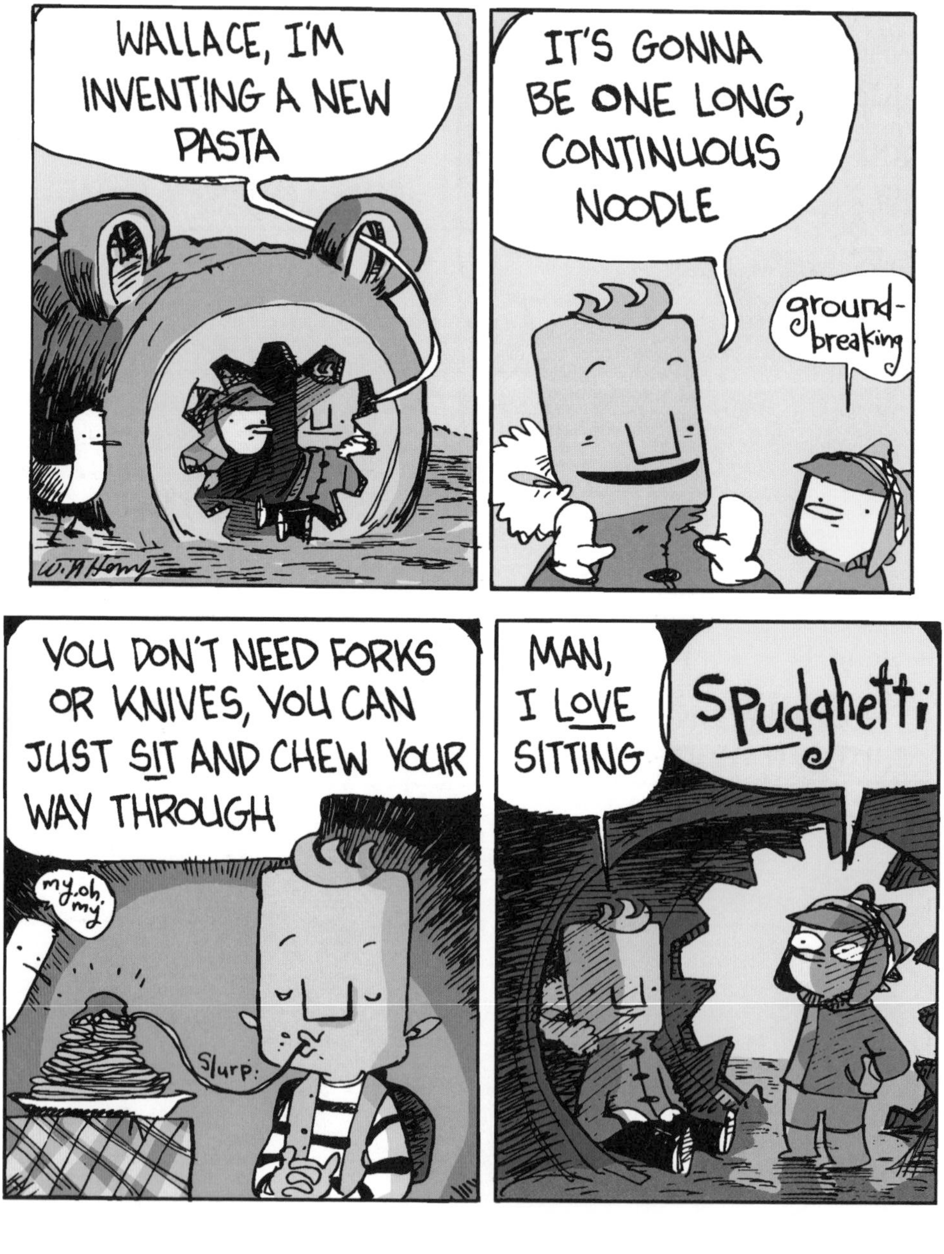
WALLACE, I'M INVENTING A NEW PASTA
IT'S GONNA BE ONE LONG, CONTINUOUS NOODLE
ground-breaking
YOU DON'T NEED FORKS OR KNIVES, YOU CAN JUST SIT AND CHEW YOUR WAY THROUGH
my, oh, my
Slurp
MAN, I LOVE SITTING
Spudghetti

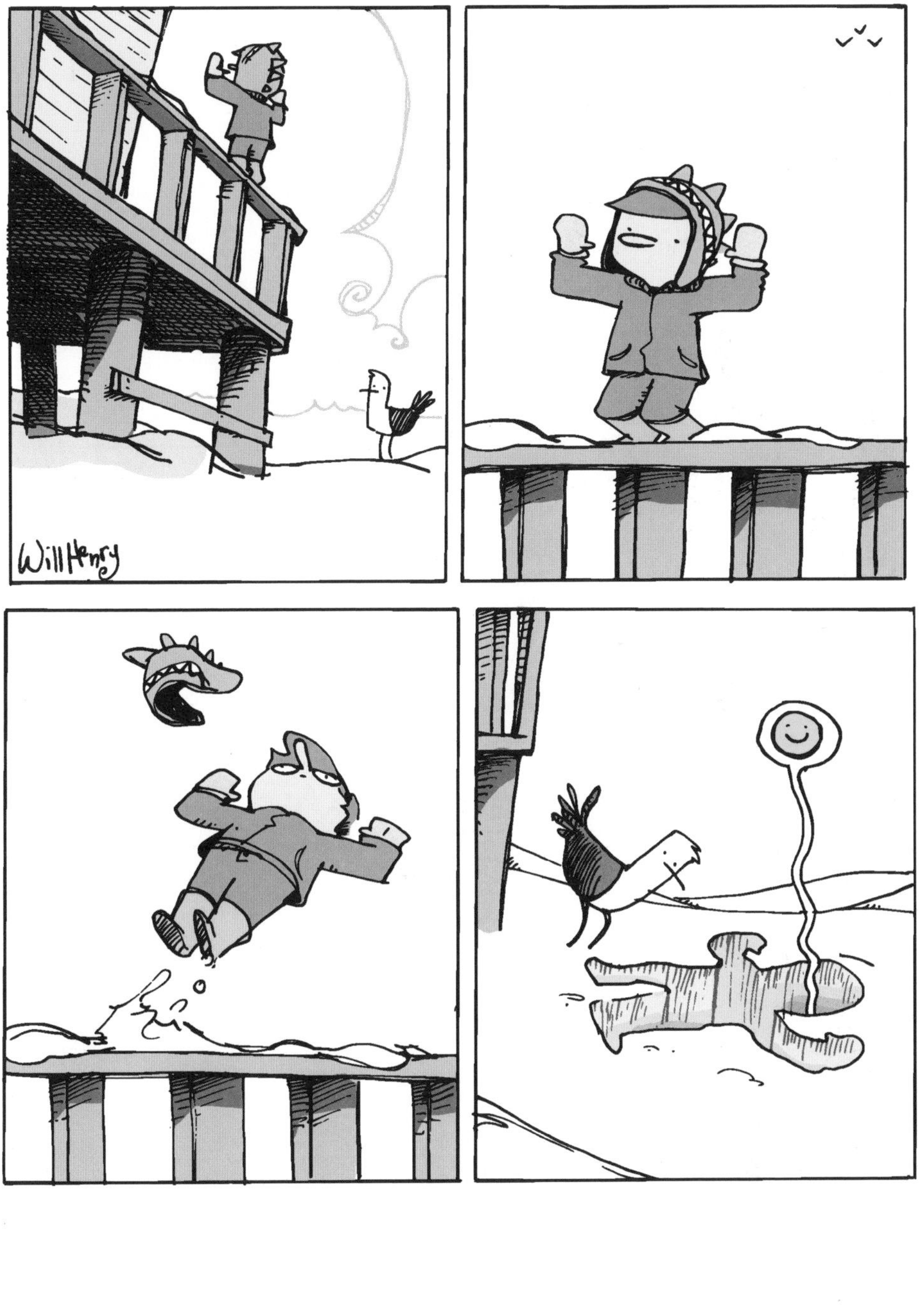
Will Henry

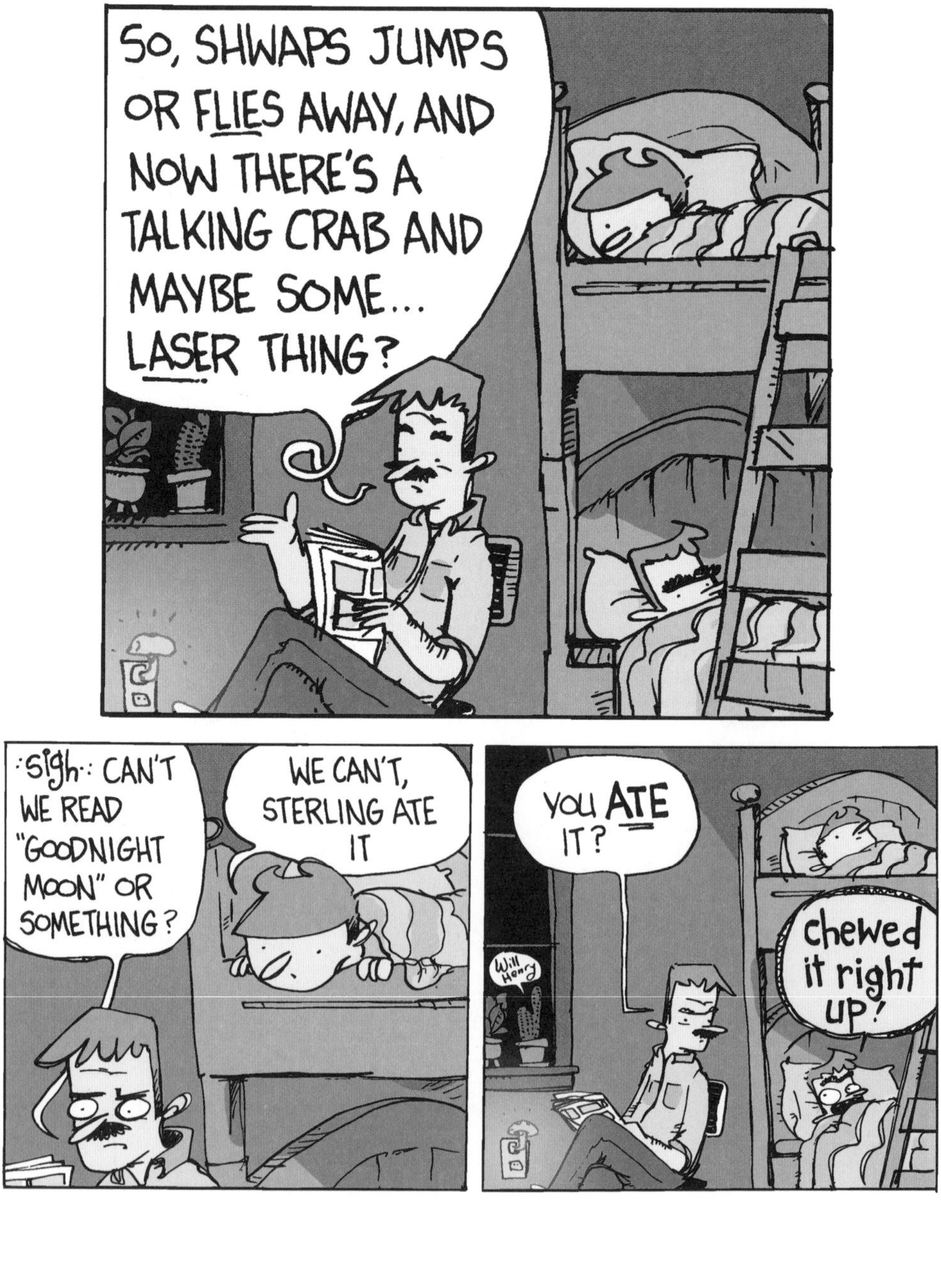
SO, SHWAPS JUMPS OR FLIES AWAY, AND NOW THERE'S A TALKING CRAB AND MAYBE SOME... LASER THING?
·sigh·: CAN'T WE READ "GOODNIGHT MOON" OR SOMETHING?
WE CAN'T, STERLING ATE IT
YOU ATE IT?
Will Henry
chewed it right up!

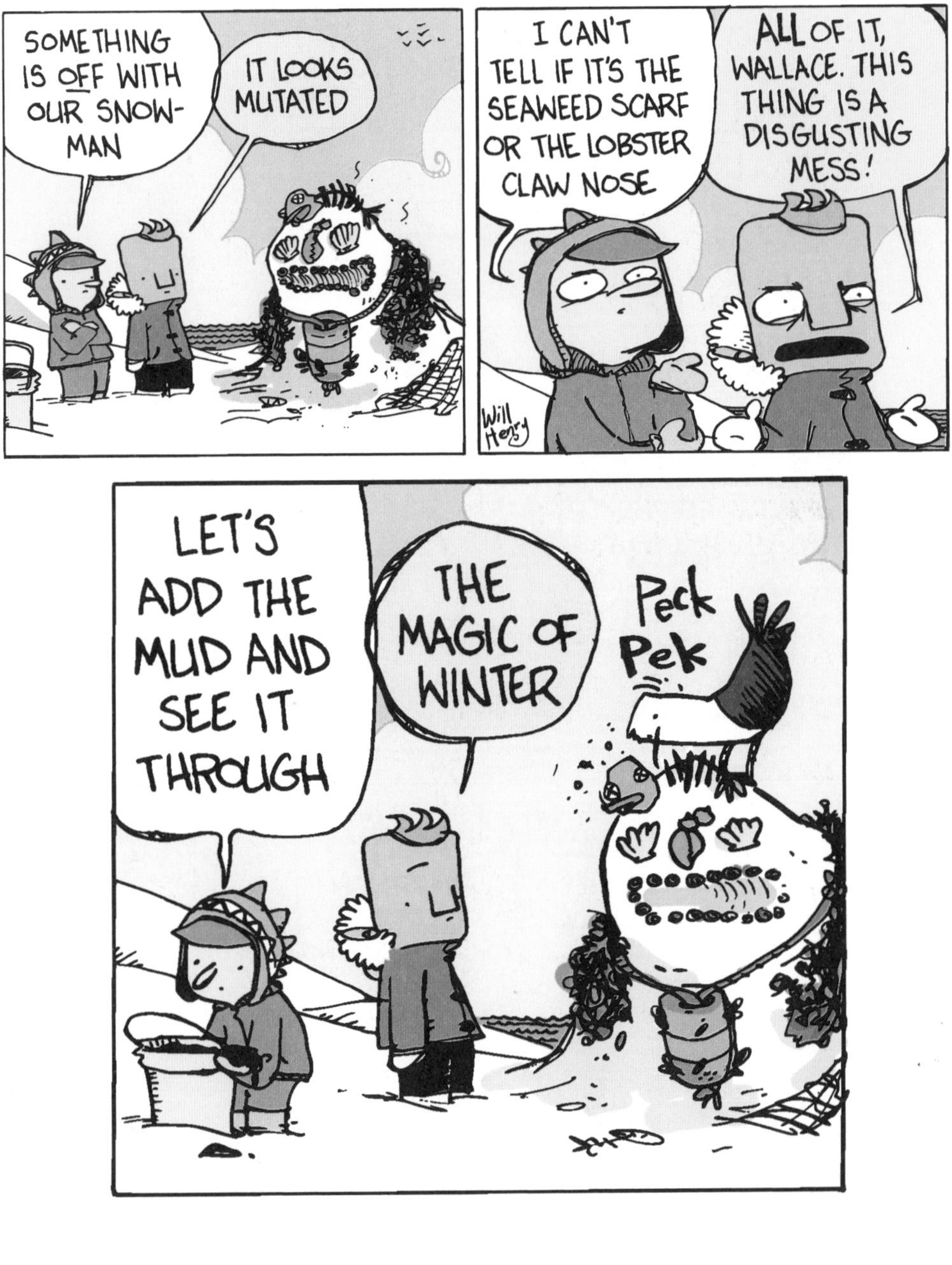
SOMETHING IS OFF WITH OUR SNOW-MAN
IT LOOKS MUTATED
I CAN'T TELL IF IT'S THE SEAWEED SCARF OR THE LOBSTER CLAW NOSE
ALL OF IT, WALLACE. THIS THING IS A DISGUSTING MESS!
Will Henry
LET'S ADD THE MUD AND SEE IT THROUGH
THE MAGIC OF WINTER
Peck
Pek

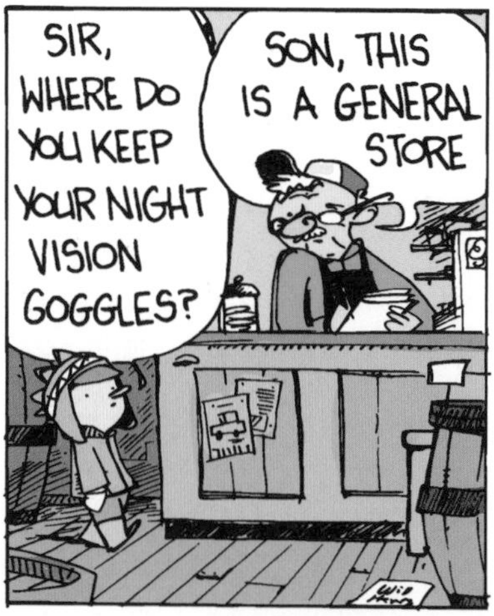
SIR, WHERE DO YOU KEEP YOUR NIGHT VISION GOGGLES?
SON, THIS IS A GENERAL STORE

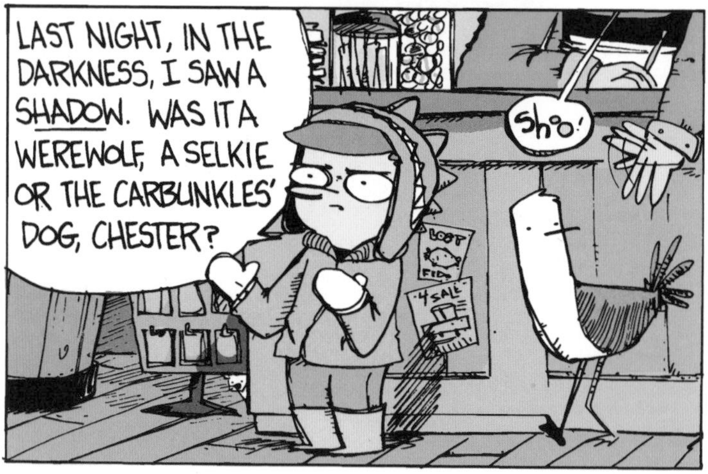
LAST NIGHT, IN THE DARKNESS, I SAW A SHADOW. WAS IT A WEREWOLF, A SELKIE OR THE CARBUNKLES' DOG, CHESTER?
Shoo!

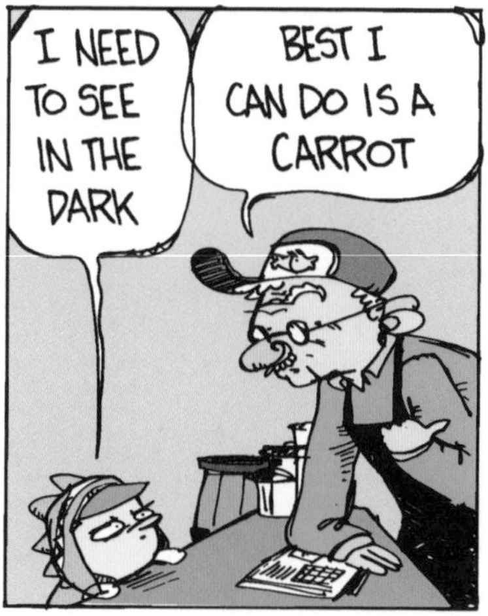
I NEED TO SEE IN THE DARK
BEST I CAN DO IS A CARROT

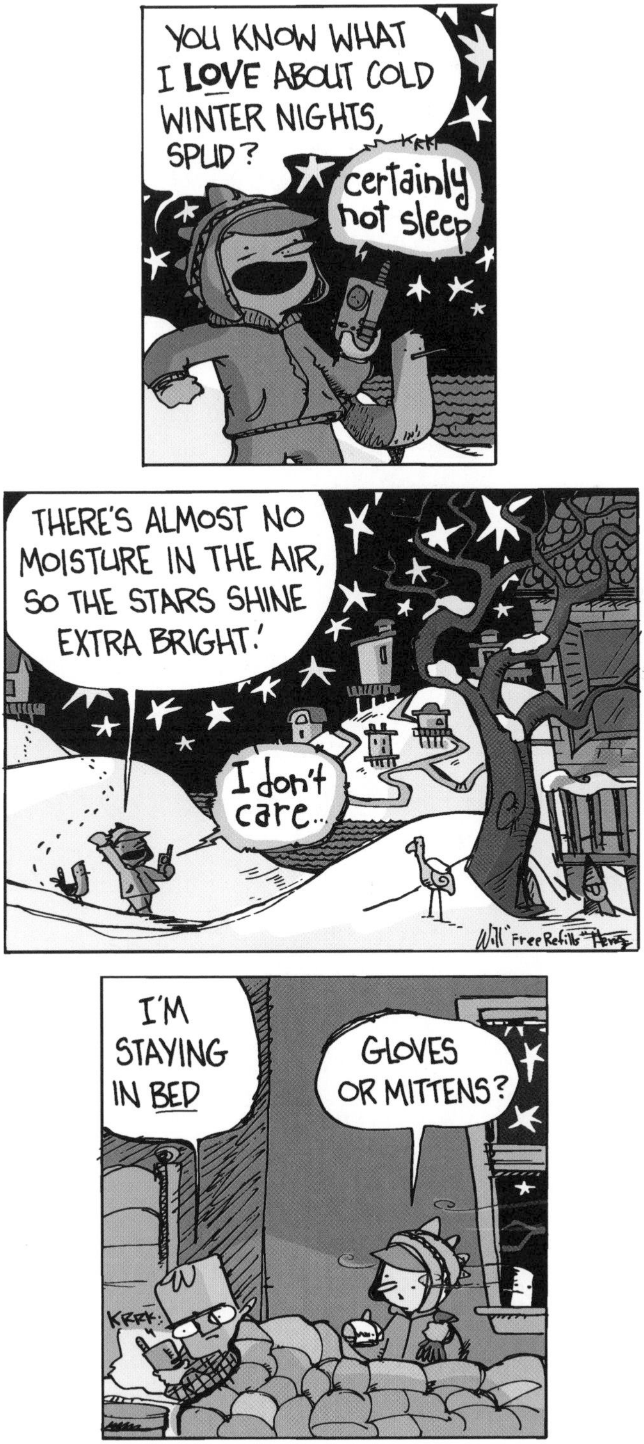
YOU KNOW WHAT I LOVE ABOUT COLD WINTER NIGHTS, SPUD?
certainly not sleep
THERE'S ALMOST NO MOISTURE IN THE AIR, SO THE STARS SHINE EXTRA BRIGHT!
I don't care...
I'M STAYING IN BED
GLOVES OR MITTENS?

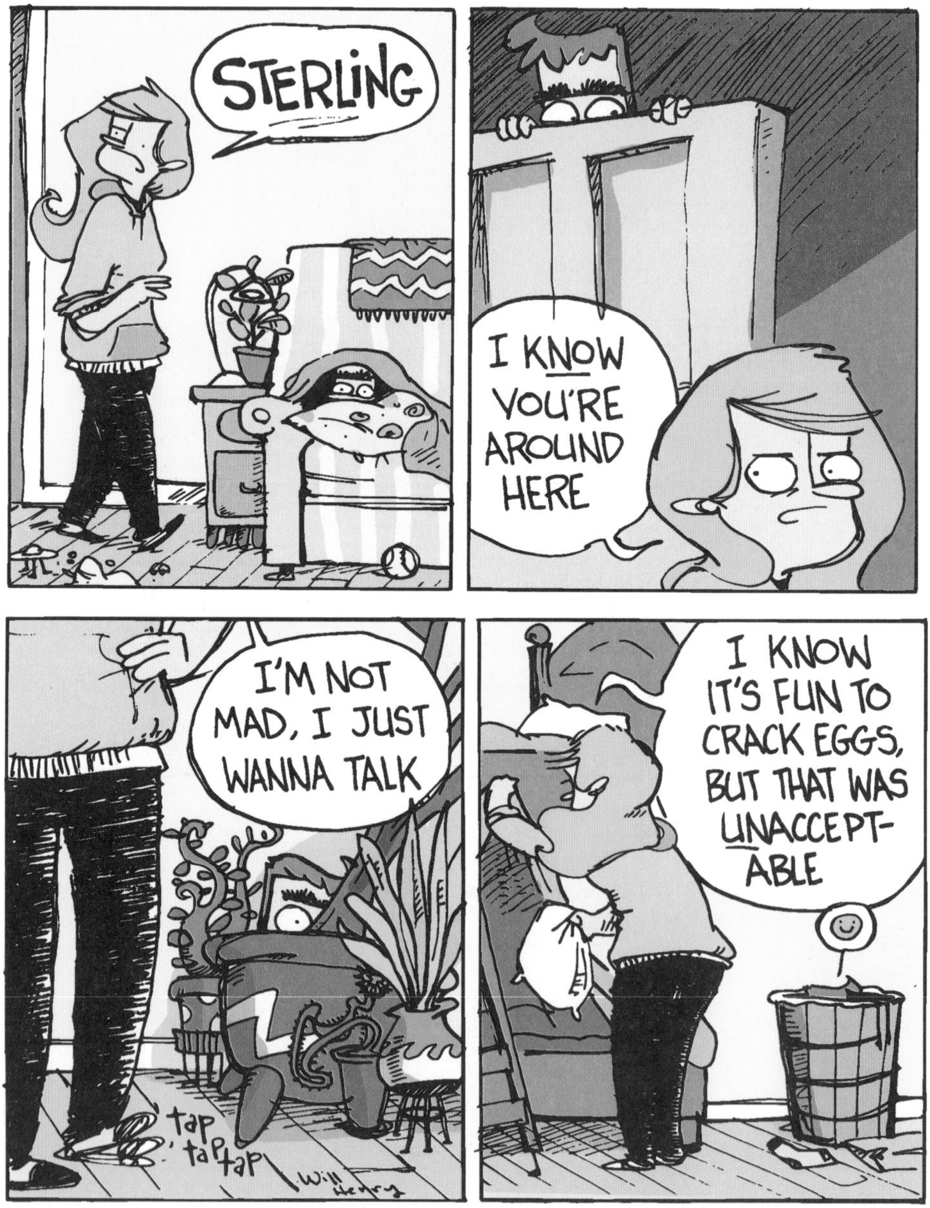
STERLING
I KNOW YOU'RE AROUND HERE
I'M NOT MAD, I JUST WANNA TALK
tap, tap tap
I KNOW IT'S FUN TO CRACK EGGS, BUT THAT WAS UNACCEPT-ABLE

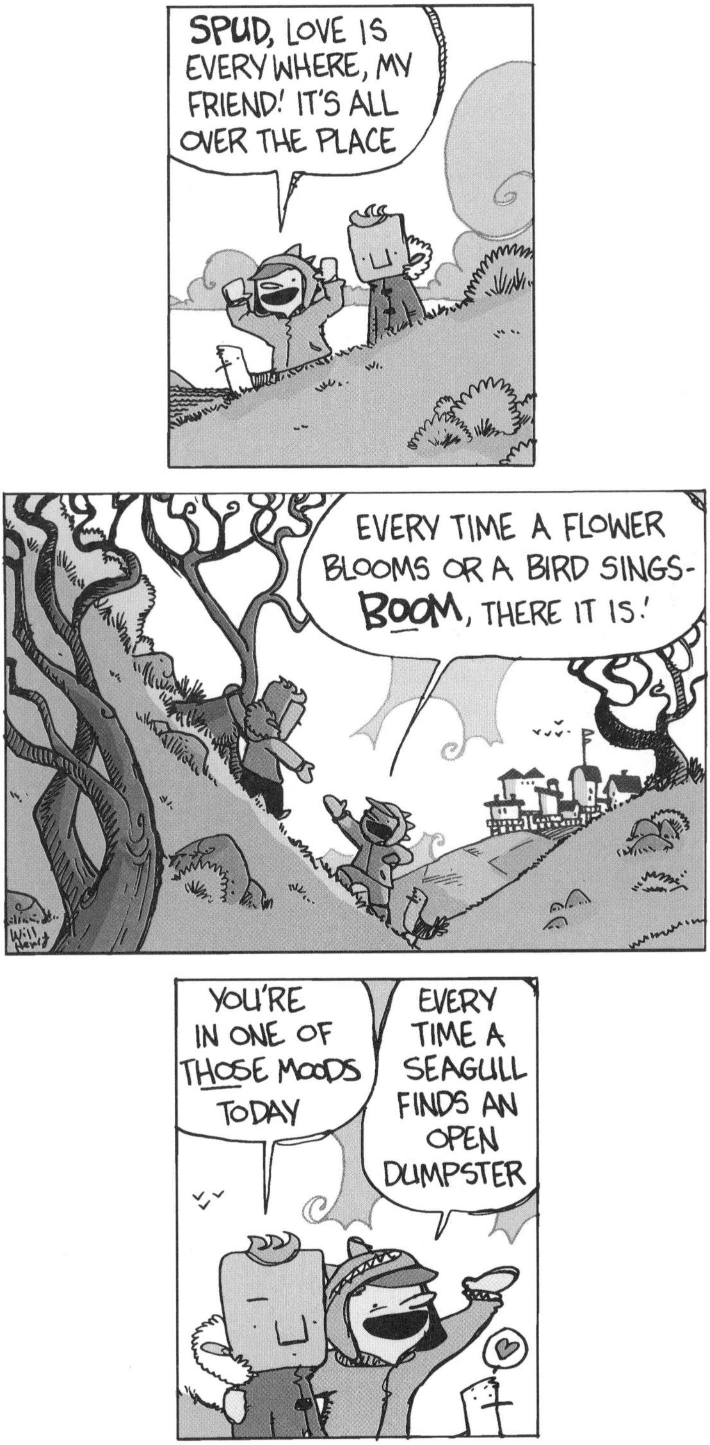
SPUD, LOVE IS EVERY WHERE, MY FRIEND! IT'S ALL OVER THE PLACE
EVERY TIME A FLOWER BLOOMS OR A BIRD SINGS- BOOM, THERE IT IS!
YOU'RE IN ONE OF THOSE MOODS TODAY
EVERY TIME A SEAGULL FINDS AN OPEN DUMPSTER

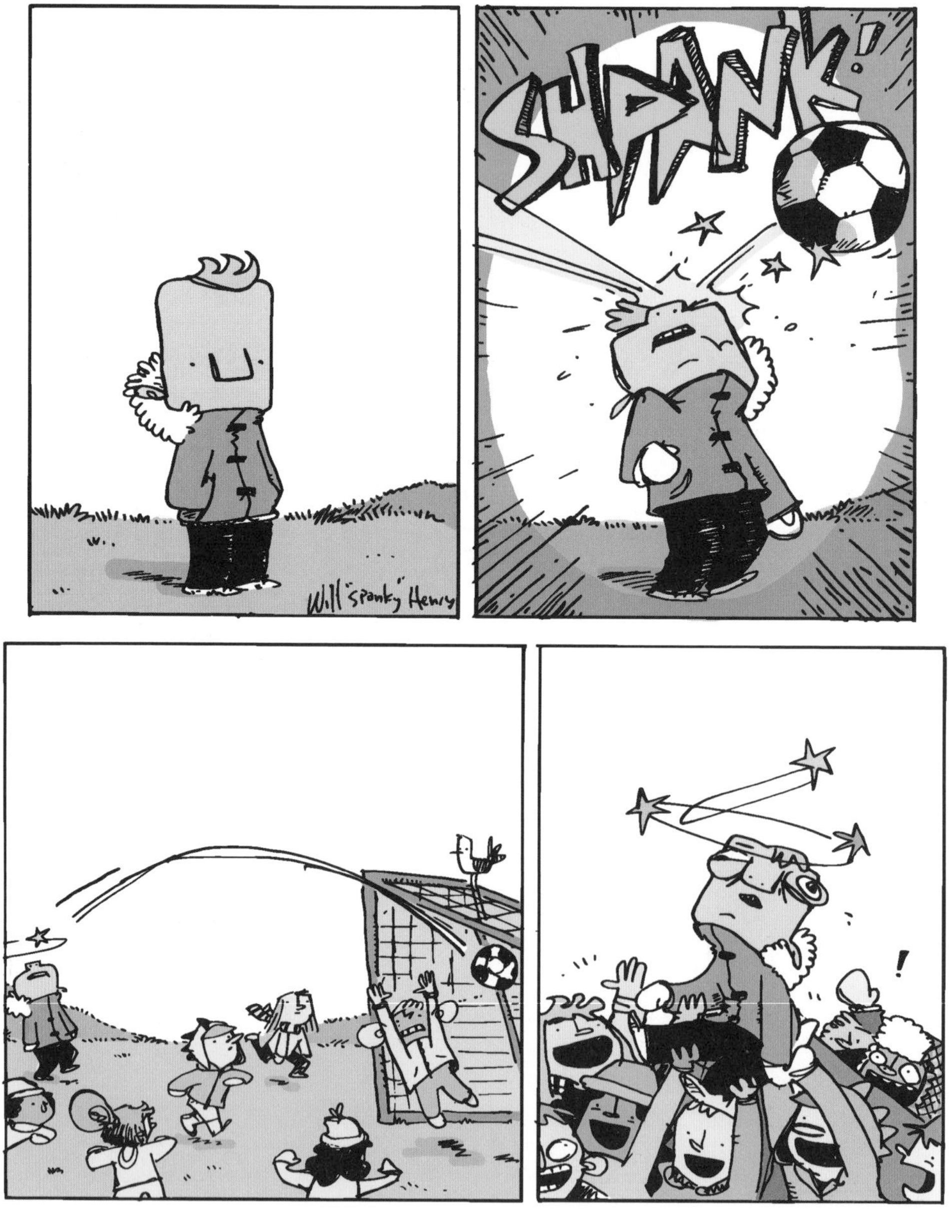
Will "spanky" Henry
SHPANK!
!

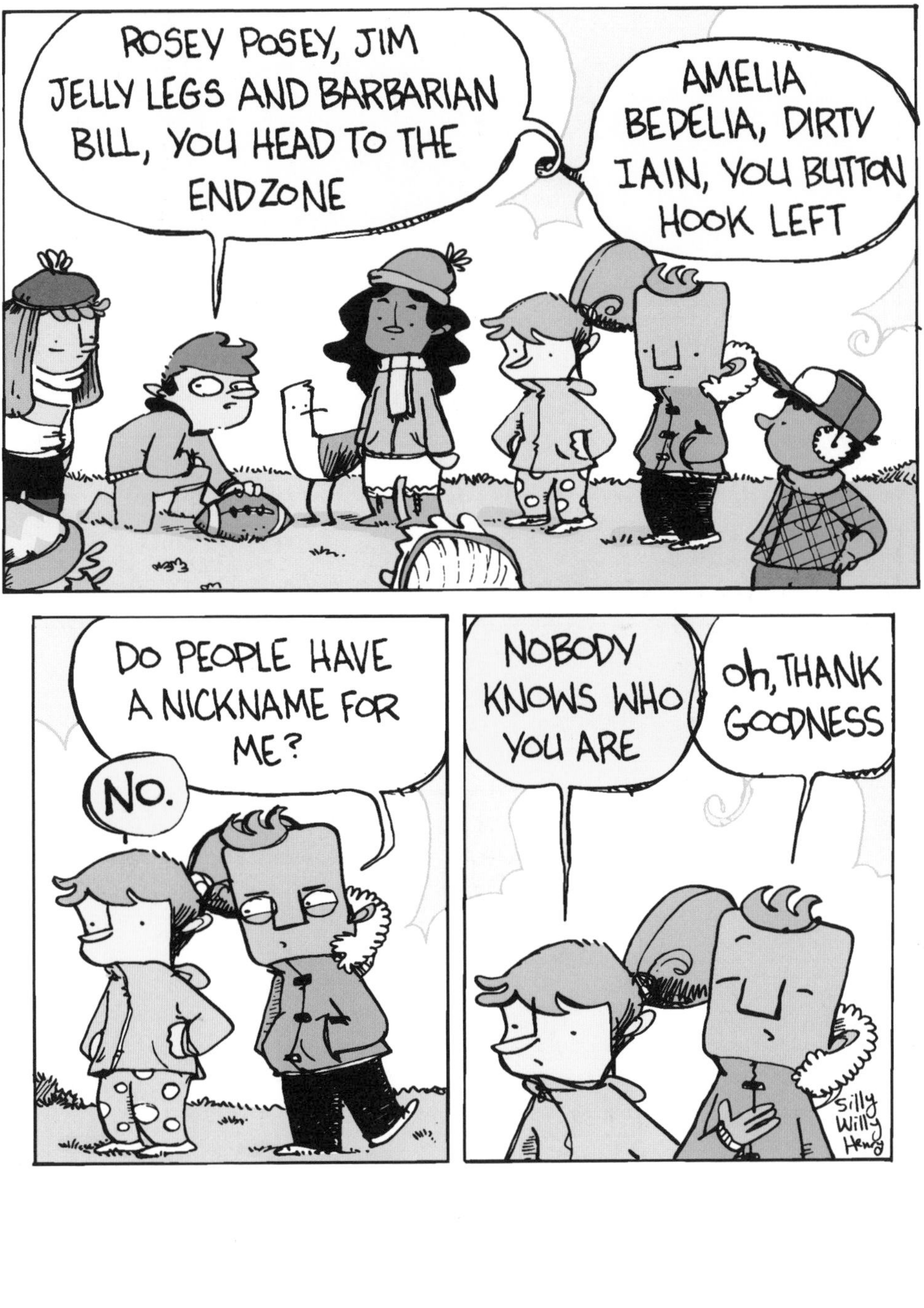
ROSEY POSEY, JIM JELLY LEGS AND BARBARIAN BILL, YOU HEAD TO THE ENDZONE
AMELIA BEDELIA, DIRTY IAIN, YOU BUTTON HOOK LEFT
DO PEOPLE HAVE A NICKNAME FOR ME?
NO.
NOBODY KNOWS WHO YOU ARE
oh, THANK GOODNESS
Silly Willy Henry

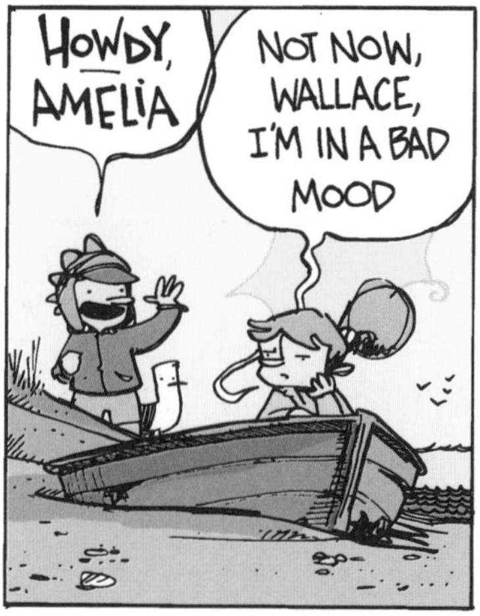
HOWDY, AMELIA
NOT NOW, WALLACE, I'M IN A BAD MOOD

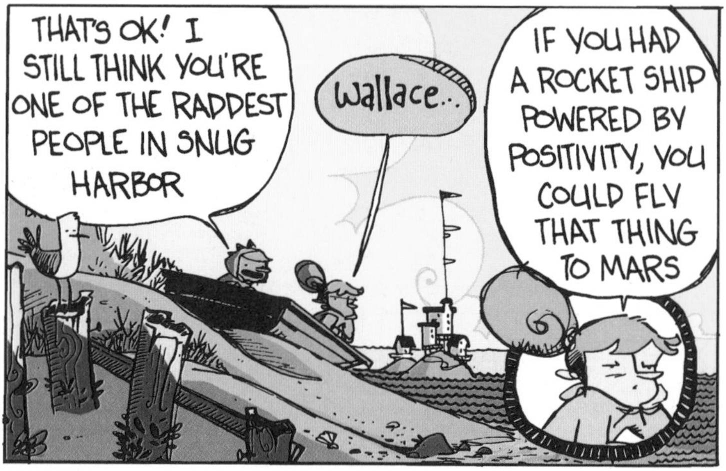
THAT'S OK! I STILL THINK YOU'RE ONE OF THE RADDEST PEOPLE IN SNUG HARBOR
wallace...
IF YOU HAD A ROCKET SHIP POWERED BY POSITIVITY, YOU COULD FLY THAT THING TO MARS

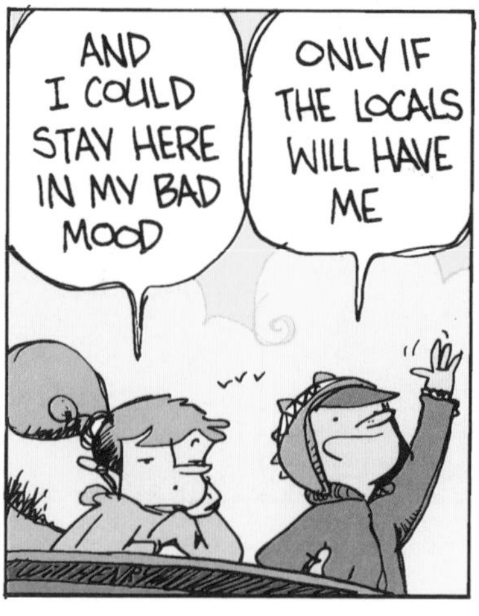
AND I COULD STAY HERE IN MY BAD MOOD
ONLY IF THE LOCALS WILL HAVE ME

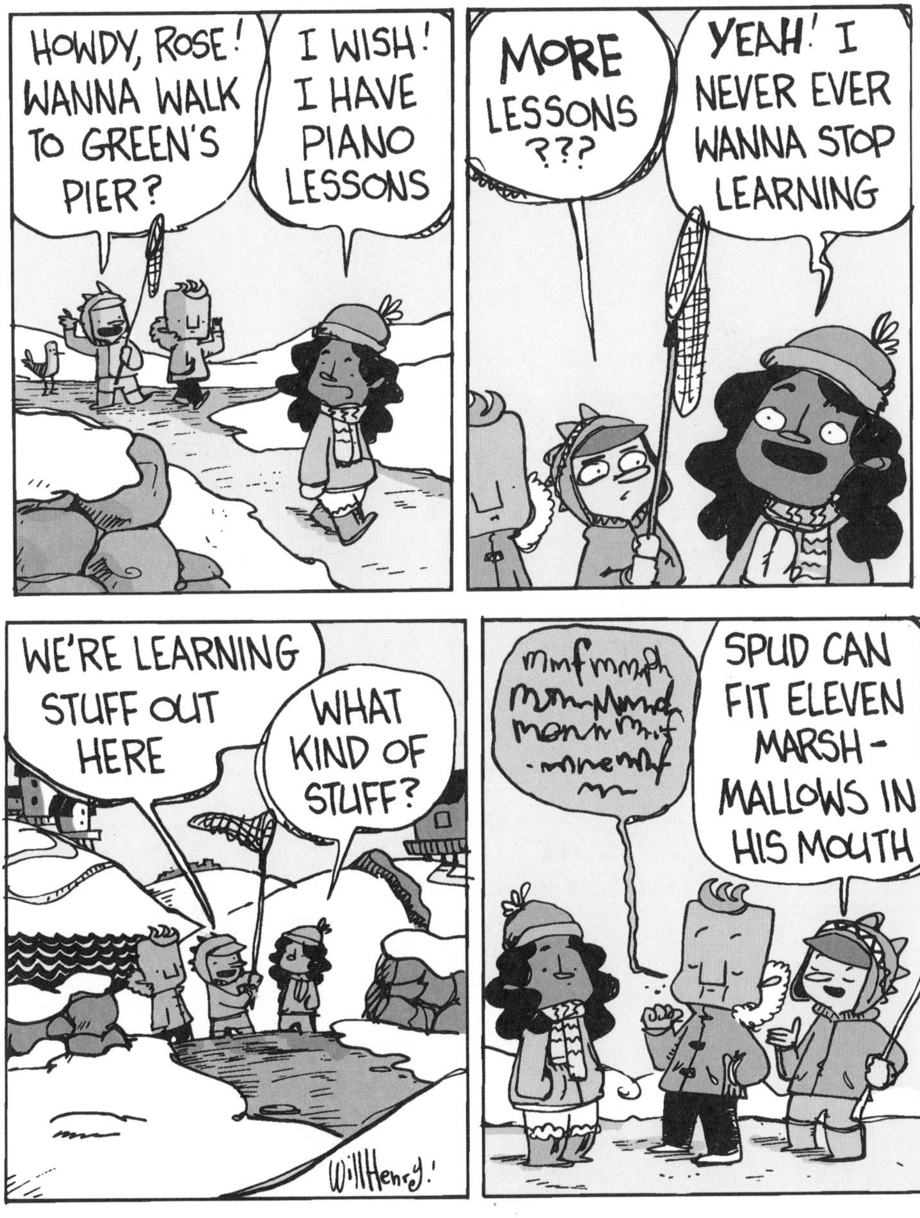
HOWDY, ROSE! WANNA WALK TO GREEN'S PIER?
I WISH! I HAVE PIANO LESSONS
MORE LESSONS ???
YEAH! I NEVER EVER WANNA STOP LEARNING
WE'RE LEARNING STUFF OUT HERE
WHAT KIND OF STUFF?
WillHenry!
SPUD CAN FIT ELEVEN MARSH-MALLOWS IN HIS MOUTH

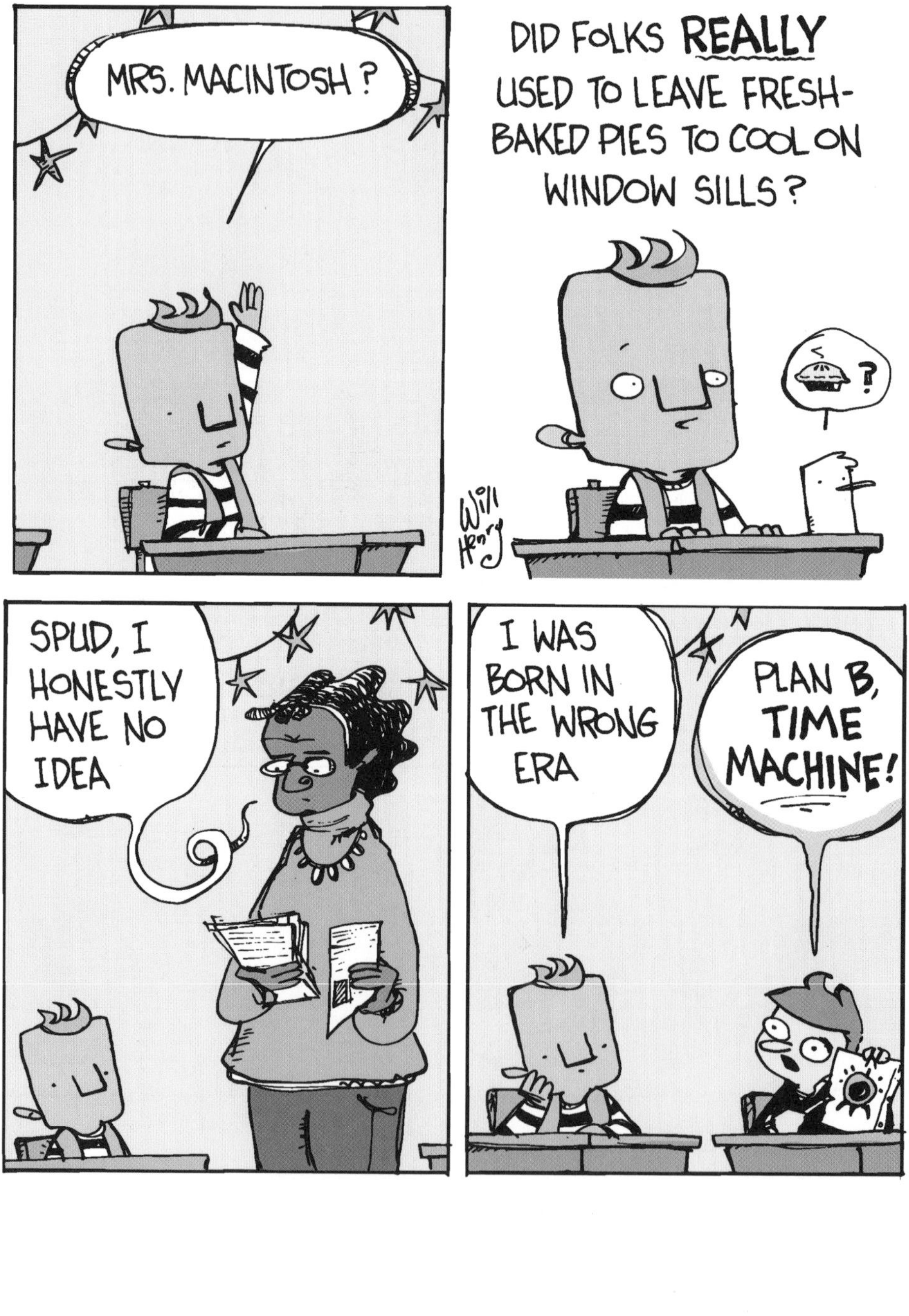
MRS. MACINTOSH ?
DID FOLKS REALLY USED TO LEAVE FRESH-BAKED PIES TO COOL ON WINDOW SILLS ?
Will Henry
SPUD, I HONESTLY HAVE NO IDEA
I WAS BORN IN THE WRONG ERA
PLAN B, TIME MACHINE!

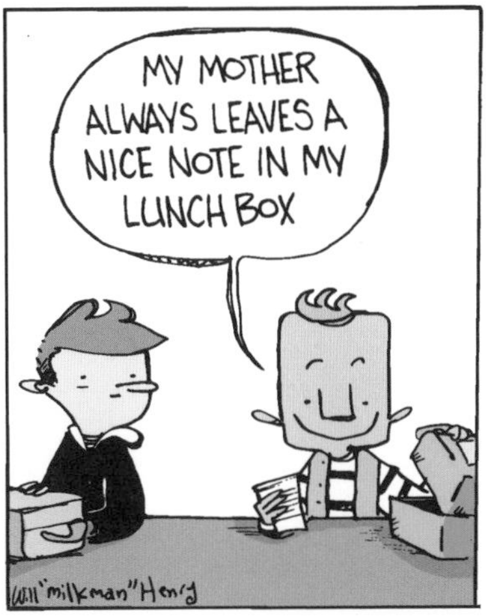
MY MOTHER ALWAYS LEAVES A NICE NOTE IN MY LUNCH BOX
Will "milkman" Henry

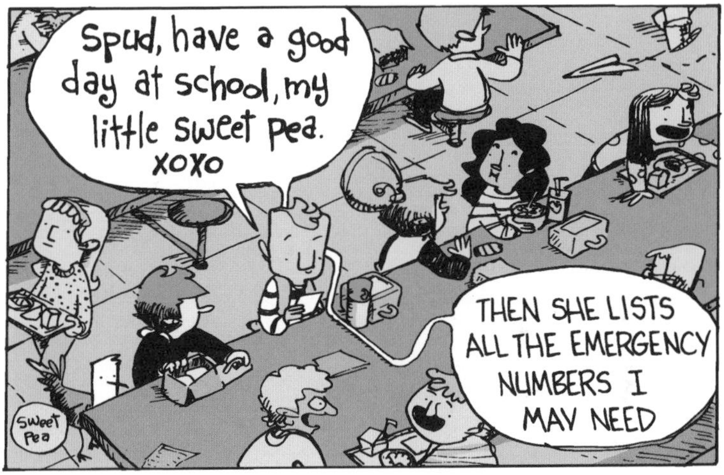
Spud, have a good day at school, my little sweet pea. XOXO
THEN SHE LISTS ALL THE EMERGENCY NUMBERS I MAY NEED
Sweet Pea

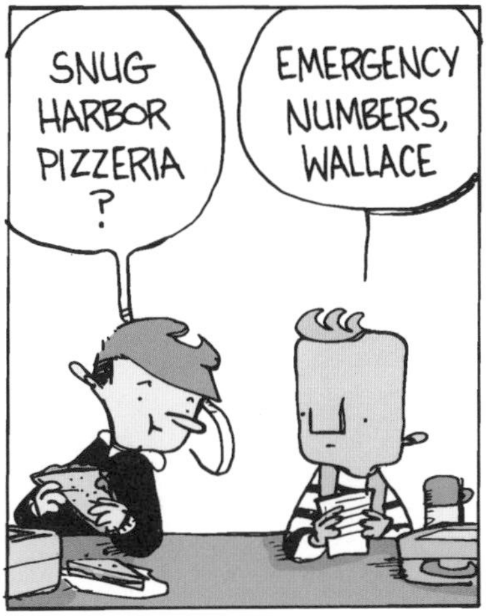
SNUG HARBOR PIZZERIA ?
EMERGENCY NUMBERS, WALLACE

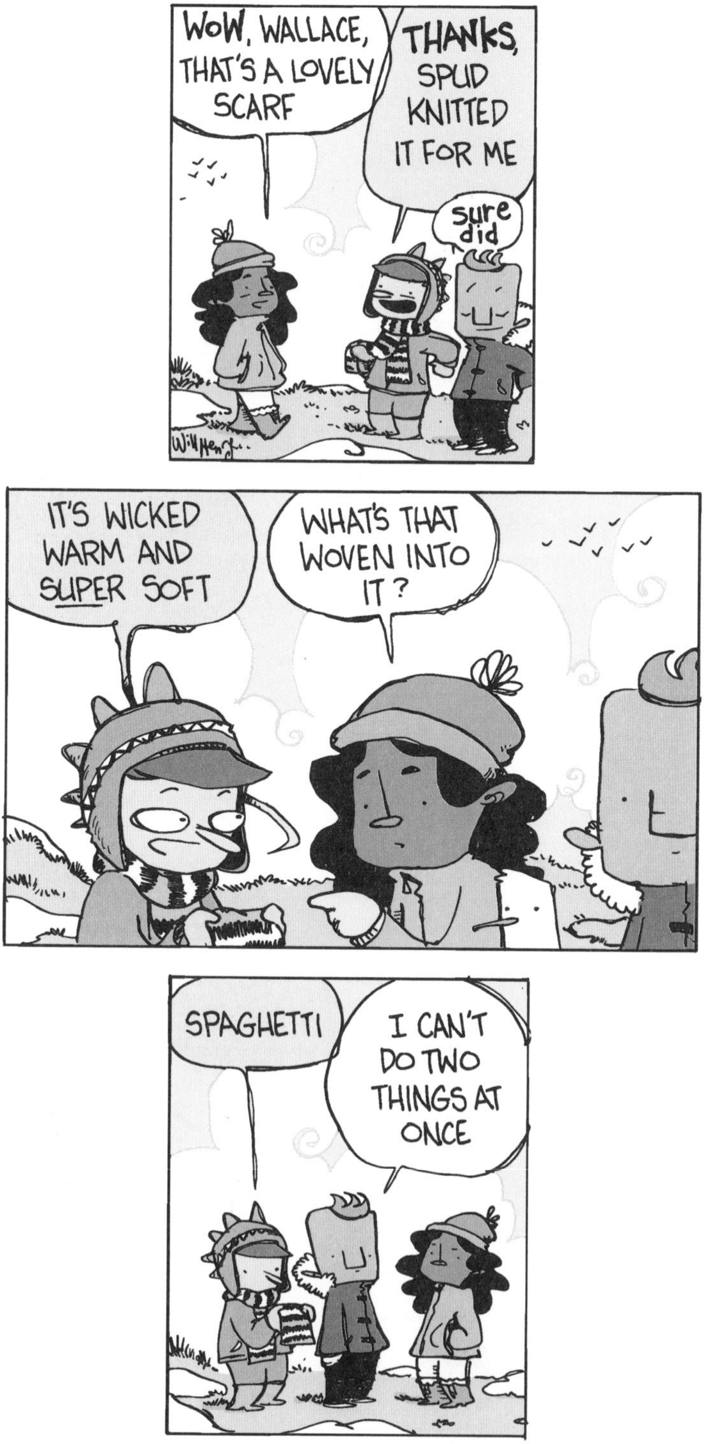
WOW, WALLACE, THAT'S A LOVELY SCARF
THANKS, SPUD KNITTED IT FOR ME
sure did
Will Henry
IT'S WICKED WARM AND SUPER SOFT
WHAT'S THAT WOVEN INTO IT?
SPAGHETTI
I CAN'T DO TWO THINGS AT ONCE

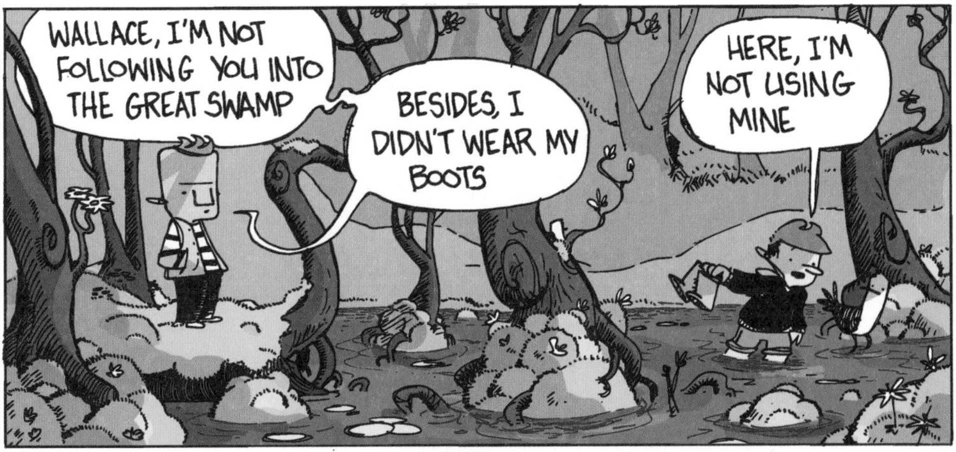
WALLACE, I'M NOT FOLLOWING YOU INTO THE GREAT SWAMP
BESIDES, I DIDN'T WEAR MY BOOTS
HERE, I'M NOT USING MINE

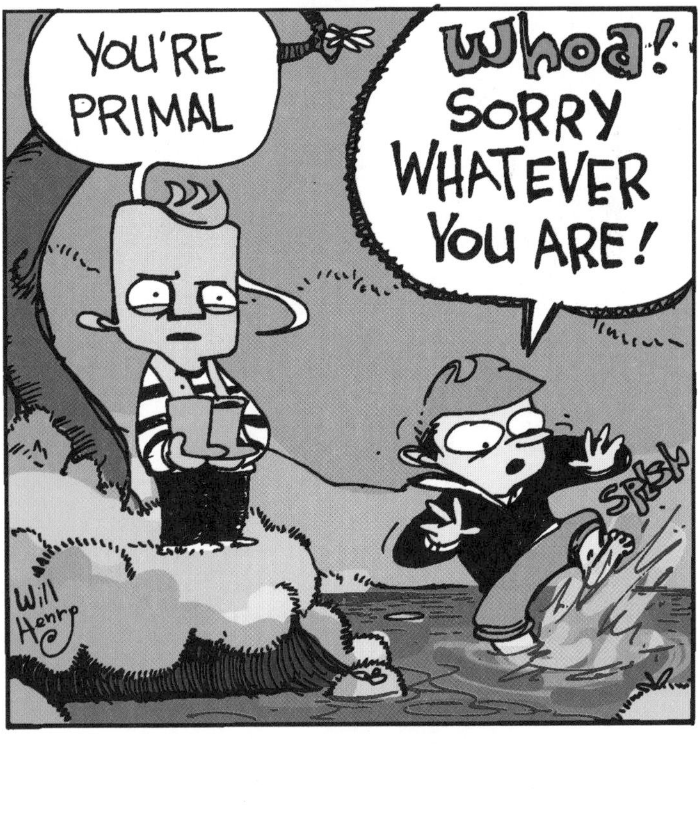
YOU'RE PRIMAL
Whoa! SORRY WHATEVER YOU ARE!
SPLSH
Will Henry

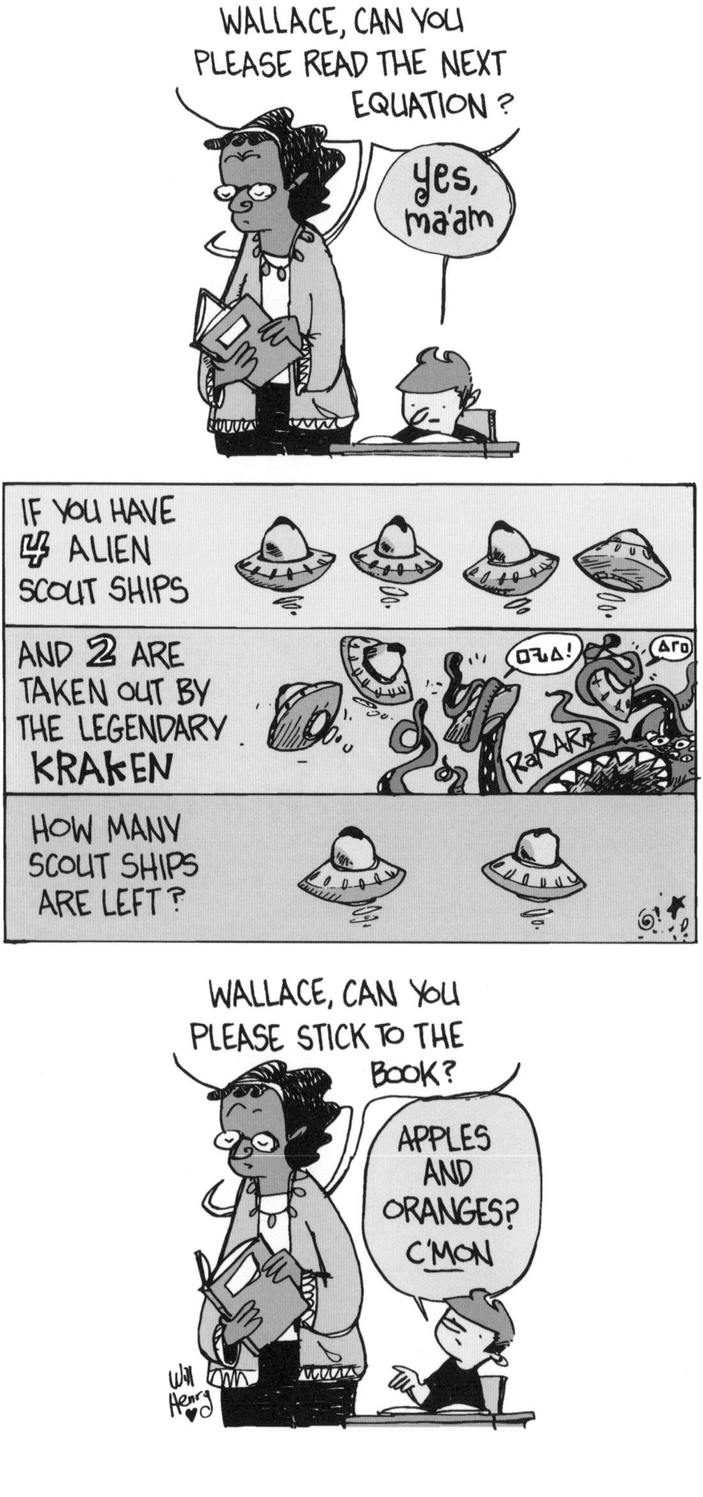
WALLACE, CAN YOU PLEASE READ THE NEXT EQUATION ?
yes, ma'am
IF YOU HAVE 4 ALIEN SCOUT SHIPS
AND 2 ARE TAKEN OUT BY THE LEGENDARY KRAKEN
RaRARR
HOW MANY SCOUT SHIPS ARE LEFT ?
WALLACE, CAN YOU PLEASE STICK TO THE BOOK?
APPLES AND ORANGES? C'MON
Will Henry

WHAT'RE YOU LOOKIN' AT, WALLACE ?
THERE'S A STORM ROLLING IN FROM THE OCEAN!
YOU CAN FEEL THE CHANGE IN PRESSURE. AND THE LIGHTNING IS PUTTING ON A SHOW!
KRAK
Will Henry
oh, Hi, SPUD
you're all NUTS!!!

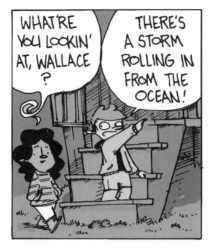

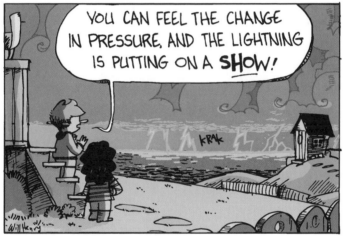

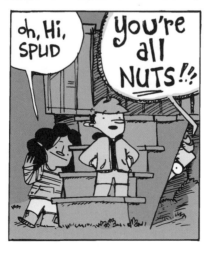

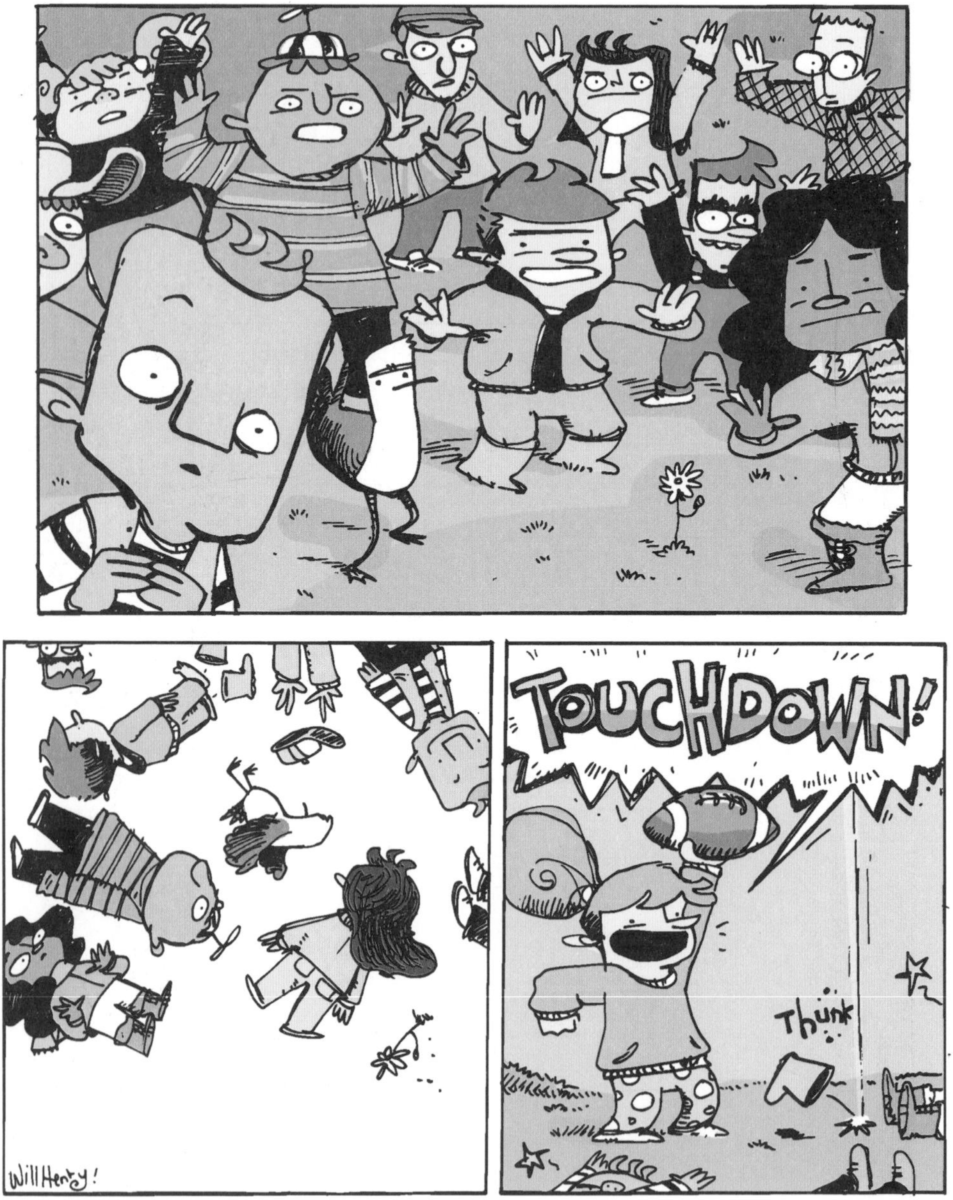

Will Henry!
TOUCHDOWN!
Thunk

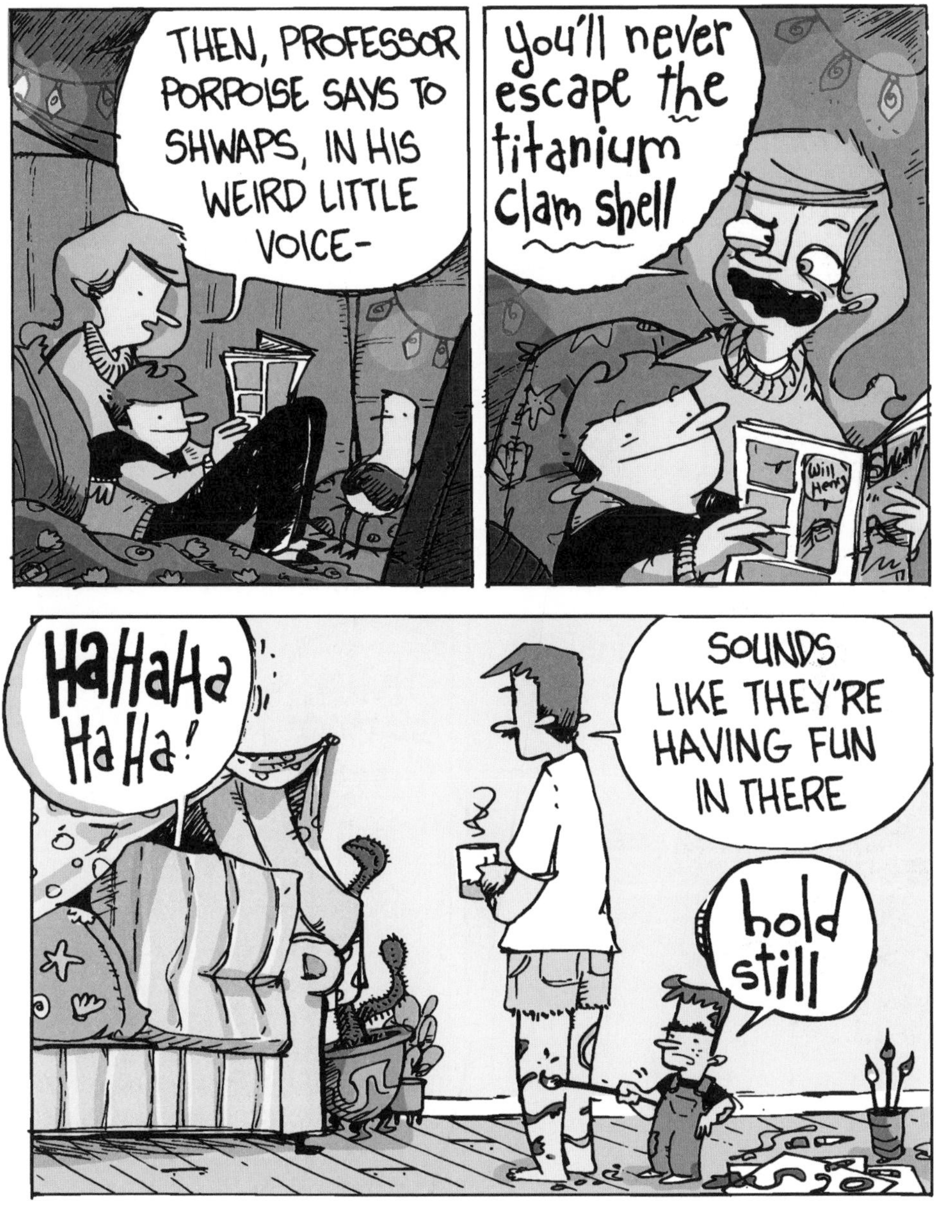
THEN, PROFESSOR PORPOISE SAYS TO SHWAPS, IN HIS WEIRD LITTLE VOICE-
you'll never escape the titanium clam shell
HaHaHa HaHa!
SOUNDS LIKE THEY'RE HAVING FUN IN THERE
hold still

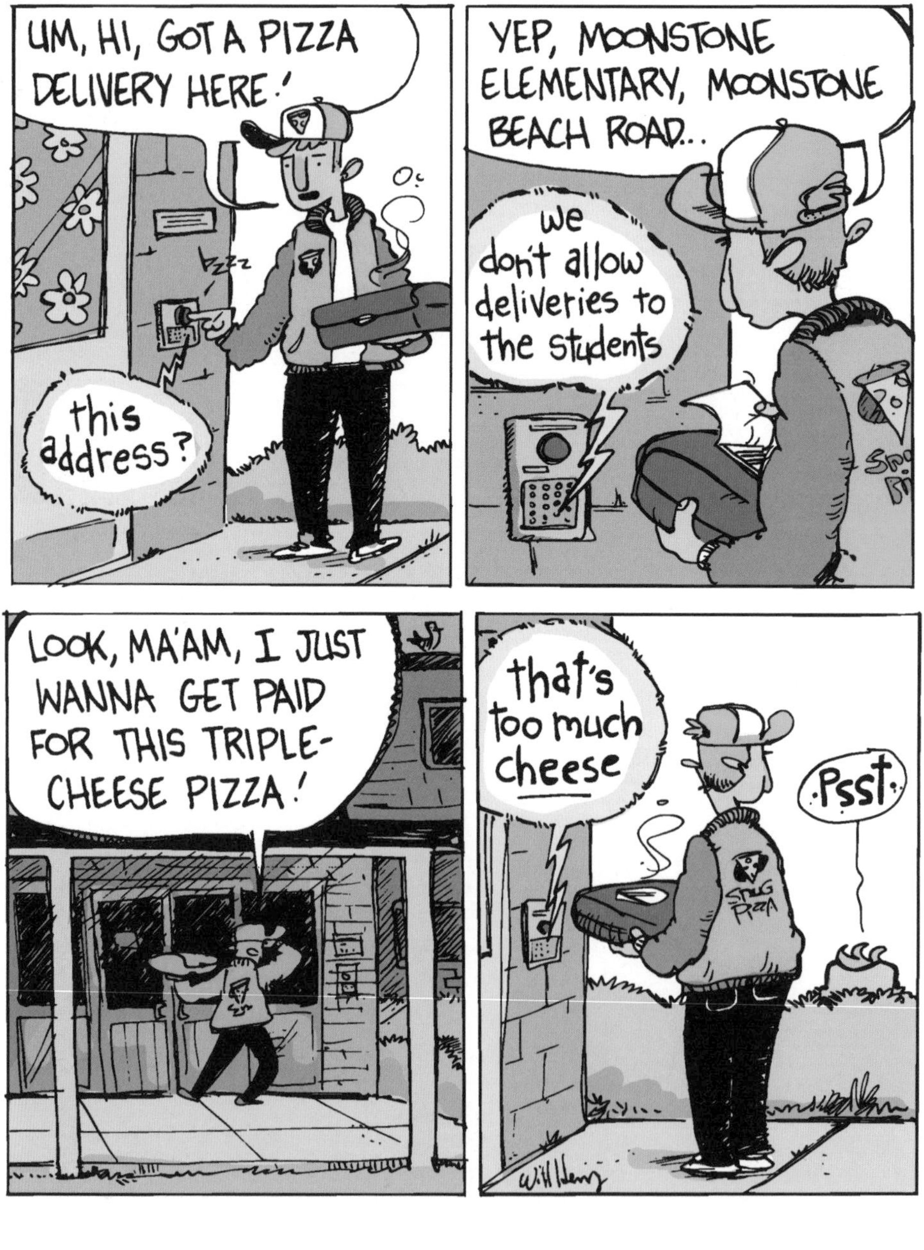
UM, HI, GOT A PIZZA DELIVERY HERE!
zzz
this address?
YEP, MOONSTONE ELEMENTARY, MOONSTONE BEACH ROAD...
we don't allow deliveries to the students
LOOK, MA'AM, I JUST WANNA GET PAID FOR THIS TRIPLE-CHEESE PIZZA!
that's too much cheese
Psst
SNUG PIZZA
Will Henry

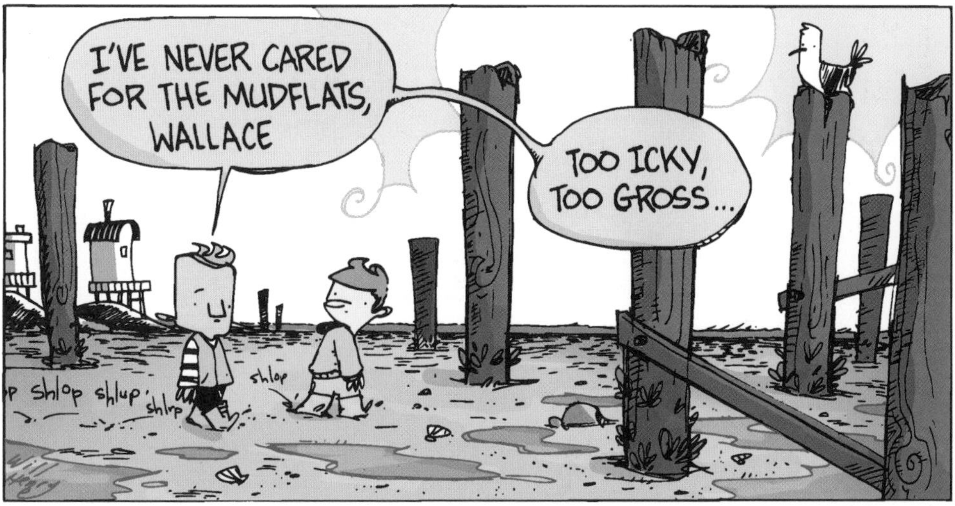
I'VE NEVER CARED FOR THE MUDFLATS, WALLACE
TOO ICKY, TOO GROSS...
shlop shlup shlup
shlop

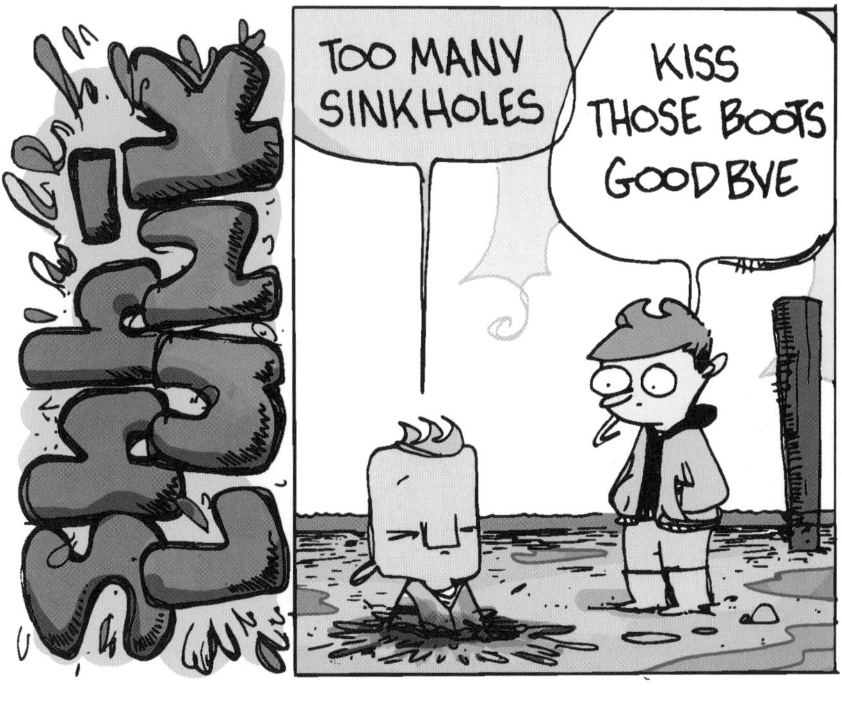
SHLUK!
TOO MANY SINKHOLES
KISS THOSE BOOTS GOODBYE

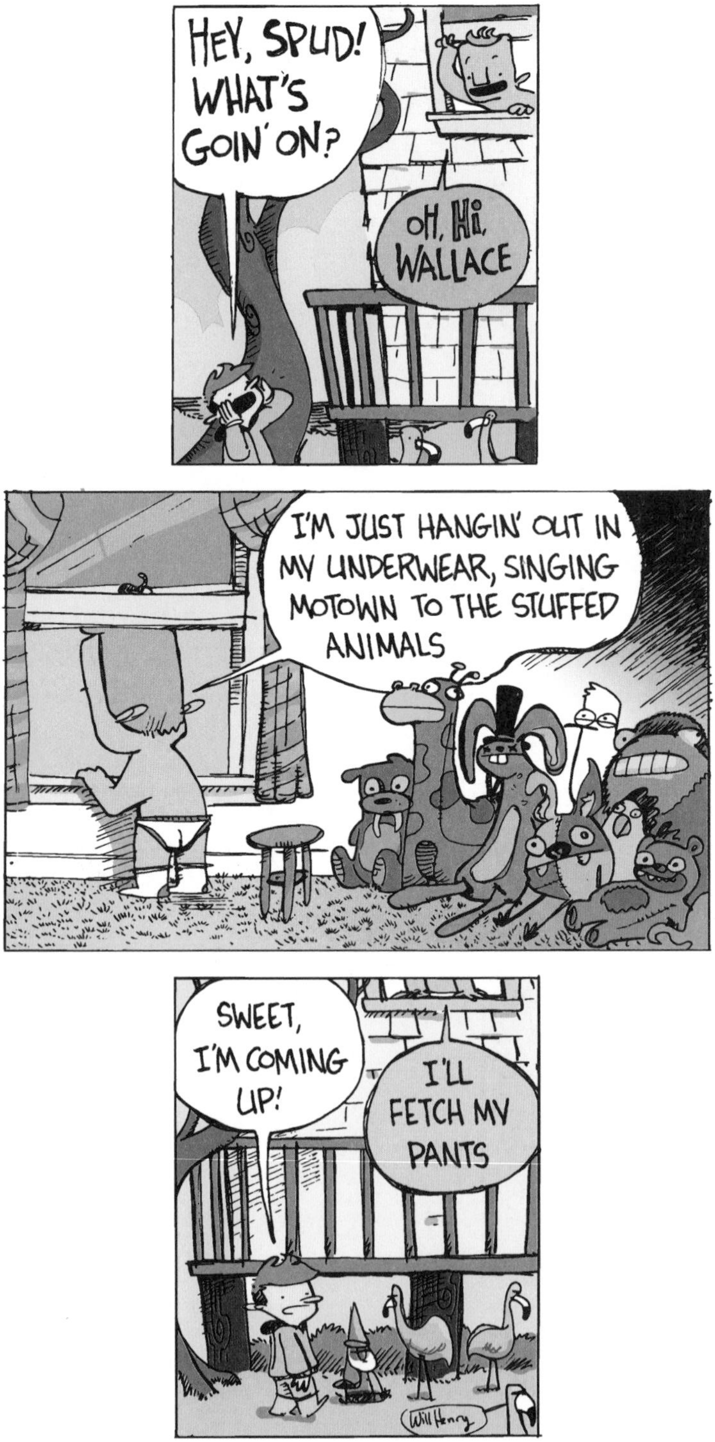
HEY, SPUD! WHAT'S GOIN' ON?
OH, HI, WALLACE
I'M JUST HANGIN' OUT IN MY UNDERWEAR, SINGING MOTOWN TO THE STUFFED ANIMALS
SWEET, I'M COMING UP!
I'LL FETCH MY PANTS
Will Henry

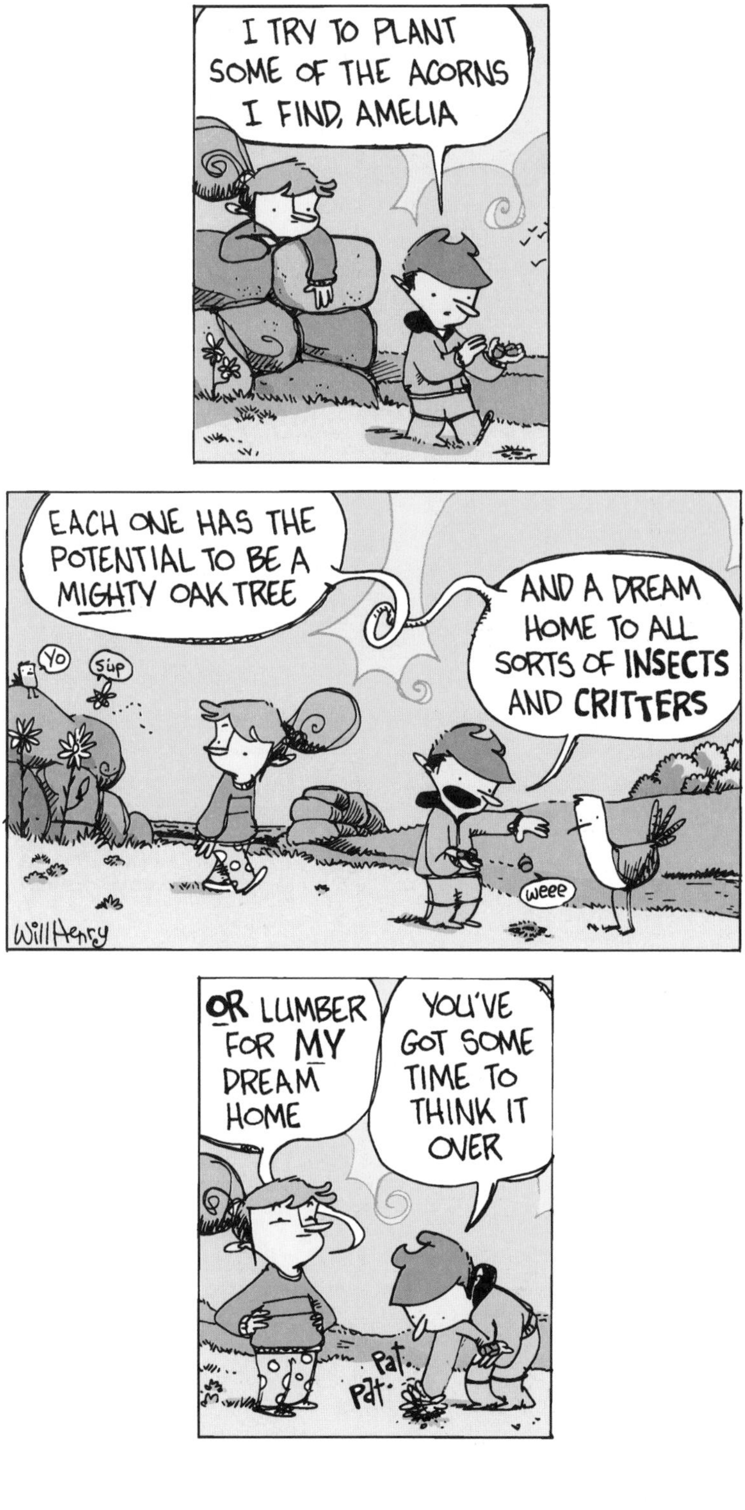
I TRY TO PLANT SOME OF THE ACORNS I FIND, AMELIA
EACH ONE HAS THE POTENTIAL TO BE A MIGHTY OAK TREE
AND A DREAM HOME TO ALL SORTS OF INSECTS AND CRITTERS
YO
SUP
WEEE
Will Henry
OR LUMBER FOR MY DREAM HOME
YOU'VE GOT SOME TIME TO THINK IT OVER
PAT
PAT

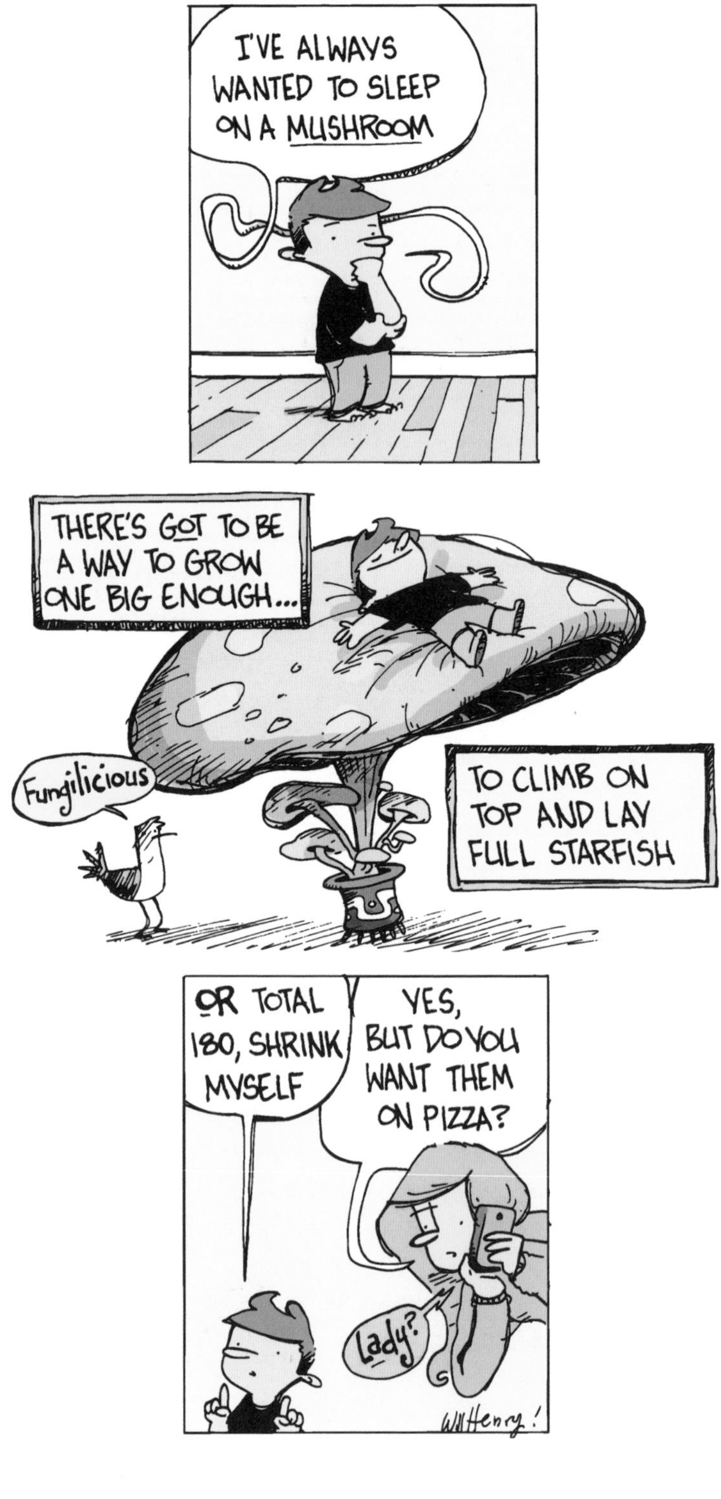
I'VE ALWAYS WANTED TO SLEEP ON A MUSHROOM
THERE'S GOT TO BE A WAY TO GROW ONE BIG ENOUGH...
Fungilicious
TO CLIMB ON TOP AND LAY FULL STARFISH
OR TOTAL 180, SHRINK MYSELF
YES, BUT DO YOU WANT THEM ON PIZZA?
Lady?

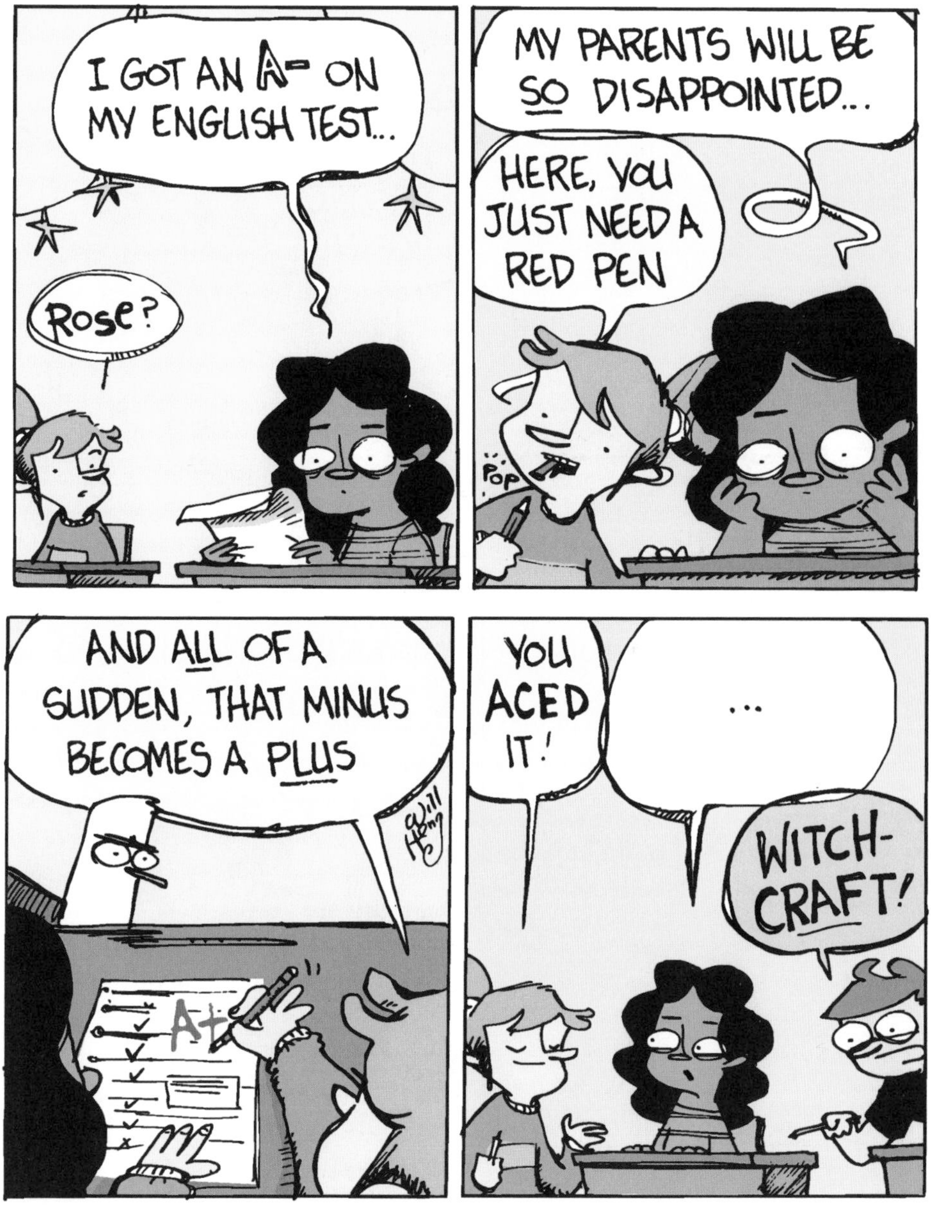
I GOT AN A- ON MY ENGLISH TEST...
Rose?
MY PARENTS WILL BE SO DISAPPOINTED...
HERE, YOU JUST NEED A RED PEN
POP
AND ALL OF A SUDDEN, THAT MINUS BECOMES A PLUS
A+
YOU ACED IT!
...
WITCH-CRAFT!

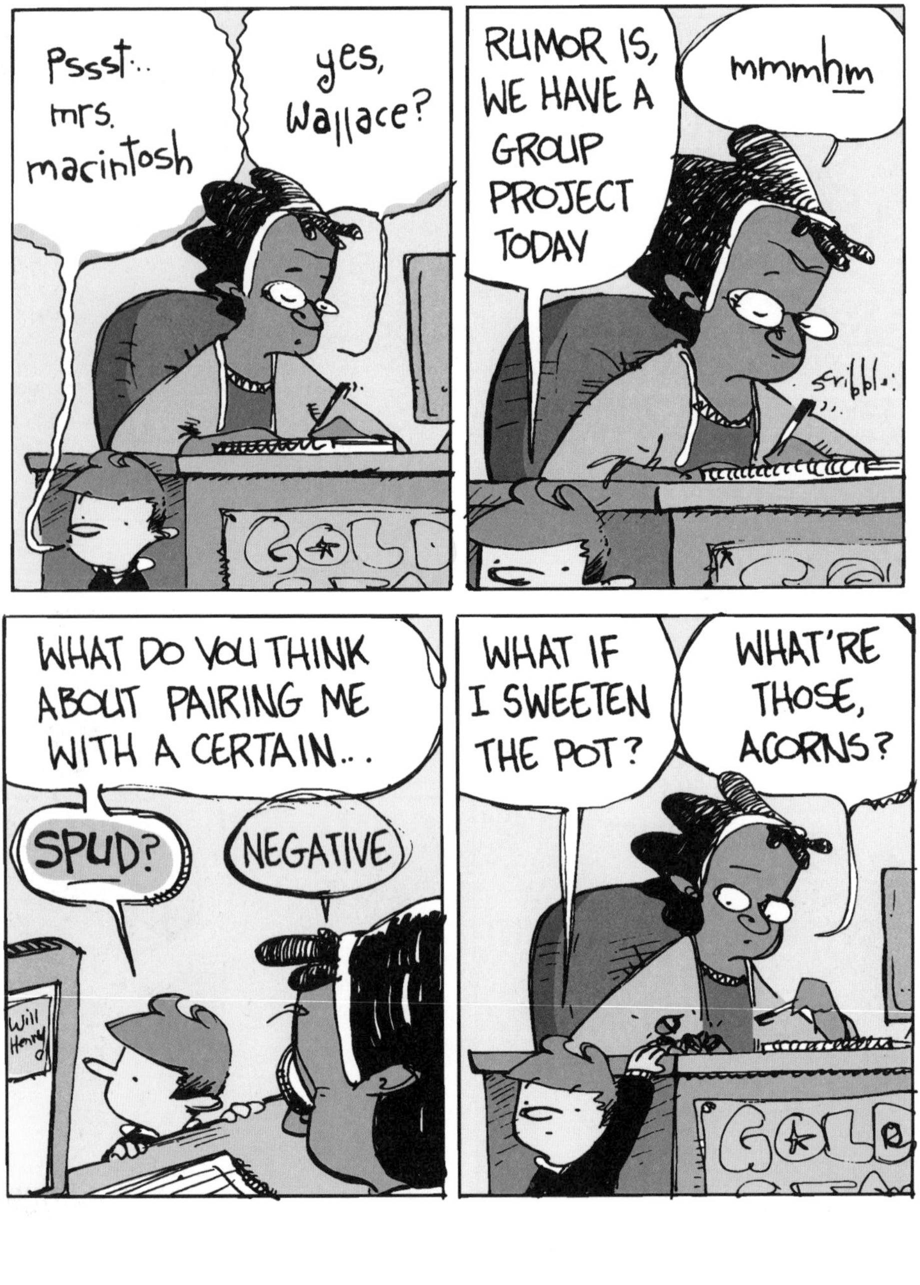
Pssst... mrs. macintosh
yes, Wallace?
RUMOR IS, WE HAVE A GROUP PROJECT TODAY
mmmhm
scribble...
WHAT DO YOU THINK ABOUT PAIRING ME WITH A CERTAIN...
SPUD?
NEGATIVE
Will Henry
WHAT IF I SWEETEN THE POT?
WHAT'RE THOSE, ACORNS?

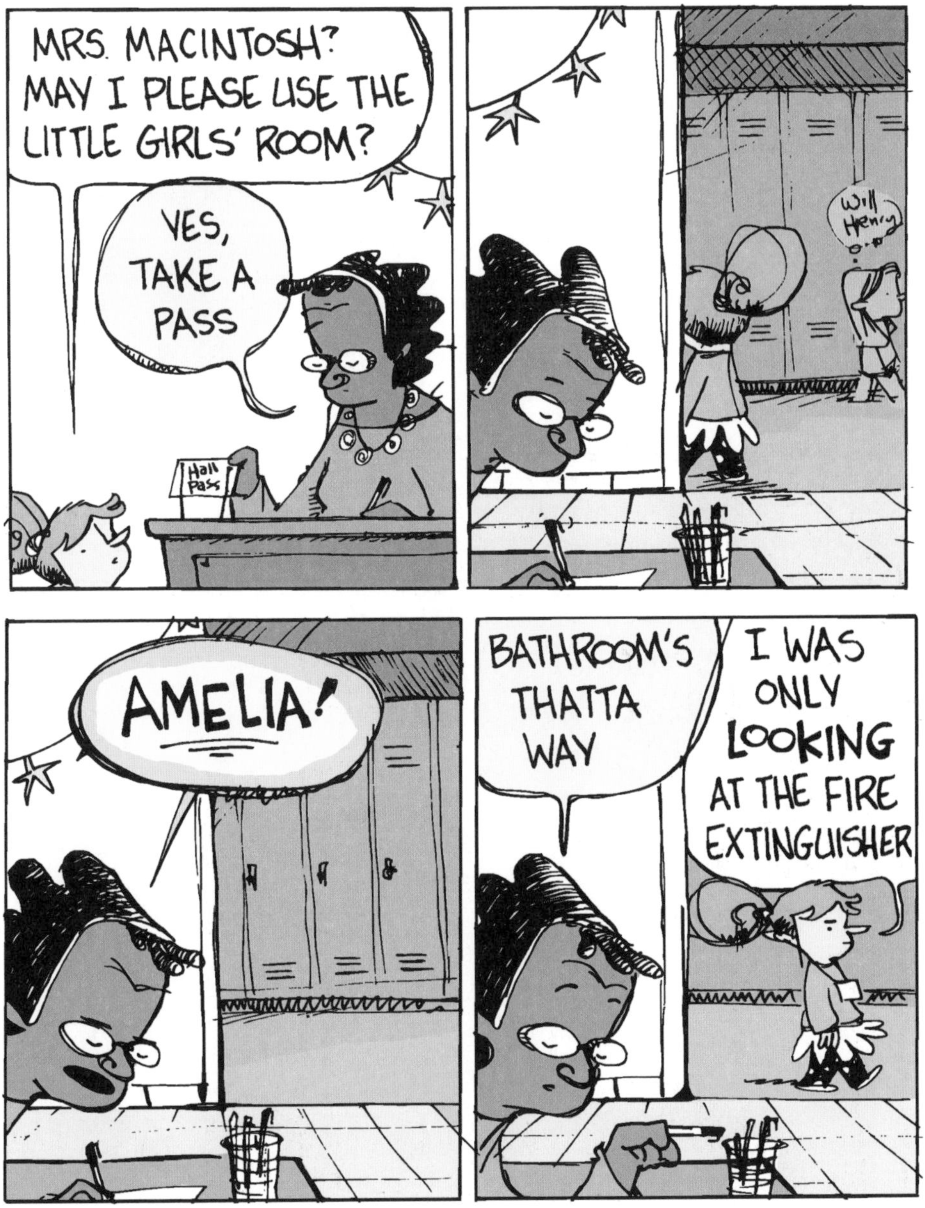
MRS. MACINTOSH? MAY I PLEASE USE THE LITTLE GIRLS' ROOM?
YES, TAKE A PASS
Hall Pass
Will Henry
AMELIA!
BATHROOM'S THATTA WAY
I WAS ONLY LOOKING AT THE FIRE EXTINGUISHER

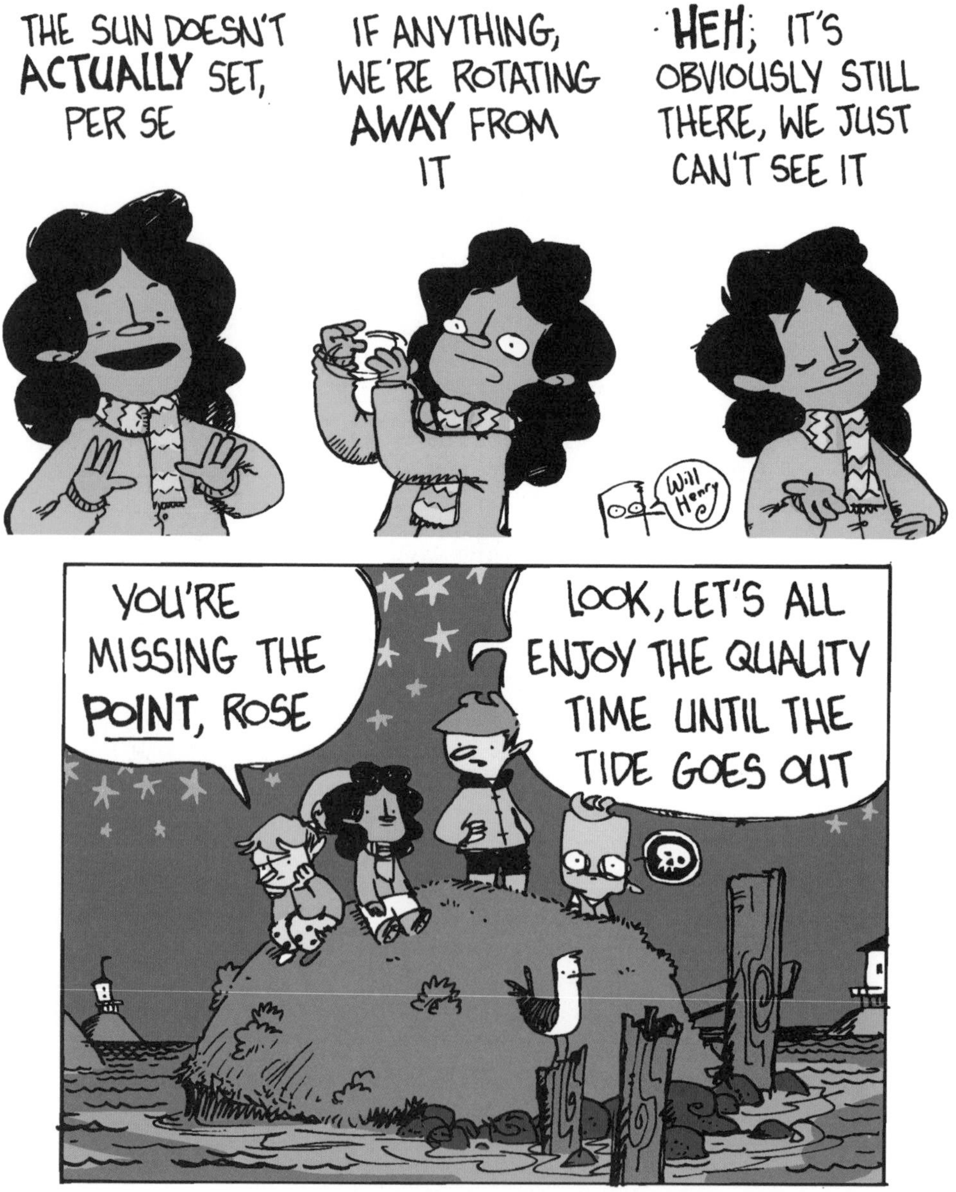
THE SUN DOESN'T ACTUALLY SET, PER SE
IF ANYTHING, WE'RE ROTATING AWAY FROM IT
HEH; IT'S OBVIOUSLY STILL THERE, WE JUST CAN'T SEE IT
Will Henry
YOU'RE MISSING THE POINT, ROSE
LOOK, LET'S ALL ENJOY THE QUALITY TIME UNTIL THE TIDE GOES OUT

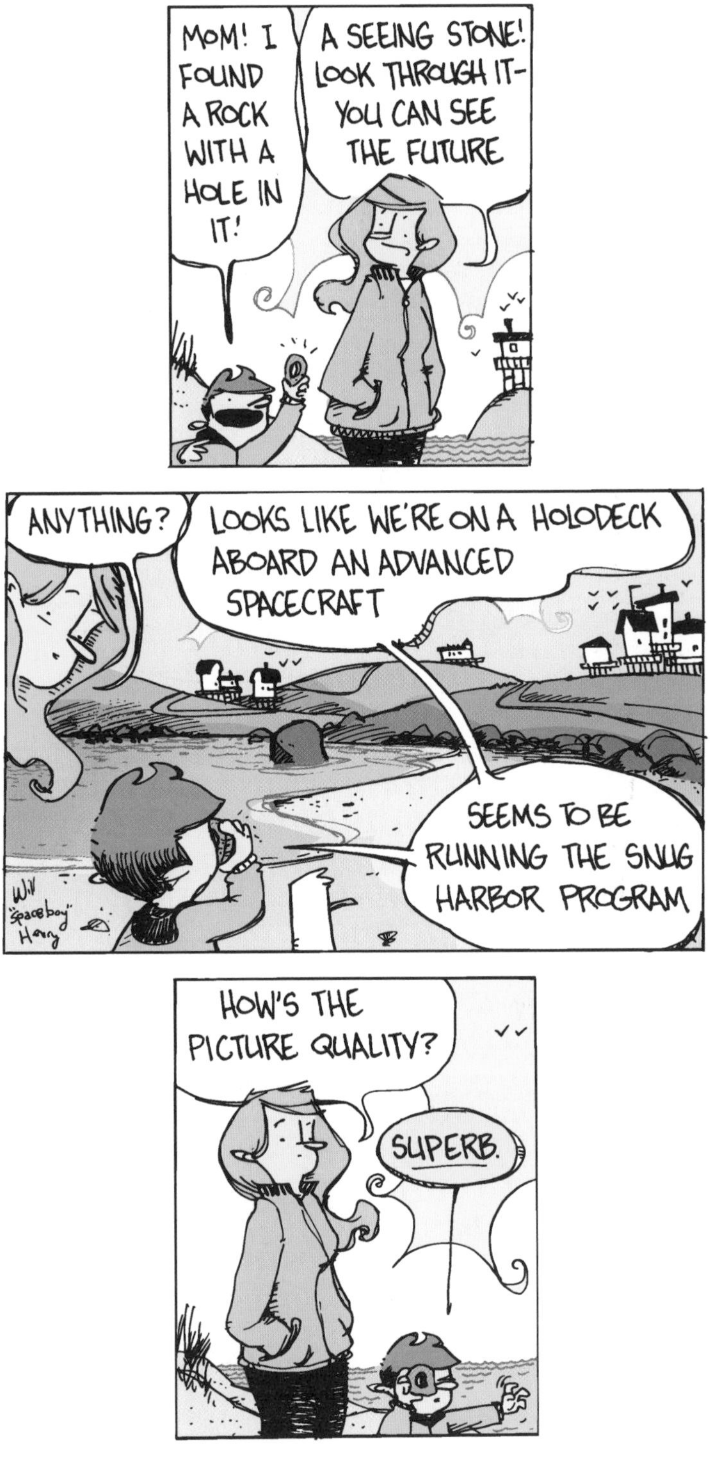
MOM! I FOUND A ROCK WITH A HOLE IN IT!
A SEEING STONE! LOOK THROUGH IT- YOU CAN SEE THE FUTURE
ANYTHING?
LOOKS LIKE WE'RE ON A HOLODECK ABOARD AN ADVANCED SPACECRAFT
SEEMS TO BE RUNNING THE SNUG HARBOR PROGRAM
Will "spaceboy" Henry
HOW'S THE PICTURE QUALITY?
SUPERB.

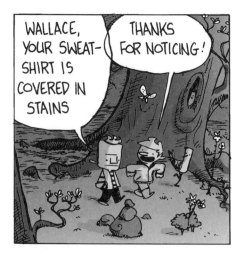

WALLACE, YOUR SWEAT-SHIRT IS COVERED IN STAINS
THANKS FOR NOTICING!
I'M LETTING IT GET GROSS AND GRIMY
IN HOPES THAT IT GROWS MOSS AND FUNGI
I'm Lichen it!
MOSS BOSS, COMIN' THROUGH
WillHenry
IT'S ATTRACTING WILDLIFE
hah QUIT IT!
Lick Lick

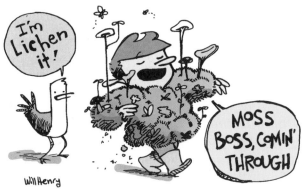

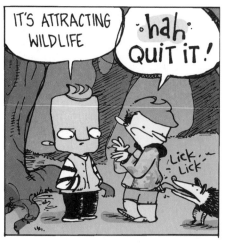

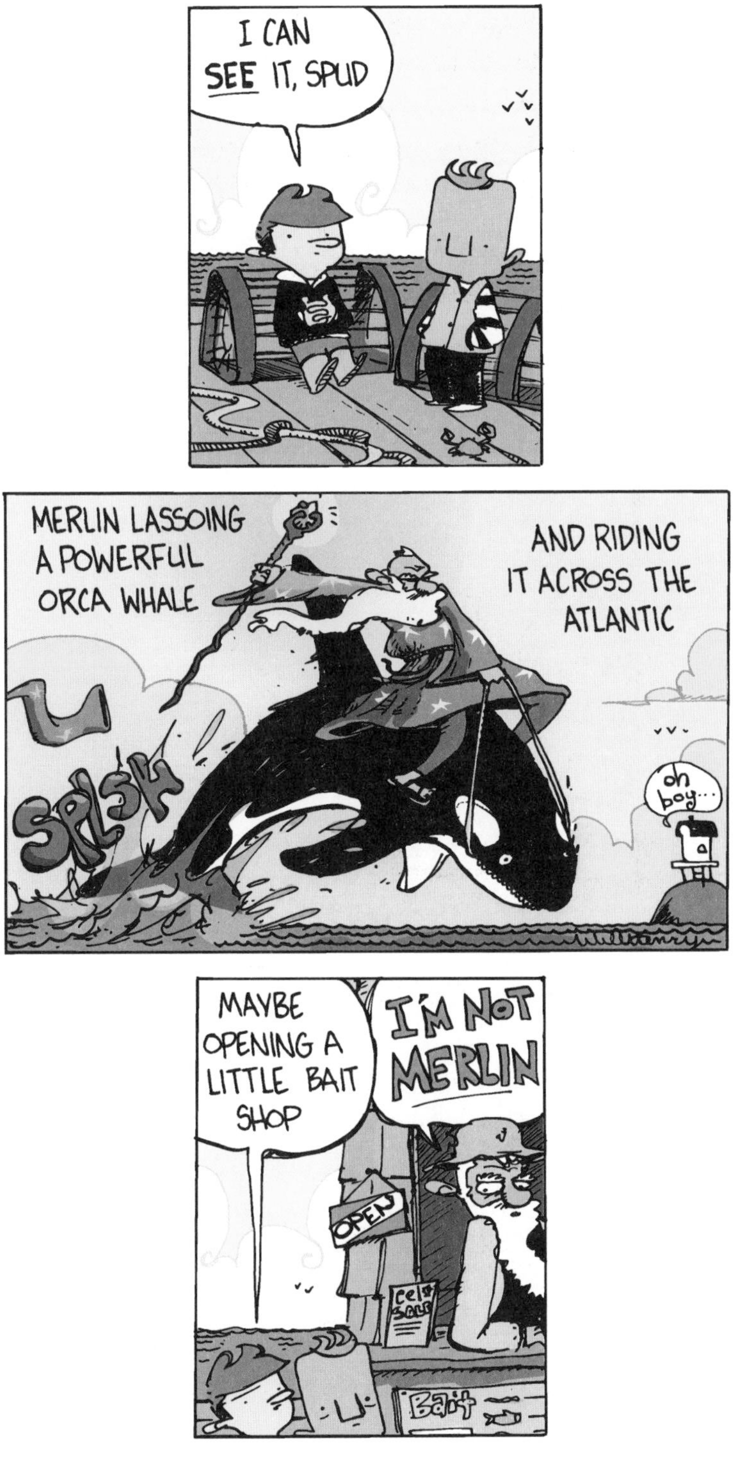
I CAN SEE IT, SPUD
MERLIN LASSOING A POWERFUL ORCA WHALE
AND RIDING IT ACROSS THE ATLANTIC
SPLSH
oh boy...
MAYBE OPENING A LITTLE BAIT SHOP
I'M NOT MERLIN
OPEN
Bait

HA HA, WALLACE! THAT'S PARK PLACE WITH TWO HOTELS! YOU OWE ME-
blrp
Will Henry
i love family game night!!!
STERLING... YOU WEREN'T EVEN PLAYING

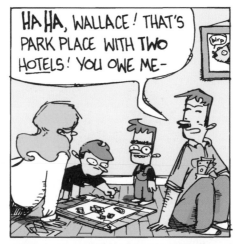

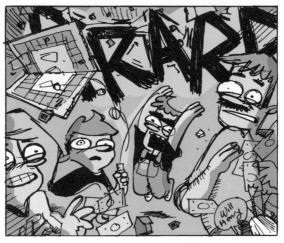

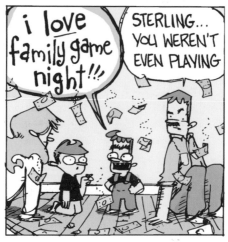

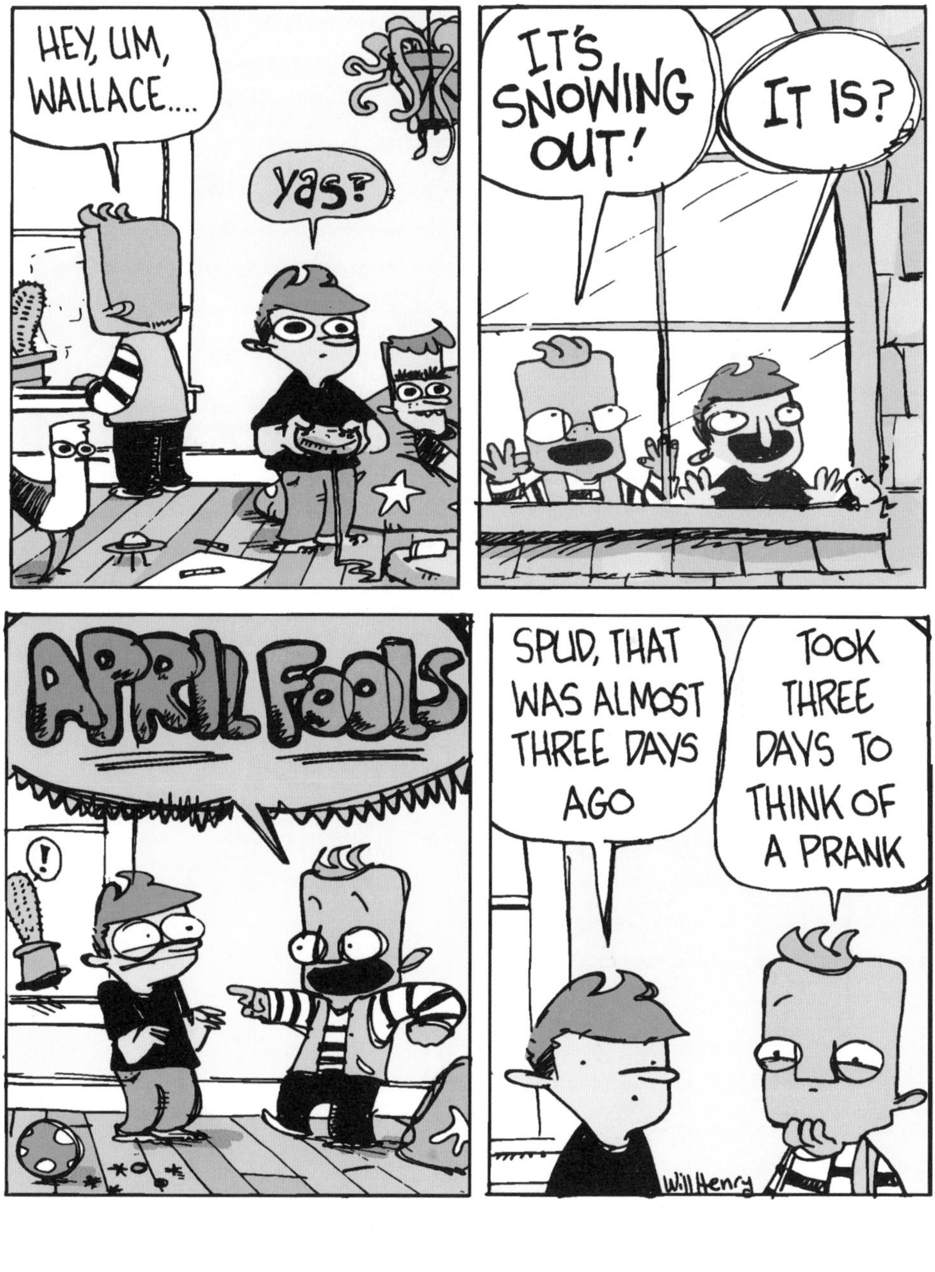
HEY, UM, WALLACE....
yas?
IT'S SNOWING OUT!
IT IS?
APRIL FOOLS
!
SPUD, THAT WAS ALMOST THREE DAYS AGO
TOOK THREE DAYS TO THINK OF A PRANK
Will Henry

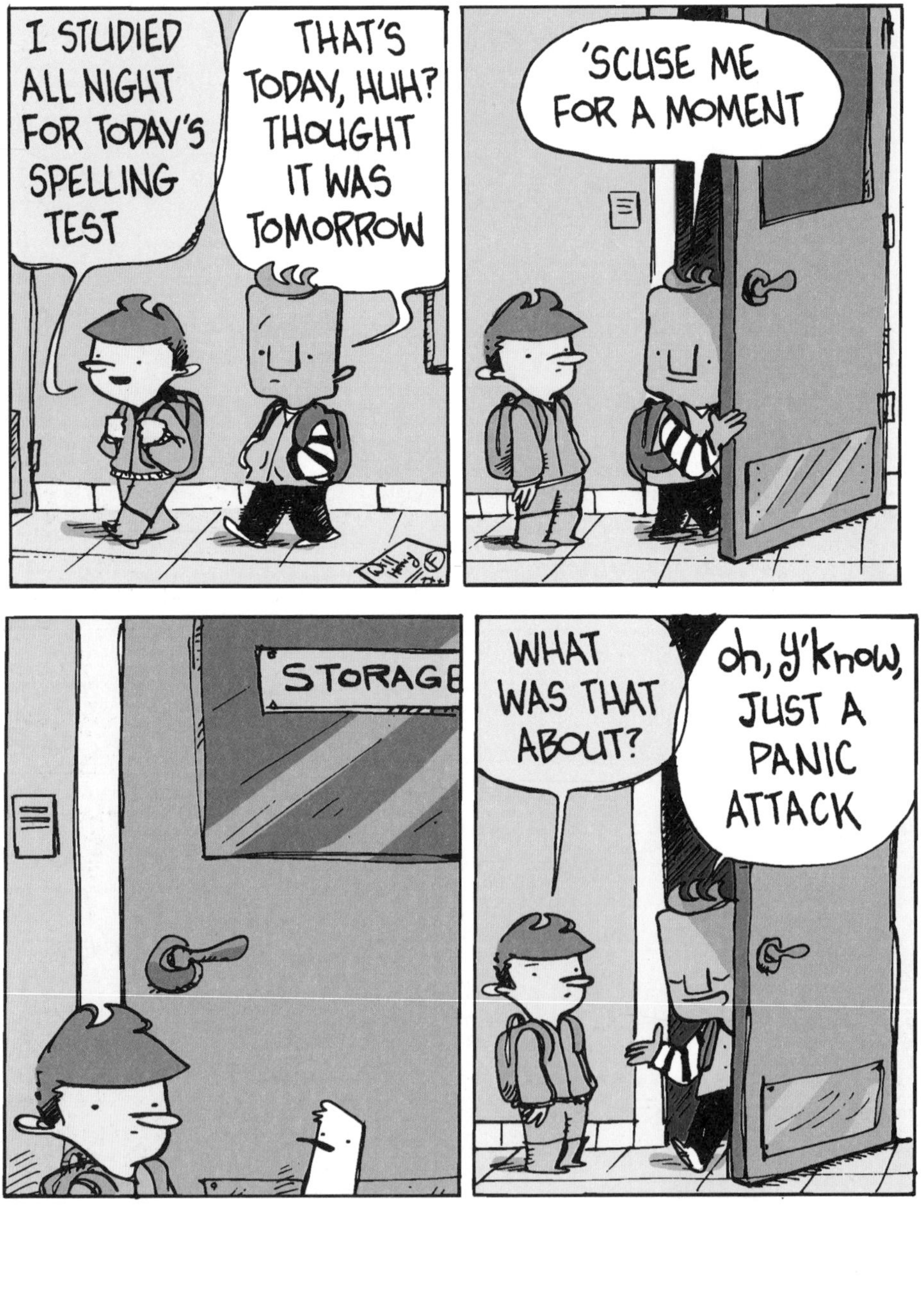
I STUDIED ALL NIGHT FOR TODAY'S SPELLING TEST
THAT'S TODAY, HUH? THOUGHT IT WAS TOMORROW
'SCUSE ME FOR A MOMENT
STORAGE
WHAT WAS THAT ABOUT?
oh, y'know, JUST A PANIC ATTACK

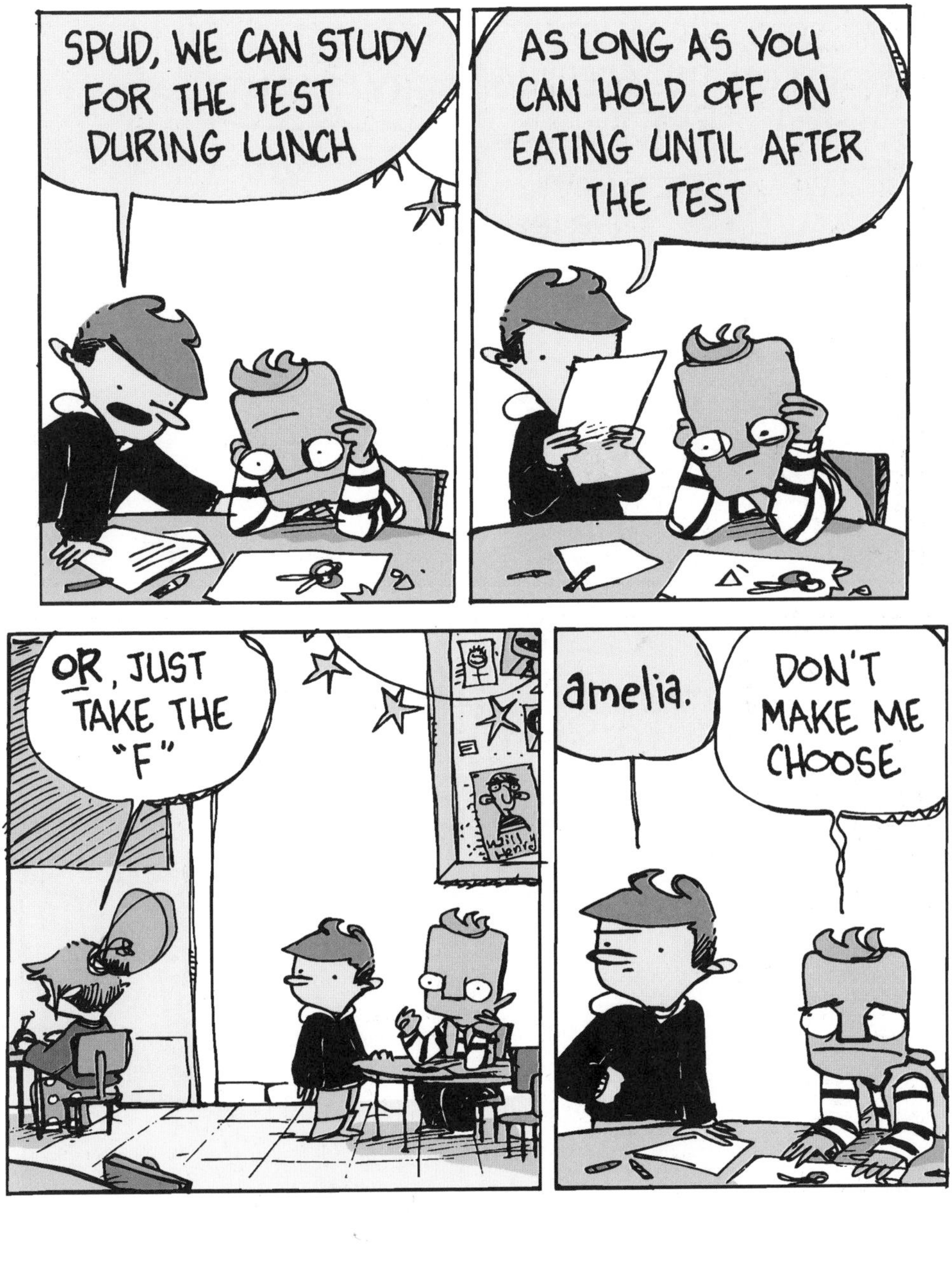
SPUD, WE CAN STUDY FOR THE TEST DURING LUNCH
AS LONG AS YOU CAN HOLD OFF ON EATING UNTIL AFTER THE TEST
OR, JUST TAKE THE "F"
Willy Henry
amelia.
DON'T MAKE ME CHOOSE

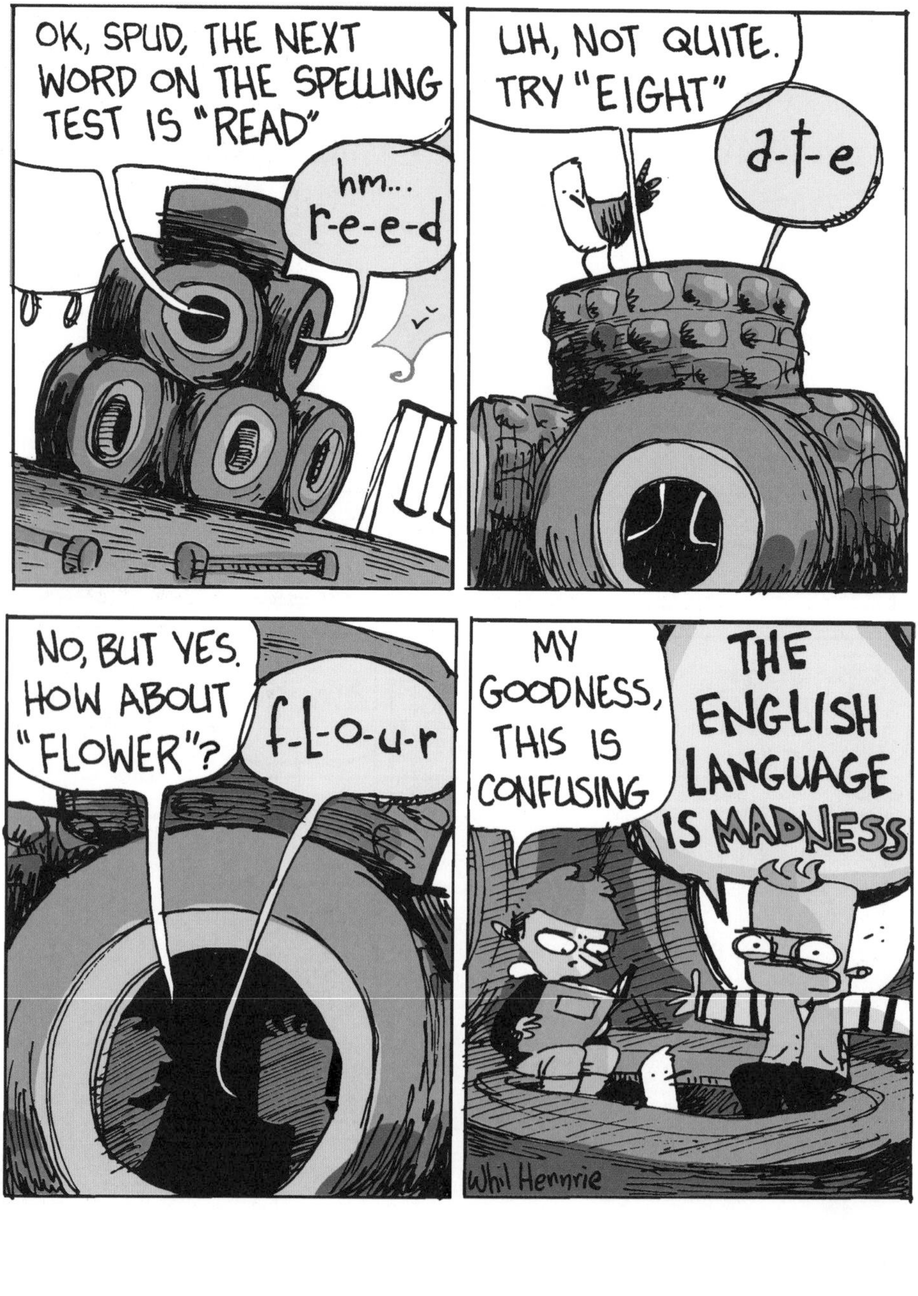
OK, SPUD, THE NEXT WORD ON THE SPELLING TEST IS "READ"
hm... r-e-e-d
UH, NOT QUITE. TRY "EIGHT"
a-t-e
NO, BUT YES. HOW ABOUT "FLOWER"?
f-l-o-u-r
MY GOODNESS, THIS IS CONFUSING
THE ENGLISH LANGUAGE IS MADNESS
Whil Hennrie

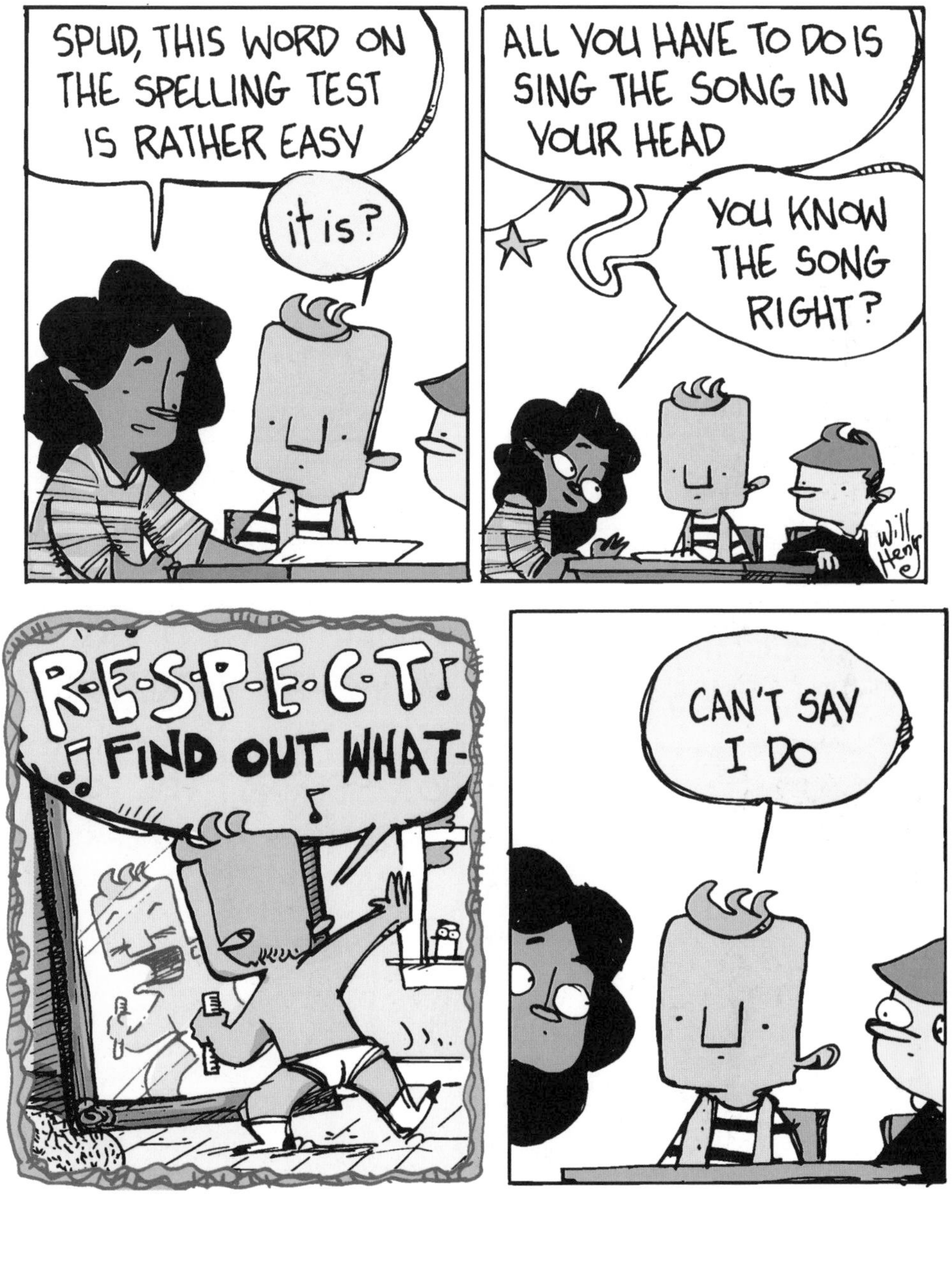
SPUD, THIS WORD ON THE SPELLING TEST IS RATHER EASY
it is?
ALL YOU HAVE TO DO IS SING THE SONG IN YOUR HEAD
YOU KNOW THE SONG RIGHT?
Will Henry
R-E-S-P-E-C-T
FIND OUT WHAT-
CAN'T SAY I DO

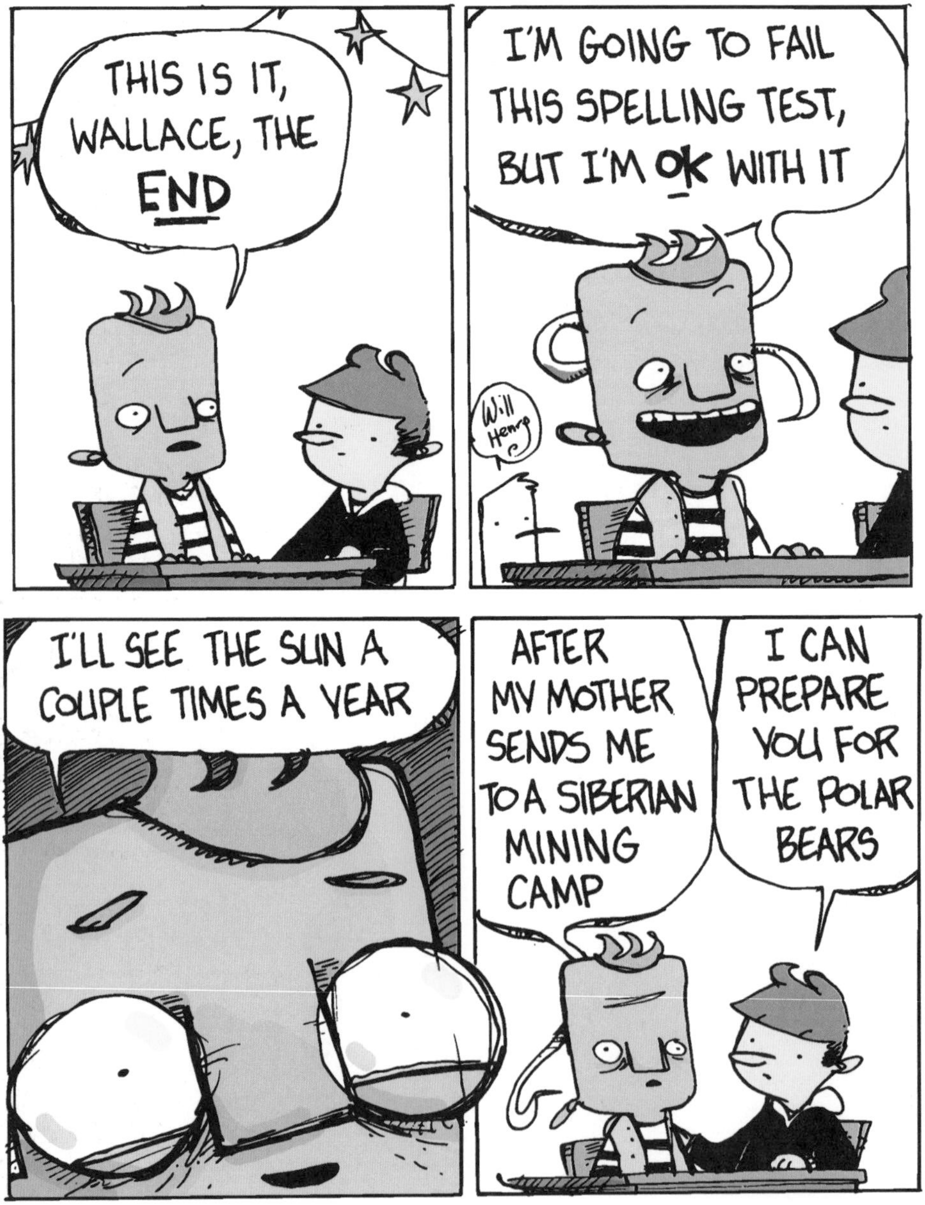
THIS IS IT, WALLACE, THE END
I'M GOING TO FAIL THIS SPELLING TEST, BUT I'M OK WITH IT
Will Henry
I'LL SEE THE SUN A COUPLE TIMES A YEAR
AFTER MY MOTHER SENDS ME TO A SIBERIAN MINING CAMP
I CAN PREPARE YOU FOR THE POLAR BEARS

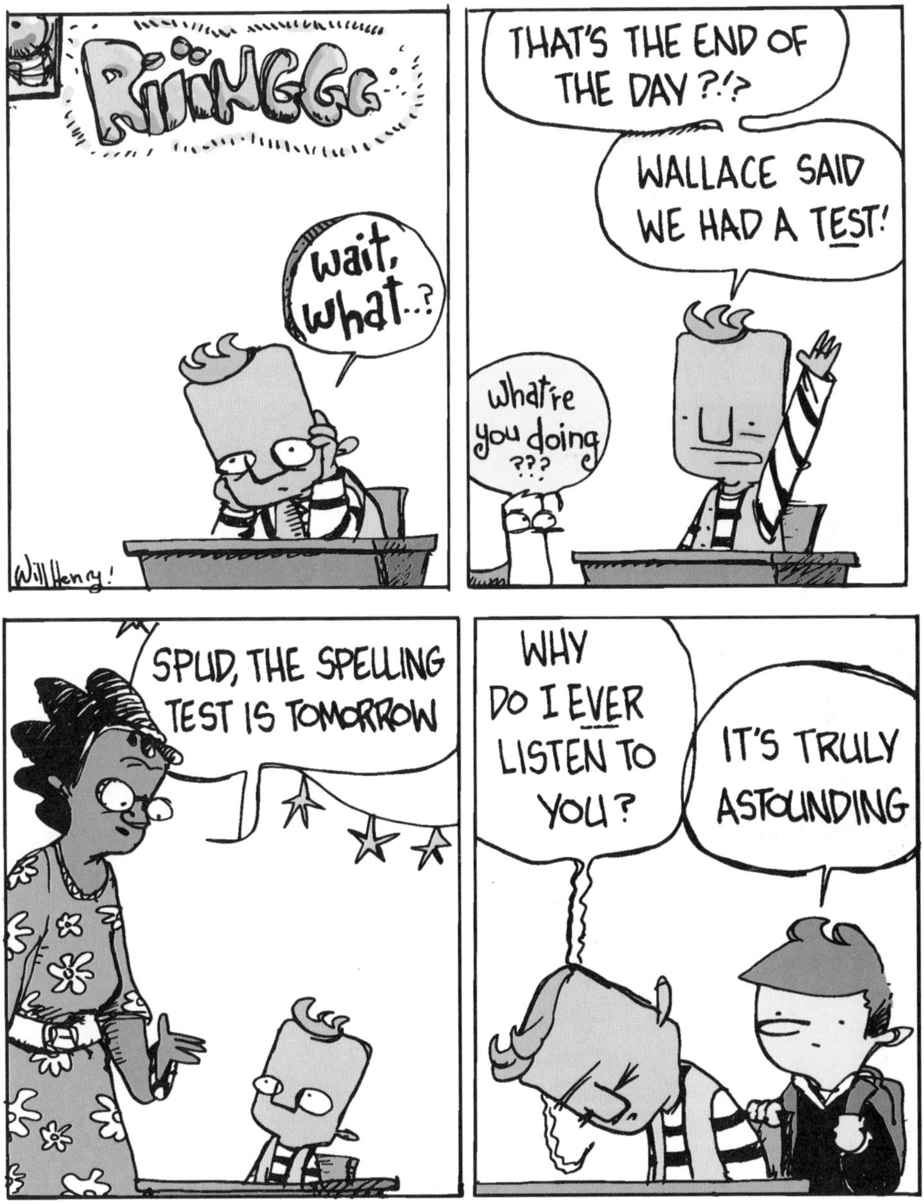
RIIINGGG
wait, what..?
Will Henry!
THAT'S THE END OF THE DAY?!?
WALLACE SAID WE HAD A TEST!
what're you doing???
SPUD, THE SPELLING TEST IS TOMORROW
WHY DO I EVER LISTEN TO YOU?
IT'S TRULY ASTOUNDING

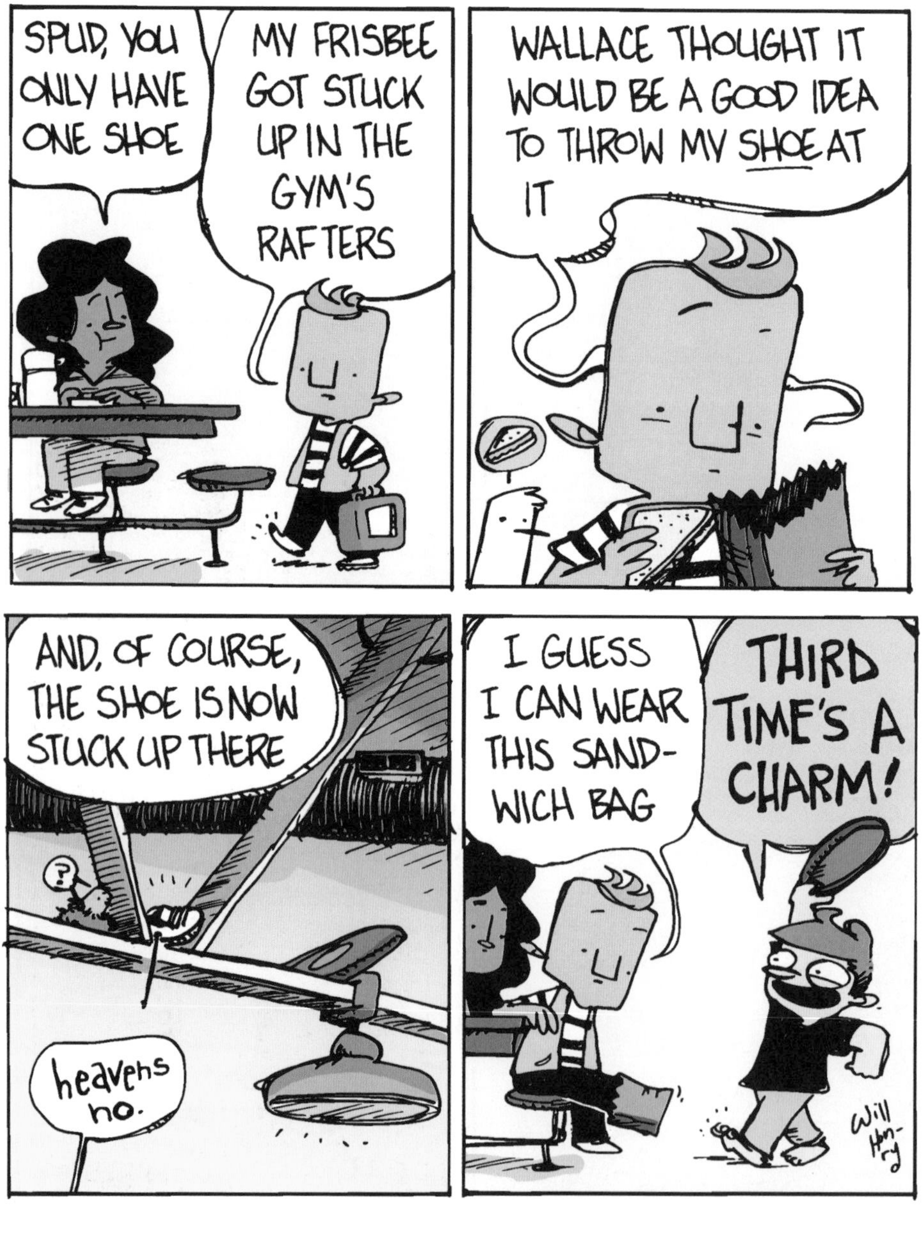
SPUD, YOU ONLY HAVE ONE SHOE
MY FRISBEE GOT STUCK UP IN THE GYM'S RAFTERS
WALLACE THOUGHT IT WOULD BE A GOOD IDEA TO THROW MY SHOE AT IT
AND, OF COURSE, THE SHOE IS NOW STUCK UP THERE
?
heavens no.
I GUESS I CAN WEAR THIS SAND-WICH BAG
THIRD TIME'S A CHARM!
Will Henry

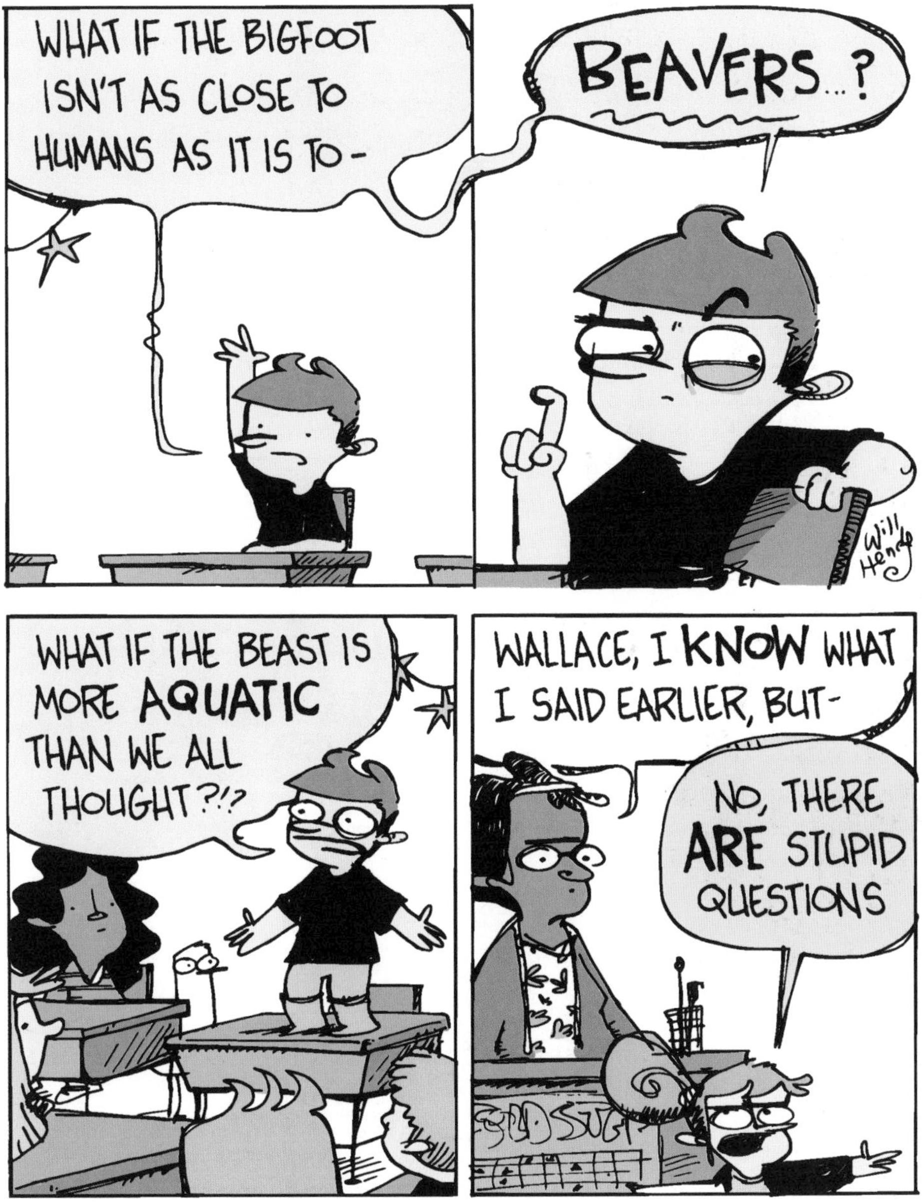
WHAT IF THE BIGFOOT ISN'T AS CLOSE TO HUMANS AS IT IS TO-
BEAVERS...?
Will Hend
WHAT IF THE BEAST IS MORE AQUATIC THAN WE ALL THOUGHT?!?
WALLACE, I KNOW WHAT I SAID EARLIER, BUT-
NO, THERE ARE STUPID QUESTIONS

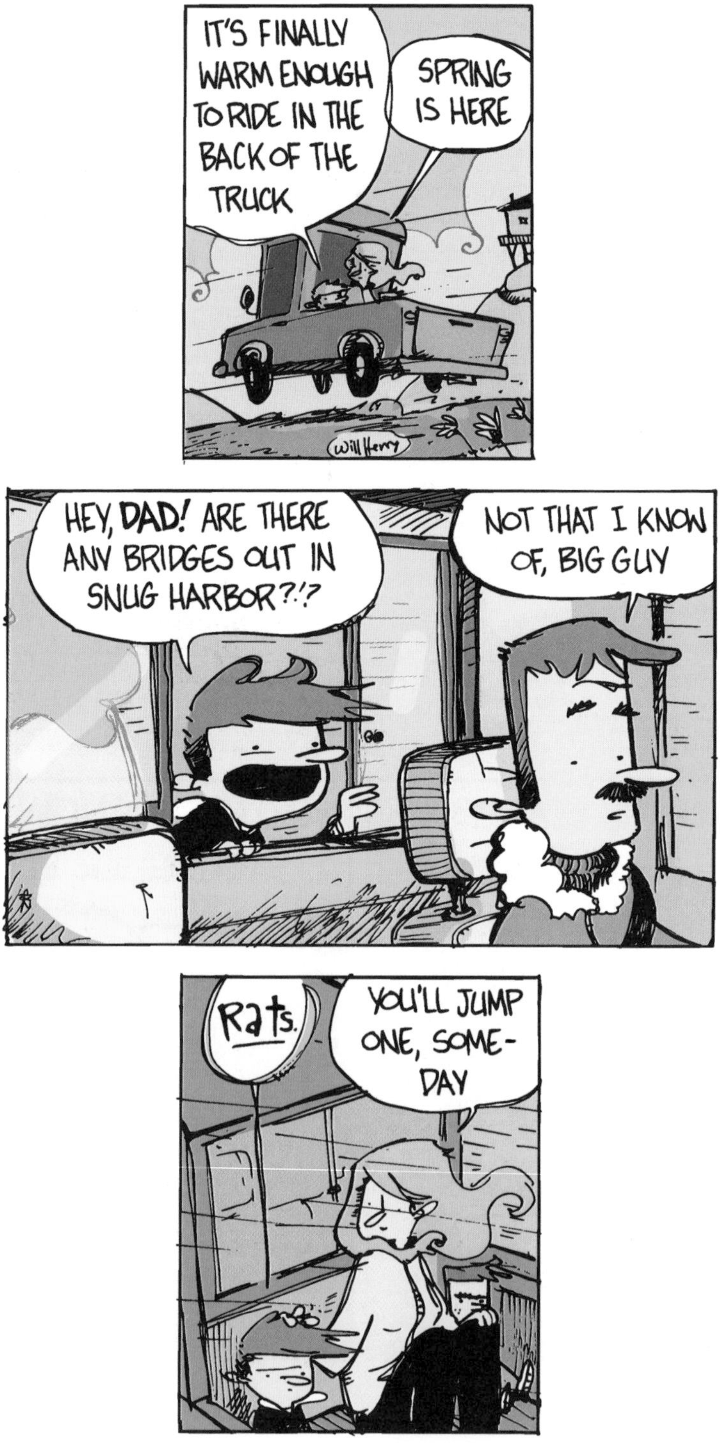
IT'S FINALLY WARM ENOUGH TO RIDE IN THE BACK OF THE TRUCK
SPRING IS HERE
Will Henry
HEY, DAD! ARE THERE ANY BRIDGES OUT IN SNUG HARBOR?!?
NOT THAT I KNOW OF, BIG GUY
Rats.
YOU'LL JUMP ONE, SOME-DAY

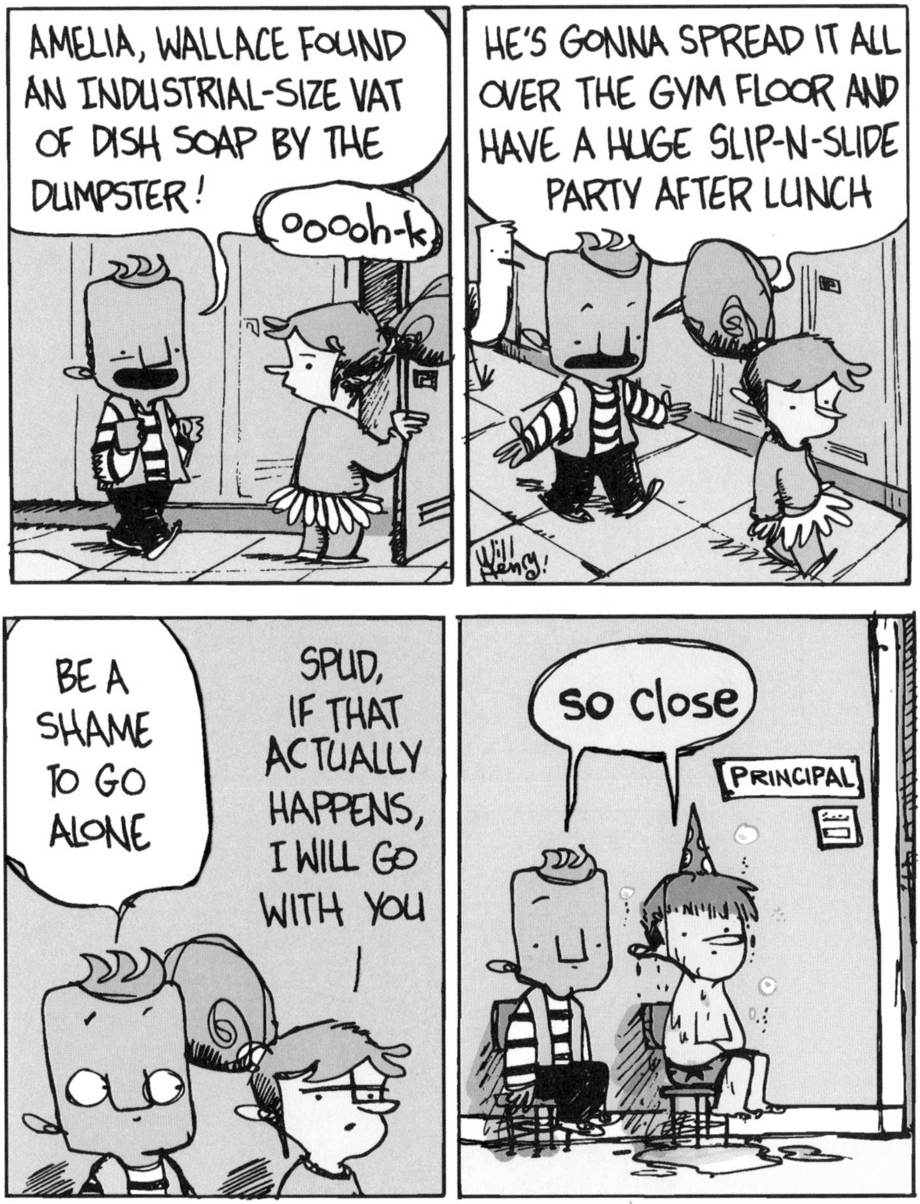

AMELIA, WALLACE FOUND AN INDUSTRIAL-SIZE VAT OF DISH SOAP BY THE DUMPSTER!
ooooh-k
HE'S GONNA SPREAD IT ALL OVER THE GYM FLOOR AND HAVE A HUGE SLIP-N-SLIDE PARTY AFTER LUNCH
Will Henry!
BE A SHAME TO GO ALONE
SPUD, IF THAT ACTUALLY HAPPENS, I WILL GO WITH YOU
so close
PRINCIPAL

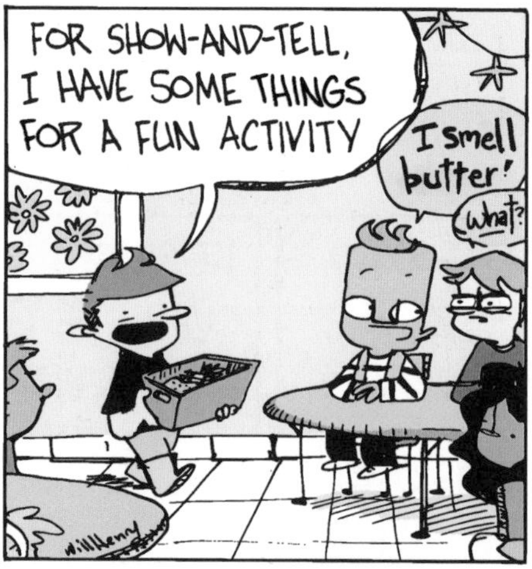
FOR SHOW-AND-TELL, I HAVE SOME THINGS FOR A FUN ACTIVITY
I smell butter!
what?

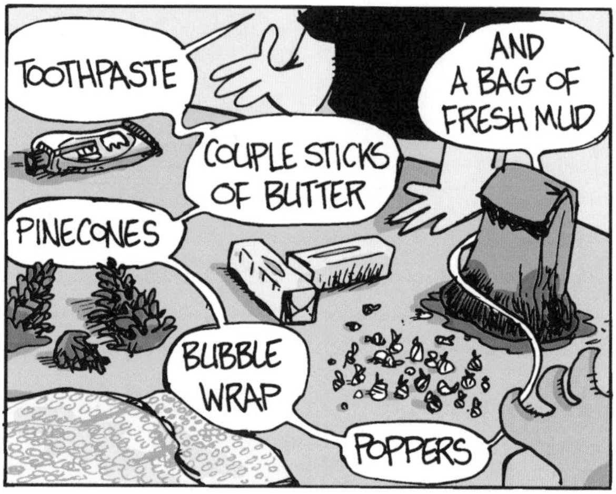
TOOTHPASTE
AND A BAG OF FRESH MUD
COUPLE STICKS OF BUTTER
PINECONES
BUBBLE WRAP
POPPERS

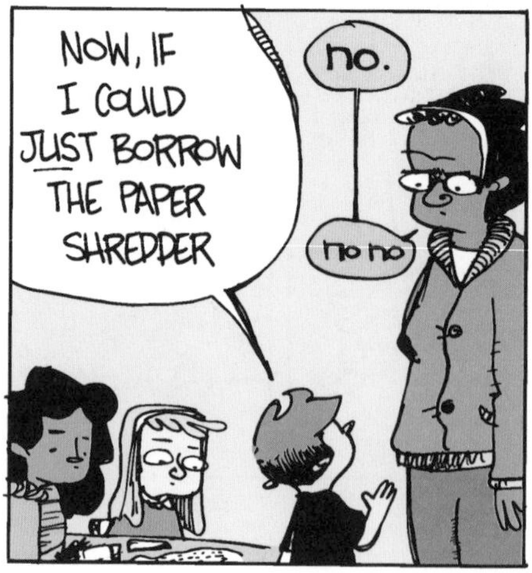
NOW, IF I COULD JUST BORROW THE PAPER SHREDDER
no.
no no

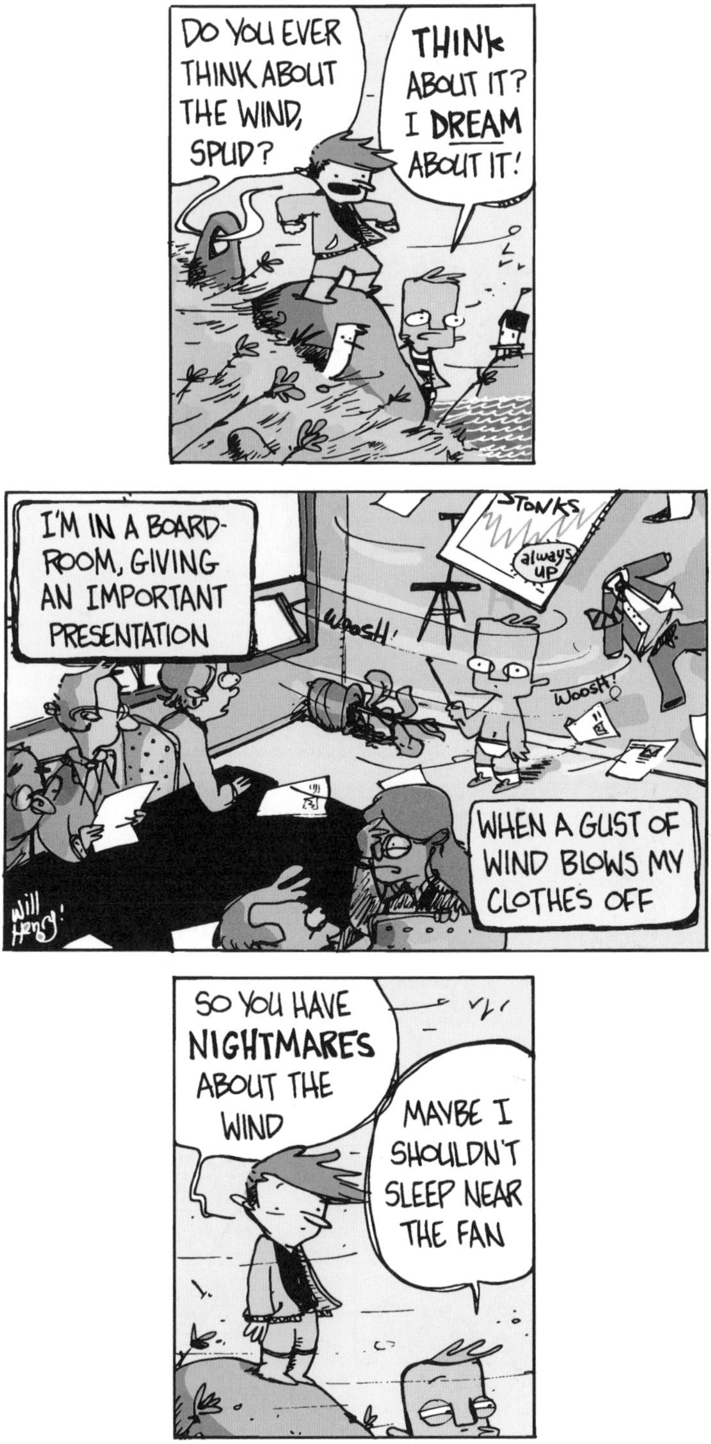
DO YOU EVER THINK ABOUT THE WIND, SPUD?
THINK ABOUT IT? I DREAM ABOUT IT!
I'M IN A BOARD-ROOM, GIVING AN IMPORTANT PRESENTATION
STONKS
always up
WOOSH!
WOOSH!
WHEN A GUST OF WIND BLOWS MY CLOTHES OFF
Will Henry!
SO YOU HAVE NIGHTMARES ABOUT THE WIND
MAYBE I SHOULDN'T SLEEP NEAR THE FAN

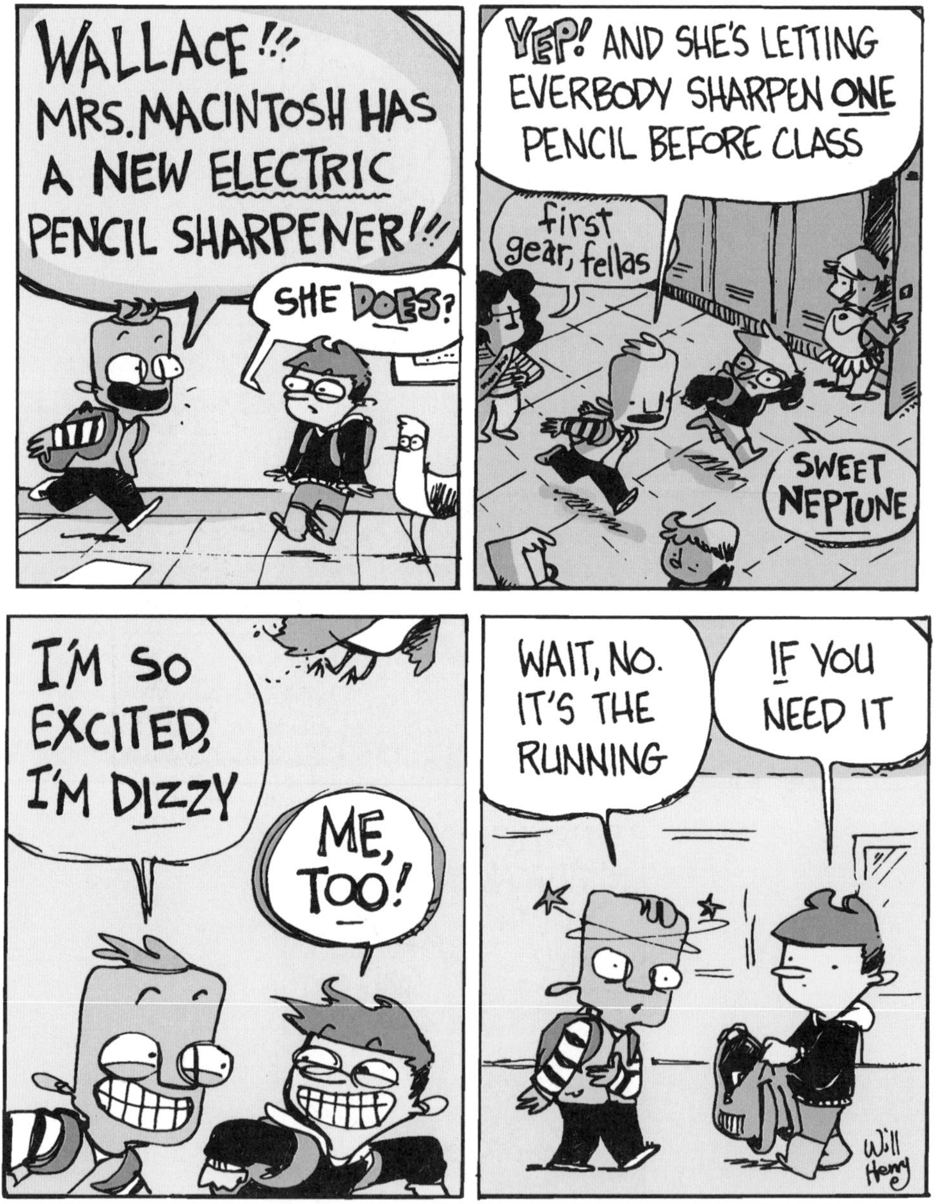
WALLACE!!!
MRS. MACINTOSH HAS A NEW ELECTRIC PENCIL SHARPENER!!!
SHE DOES?
YEP! AND SHE'S LETTING EVERBODY SHARPEN ONE PENCIL BEFORE CLASS
first gear, fellas
SWEET NEPTUNE
I'M SO EXCITED, I'M DIZZY
ME, TOO!
WAIT, NO. IT'S THE RUNNING
IF YOU NEED IT
Will Henry

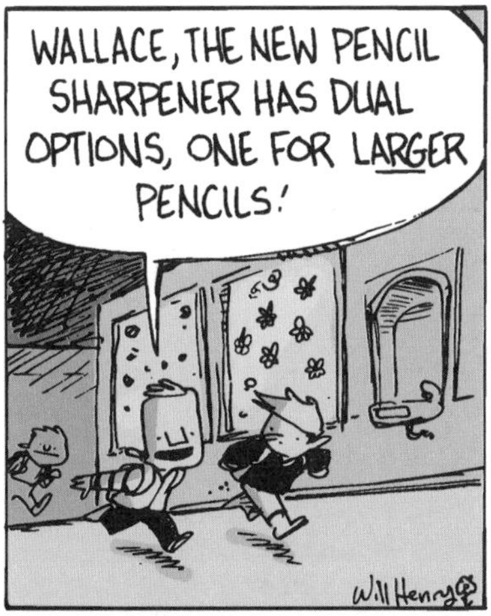
WALLACE, THE NEW PENCIL SHARPENER HAS DUAL OPTIONS, ONE FOR LARGER PENCILS!
Will Henry

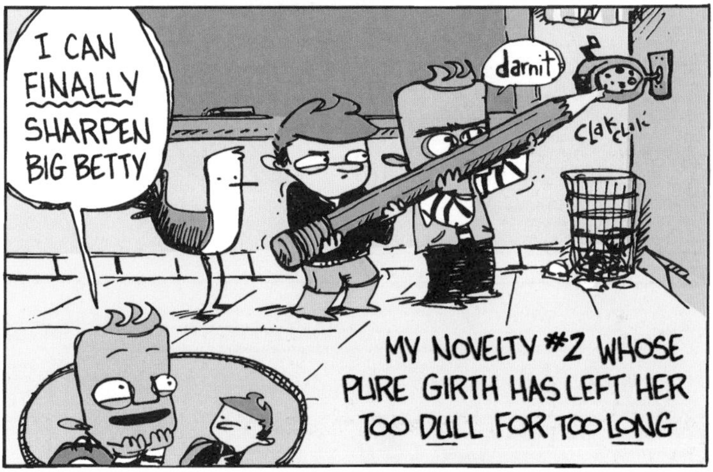
I CAN FINALLY SHARPEN BIG BETTY
darnit
clakclak
MY NOVELTY #2 WHOSE PURE GIRTH HAS LEFT HER TOO DULL FOR TOO LONG

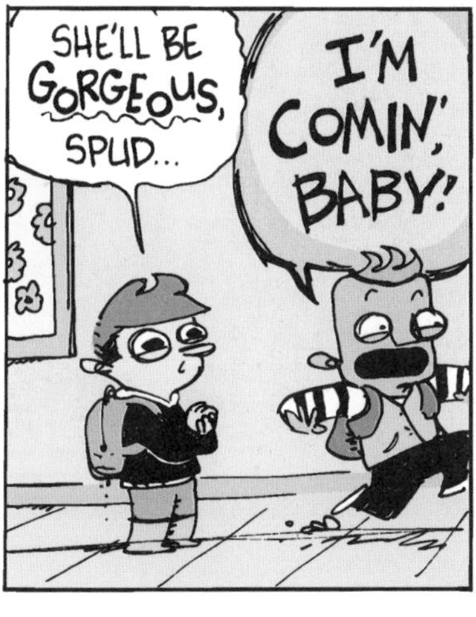
SHE'LL BE GORGEOUS, SPUD...
I'M COMIN', BABY!

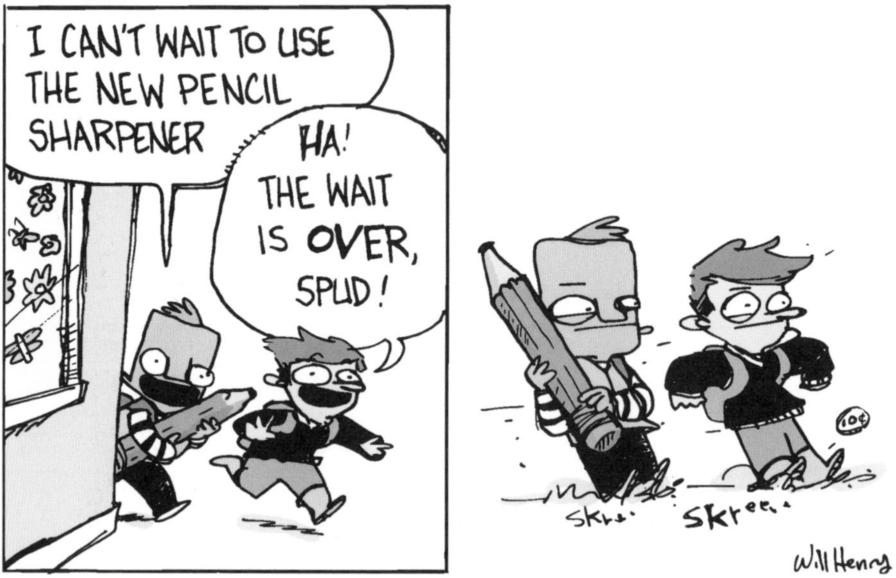
I CAN'T WAIT TO USE THE NEW PENCIL SHARPENER
HA! THE WAIT IS OVER, SPUD!
SKree..
Will Henry

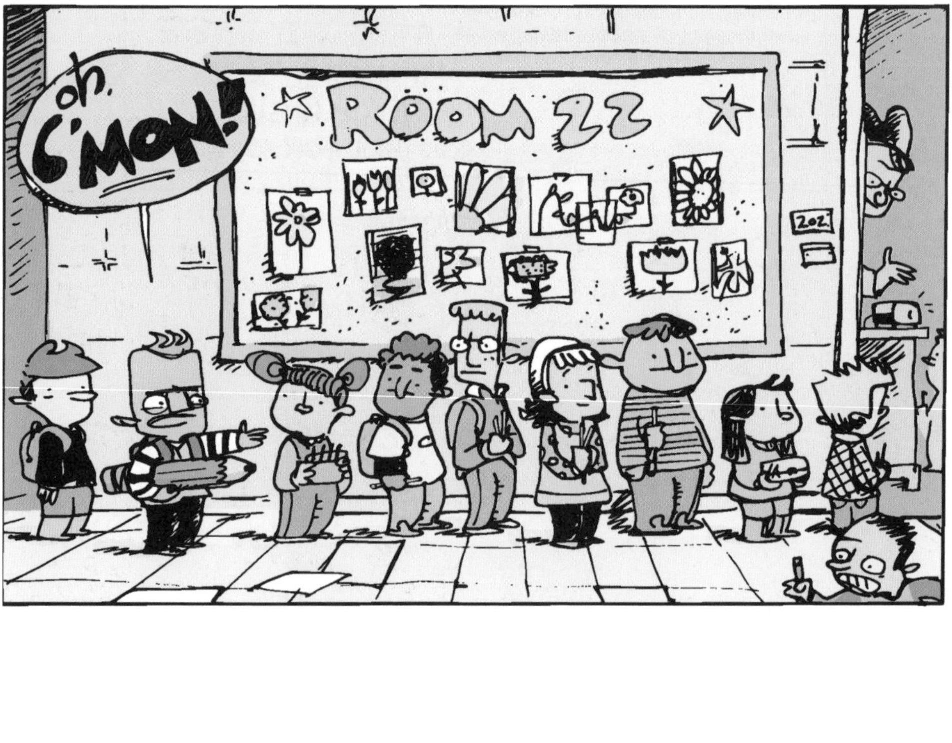
oh, C'MON!
ROOM 22

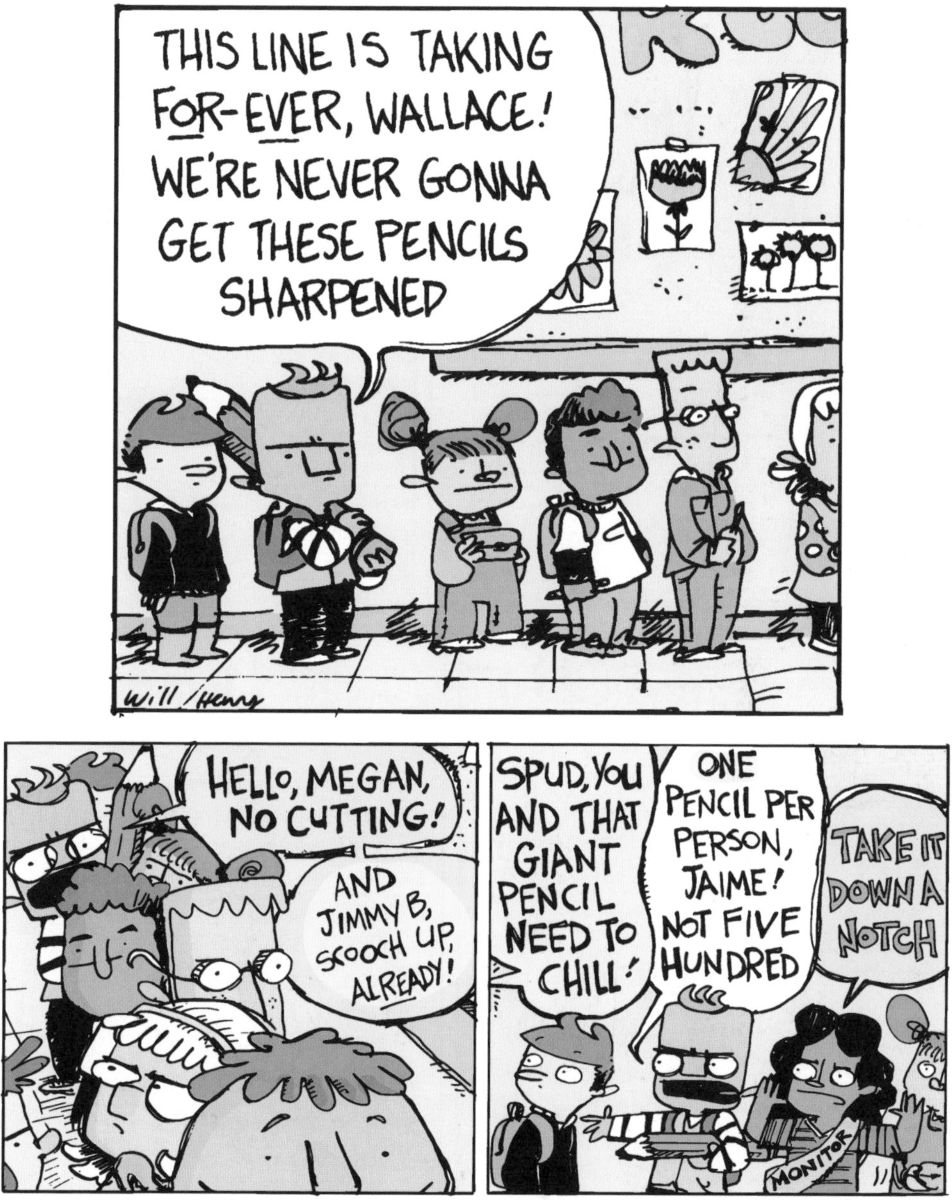
THIS LINE IS TAKING FOR-EVER, WALLACE! WE'RE NEVER GONNA GET THESE PENCILS SHARPENED
Will/Henry
HELLO, MEGAN, NO CUTTING!
AND JIMMY B, SCOOCH UP, ALREADY!
SPUD, YOU AND THAT GIANT PENCIL NEED TO CHILL!
ONE PENCIL PER PERSON, JAIME! NOT FIVE HUNDRED
TAKE IT DOWN A NOTCH
MONITOR

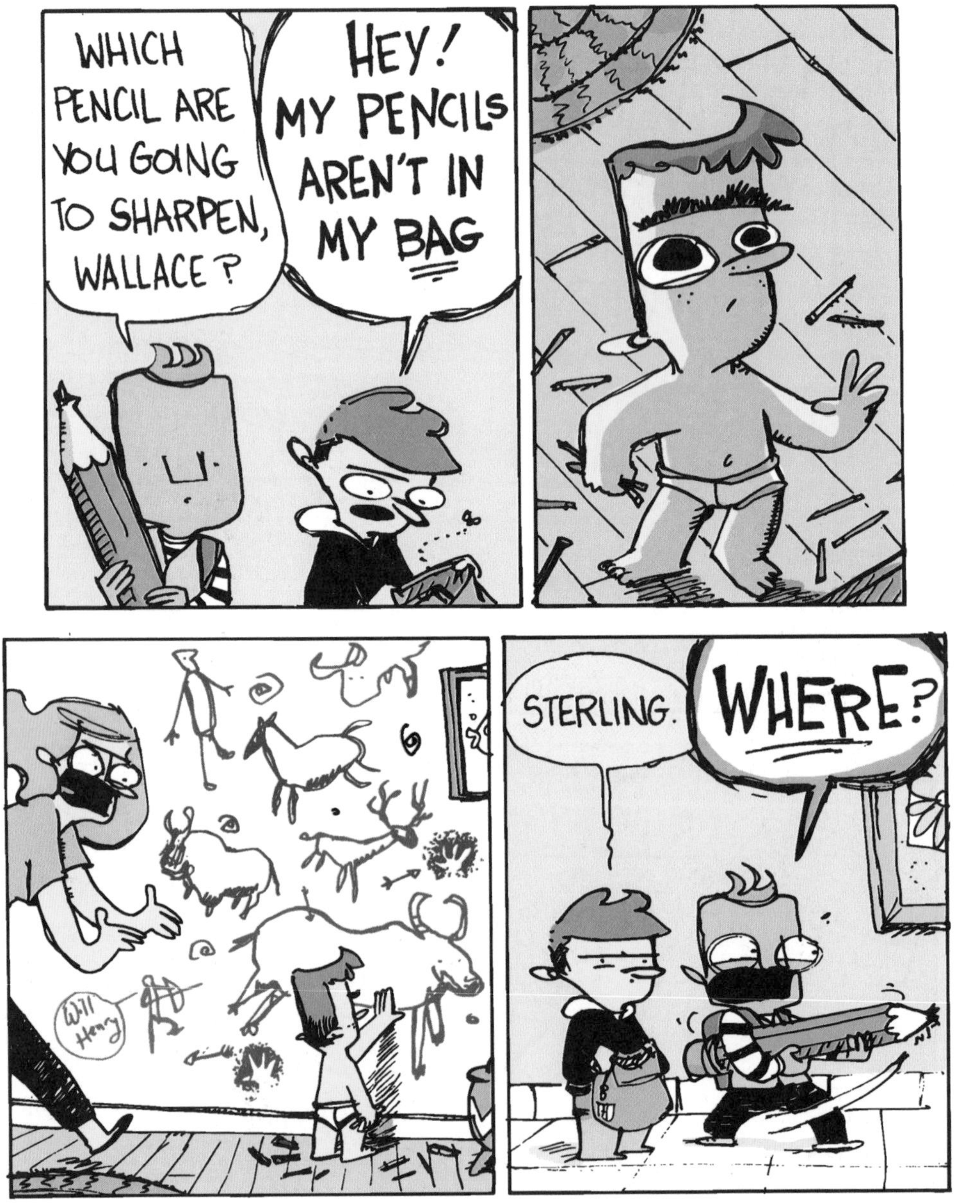
WHICH PENCIL ARE YOU GOING TO SHARPEN, WALLACE?
HEY! MY PENCILS AREN'T IN MY BAG
Will Henry
STERLING.
WHERE?

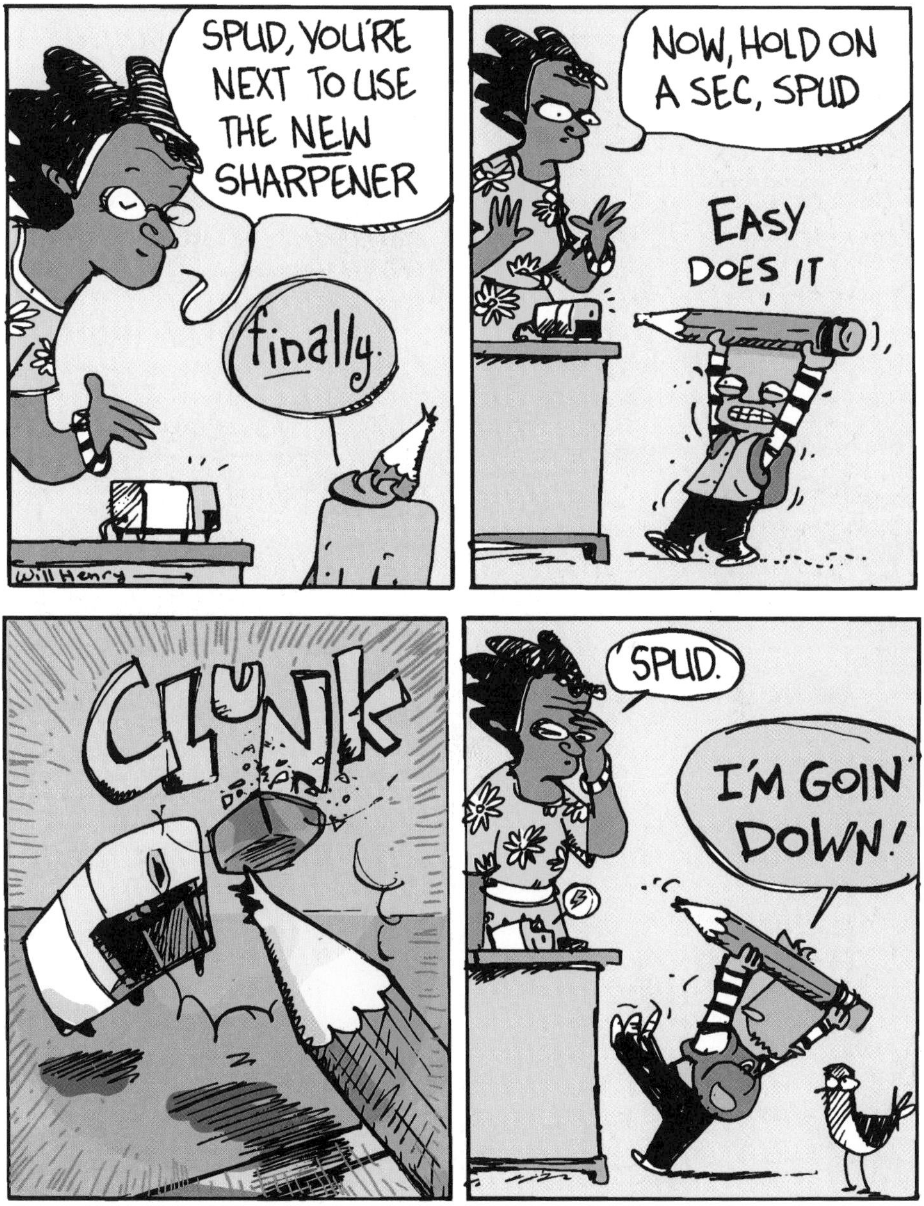
SPUD, YOU'RE NEXT TO USE THE NEW SHARPENER
finally.
Will Henry
NOW, HOLD ON A SEC, SPUD
EASY DOES IT
CLUNK
SPUD.
I'M GOIN' DOWN!

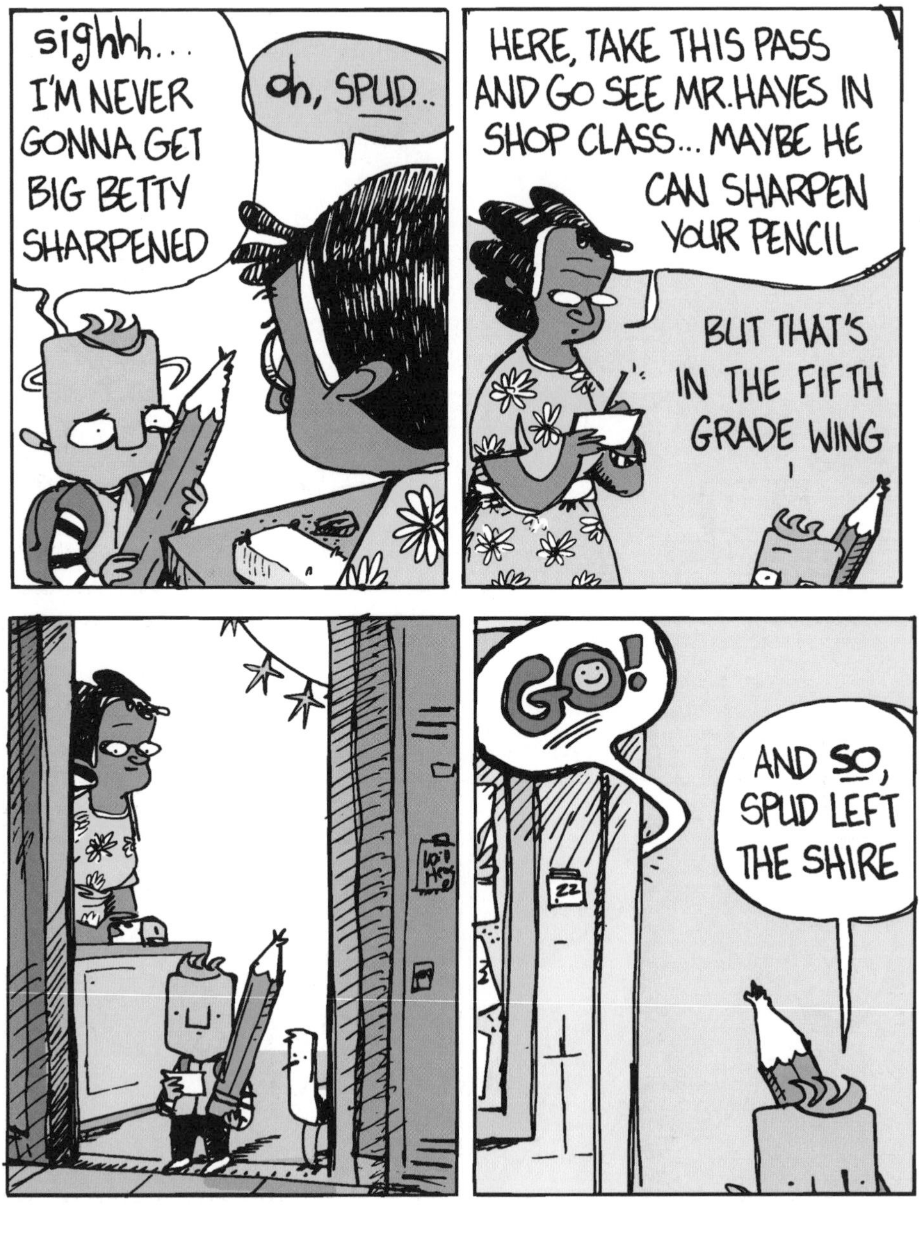
sighhh... I'M NEVER GONNA GET BIG BETTY SHARPENED
oh, SPUD...
HERE, TAKE THIS PASS AND GO SEE MR. HAYES IN SHOP CLASS... MAYBE HE CAN SHARPEN YOUR PENCIL
BUT THAT'S IN THE FIFTH GRADE WING
GO!
AND SO, SPUD LEFT THE SHIRE

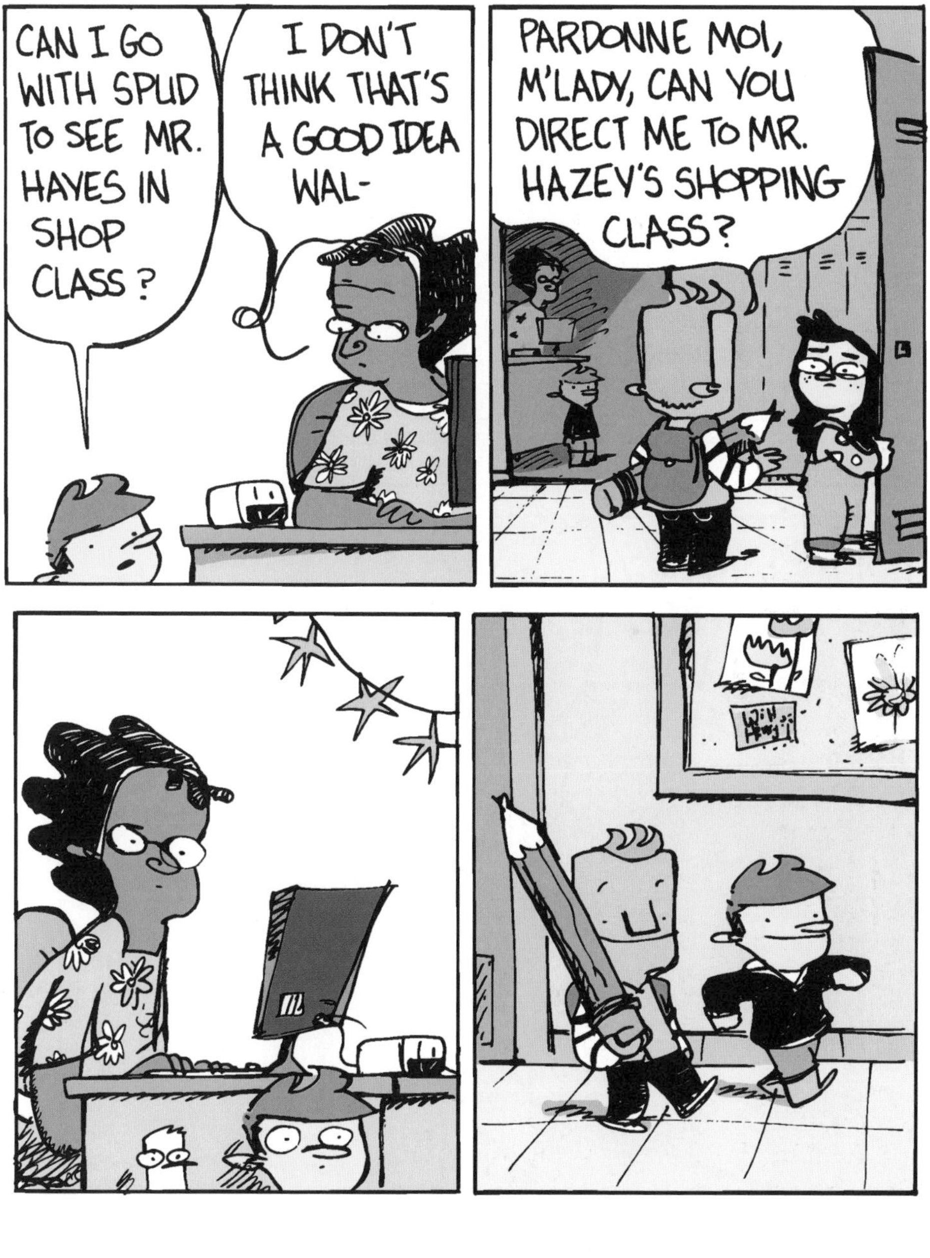
CAN I GO WITH SPUD TO SEE MR. HAYES IN SHOP CLASS?
I DON'T THINK THAT'S A GOOD IDEA WAL-
PARDONNE MOI, M'LADY, CAN YOU DIRECT ME TO MR. HAZEY'S SHOPPING CLASS?

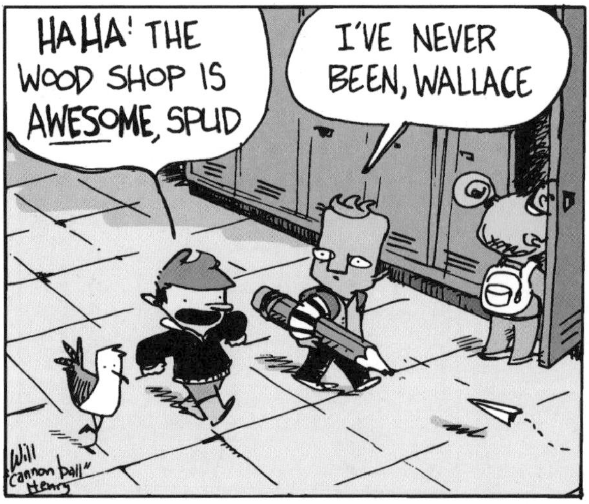
HAHA! THE WOOD SHOP IS AWESOME, SPUD
I'VE NEVER BEEN, WALLACE
Will "cannon ball" Henry

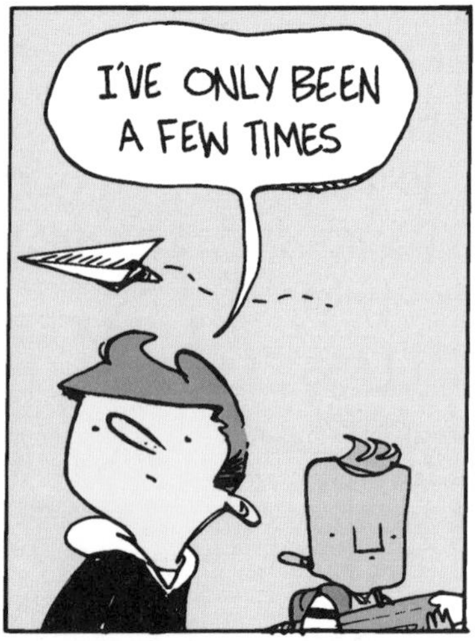
I'VE ONLY BEEN A FEW TIMES

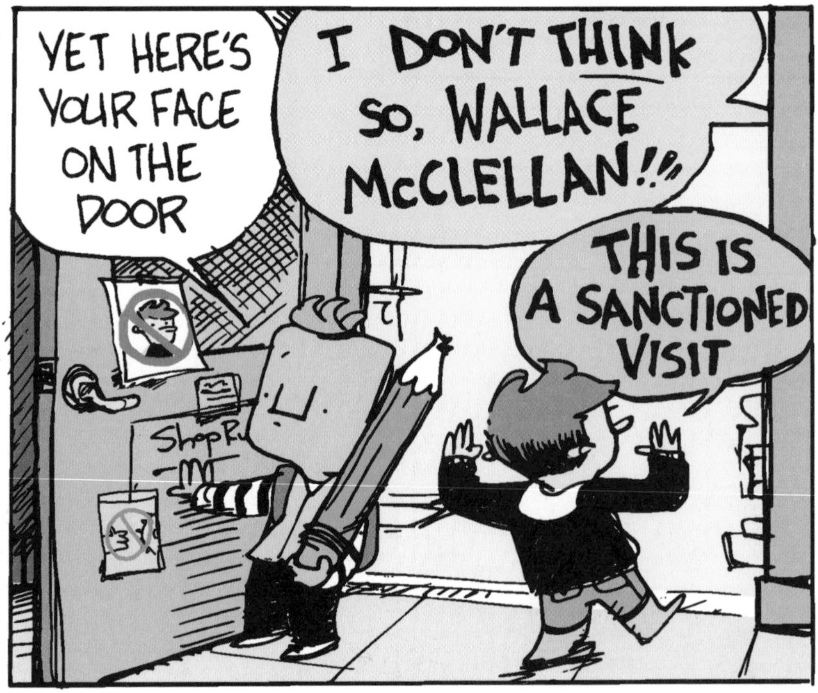
YET HERE'S YOUR FACE ON THE DOOR
I DON'T THINK SO, WALLACE McCLELLAN!!
THIS IS A SANCTIONED VISIT

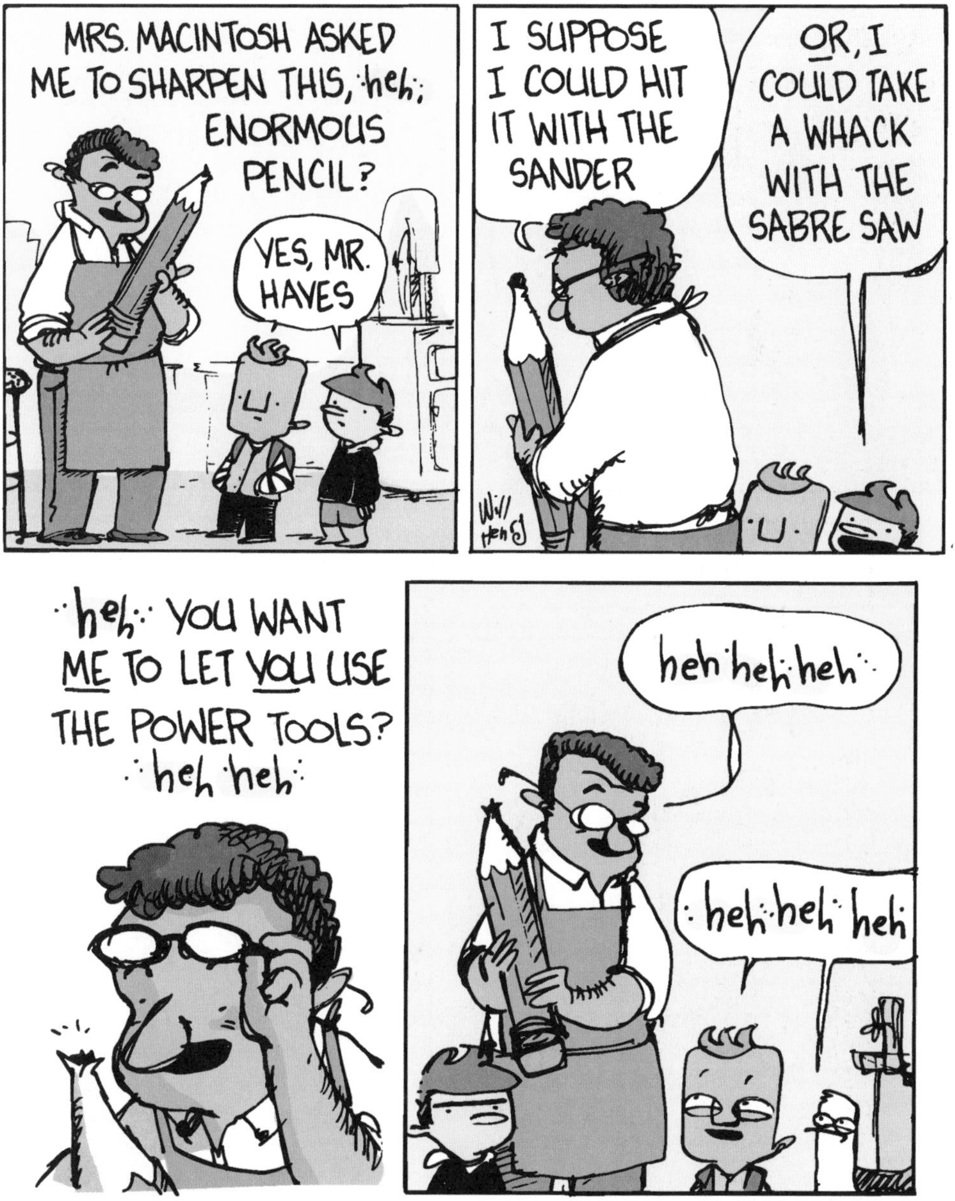
MRS. MACINTOSH ASKED ME TO SHARPEN THIS, heh ENORMOUS PENCIL?
YES, MR. HAYES
I SUPPOSE I COULD HIT IT WITH THE SANDER
OR, I COULD TAKE A WHACK WITH THE SABRE SAW
heh YOU WANT ME TO LET YOU USE THE POWER TOOLS? heh heh
heh heh heh
heh heh heh

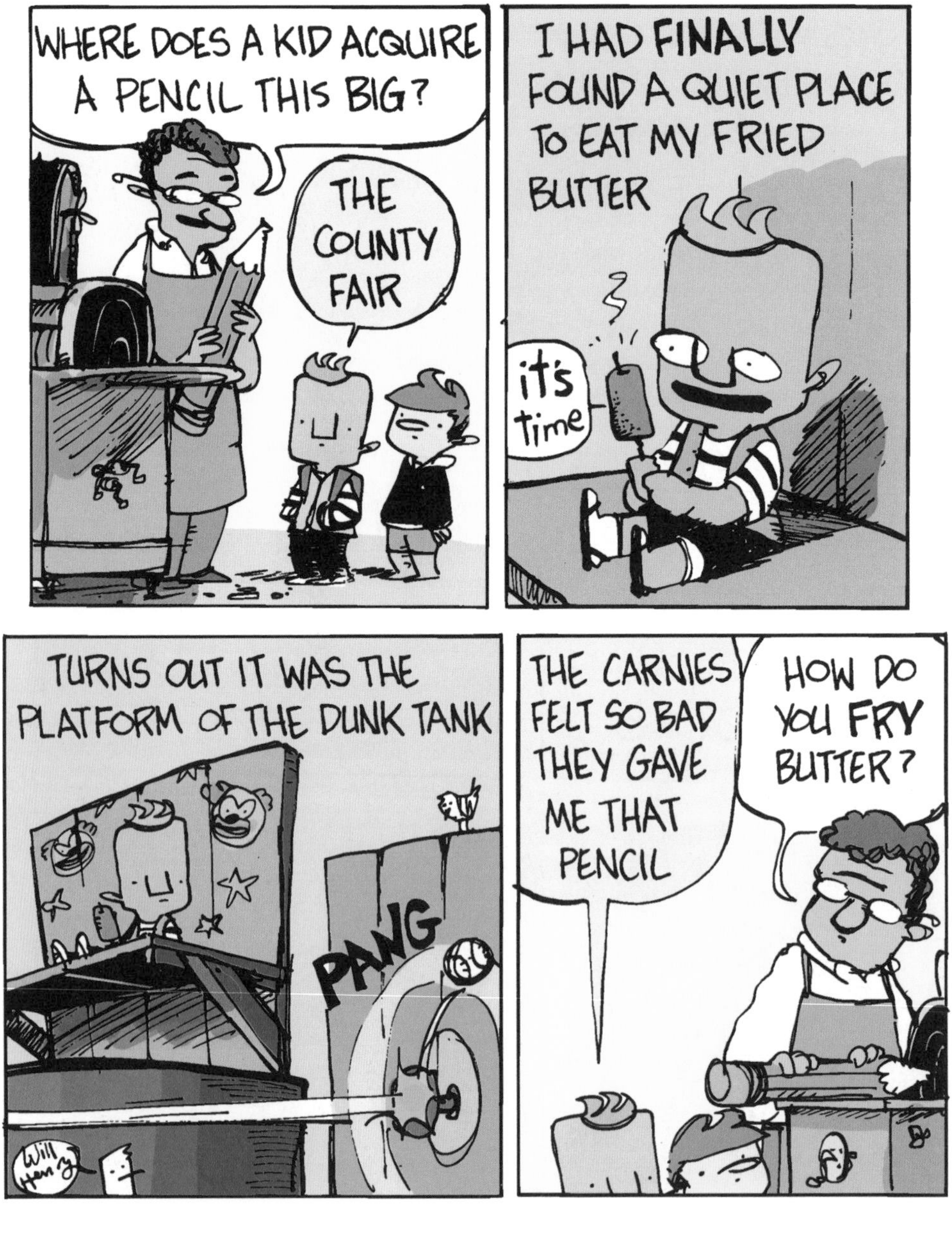
WHERE DOES A KID ACQUIRE A PENCIL THIS BIG?
THE COUNTY FAIR
I HAD FINALLY FOUND A QUIET PLACE TO EAT MY FRIED BUTTER
it's time
TURNS OUT IT WAS THE PLATFORM OF THE DUNK TANK
PANG
Will Henry
THE CARNIES FELT SO BAD THEY GAVE ME THAT PENCIL
HOW DO YOU FRY BUTTER?

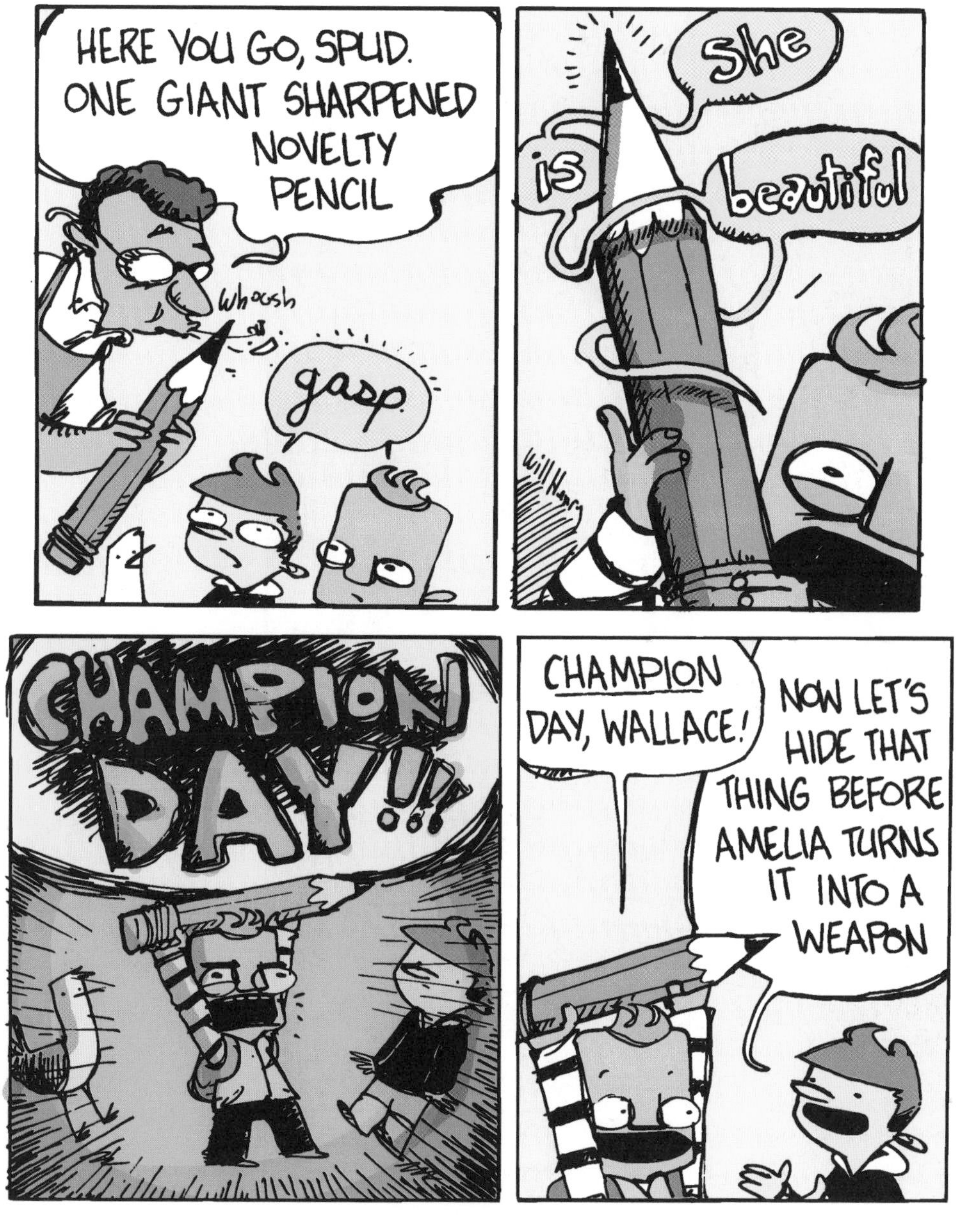
HERE YOU GO, SPUD. ONE GIANT SHARPENED NOVELTY PENCIL
Whoosh
gasp
she
is
beautiful
CHAMPION DAY!!!
CHAMPION DAY, WALLACE!
NOW LET'S HIDE THAT THING BEFORE AMELIA TURNS IT INTO A WEAPON

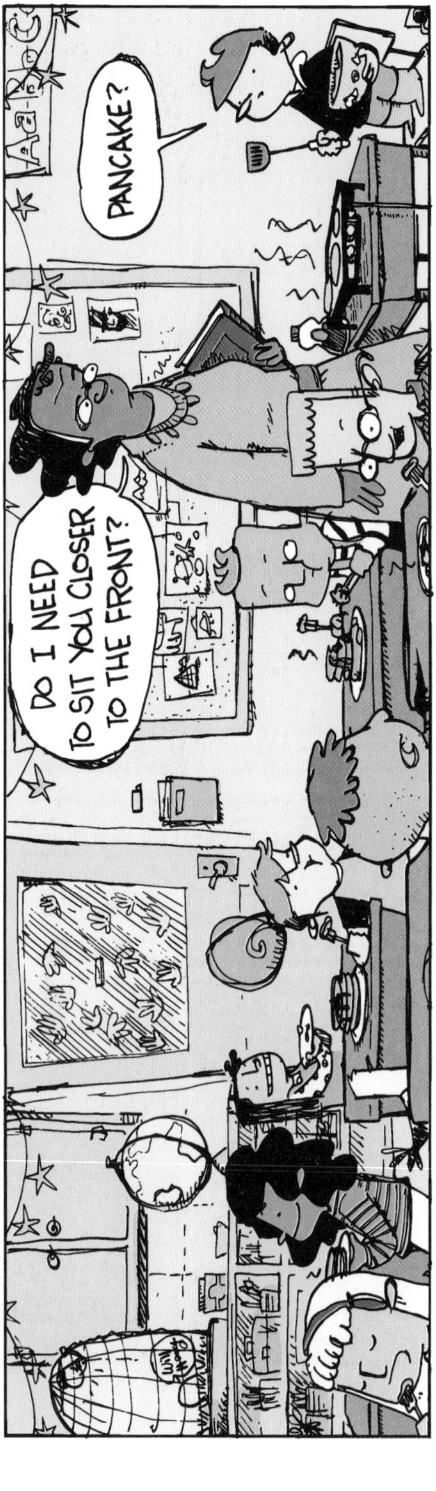
DO I NEED TO SIT YOU CLOSER TO THE FRONT?
PANCAKE?

APRIL SHOWERS BRING
MAY FLOWERS

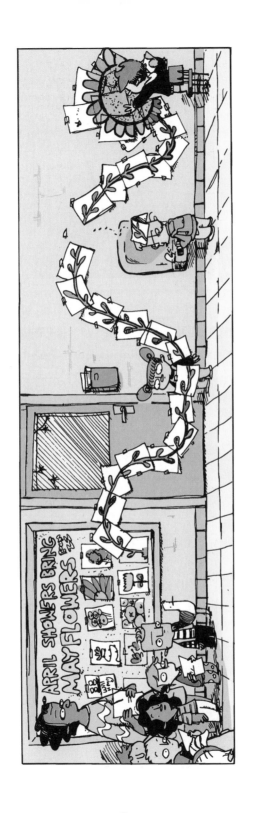

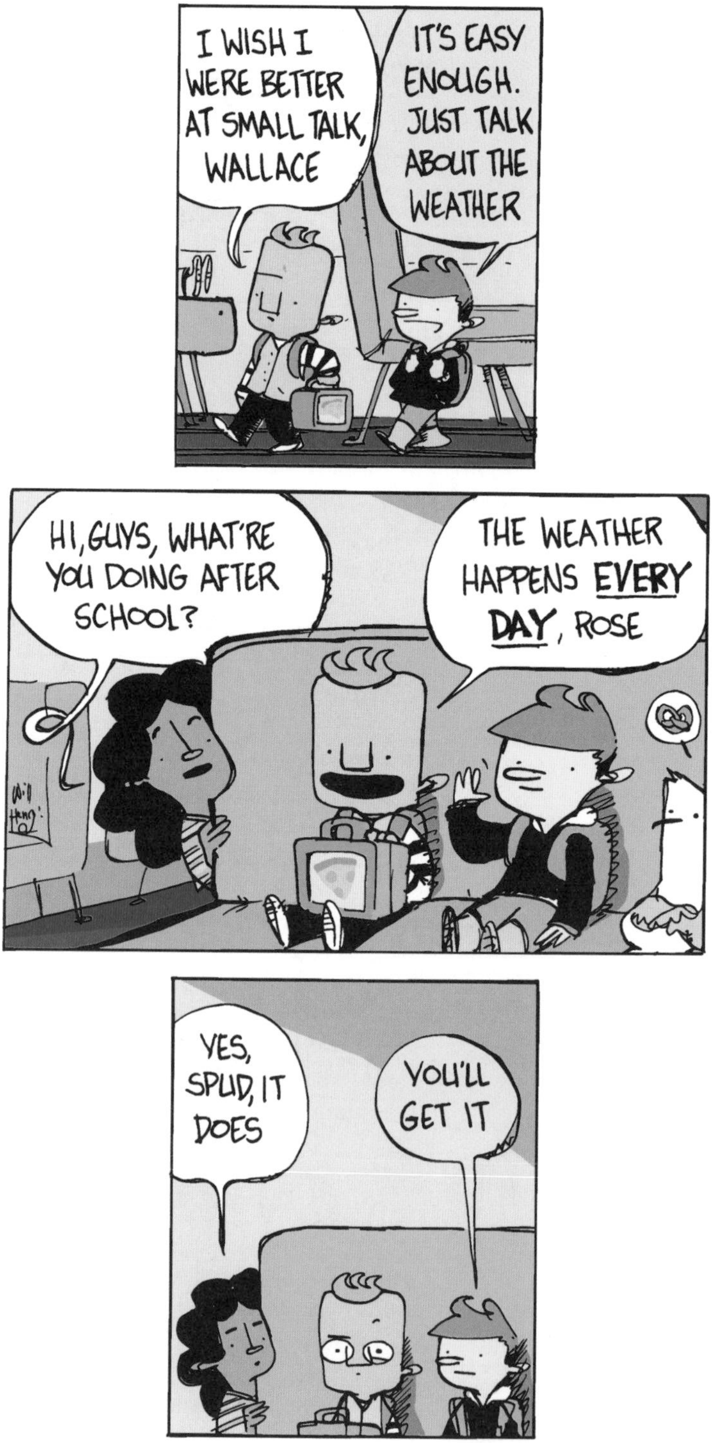
I WISH I WERE BETTER AT SMALL TALK, WALLACE
IT'S EASY ENOUGH. JUST TALK ABOUT THE WEATHER
HI, GUYS, WHAT'RE YOU DOING AFTER SCHOOL?
THE WEATHER HAPPENS **EVERY DAY**, ROSE
YES, SPUD, IT DOES
YOU'LL GET IT

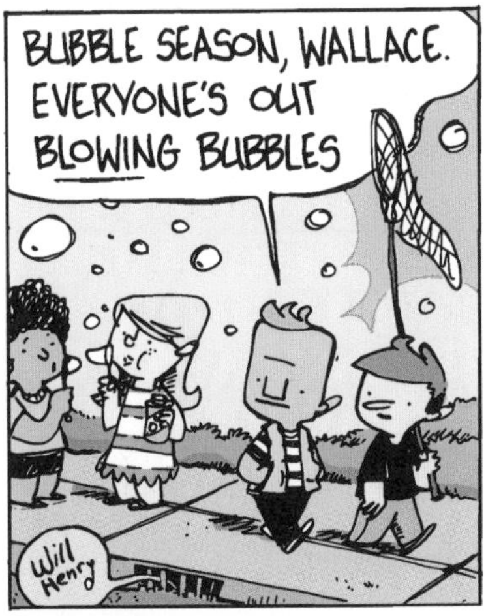
BUBBLE SEASON, WALLACE. EVERYONE'S OUT BLOWING BUBBLES
Will Henry

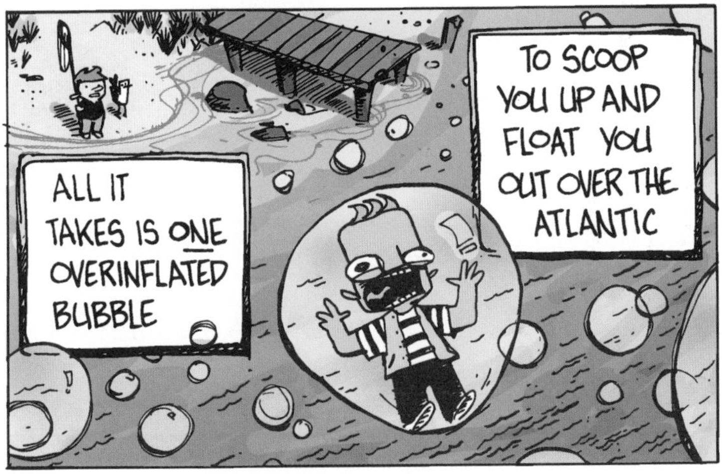
ALL IT TAKES IS ONE OVERINFLATED BUBBLE
TO SCOOP YOU UP AND FLOAT YOU OUT OVER THE ATLANTIC

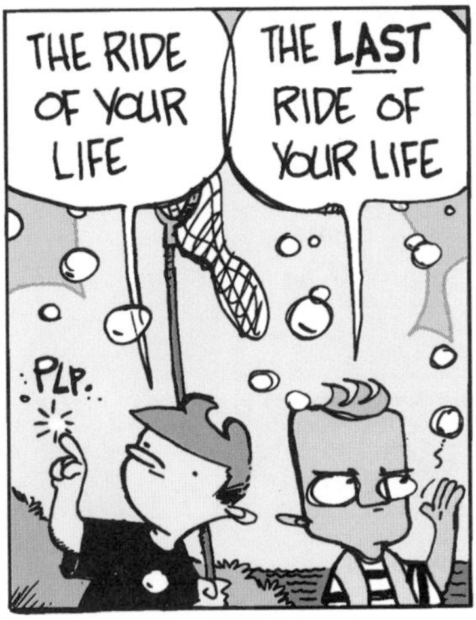
THE RIDE OF YOUR LIFE
THE LAST RIDE OF YOUR LIFE
PLP.

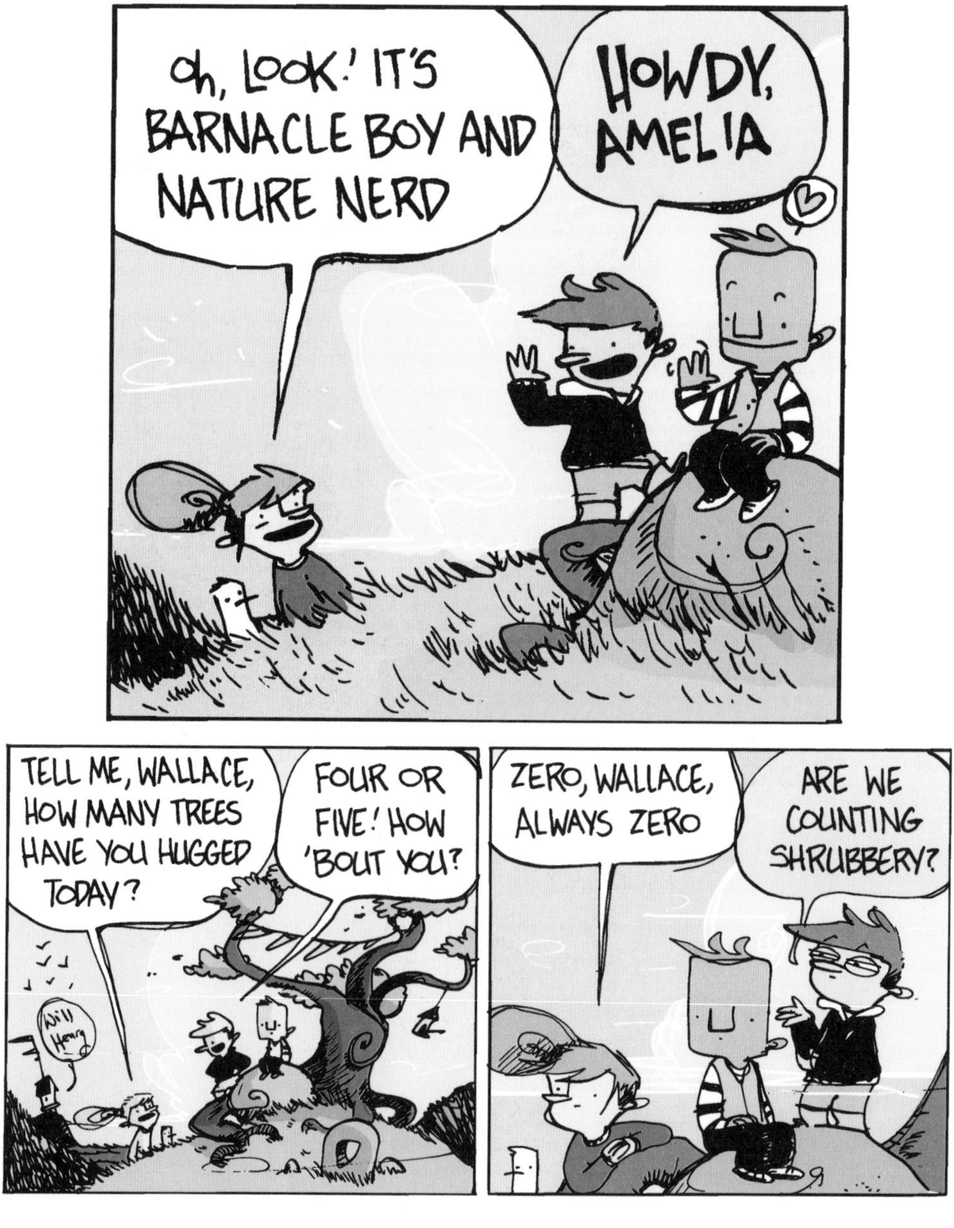
Oh, LOOK! IT'S BARNACLE BOY AND NATURE NERD
HOWDY, AMELIA
TELL ME, WALLACE, HOW MANY TREES HAVE YOU HUGGED TODAY?
FOUR OR FIVE! HOW 'BOUT YOU?
Will Henry
ZERO, WALLACE, ALWAYS ZERO
ARE WE COUNTING SHRUBBERY?

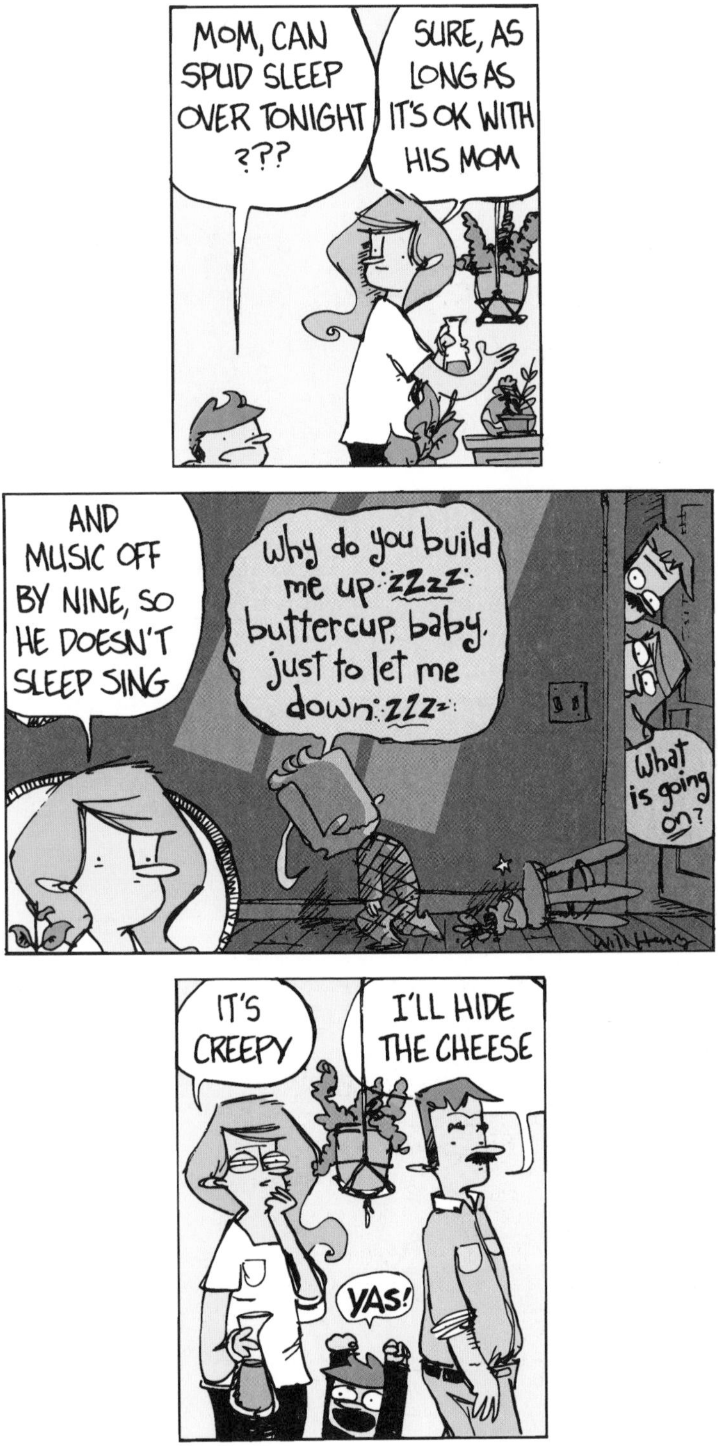
MOM, CAN SPUD SLEEP OVER TONIGHT ???
SURE, AS LONG AS IT'S OK WITH HIS MOM
AND MUSIC OFF BY NINE, SO HE DOESN'T SLEEP SING
Why do you build me up zzzz buttercup, baby, just to let me down zzz
What is going on?
IT'S CREEPY
I'LL HIDE THE CHEESE
YAS!

ROSE! ROOM TEN'S CLASS HAMSTER ESCAPED!!
HER NAME IS PEBBLES AND SHE IS ADORABLE!
Gasp
MATTY HASKINS WAS FEEDING HER WHEN SHE RAN OUT THE DOOR!
HM ... WHERE WOULD A SCARED, HUNGRY HAMSTER WANT TO GO?
I DUNNO, ROSE...
LET'S ASK ONE
TO THE CAFETERIA

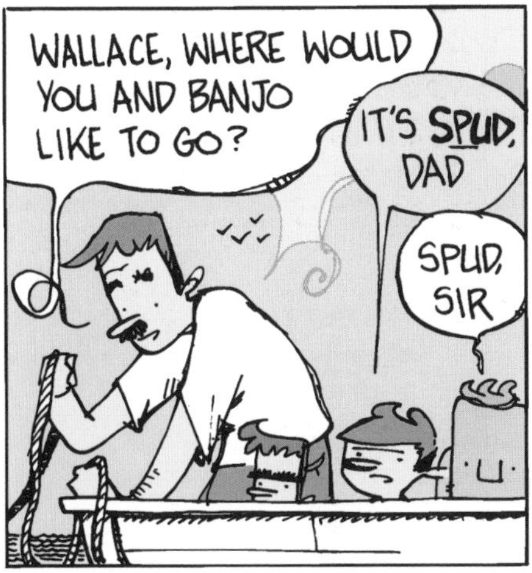
WALLACE, WHERE WOULD YOU AND BANJO LIKE TO GO?
IT'S SPUD, DAD
SPUD, SIR

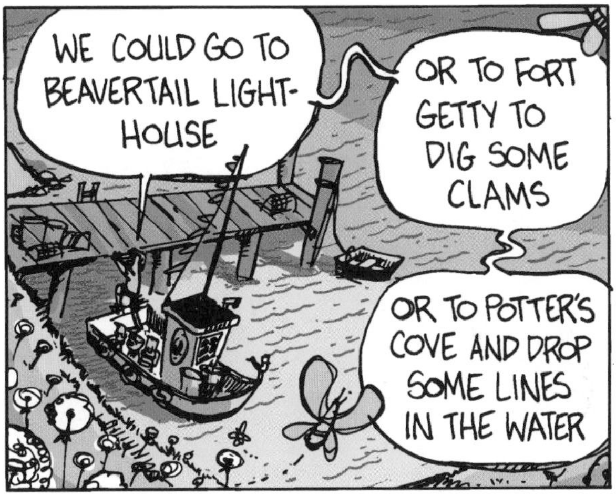
WE COULD GO TO BEAVERTAIL LIGHT-HOUSE
OR TO FORT GETTY TO DIG SOME CLAMS
OR TO POTTER'S COVE AND DROP SOME LINES IN THE WATER

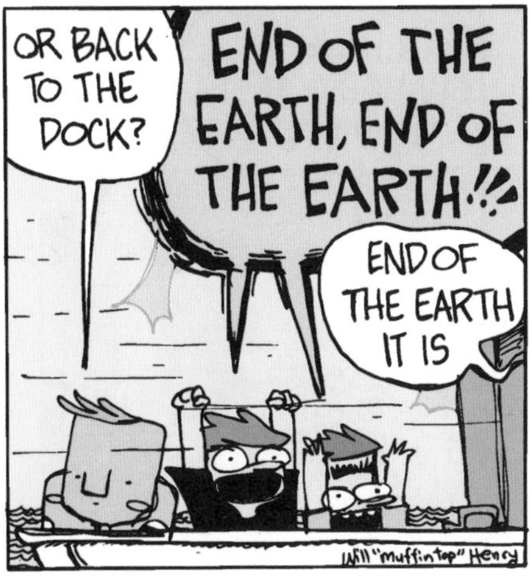
OR BACK TO THE DOCK?
END OF THE EARTH, END OF THE EARTH!!!
END OF THE EARTH IT IS
Will "muffintop" Henry

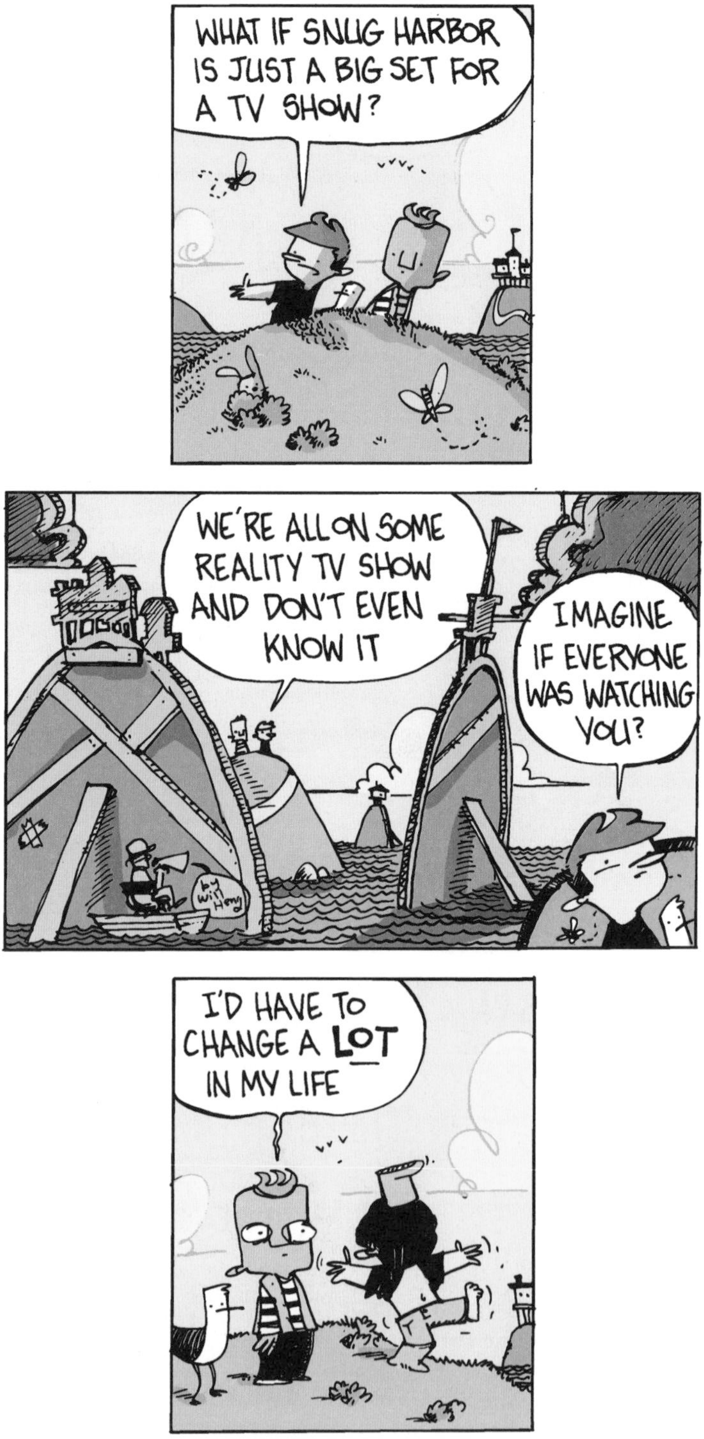
WHAT IF SNUG HARBOR IS JUST A BIG SET FOR A TV SHOW?
WE'RE ALL ON SOME REALITY TV SHOW AND DON'T EVEN KNOW IT
IMAGINE IF EVERYONE WAS WATCHING YOU?
by Will Henry
I'D HAVE TO CHANGE A LOT IN MY LIFE

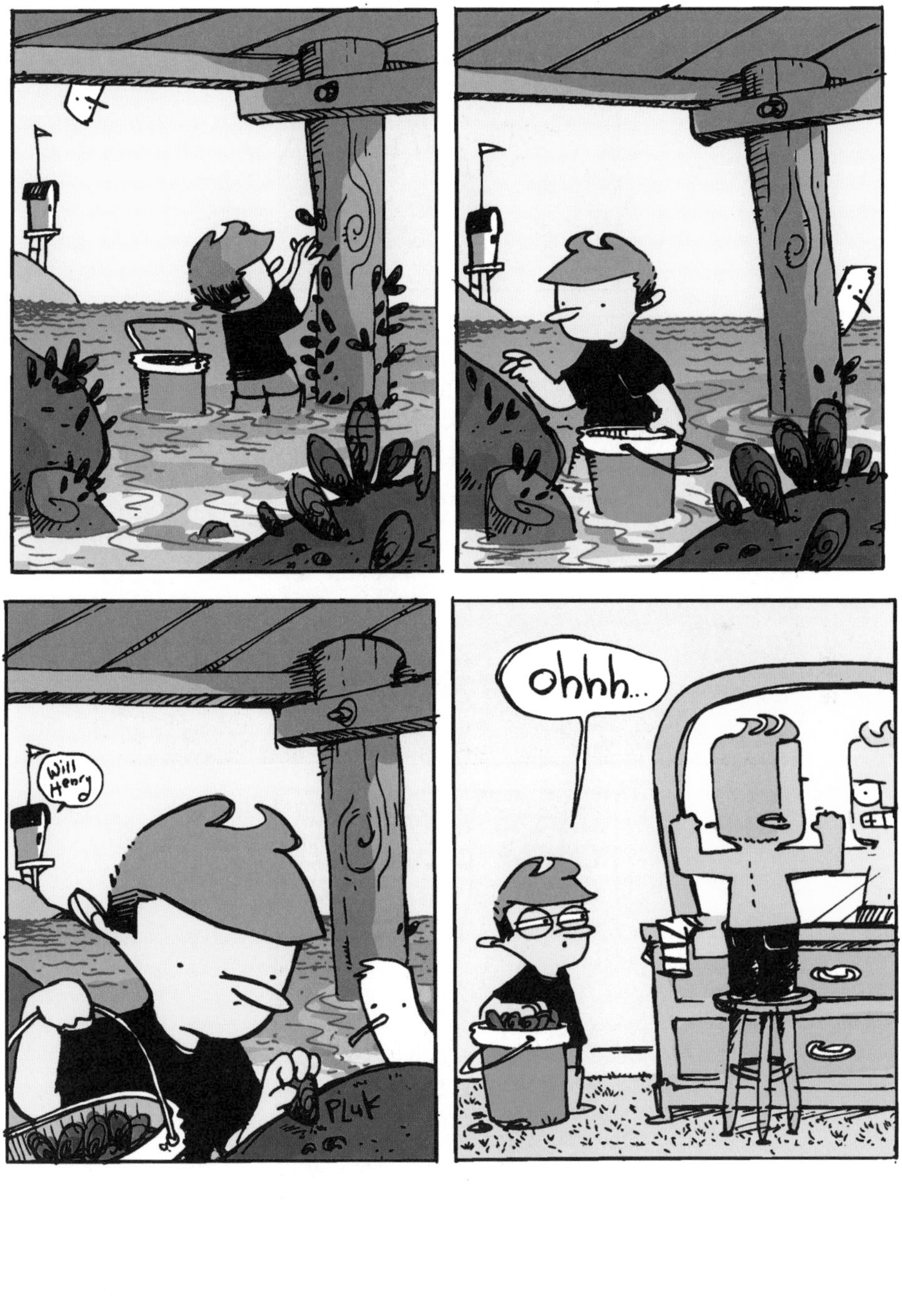
Will Henry
PLUK
ohhh...

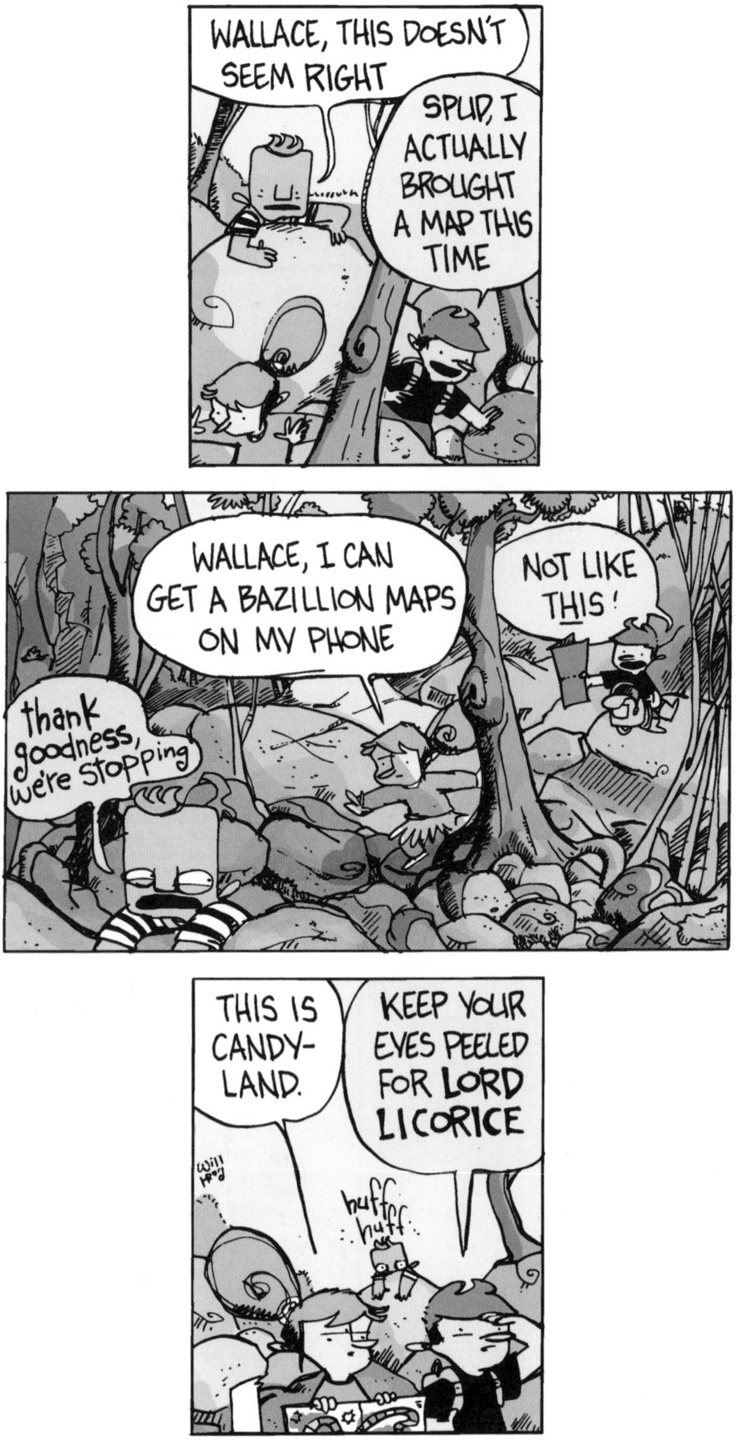
WALLACE, THIS DOESN'T SEEM RIGHT
SPUD, I ACTUALLY BROUGHT A MAP THIS TIME
WALLACE, I CAN GET A BAZILLION MAPS ON MY PHONE
NOT LIKE THIS!
thank goodness, we're stopping
THIS IS CANDY-LAND.
KEEP YOUR EYES PEELED FOR LORD LICORICE
huff huff

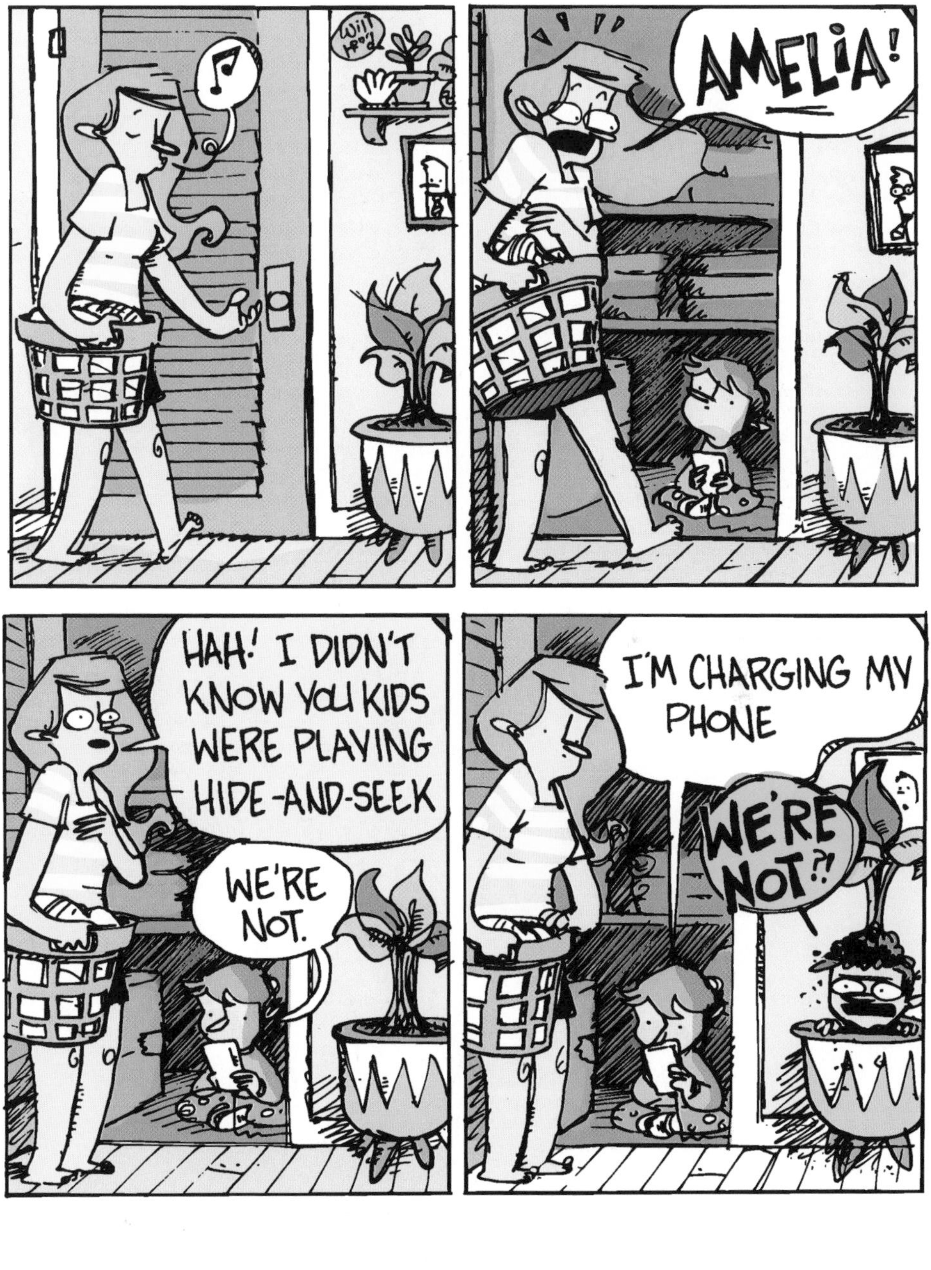
WILT HEED
AMELIA!
HAH! I DIDN'T KNOW YOU KIDS WERE PLAYING HIDE-AND-SEEK
WE'RE NOT.
I'M CHARGING MY PHONE
WE'RE NOT?!

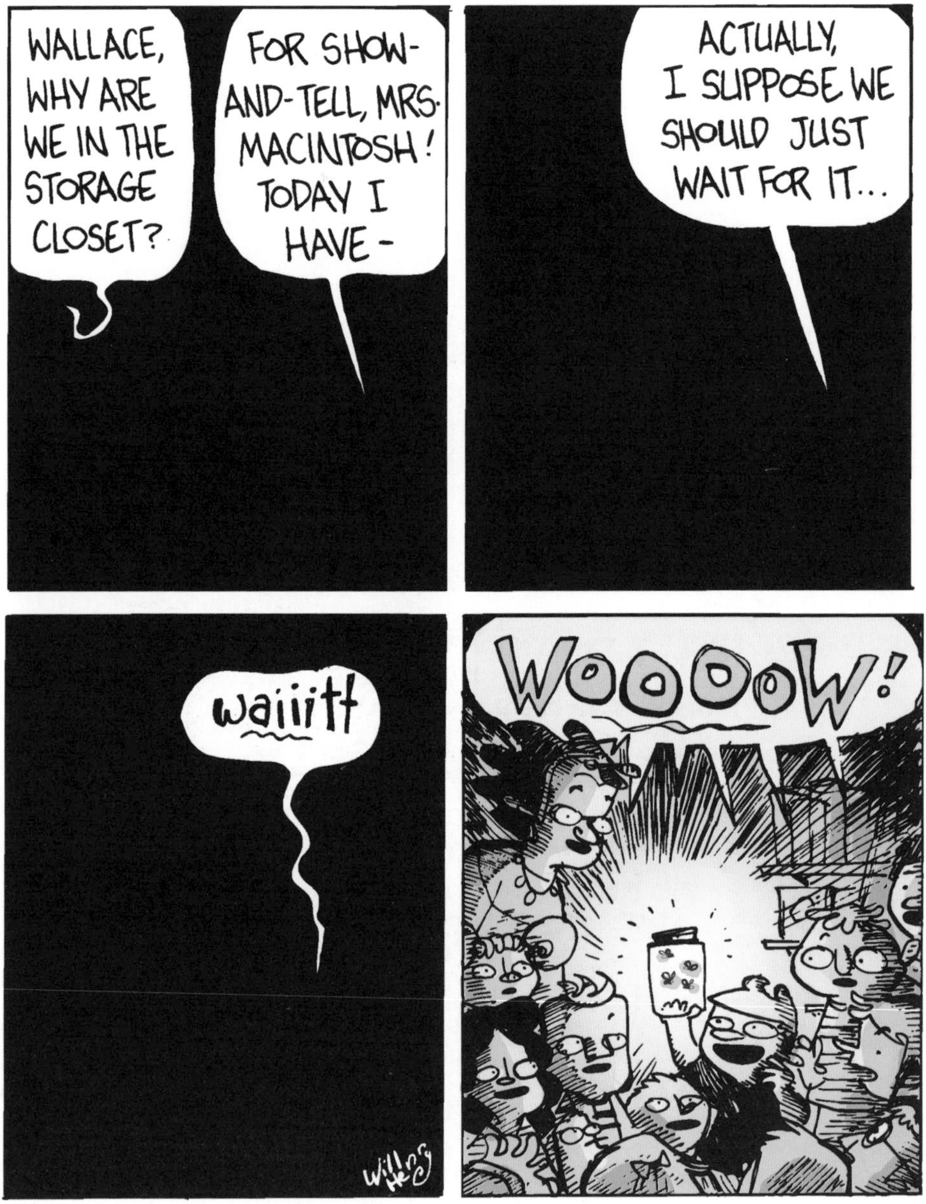
WALLACE, WHY ARE WE IN THE STORAGE CLOSET?
FOR SHOW-AND-TELL, MRS. MACINTOSH! TODAY I HAVE -
ACTUALLY, I SUPPOSE WE SHOULD JUST WAIT FOR IT...
waiiitt
WOOOOW!

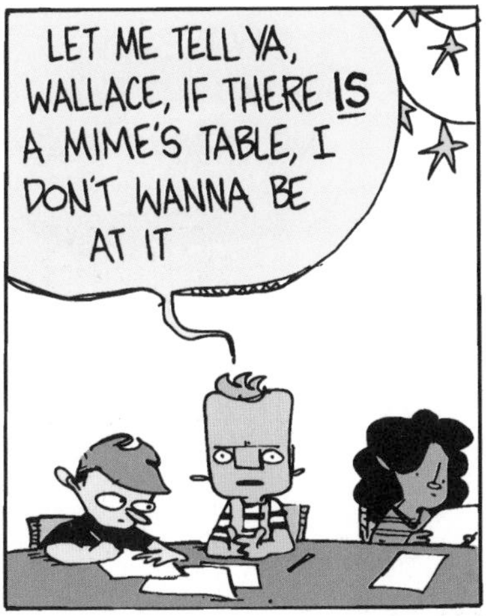
LET ME TELL YA, WALLACE, IF THERE IS A MIME'S TABLE, I DON'T WANNA BE AT IT

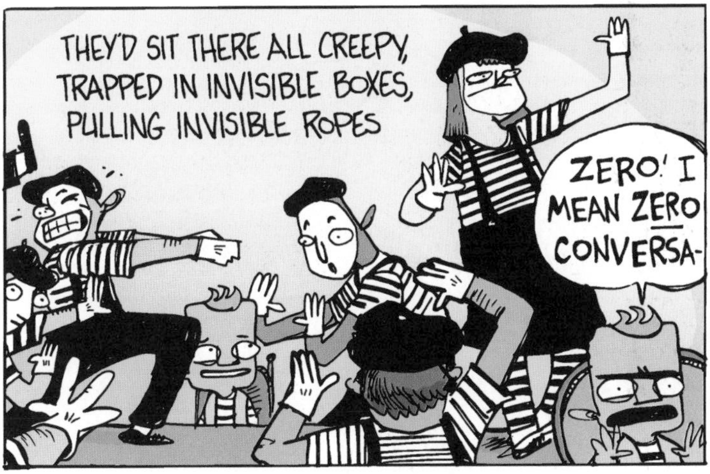
THEY'D SIT THERE ALL CREEPY, TRAPPED IN INVISIBLE BOXES, PULLING INVISIBLE ROPES
ZERO! I MEAN ZERO CONVERSA-

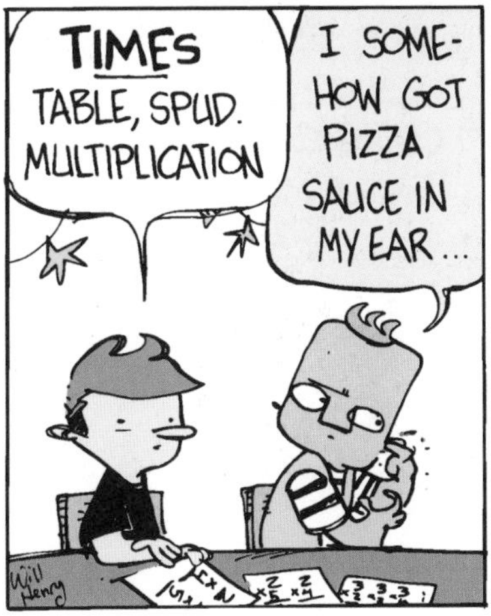
TIMES TABLE, SPUD. MULTIPLICATION
I SOME-HOW GOT PIZZA SAUCE IN MY EAR...
Will Henry

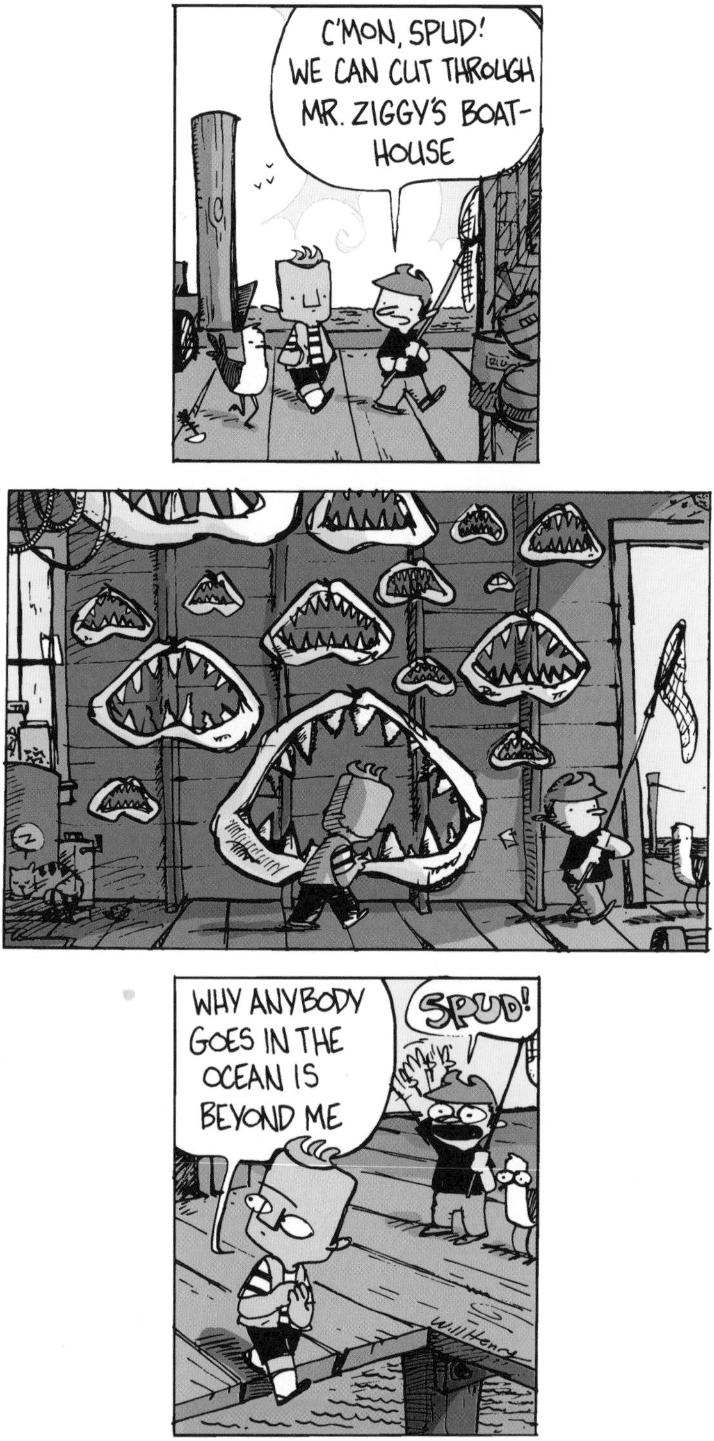
C'MON, SPUD! WE CAN CUT THROUGH MR. ZIGGY'S BOAT-HOUSE
WHY ANYBODY GOES IN THE OCEAN IS BEYOND ME
SPUD!
Will Henry

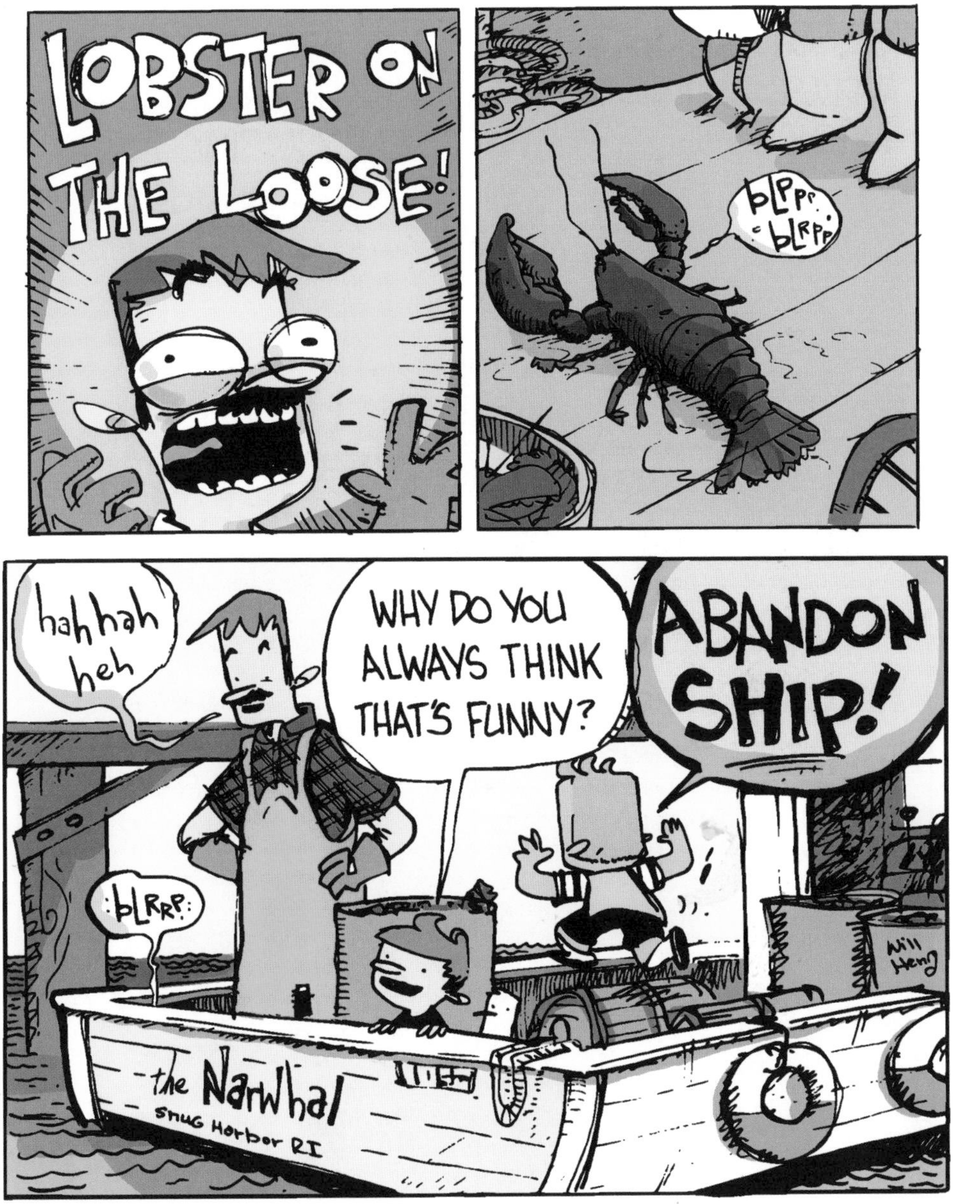
LOBSTER ON THE LOOSE!
bLPpr
bLRPP
hahhah heh
WHY DO YOU ALWAYS THINK THAT'S FUNNY?
ABANDON SHIP!
bLRRP
the Narwhal
SNUG Harbor RI
Will Henry

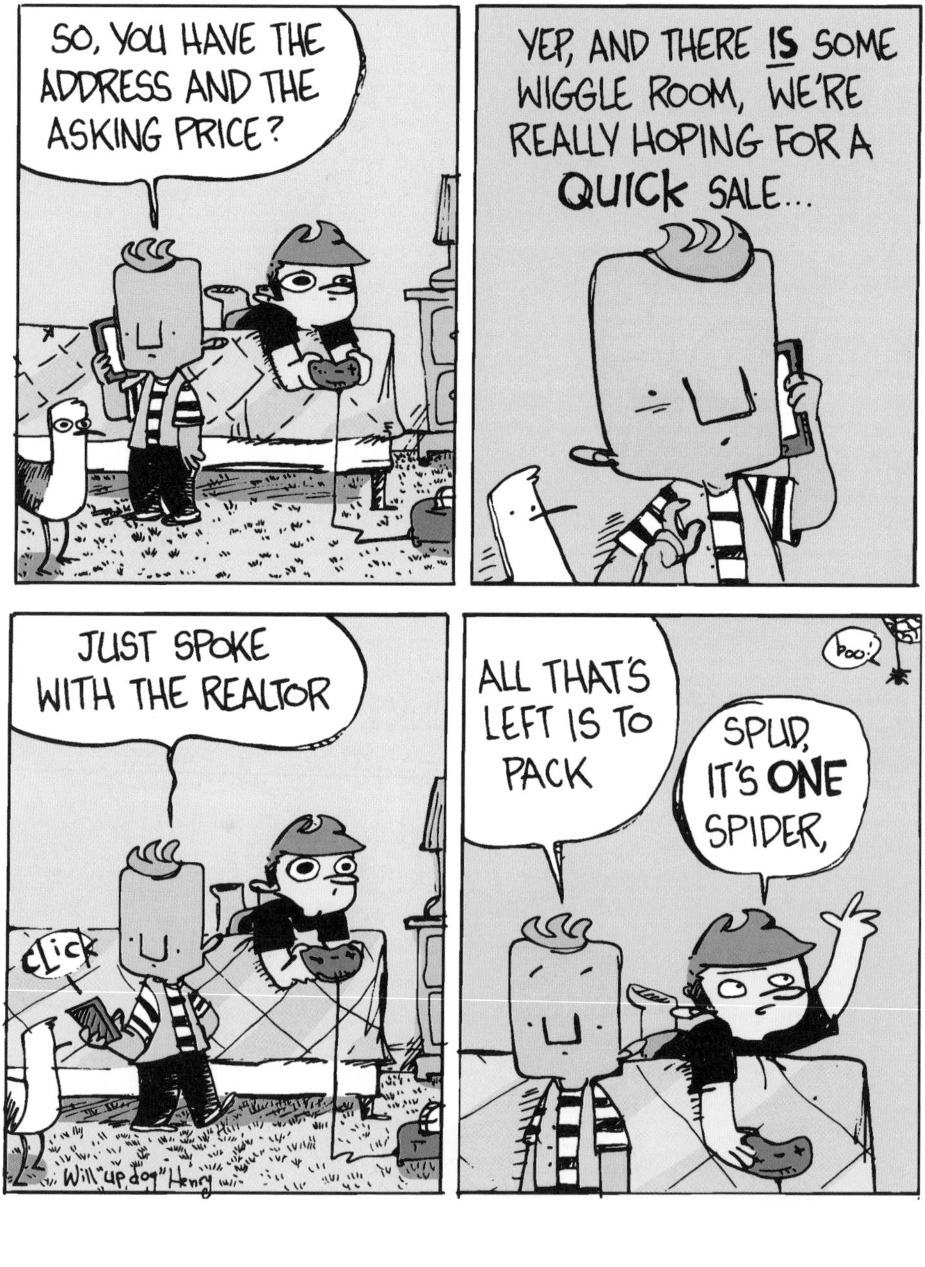
SO, YOU HAVE THE ADDRESS AND THE ASKING PRICE?
YEP, AND THERE IS SOME WIGGLE ROOM, WE'RE REALLY HOPING FOR A QUICK SALE...
JUST SPOKE WITH THE REALTOR
CLICK
Will "up dog" Henry
boo!
ALL THAT'S LEFT IS TO PACK
SPUD, IT'S ONE SPIDER,

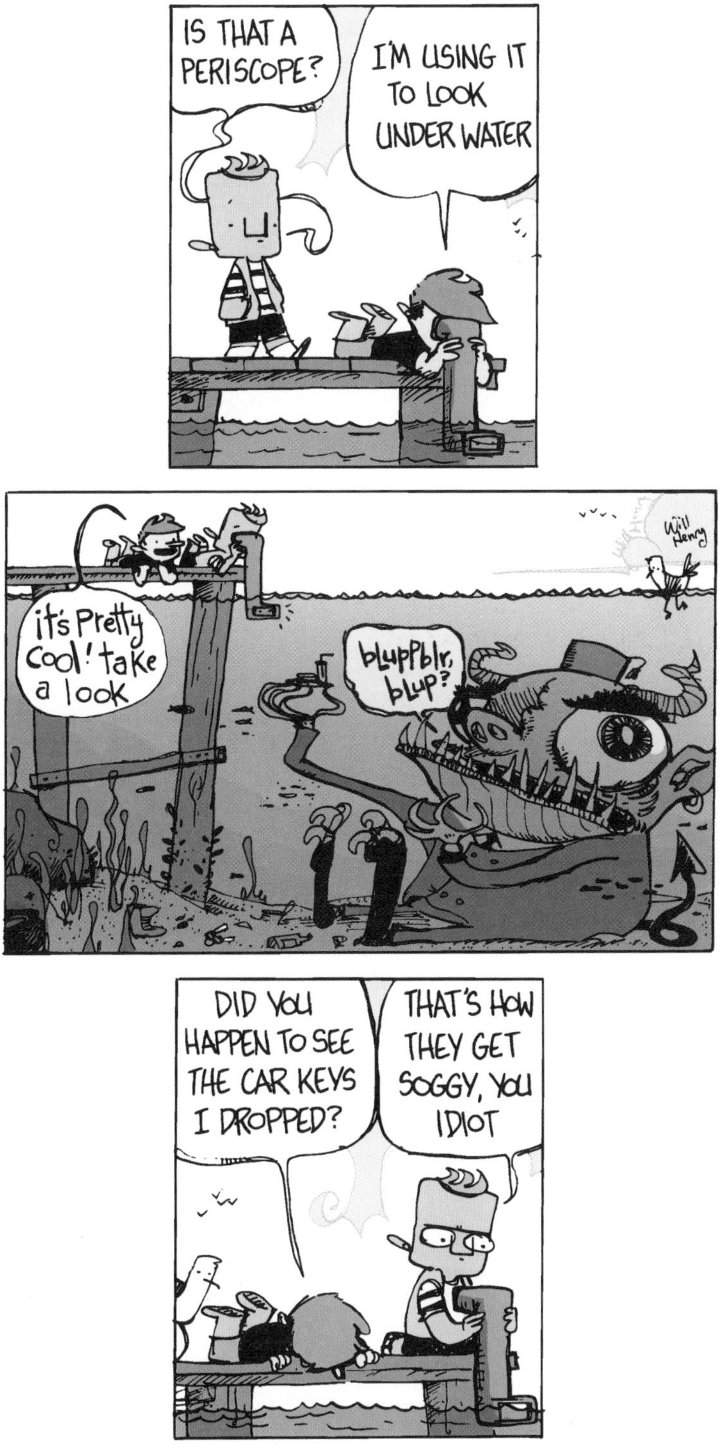
IS THAT A PERISCOPE?
I'M USING IT TO LOOK UNDER WATER
it's Pretty cool! take a look
bluppblr, blup?
Will Henry
DID YOU HAPPEN TO SEE THE CAR KEYS I DROPPED?
THAT'S HOW THEY GET SOGGY, YOU IDIOT

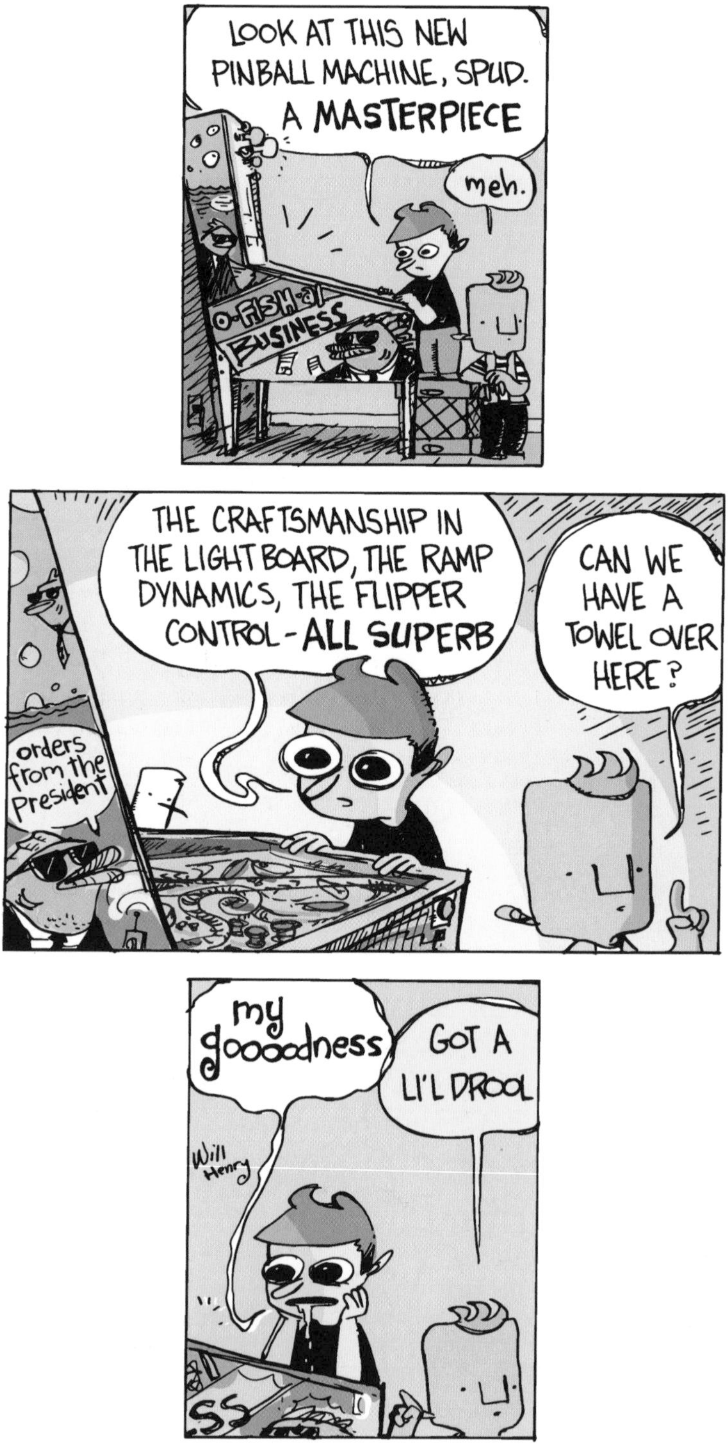
LOOK AT THIS NEW PINBALL MACHINE, SPUD. A **MASTERPIECE**
meh.
O-FISH-aL BUSINESS
THE CRAFTSMANSHIP IN THE LIGHTBOARD, THE RAMP DYNAMICS, THE FLIPPER CONTROL-**ALL SUPERB**
CAN WE HAVE A TOWEL OVER HERE?
orders from the President
my goooodness
GOT A LI'L DROOL
Will Henry

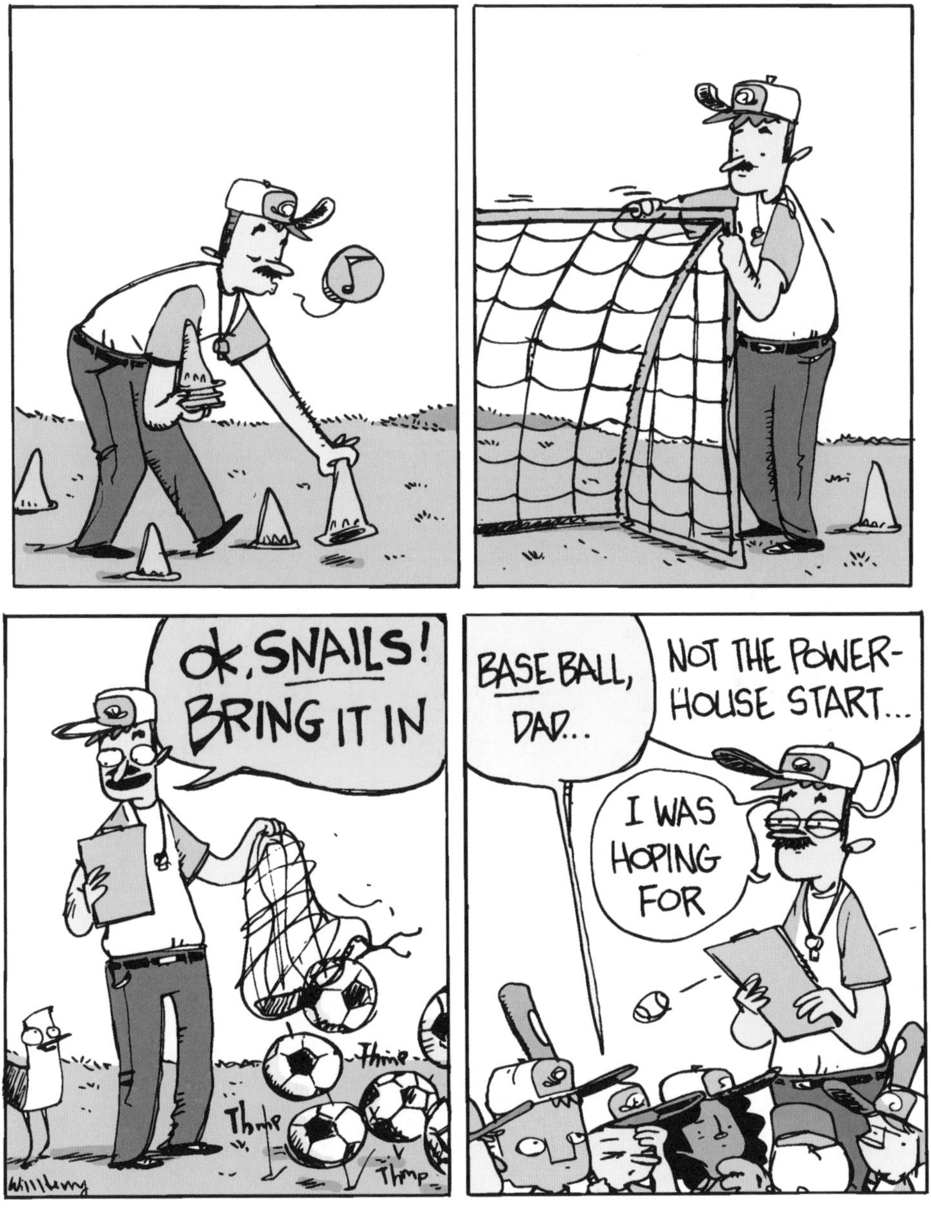

OK, SNAILS! BRING IT IN
THMP
THMP
THMP
BASEBALL, DAD...
NOT THE POWER-HOUSE START...
I WAS HOPING FOR

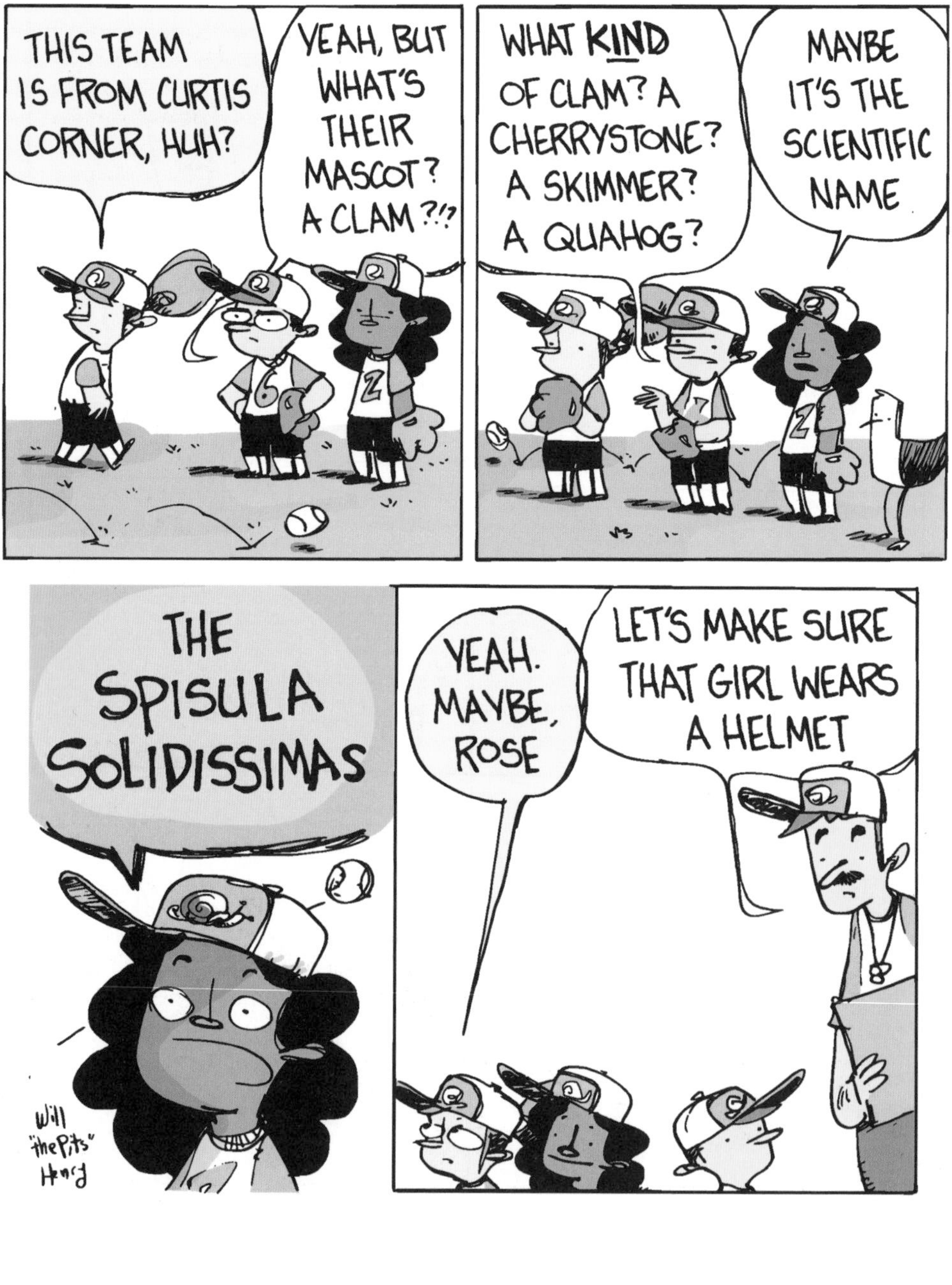
THIS TEAM IS FROM CURTIS CORNER, HUH?
YEAH, BUT WHAT'S THEIR MASCOT? A CLAM?!?
WHAT KIND OF CLAM? A CHERRYSTONE? A SKIMMER? A QUAHOG?
MAYBE IT'S THE SCIENTIFIC NAME
THE SPISULA SOLIDISSIMAS
YEAH. MAYBE, ROSE
LET'S MAKE SURE THAT GIRL WEARS A HELMET
Will "the Pits" Henry

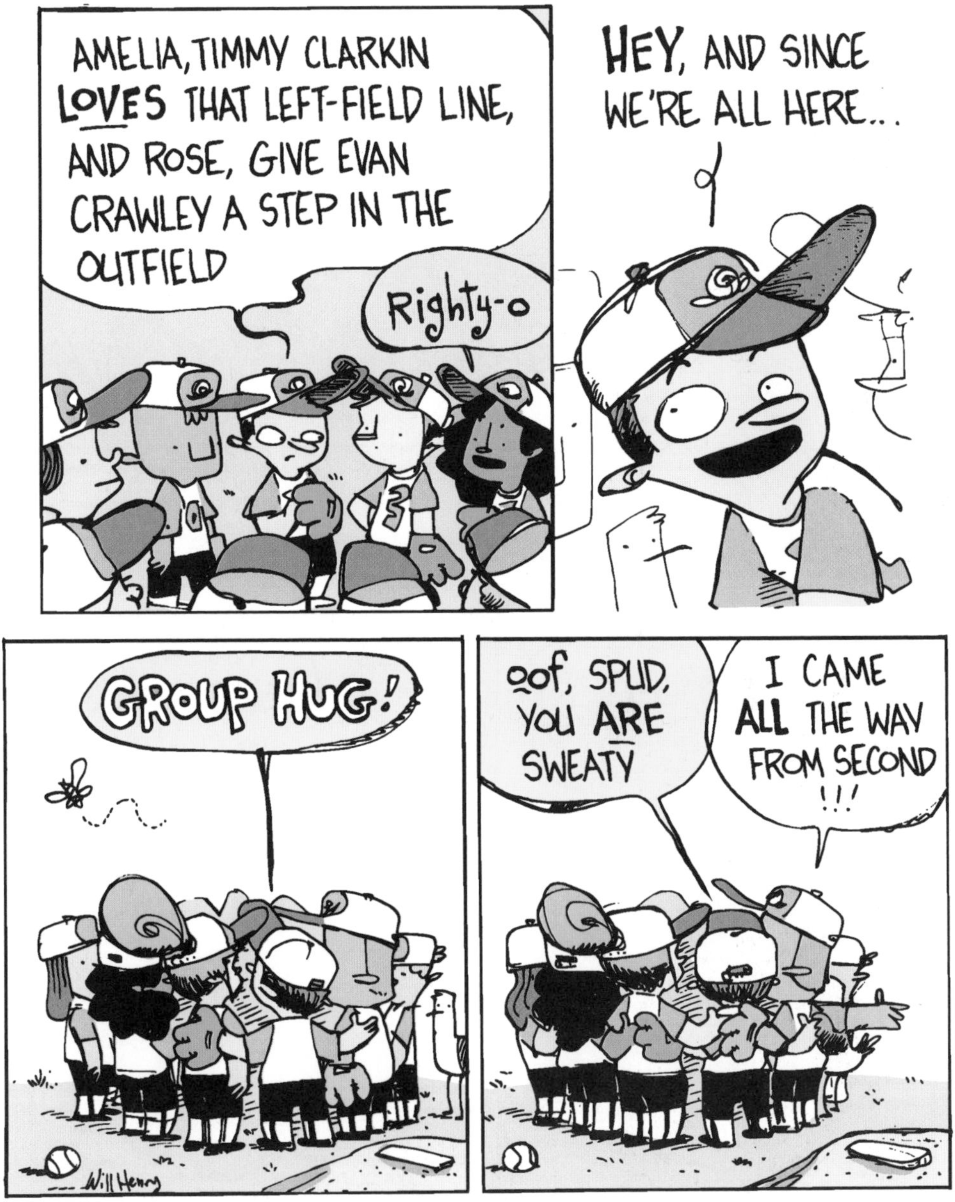

AMELIA, TIMMY CLARKIN LOVES THAT LEFT-FIELD LINE, AND ROSE, GIVE EVAN CRAWLEY A STEP IN THE OUTFIELD
Righty-o
HEY, AND SINCE WE'RE ALL HERE...
GROUP HUG!
oof, SPUD, YOU ARE SWEATY
I CAME ALL THE WAY FROM SECOND !!!
Will Henry

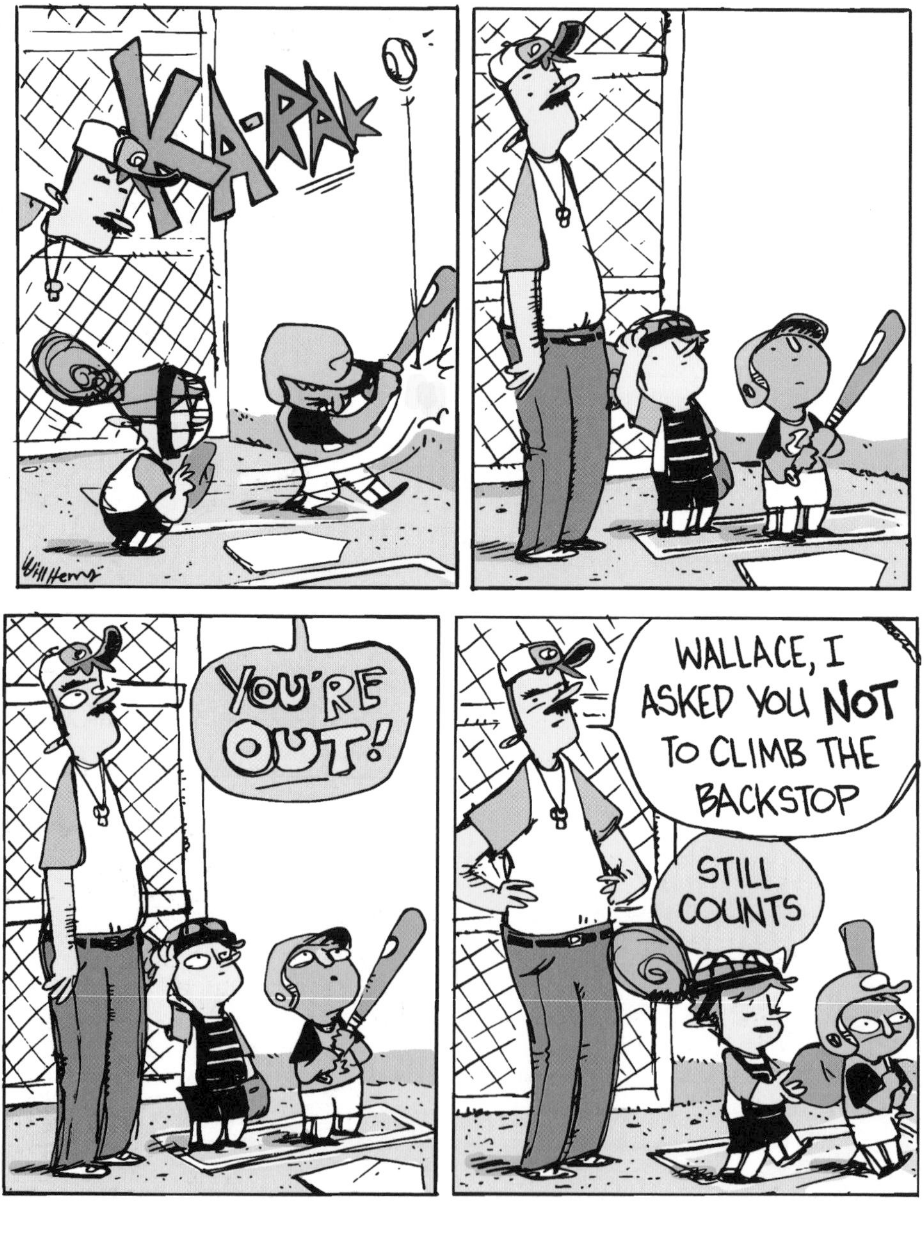
KA-RAK
YOU'RE OUT!
WALLACE, I ASKED YOU NOT TO CLIMB THE BACKSTOP
STILL COUNTS

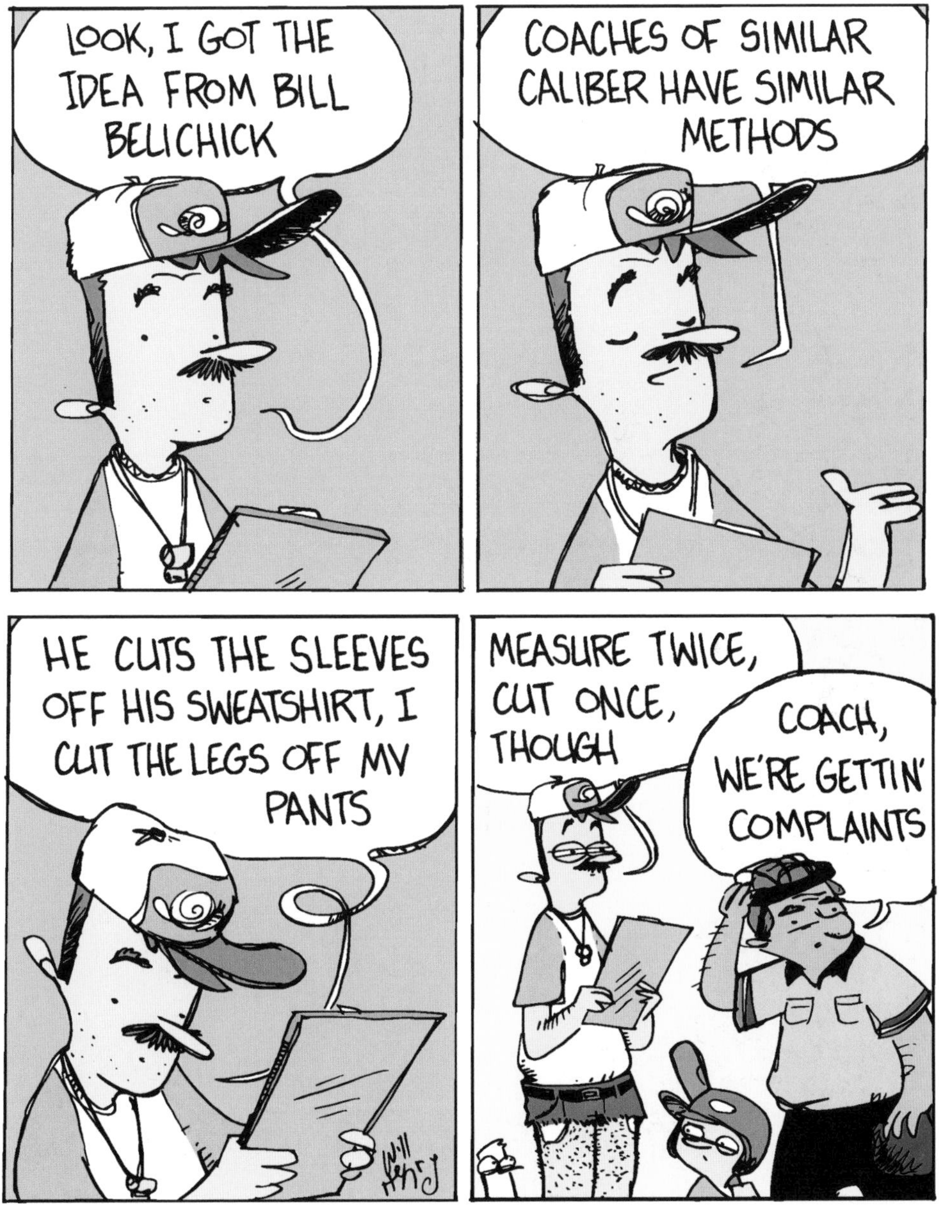
LOOK, I GOT THE IDEA FROM BILL BELICHICK
COACHES OF SIMILAR CALIBER HAVE SIMILAR METHODS
HE CUTS THE SLEEVES OFF HIS SWEATSHIRT, I CUT THE LEGS OFF MY PANTS
MEASURE TWICE, CUT ONCE, THOUGH
COACH, WE'RE GETTIN' COMPLAINTS

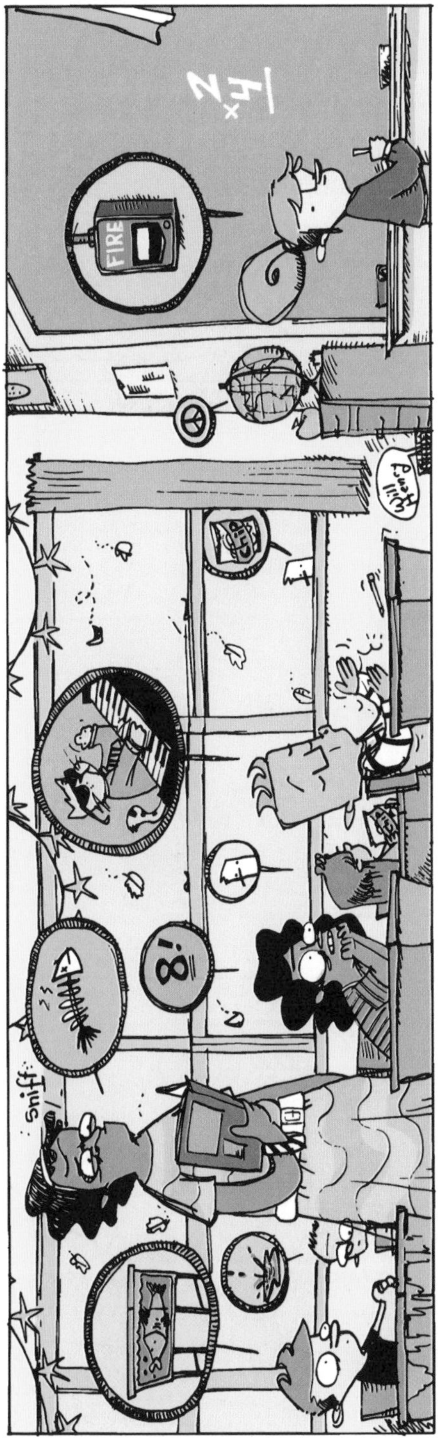
sniff
FIRE

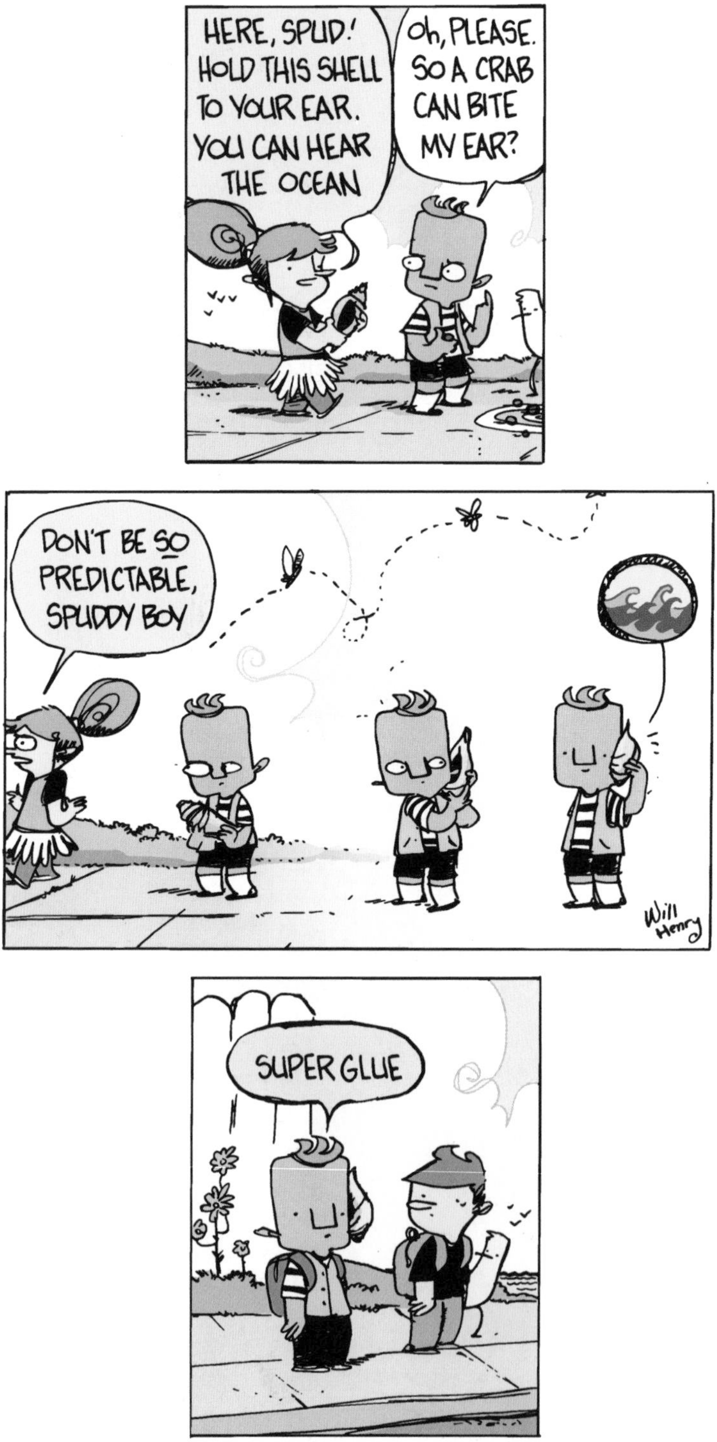
HERE, SPUD! HOLD THIS SHELL TO YOUR EAR. YOU CAN HEAR THE OCEAN
Oh, PLEASE. SO A CRAB CAN BITE MY EAR?
DON'T BE SO PREDICTABLE, SPUDDY BOY
Will Henry
SUPER GLUE

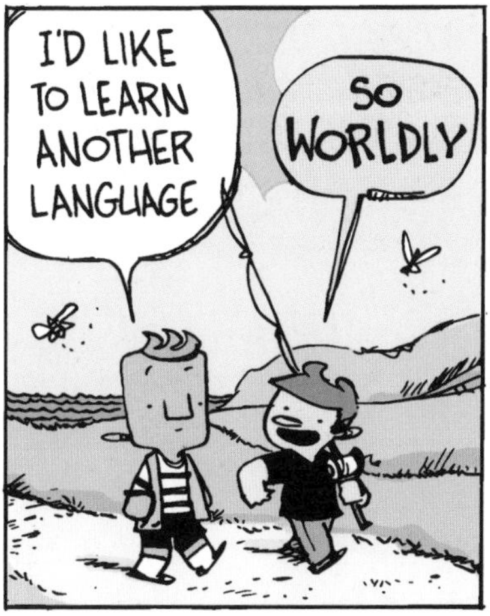
I'D LIKE TO LEARN ANOTHER LANGUAGE
SO WORLDLY

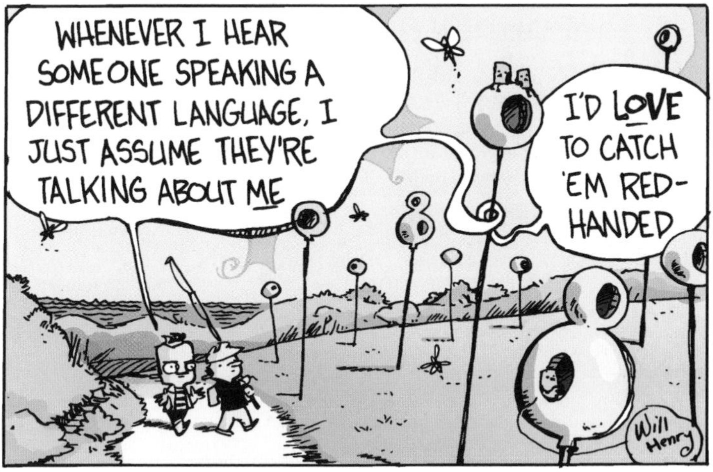
WHENEVER I HEAR SOMEONE SPEAKING A DIFFERENT LANGUAGE, I JUST ASSUME THEY'RE TALKING ABOUT ME
I'D LOVE TO CATCH 'EM RED-HANDED
Will Henry

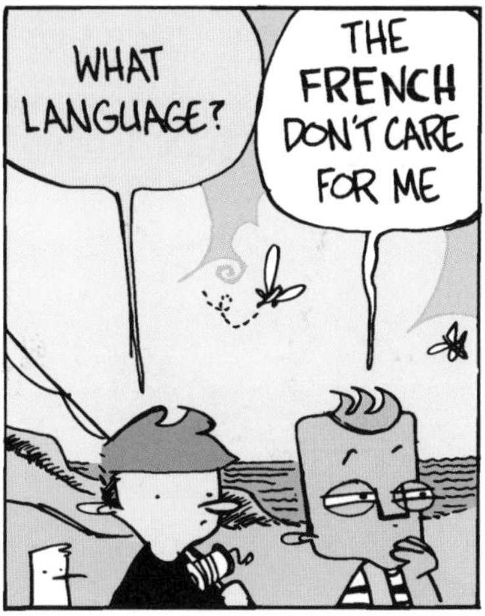
WHAT LANGUAGE?
THE FRENCH DON'T CARE FOR ME

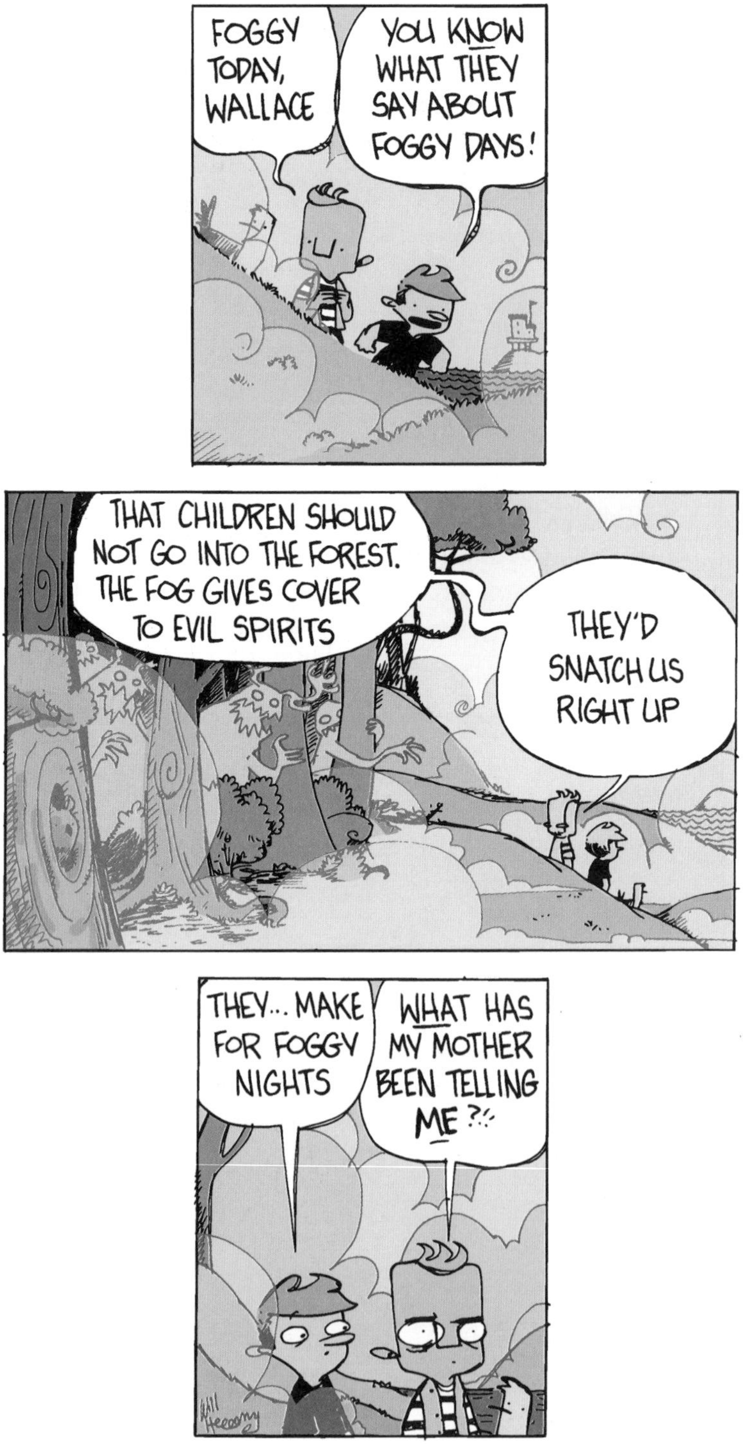
FOGGY TODAY, WALLACE
YOU KNOW WHAT THEY SAY ABOUT FOGGY DAYS!
THAT CHILDREN SHOULD NOT GO INTO THE FOREST. THE FOG GIVES COVER TO EVIL SPIRITS
THEY'D SNATCH US RIGHT UP
THEY... MAKE FOR FOGGY NIGHTS
WHAT HAS MY MOTHER BEEN TELLING ME ?!

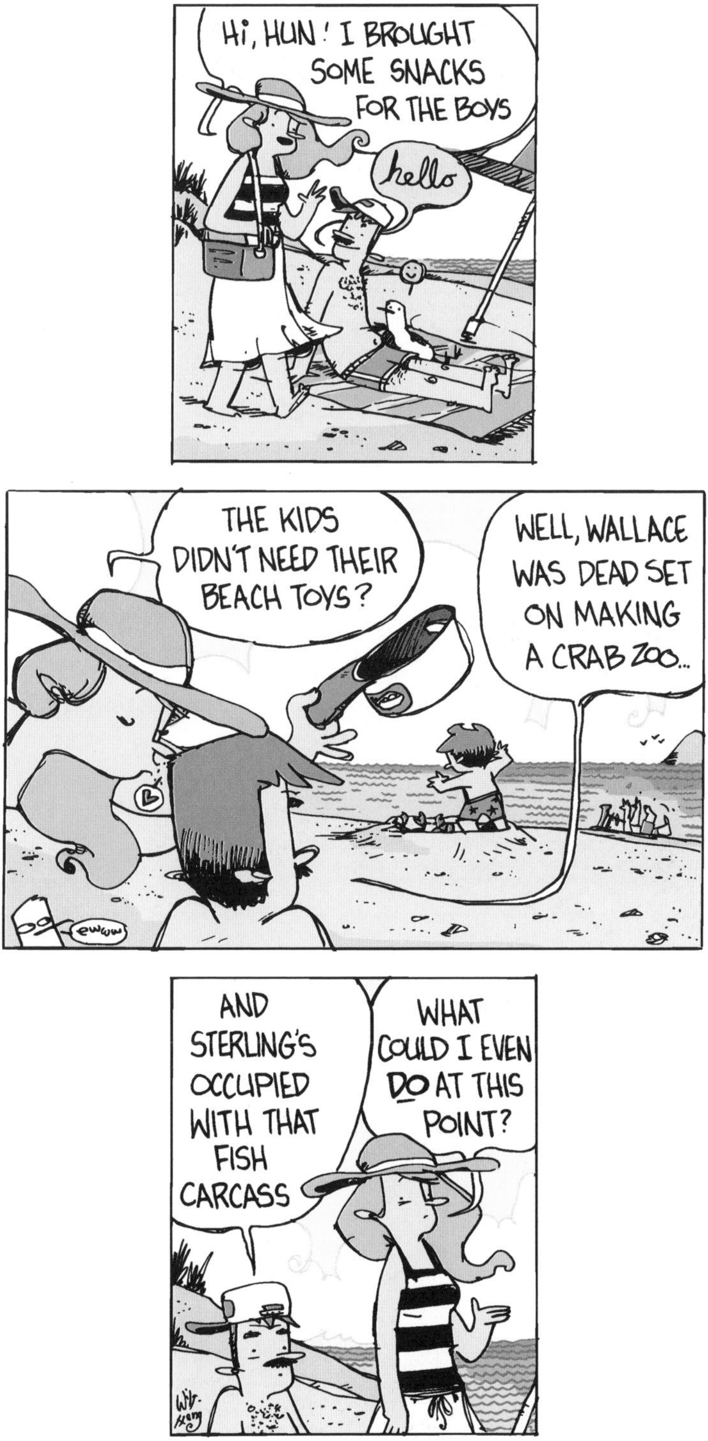

HI, HUN! I BROUGHT SOME SNACKS FOR THE BOYS
hello
THE KIDS DIDN'T NEED THEIR BEACH TOYS?
WELL, WALLACE WAS DEAD SET ON MAKING A CRAB ZOO...
ewww
AND STERLING'S OCCUPIED WITH THAT FISH CARCASS
WHAT COULD I EVEN DO AT THIS POINT?

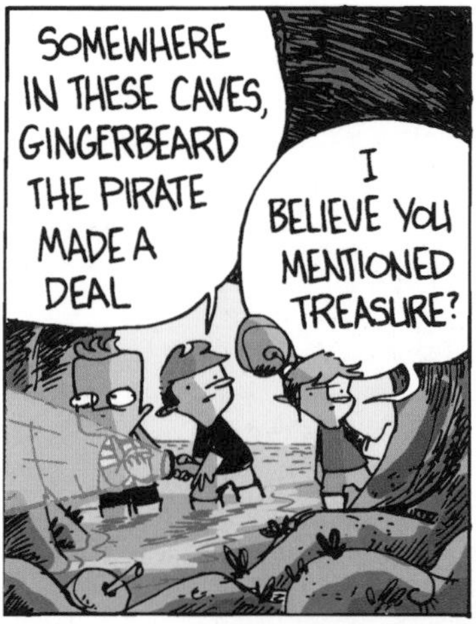
SOMEWHERE IN THESE CAVES, GINGERBEARD THE PIRATE MADE A DEAL
I BELIEVE YOU MENTIONED TREASURE?

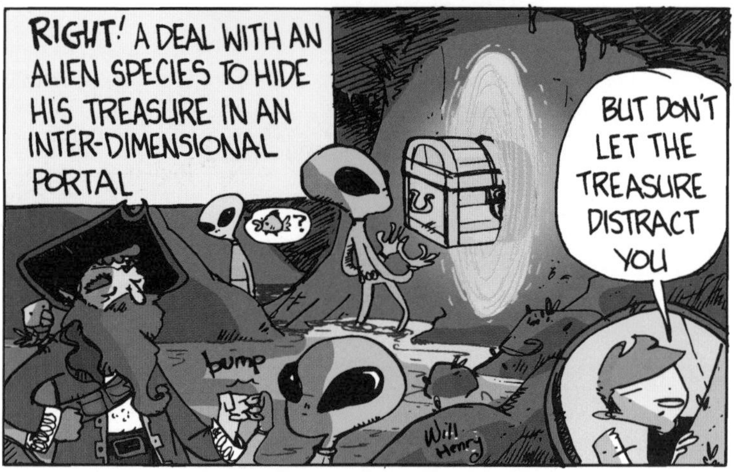
RIGHT! A DEAL WITH AN ALIEN SPECIES TO HIDE HIS TREASURE IN AN INTER-DIMENSIONAL PORTAL
BUT DON'T LET THE TREASURE DISTRACT YOU
bump
Will Henry

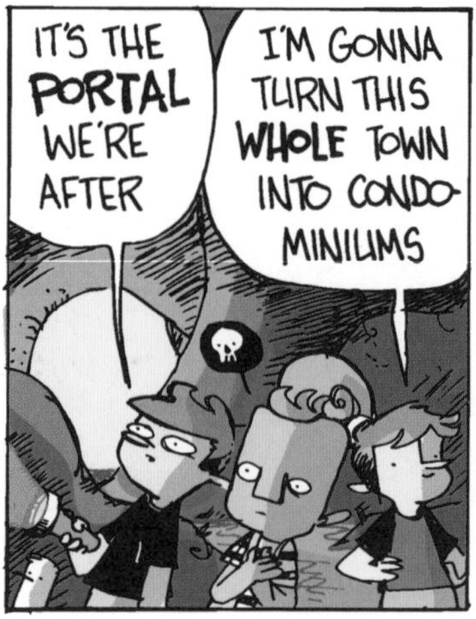
IT'S THE **PORTAL** WE'RE AFTER
I'M GONNA TURN THIS **WHOLE** TOWN INTO CONDO-MINIUMS

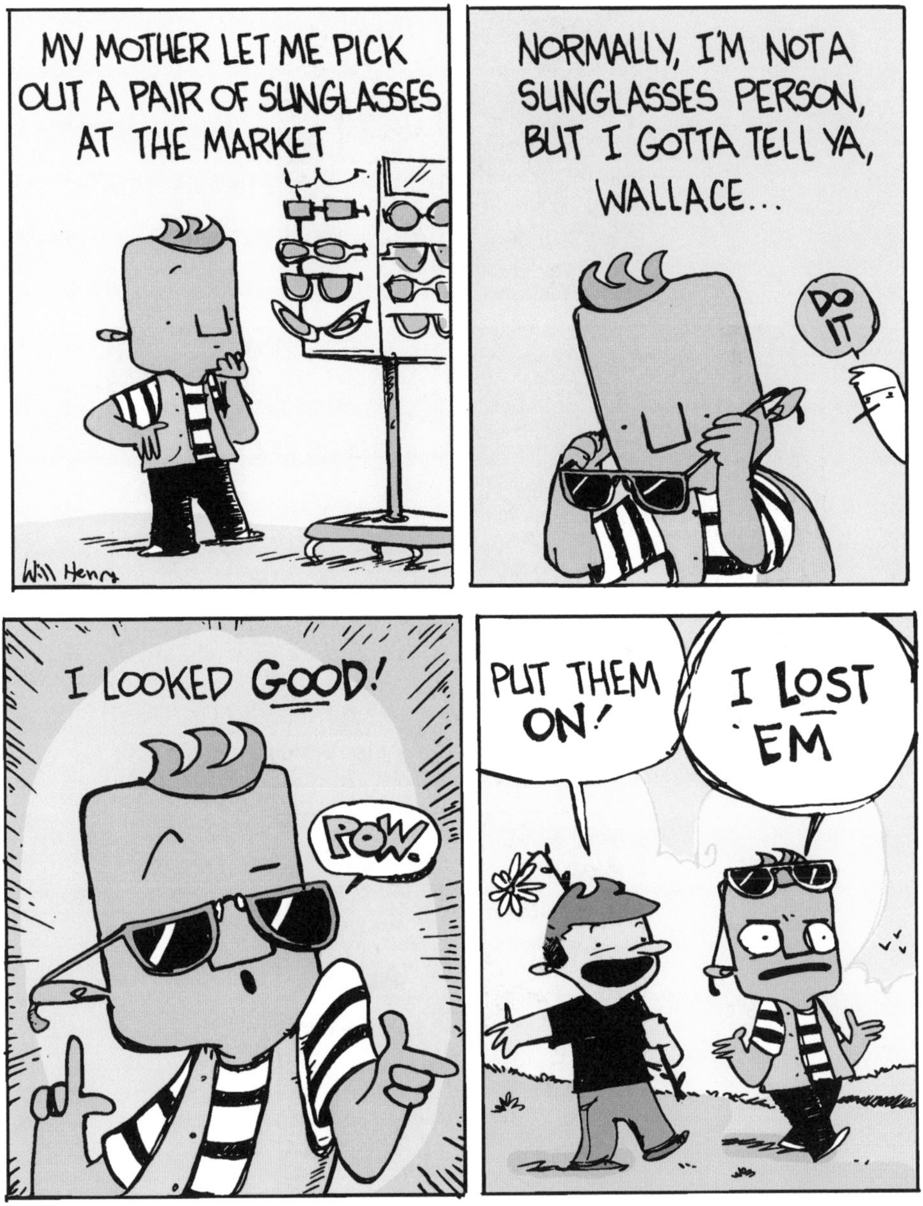
MY MOTHER LET ME PICK OUT A PAIR OF SUNGLASSES AT THE MARKET
Will Henry
NORMALLY, I'M NOT A SUNGLASSES PERSON, BUT I GOTTA TELL YA, WALLACE...
DO IT
I LOOKED GOOD!
POW
PUT THEM ON!
I LOST 'EM

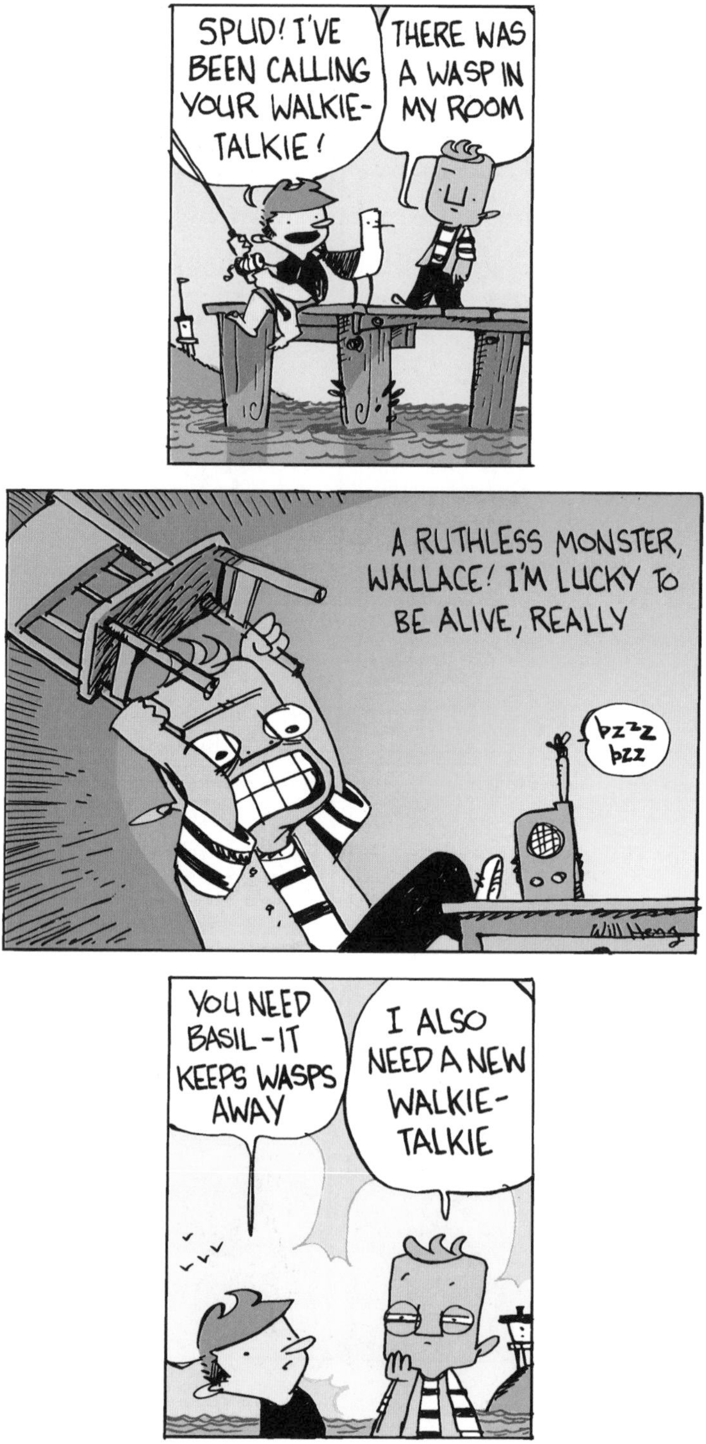
SPUD! I'VE BEEN CALLING YOUR WALKIE-TALKIE!
THERE WAS A WASP IN MY ROOM
A RUTHLESS MONSTER, WALLACE! I'M LUCKY TO BE ALIVE, REALLY
bzzz bzz
YOU NEED BASIL - IT KEEPS WASPS AWAY
I ALSO NEED A NEW WALKIE-TALKIE

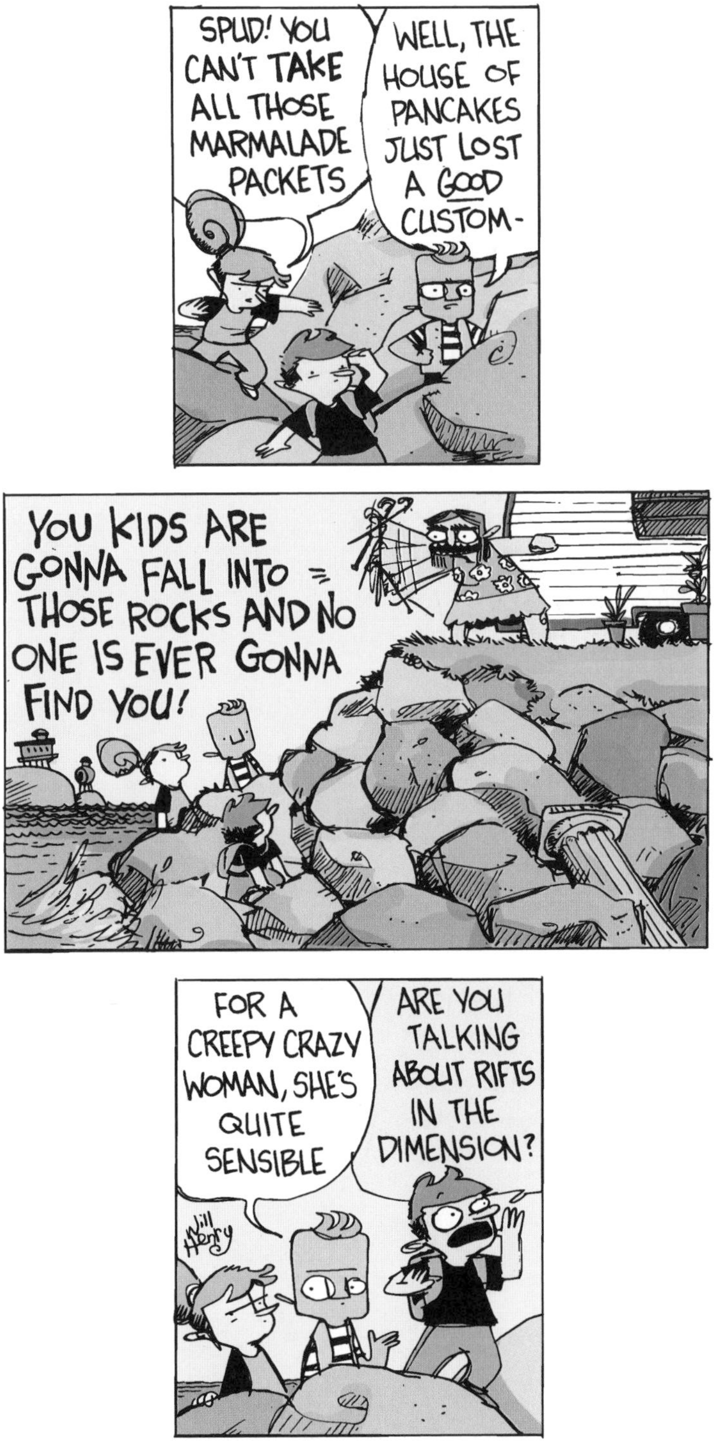
SPUD! YOU CAN'T TAKE ALL THOSE MARMALADE PACKETS
WELL, THE HOUSE OF PANCAKES JUST LOST A GOOD CUSTOM-
YOU KIDS ARE GONNA FALL INTO THOSE ROCKS AND NO ONE IS EVER GONNA FIND YOU!
FOR A CREEPY CRAZY WOMAN, SHE'S QUITE SENSIBLE
ARE YOU TALKING ABOUT RIFTS IN THE DIMENSION?
Jill Henry

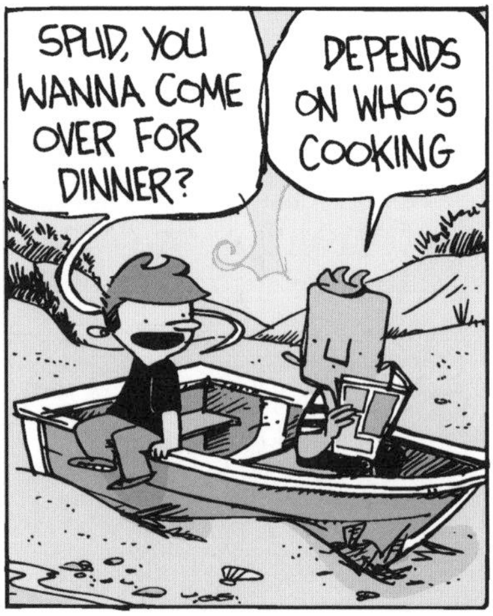
SPUD, YOU WANNA COME OVER FOR DINNER?
DEPENDS ON WHO'S COOKING

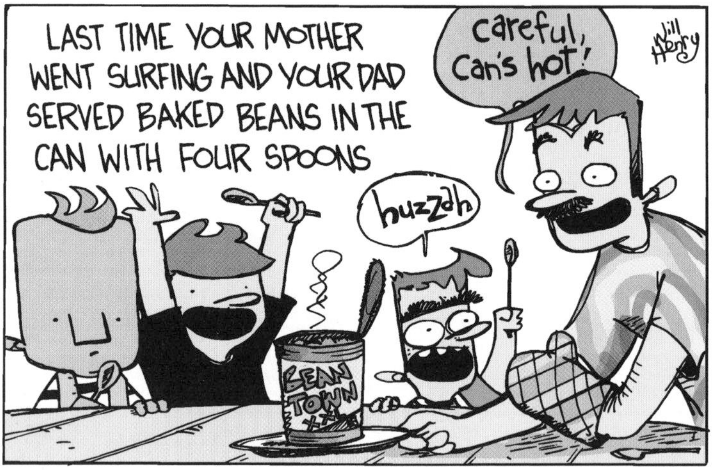
LAST TIME YOUR MOTHER WENT SURFING AND YOUR DAD SERVED BAKED BEANS IN THE CAN WITH FOUR SPOONS
careful, Can's hot!
huzzah
BEAN TOWN
Will Henry

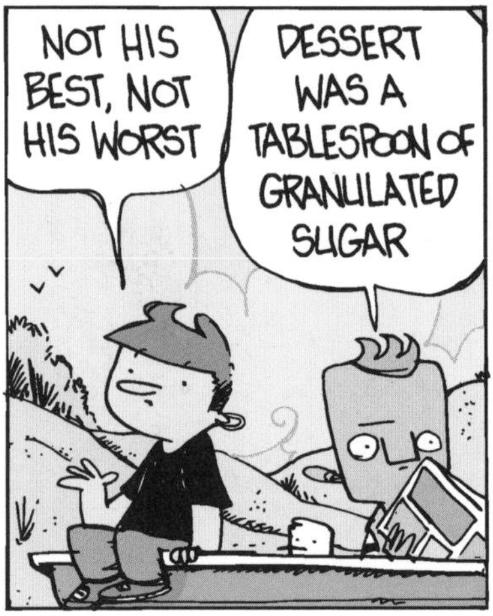
NOT HIS BEST, NOT HIS WORST
DESSERT WAS A TABLESPOON OF GRANULATED SUGAR

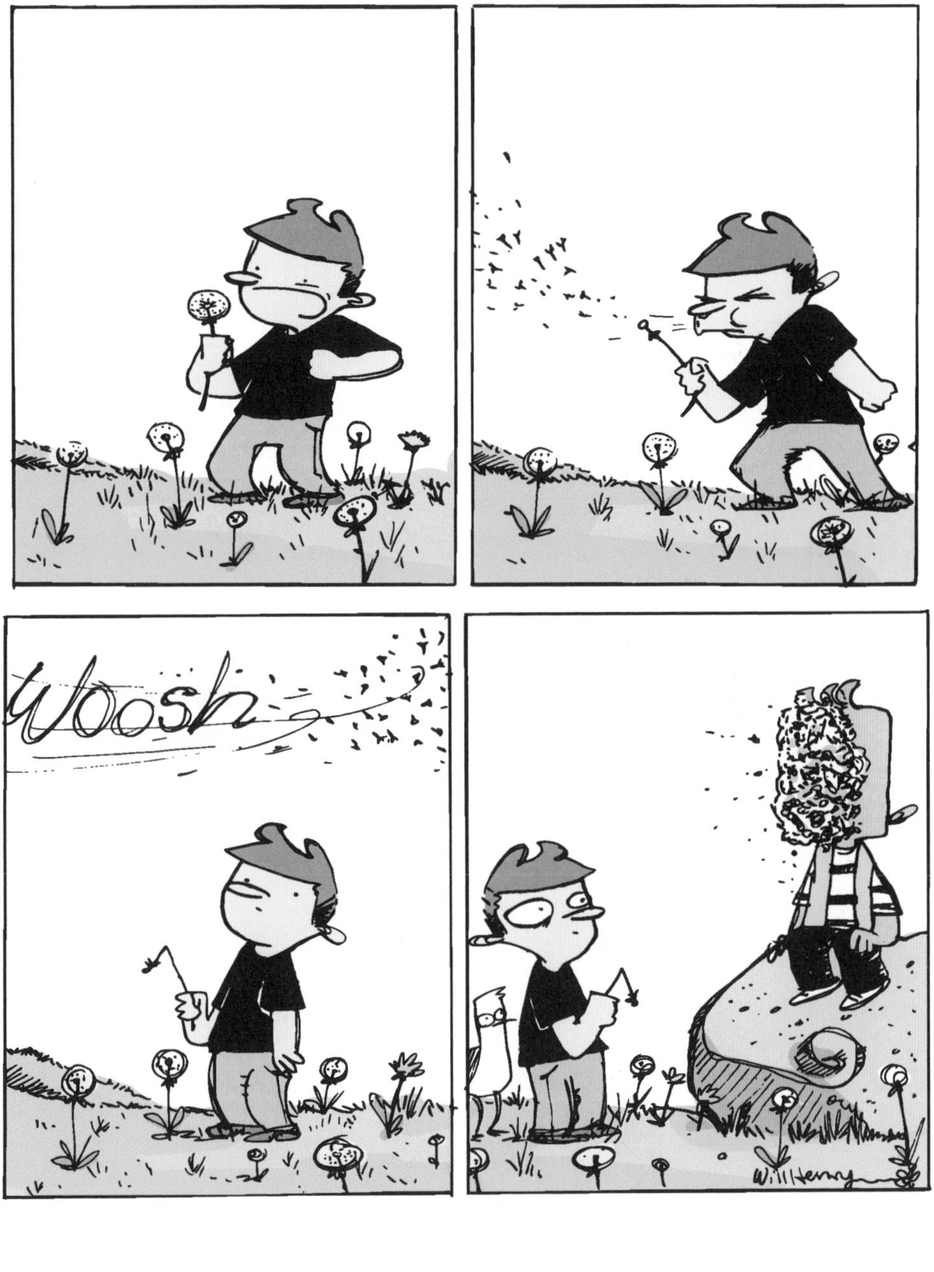
Woosh
Will Henry

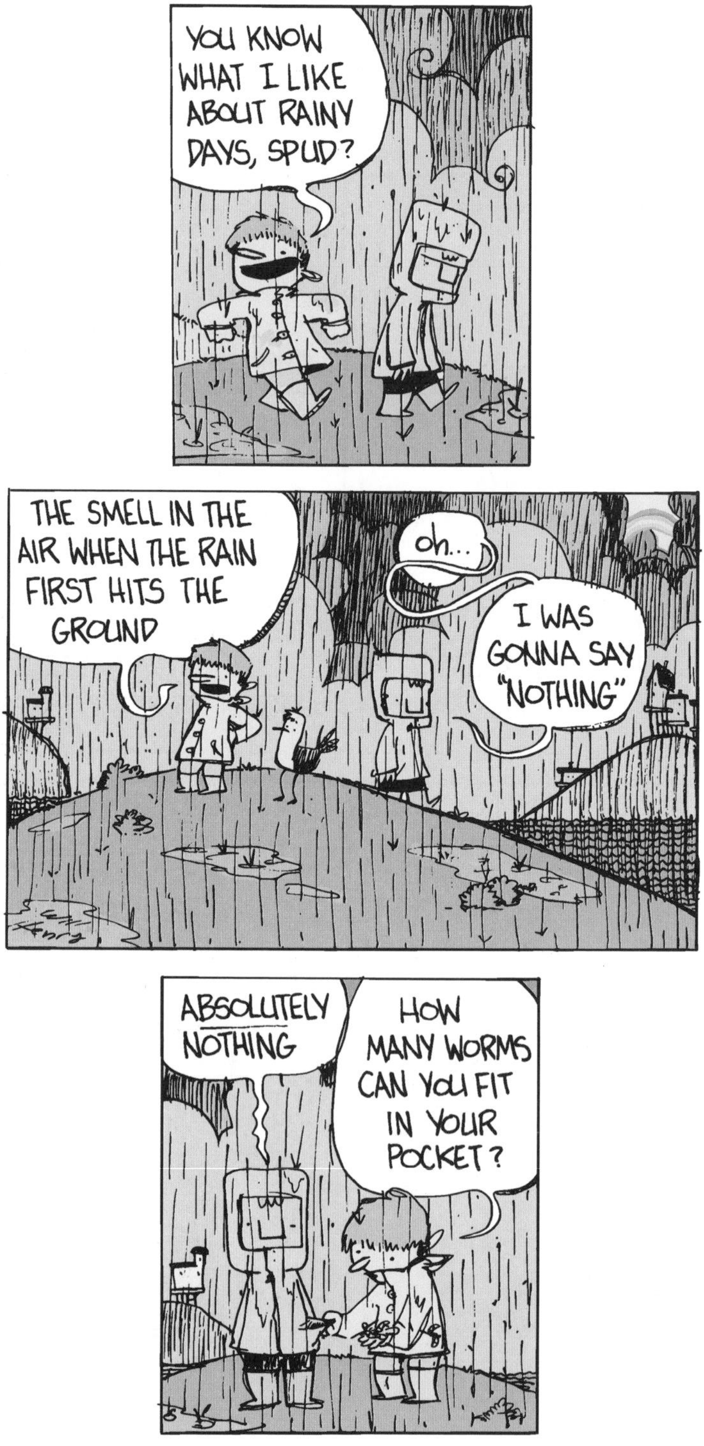
YOU KNOW WHAT I LIKE ABOUT RAINY DAYS, SPUD?
THE SMELL IN THE AIR WHEN THE RAIN FIRST HITS THE GROUND
oh...
I WAS GONNA SAY "NOTHING"
ABSOLUTELY NOTHING
HOW MANY WORMS CAN YOU FIT IN YOUR POCKET?

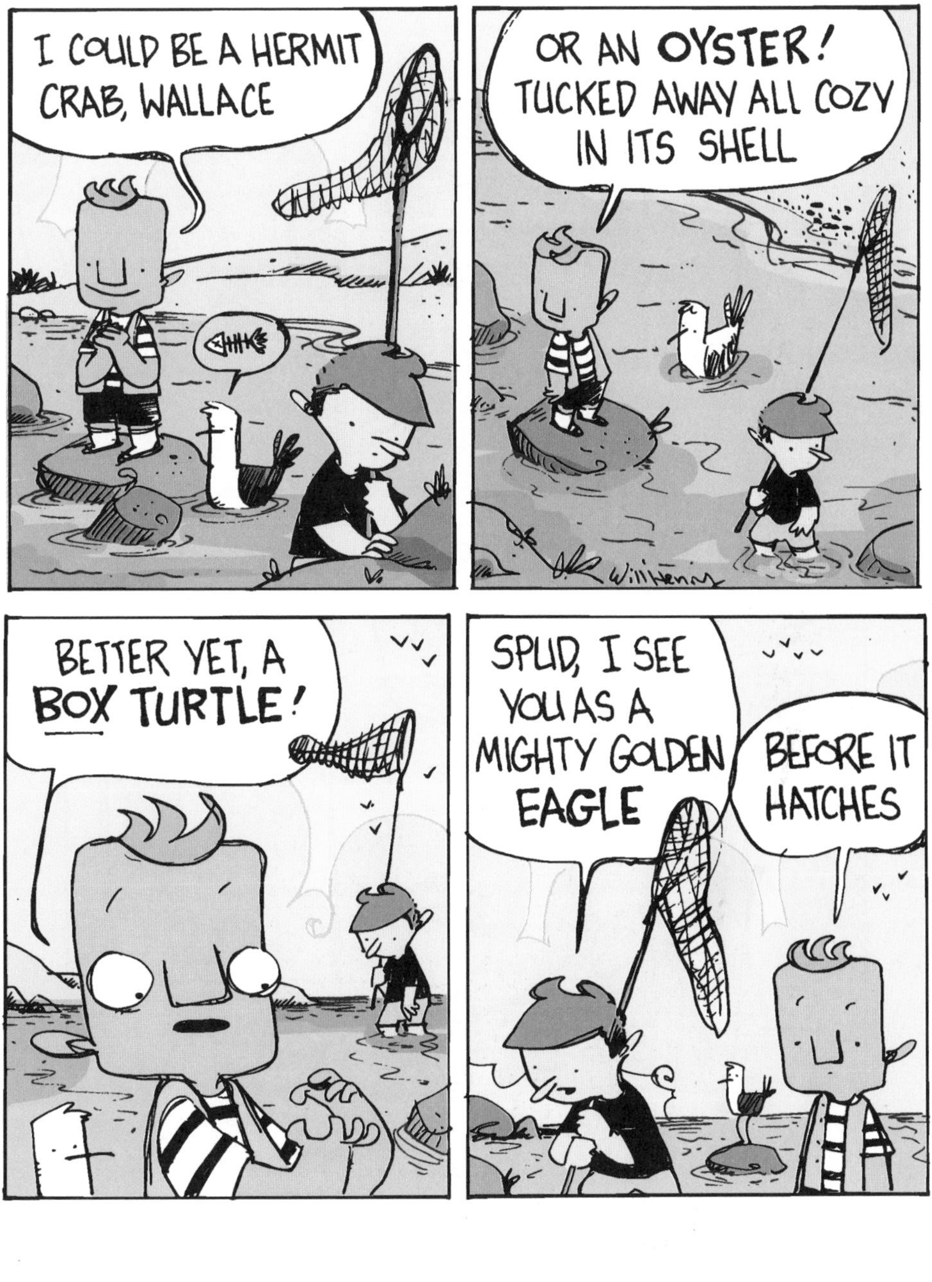
I COULD BE A HERMIT CRAB, WALLACE
OR AN OYSTER! TUCKED AWAY ALL COZY IN ITS SHELL
BETTER YET, A BOX TURTLE!
SPUD, I SEE YOU AS A MIGHTY GOLDEN EAGLE
BEFORE IT HATCHES

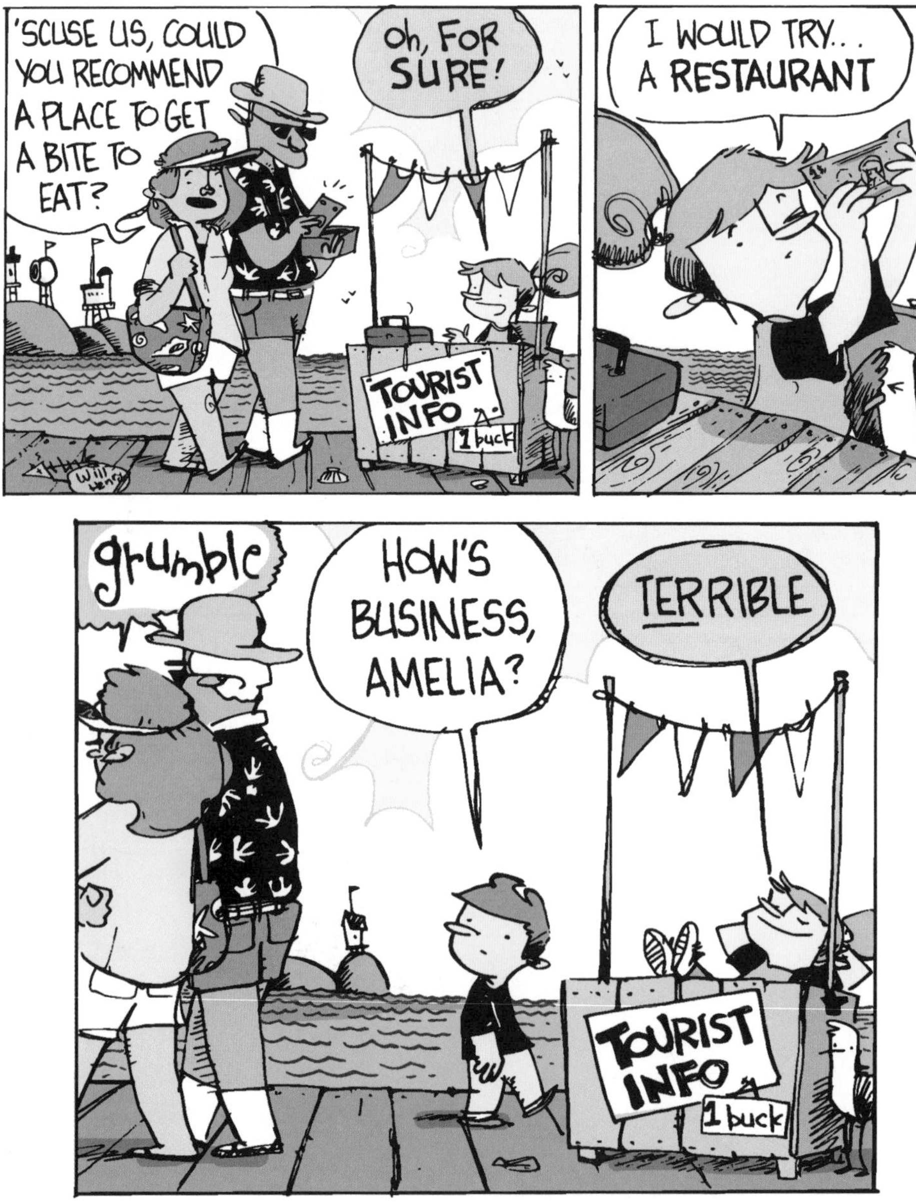
'SCUSE US, COULD YOU RECOMMEND A PLACE TO GET A BITE TO EAT?
Oh, FOR SURE!
TOURIST INFO
1 buck
I WOULD TRY... A RESTAURANT
grumble
HOW'S BUSINESS, AMELIA?
TERRIBLE
TOURIST INFO
1 buck

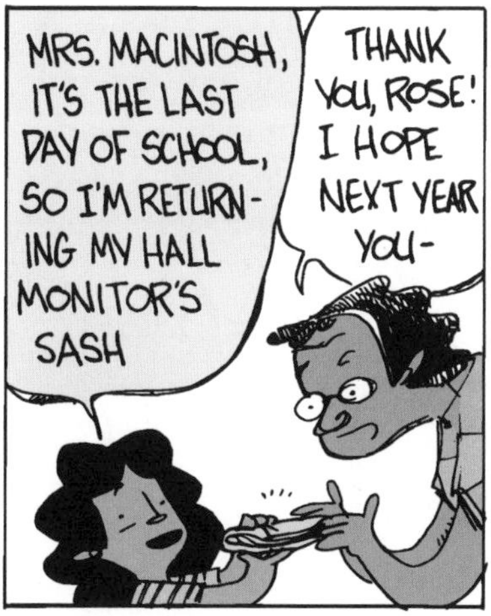
MRS. MACINTOSH, IT'S THE LAST DAY OF SCHOOL, SO I'M RETURNING MY HALL MONITOR'S SASH
THANK YOU, ROSE! I HOPE NEXT YEAR YOU-

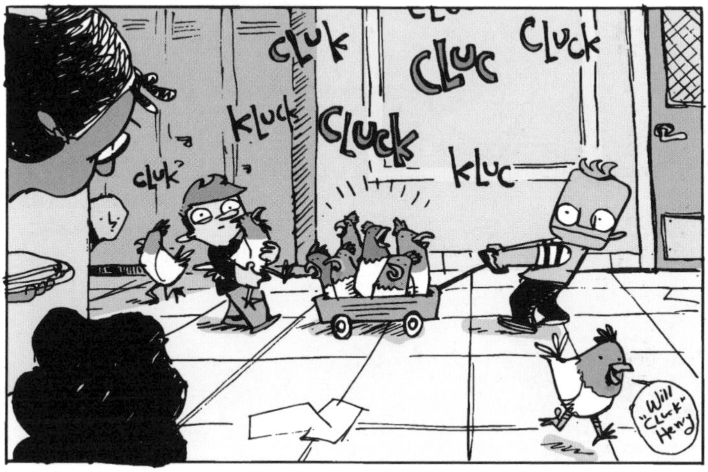
CLUK
CLUC
CLUCK
KLUCK
CLUCK
CLUK?
KLUC
"Will "Cluck" Henry

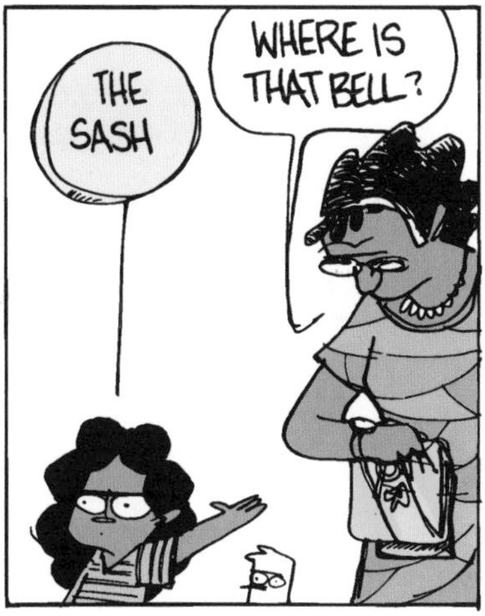
THE SASH
WHERE IS THAT BELL?

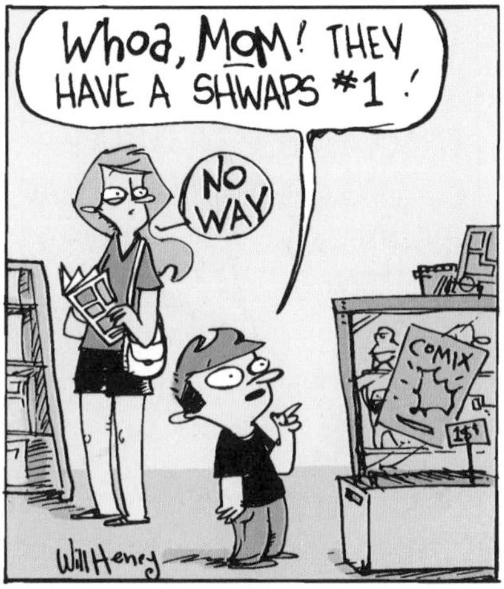
Whoa, MOM! THEY HAVE A SHWAPS #1!
NO WAY
COMIX
Will Henry

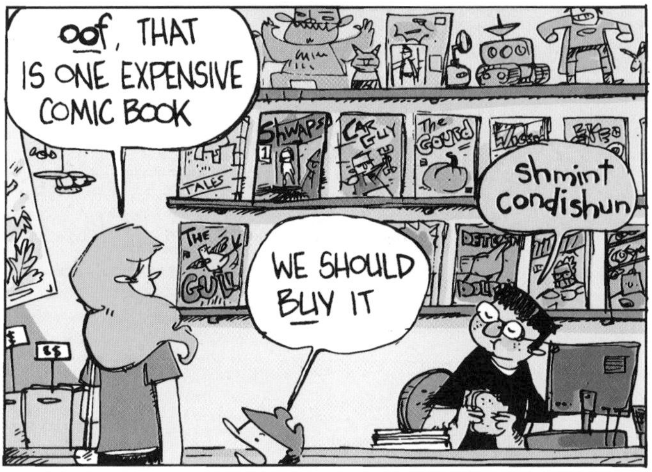
oof, THAT IS ONE EXPENSIVE COMIC BOOK
SHWAPS
CAR GUY
The GOURD
TALES
THE GULL
shmint condishun
WE SHOULD BUY IT

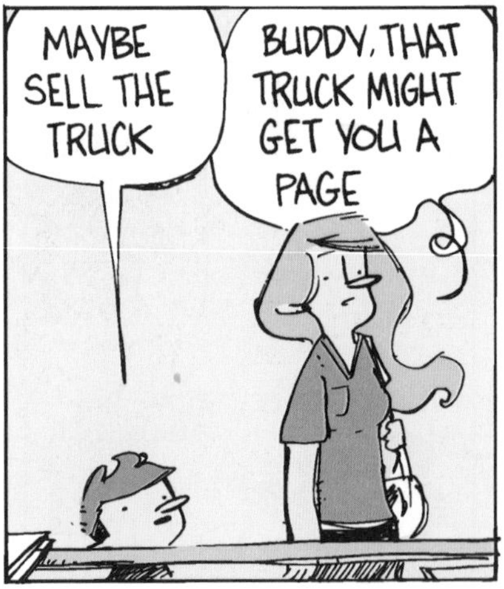
MAYBE SELL THE TRUCK
BUDDY, THAT TRUCK MIGHT GET YOU A PAGE

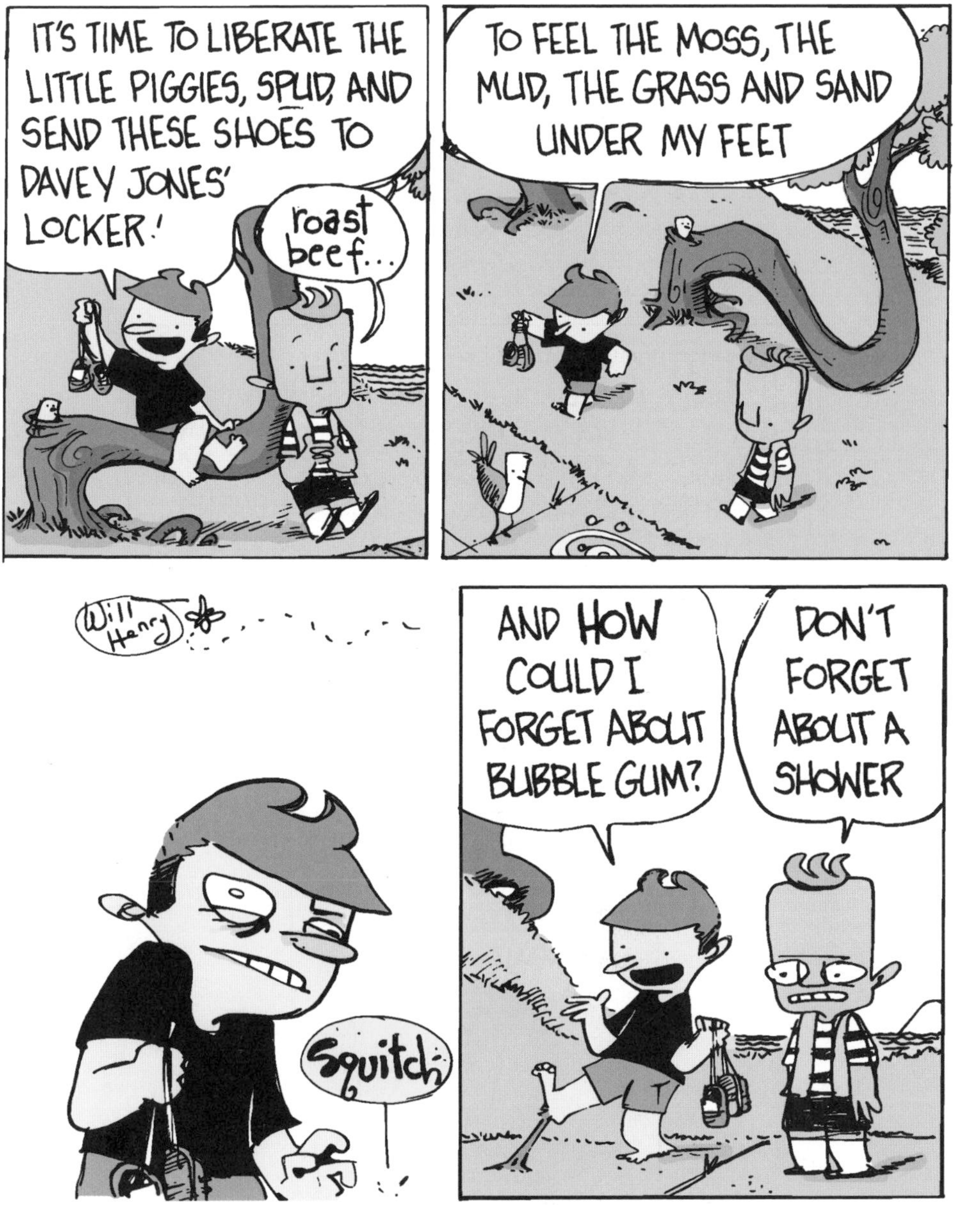
IT'S TIME TO LIBERATE THE LITTLE PIGGIES, SPUD, AND SEND THESE SHOES TO DAVEY JONES' LOCKER!
roast beef...
TO FEEL THE MOSS, THE MUD, THE GRASS AND SAND UNDER MY FEET
Will Henry
Squitch
AND HOW COULD I FORGET ABOUT BUBBLE GUM?
DON'T FORGET ABOUT A SHOWER

AMELIA! WANNA WATCH ME THROW MY SHOES OFF THE DOCKS?
sighh... NOTHIN' ELSE TO DO IN THIS TOWN
IT'S ALL COMIN' TOGETHER
SPUD, GOOD TO SEE YOU'RE STILL ROCKIN' THE SOCKS WITH SANDALS
AMELIA, THESE PROTECT ME FROM TICKS, POISON IVY, SUNBURNS...
Willy Henry
HOW 'BOUT FROM LOOKING LIKE A MIDDLE-AGED MAN?
GOT THESE CHERUB CHEEKS FOR THAT

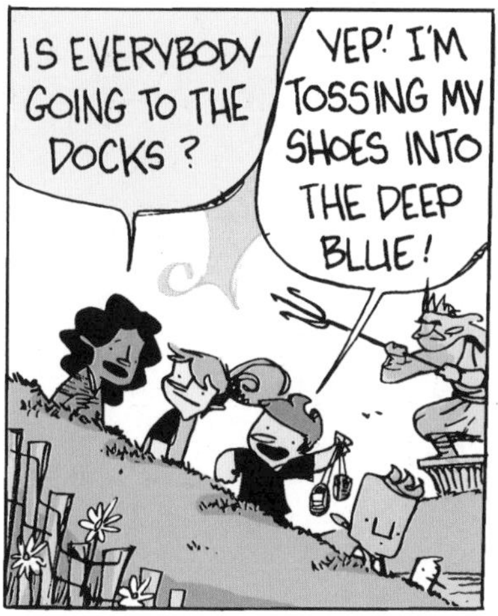
IS EVERYBODY GOING TO THE DOCKS ?
YEP! I'M TOSSING MY SHOES INTO THE DEEP BLUE!

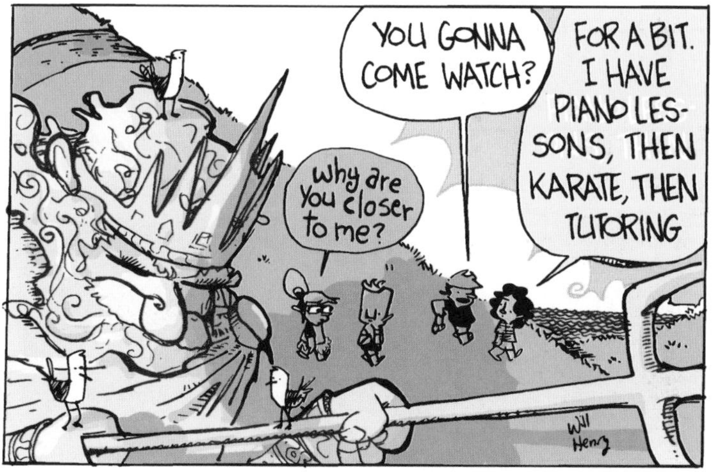
YOU GONNA COME WATCH?
FOR A BIT. I HAVE PIANO LES-SONS, THEN KARATE, THEN TUTORING
why are you closer to me?
Will Henry

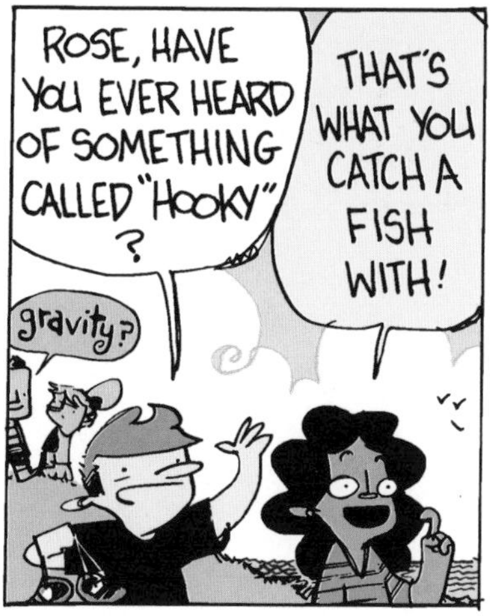
ROSE, HAVE YOU EVER HEARD OF SOMETHING CALLED "HOOKY" ?
THAT'S WHAT YOU CATCH A FISH WITH!
gravity?

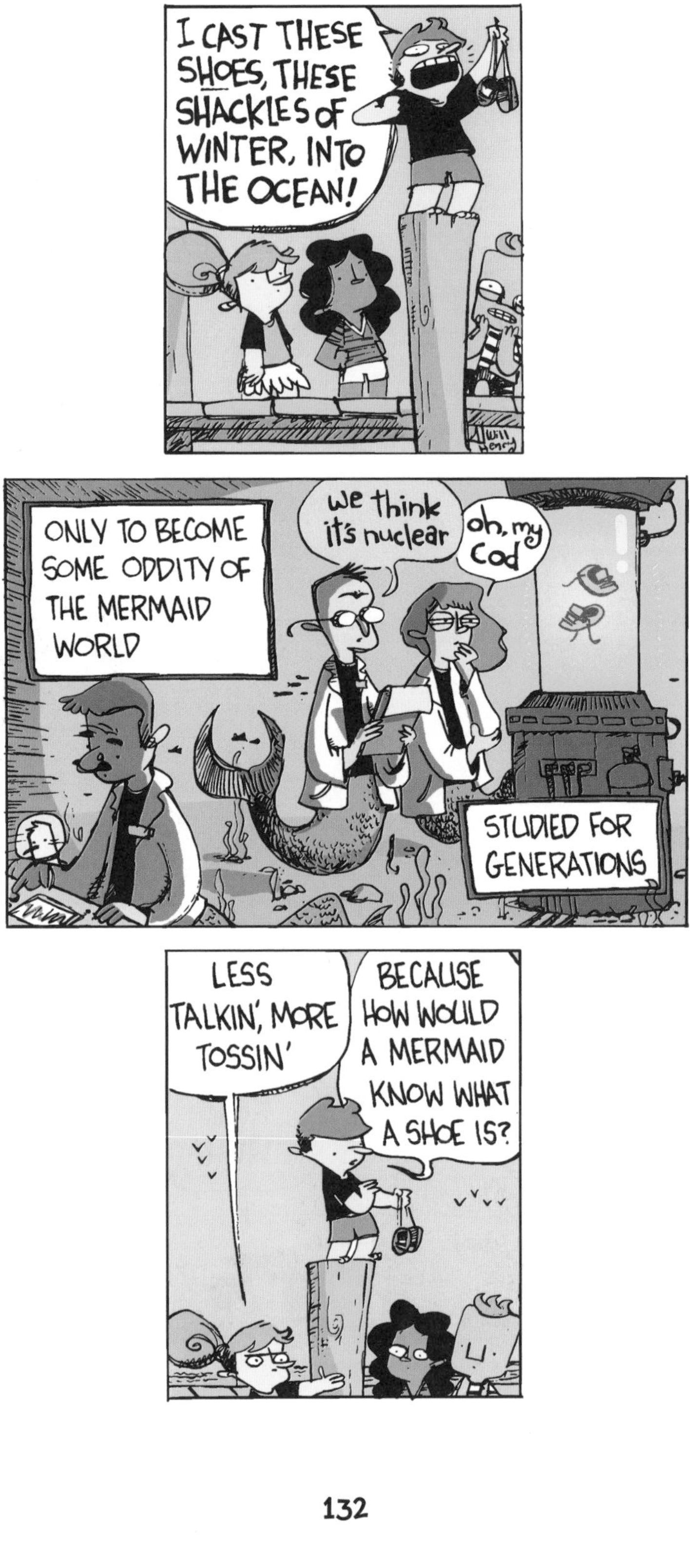
I CAST THESE SHOES, THESE SHACKLES OF WINTER, INTO THE OCEAN!
ONLY TO BECOME SOME ODDITY OF THE MERMAID WORLD
we think it's nuclear
oh, my Cod
STUDIED FOR GENERATIONS
LESS TALKIN', MORE TOSSIN'
BECAUSE HOW WOULD A MERMAID KNOW WHAT A SHOE IS?

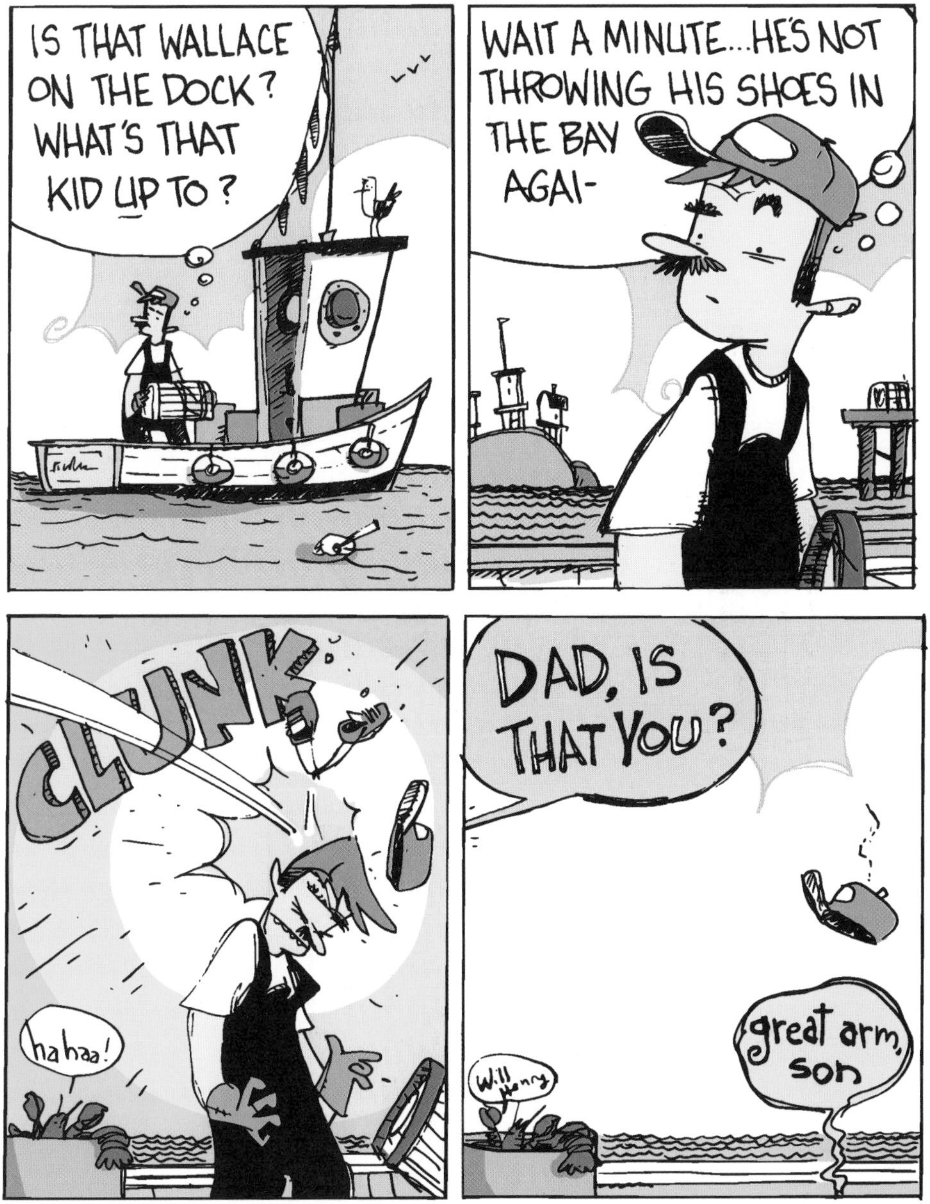
IS THAT WALLACE ON THE DOCK? WHAT'S THAT KID UP TO?
WAIT A MINUTE...HE'S NOT THROWING HIS SHOES IN THE BAY AGAI-
CLUNK
ha haa!
DAD, IS THAT YOU?
Will Henry
great arm, son

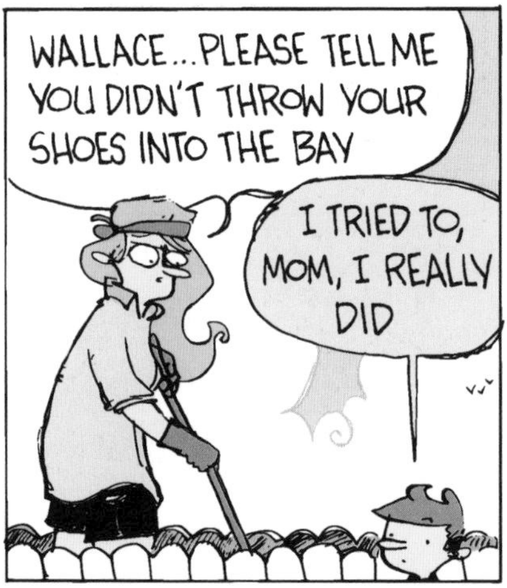
WALLACE...PLEASE TELL ME YOU DIDN'T THROW YOUR SHOES INTO THE BAY
I TRIED TO, MOM, I REALLY DID

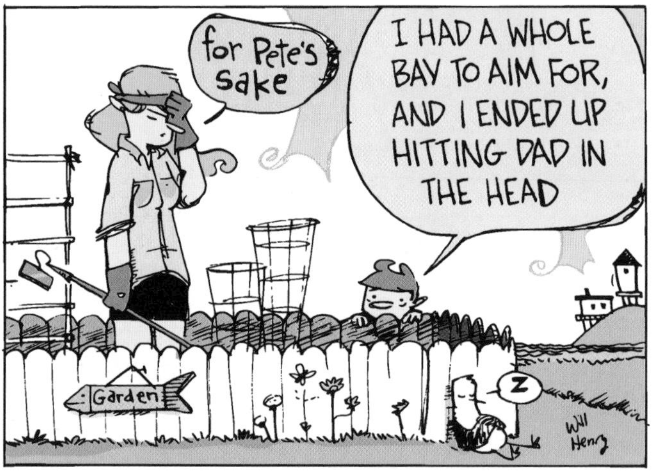
for Pete's sake
I HAD A WHOLE BAY TO AIM FOR, AND I ENDED UP HITTING DAD IN THE HEAD
Garden
Z
Will Henry

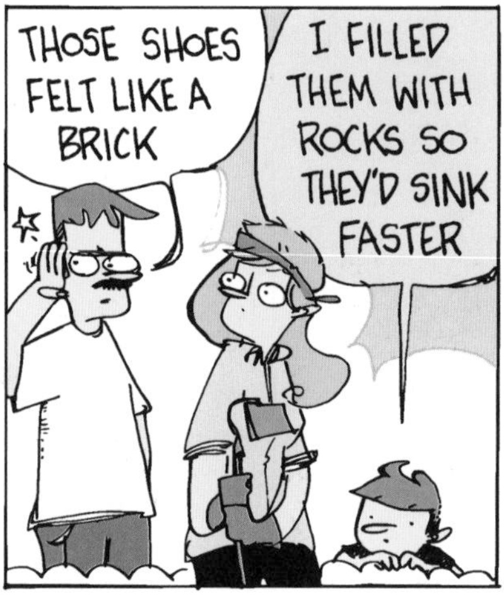
THOSE SHOES FELT LIKE A BRICK
I FILLED THEM WITH ROCKS SO THEY'D SINK FASTER

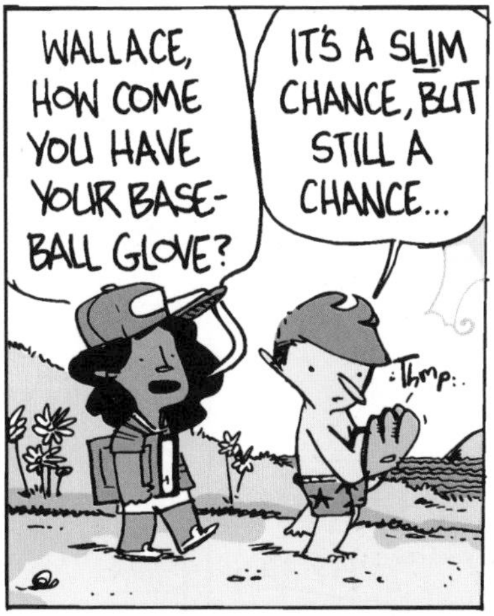
WALLACE, HOW COME YOU HAVE YOUR BASE-BALL GLOVE?
IT'S A SLIM CHANCE, BUT STILL A CHANCE...
Thmp

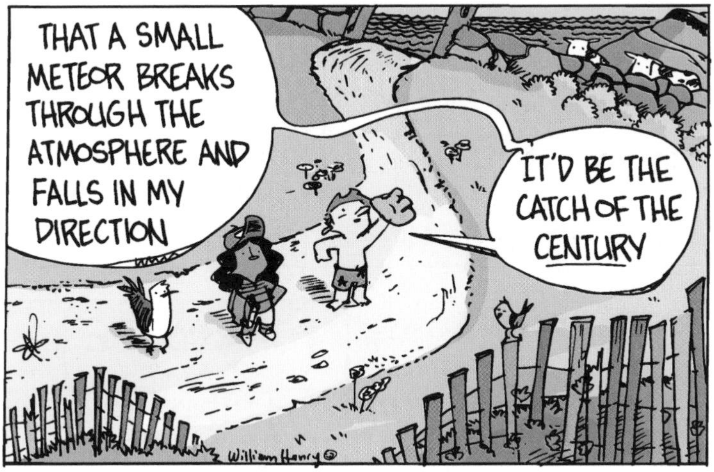
THAT A SMALL METEOR BREAKS THROUGH THE ATMOSPHERE AND FALLS IN MY DIRECTION
IT'D BE THE CATCH OF THE CENTURY
William Henry

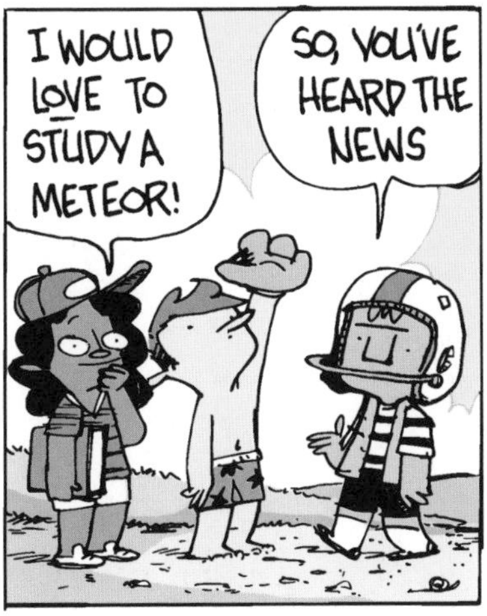
I WOULD LOVE TO STUDY A METEOR!
SO, YOU'VE HEARD THE NEWS

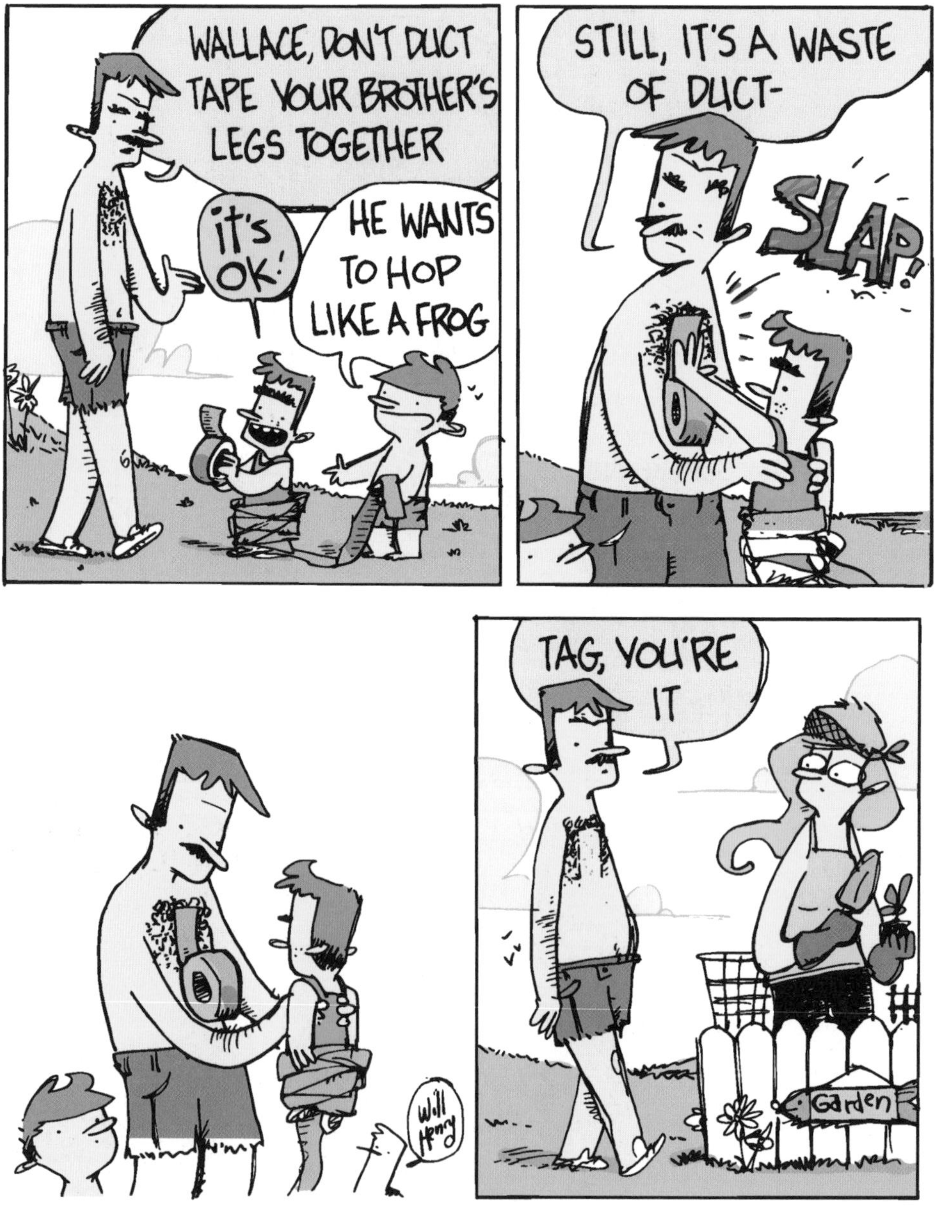
WALLACE, DON'T DUCT TAPE YOUR BROTHER'S LEGS TOGETHER
it's OK!
HE WANTS TO HOP LIKE A FROG
STILL, IT'S A WASTE OF DUCT-
SLAP!
Will Henry
TAG, YOU'RE IT
Garden

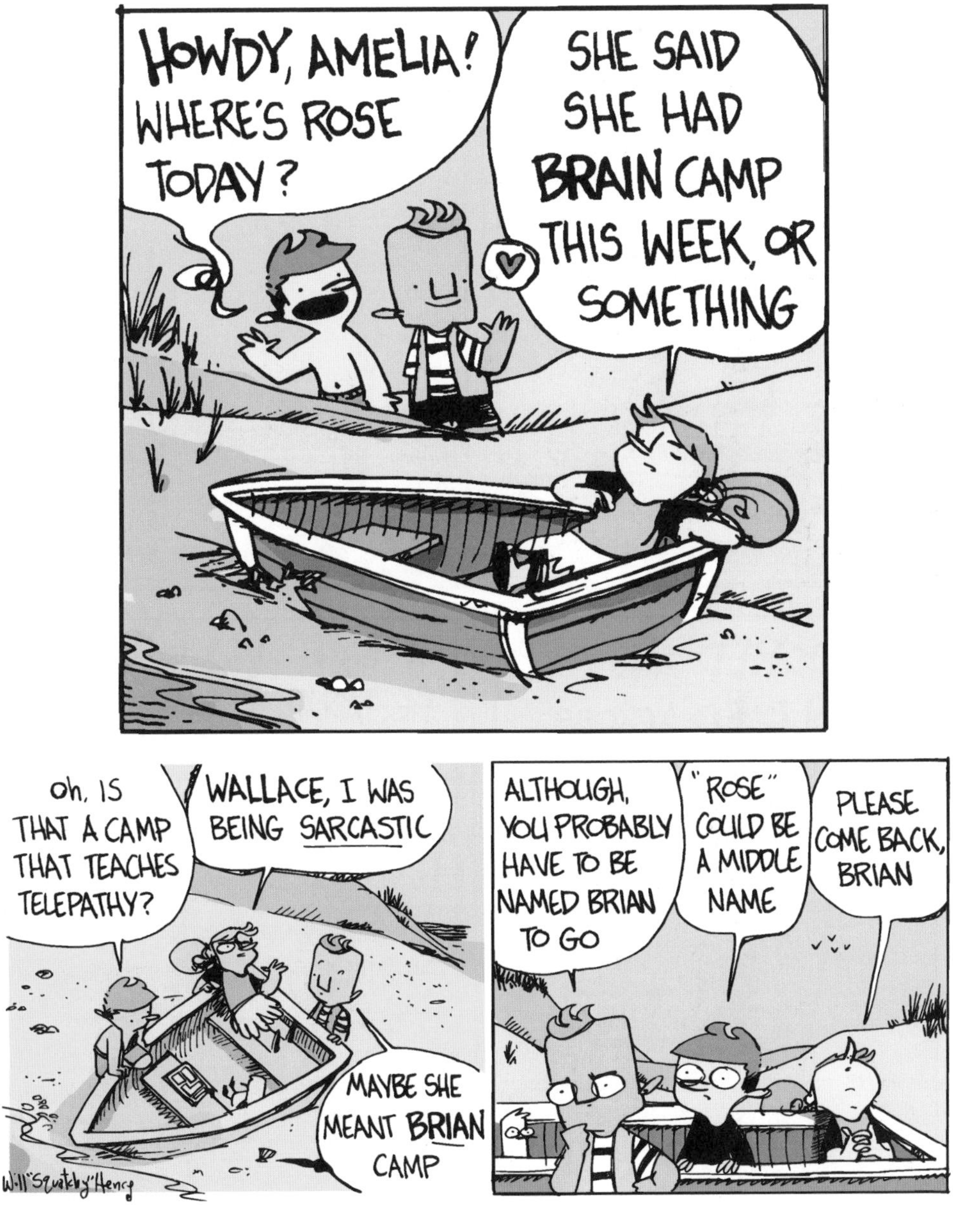
HOWDY, AMELIA! WHERE'S ROSE TODAY?
SHE SAID SHE HAD BRAIN CAMP THIS WEEK, OR SOMETHING
Oh, IS THAT A CAMP THAT TEACHES TELEPATHY?
WALLACE, I WAS BEING SARCASTIC
MAYBE SHE MEANT BRIAN CAMP
Will "Squatchy" Henry
ALTHOUGH, YOU PROBABLY HAVE TO BE NAMED BRIAN TO GO
"ROSE" COULD BE A MIDDLE NAME
PLEASE COME BACK, BRIAN

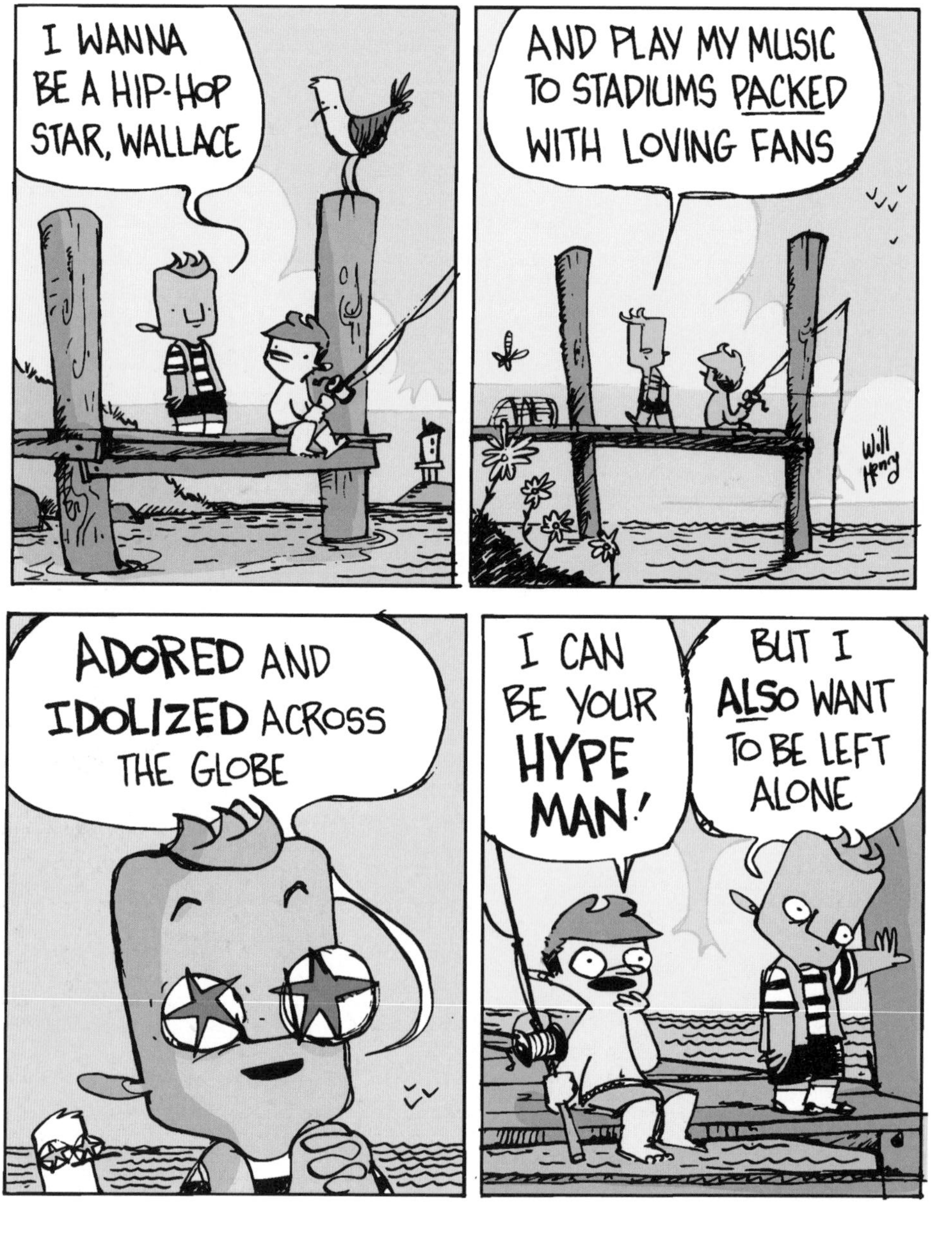
I WANNA BE A HIP-HOP STAR, WALLACE
AND PLAY MY MUSIC TO STADIUMS PACKED WITH LOVING FANS
Will Henry
ADORED AND IDOLIZED ACROSS THE GLOBE
I CAN BE YOUR HYPE MAN!
BUT I ALSO WANT TO BE LEFT ALONE

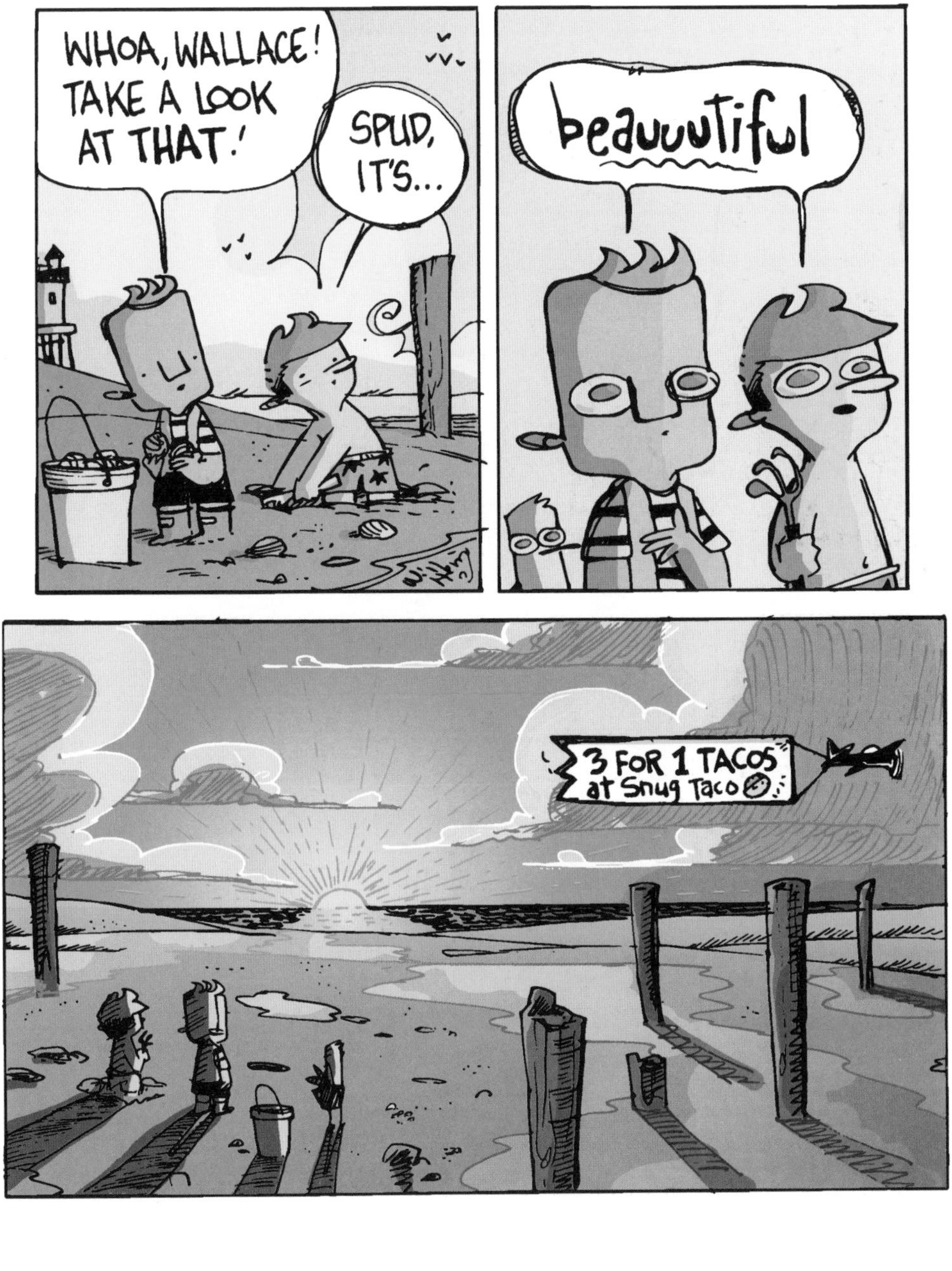
WHOA, WALLACE! TAKE A LOOK AT THAT!
SPUD, IT'S...
beauuutiful
3 FOR 1 TACOS at Snug Taco

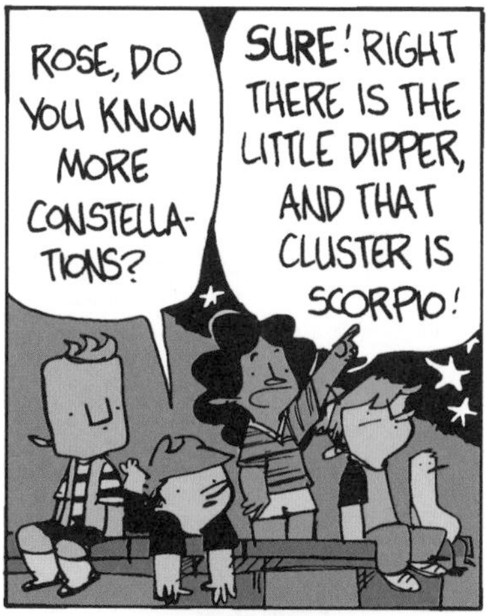
ROSE, DO YOU KNOW MORE CONSTELLA-TIONS?
SURE! RIGHT THERE IS THE LITTLE DIPPER, AND THAT CLUSTER IS SCORPIO!

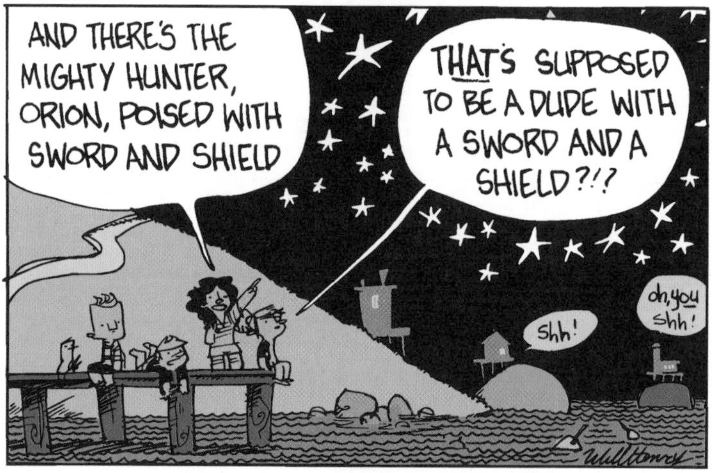
AND THERE'S THE MIGHTY HUNTER, ORION, POISED WITH SWORD AND SHIELD
THAT'S SUPPOSED TO BE A DUDE WITH A SWORD AND A SHIELD?!?
Shh!
oh, you shh!

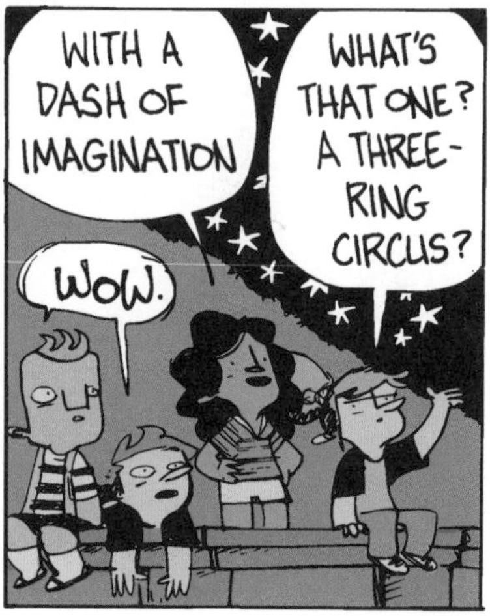
WITH A DASH OF IMAGINATION
WHAT'S THAT ONE? A THREE-RING CIRCUS?
WOW.

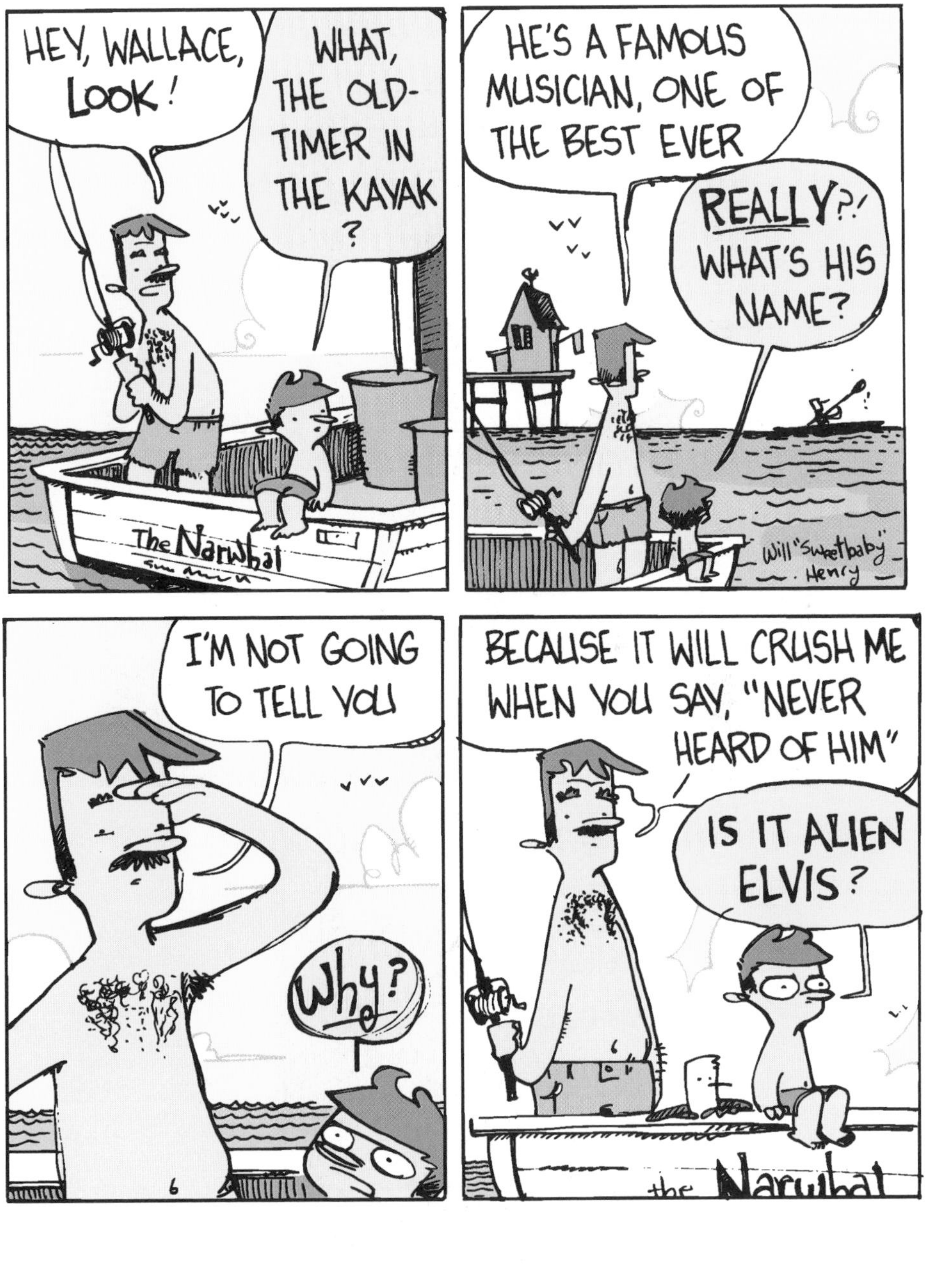
HEY, WALLACE, LOOK!
WHAT, THE OLD-TIMER IN THE KAYAK ?
The Narwhal
HE'S A FAMOUS MUSICIAN, ONE OF THE BEST EVER
REALLY?! WHAT'S HIS NAME?
Will "Sweetbaby" Henry
I'M NOT GOING TO TELL YOU
Why?
BECAUSE IT WILL CRUSH ME WHEN YOU SAY, "NEVER HEARD OF HIM"
IS IT ALIEN ELVIS ?
the Narwhal

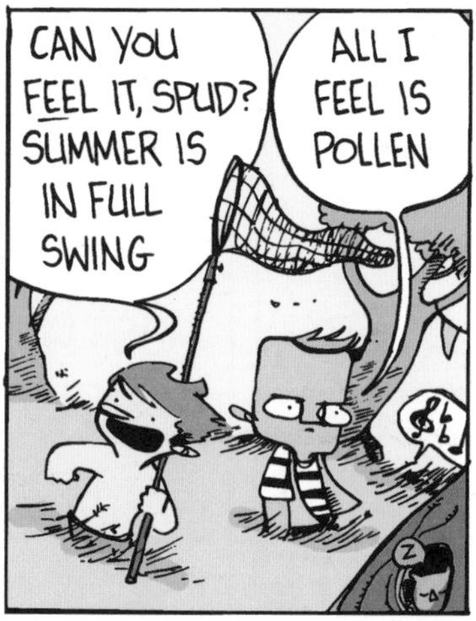
CAN YOU FEEL IT, SPUD? SUMMER IS IN FULL SWING
ALL I FEEL IS POLLEN

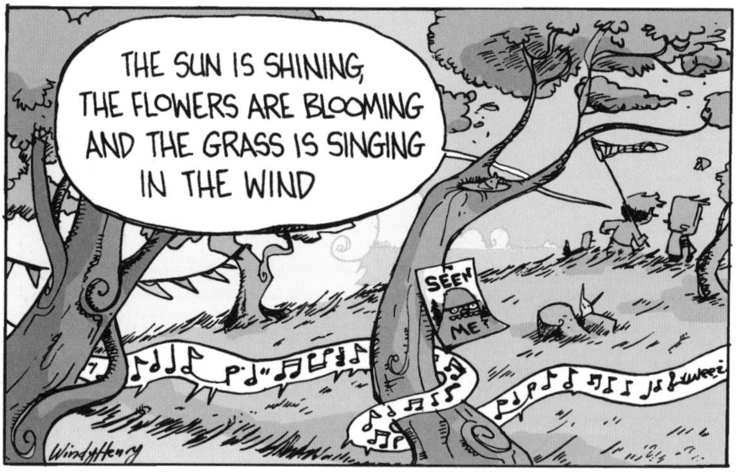
THE SUN IS SHINING, THE FLOWERS ARE BLOOMING AND THE GRASS IS SINGING IN THE WIND
SEEN ME?

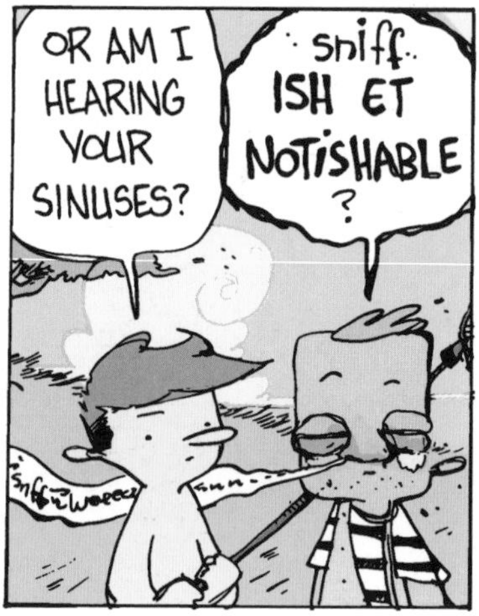
OR AM I HEARING YOUR SINUSES?
sniff
ISH ET NOTISHABLE?

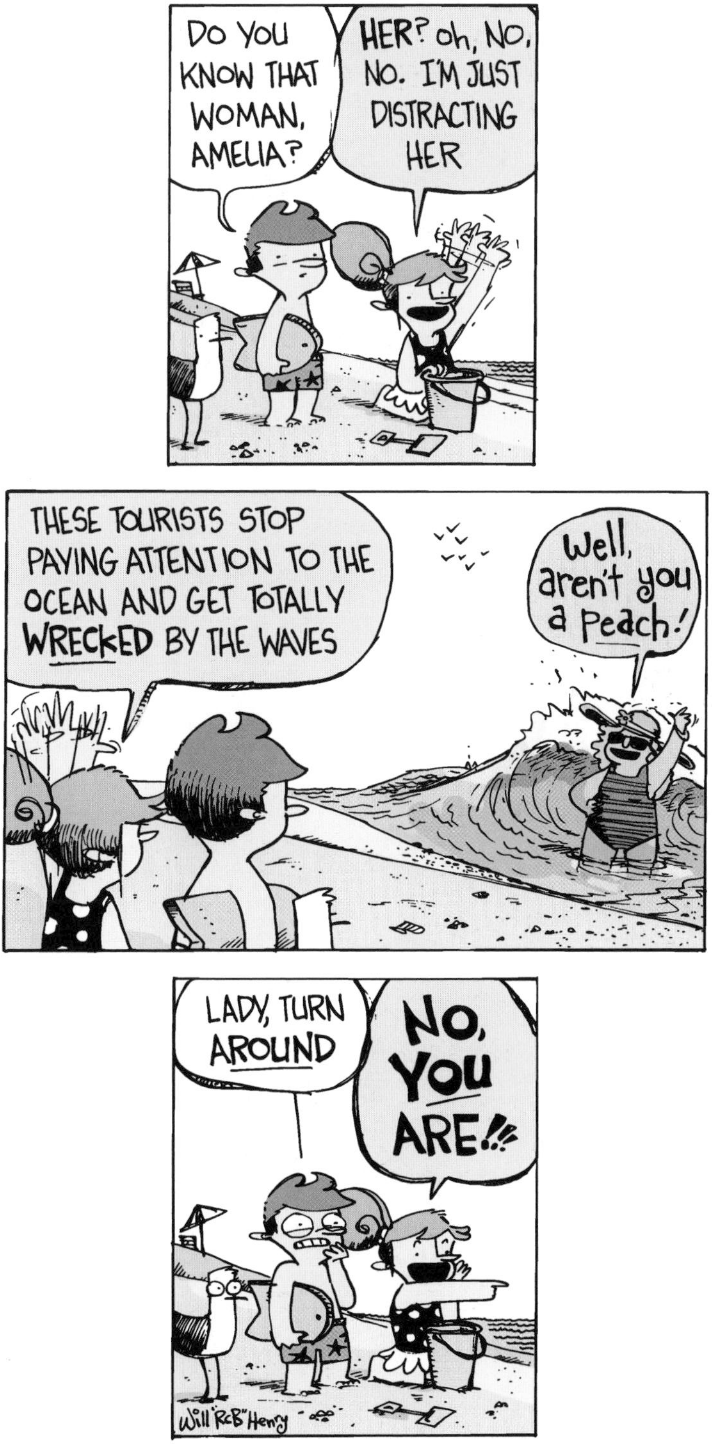
DO YOU KNOW THAT WOMAN, AMELIA?
HER? oh, NO, NO. I'M JUST DISTRACTING HER
THESE TOURISTS STOP PAYING ATTENTION TO THE OCEAN AND GET TOTALLY WRECKED BY THE WAVES
Well, aren't you a Peach!
LADY, TURN AROUND
NO, YOU ARE!!
Will "RCB" Henry

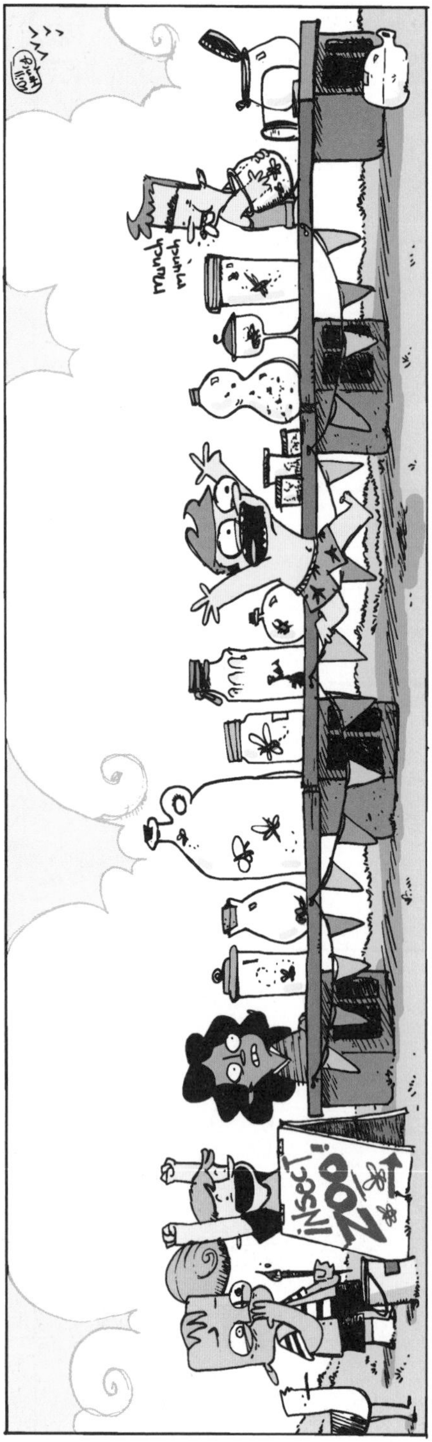
munch munch
INSECT ZOO!

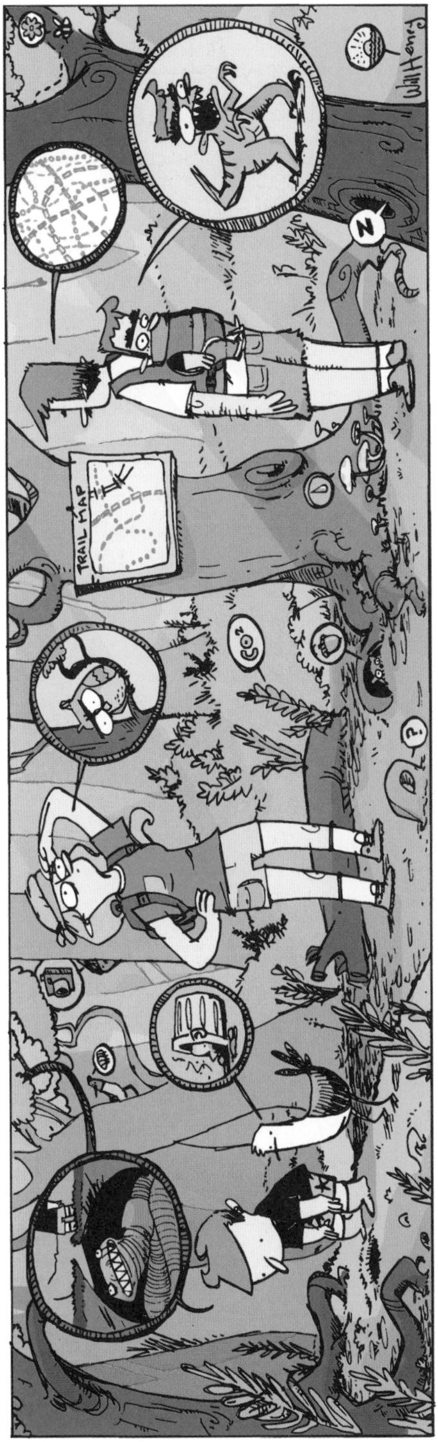
TRAIL MAP
Will Henry

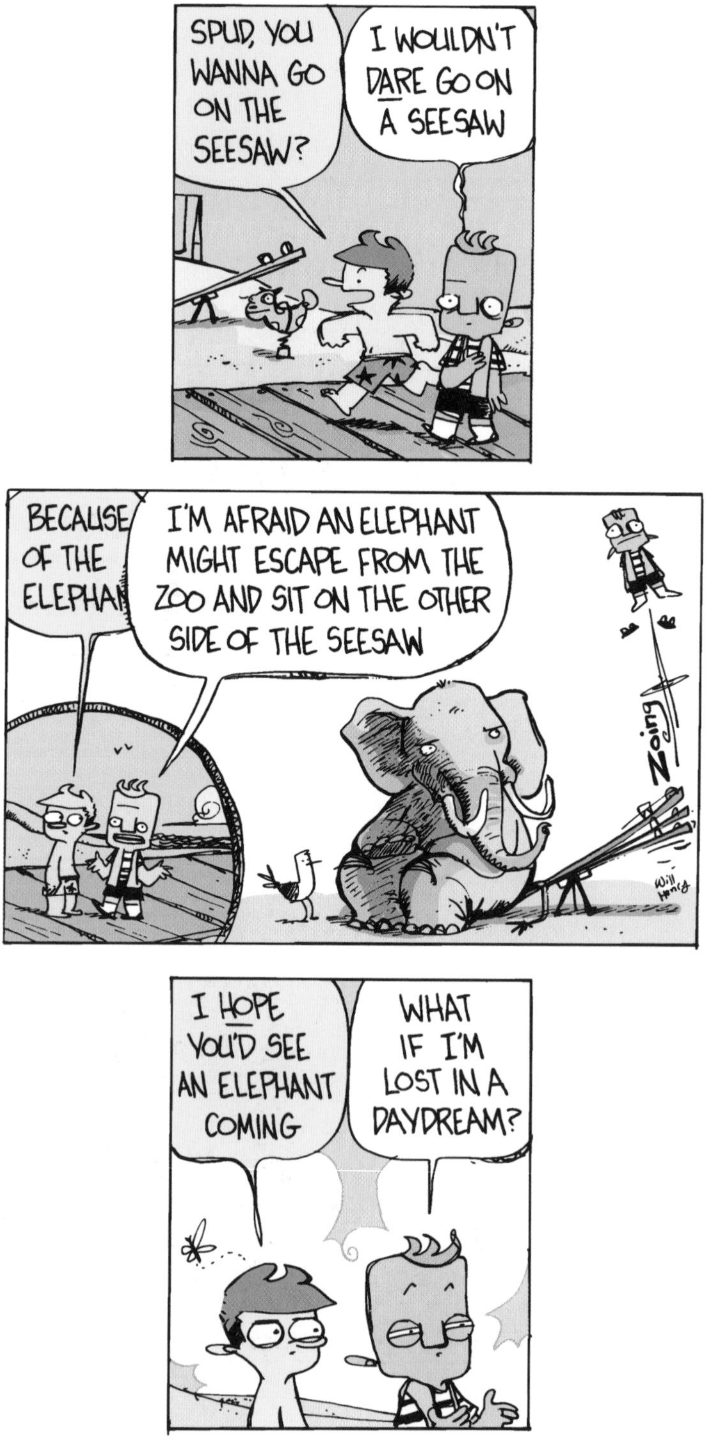
SPUD, YOU WANNA GO ON THE SEESAW?
I WOULDN'T DARE GO ON A SEESAW
BECAUSE OF THE ELEPHANT
I'M AFRAID AN ELEPHANT MIGHT ESCAPE FROM THE ZOO AND SIT ON THE OTHER SIDE OF THE SEESAW
Zoing
I HOPE YOU'D SEE AN ELEPHANT COMING
WHAT IF I'M LOST IN A DAYDREAM?

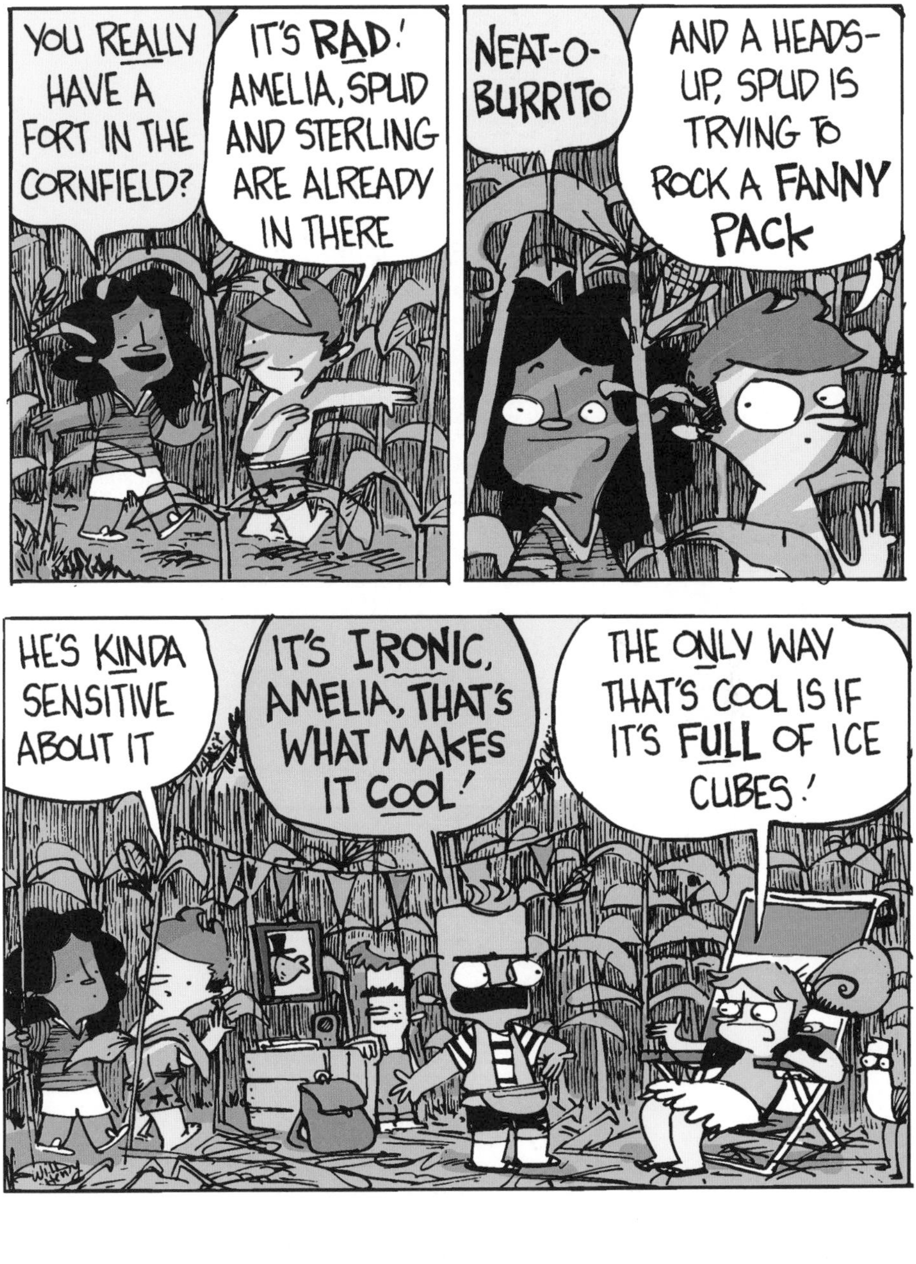
YOU REALLY HAVE A FORT IN THE CORNFIELD?
IT'S RAD! AMELIA, SPUD AND STERLING ARE ALREADY IN THERE
NEAT-O-BURRITO
AND A HEADS-UP, SPUD IS TRYING TO ROCK A FANNY PACK
HE'S KINDA SENSITIVE ABOUT IT
IT'S IRONIC, AMELIA, THAT'S WHAT MAKES IT COOL!
THE ONLY WAY THAT'S COOL IS IF IT'S FULL OF ICE CUBES!

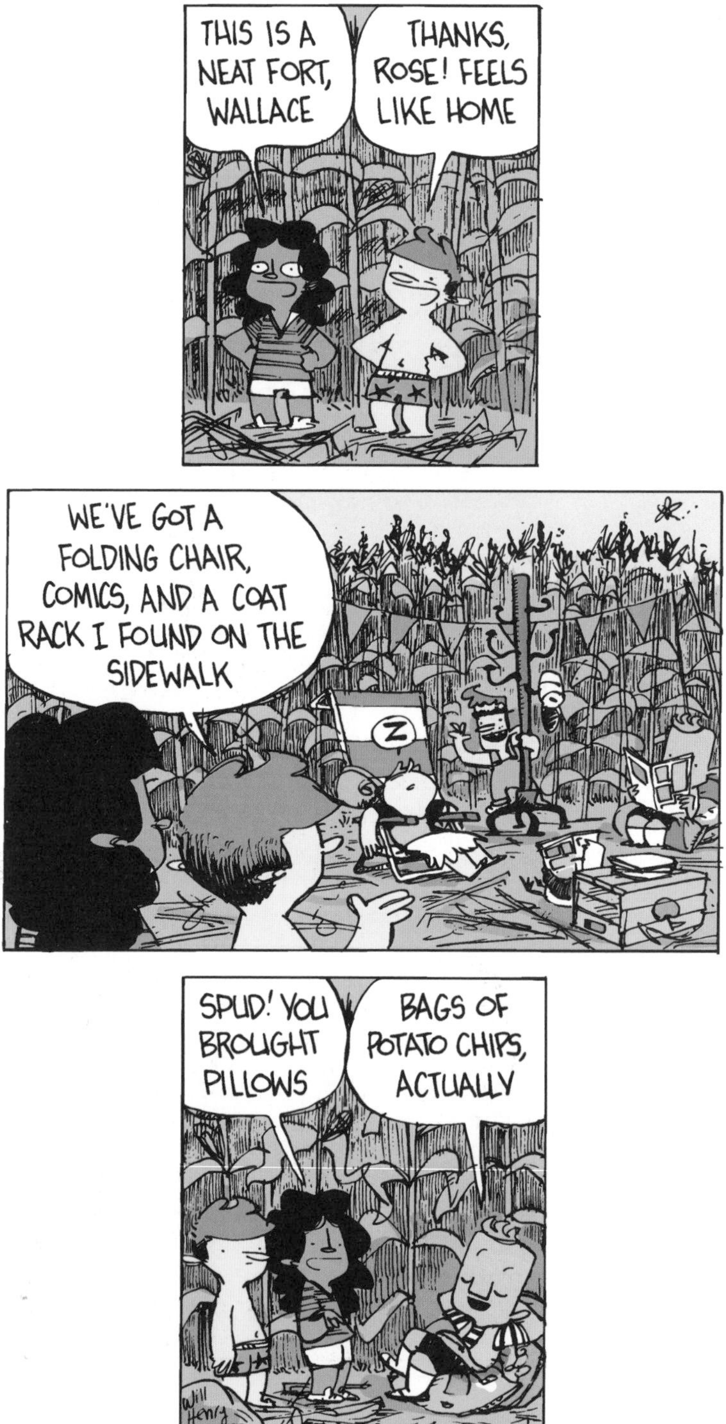

THIS IS A NEAT FORT, WALLACE
THANKS, ROSE! FEELS LIKE HOME
WE'VE GOT A FOLDING CHAIR, COMICS, AND A COAT RACK I FOUND ON THE SIDEWALK
Z
SPUD! YOU BROUGHT PILLOWS
BAGS OF POTATO CHIPS, ACTUALLY
Will Henry

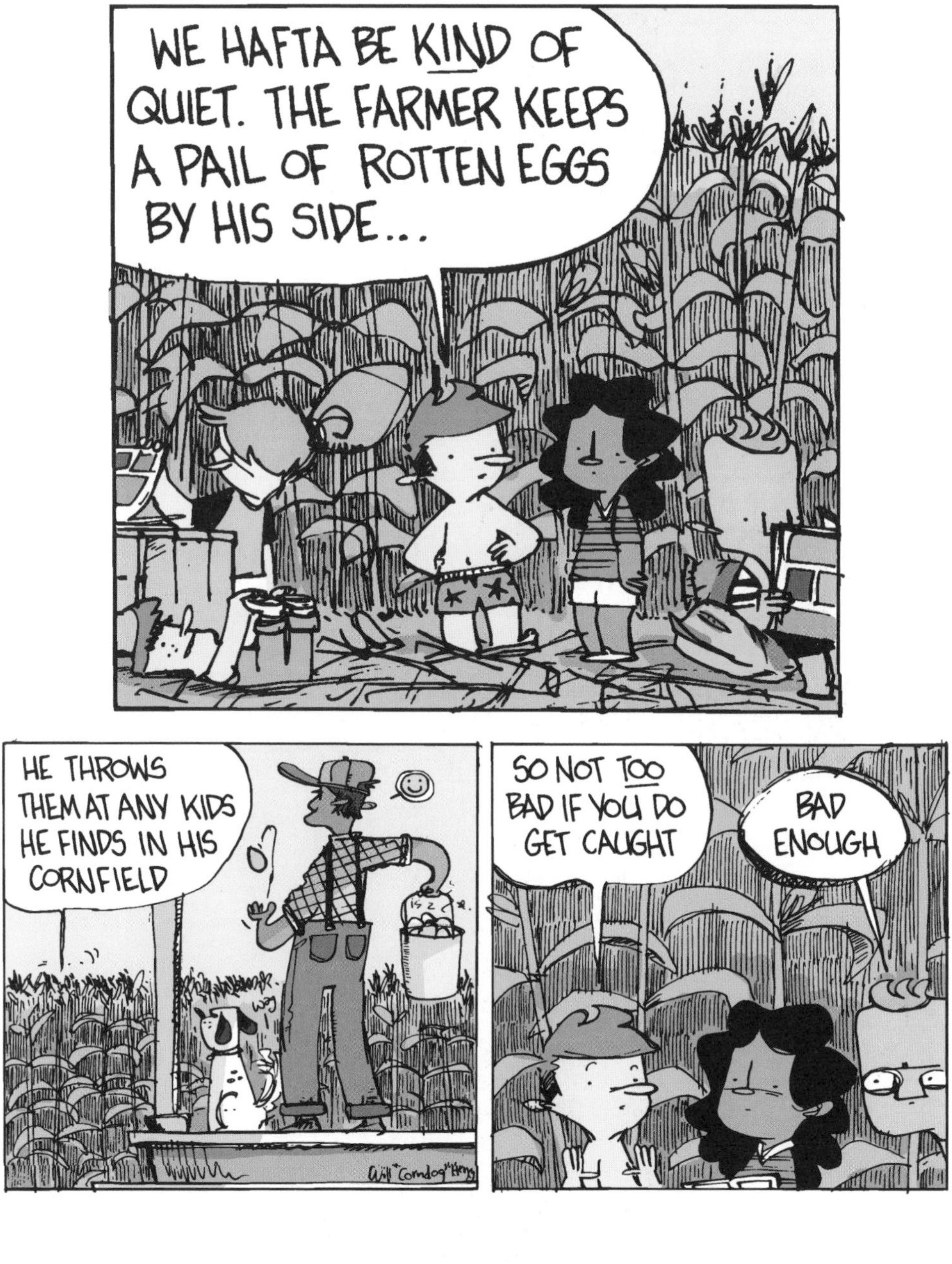
WE HAFTA BE KIND OF QUIET. THE FARMER KEEPS A PAIL OF ROTTEN EGGS BY HIS SIDE...
HE THROWS THEM AT ANY KIDS HE FINDS IN HIS CORNFIELD
wag
SO NOT TOO BAD IF YOU DO GET CAUGHT
BAD ENOUGH

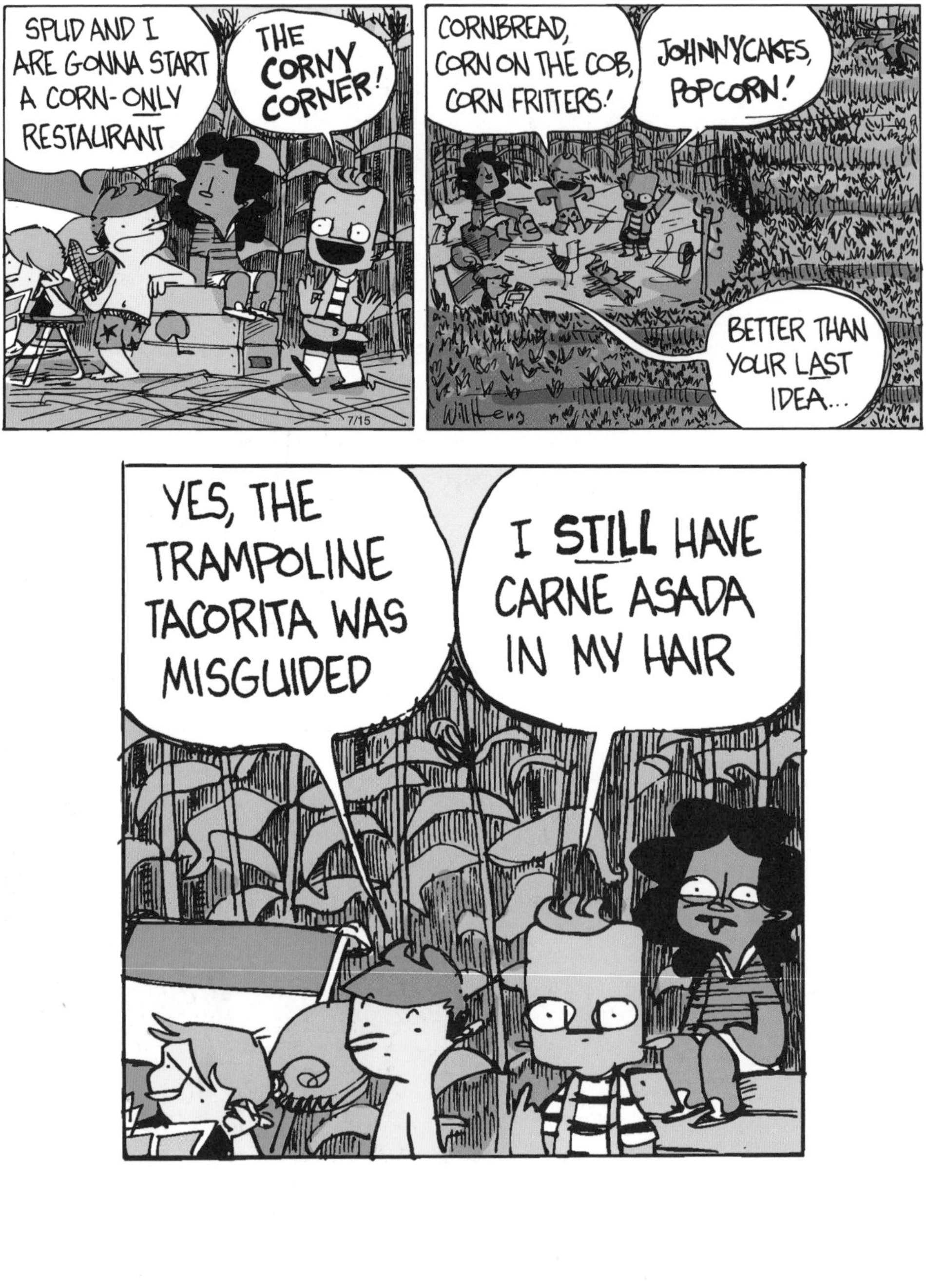
SPUD AND I ARE GONNA START A CORN-ONLY RESTAURANT
THE CORNY CORNER!
7/15
CORNBREAD, CORN ON THE COB, CORN FRITTERS!
JOHNNYCAKES, POPCORN!
BETTER THAN YOUR LAST IDEA...
YES, THE TRAMPOLINE TACORITA WAS MISGUIDED
I STILL HAVE CARNE ASADA IN MY HAIR

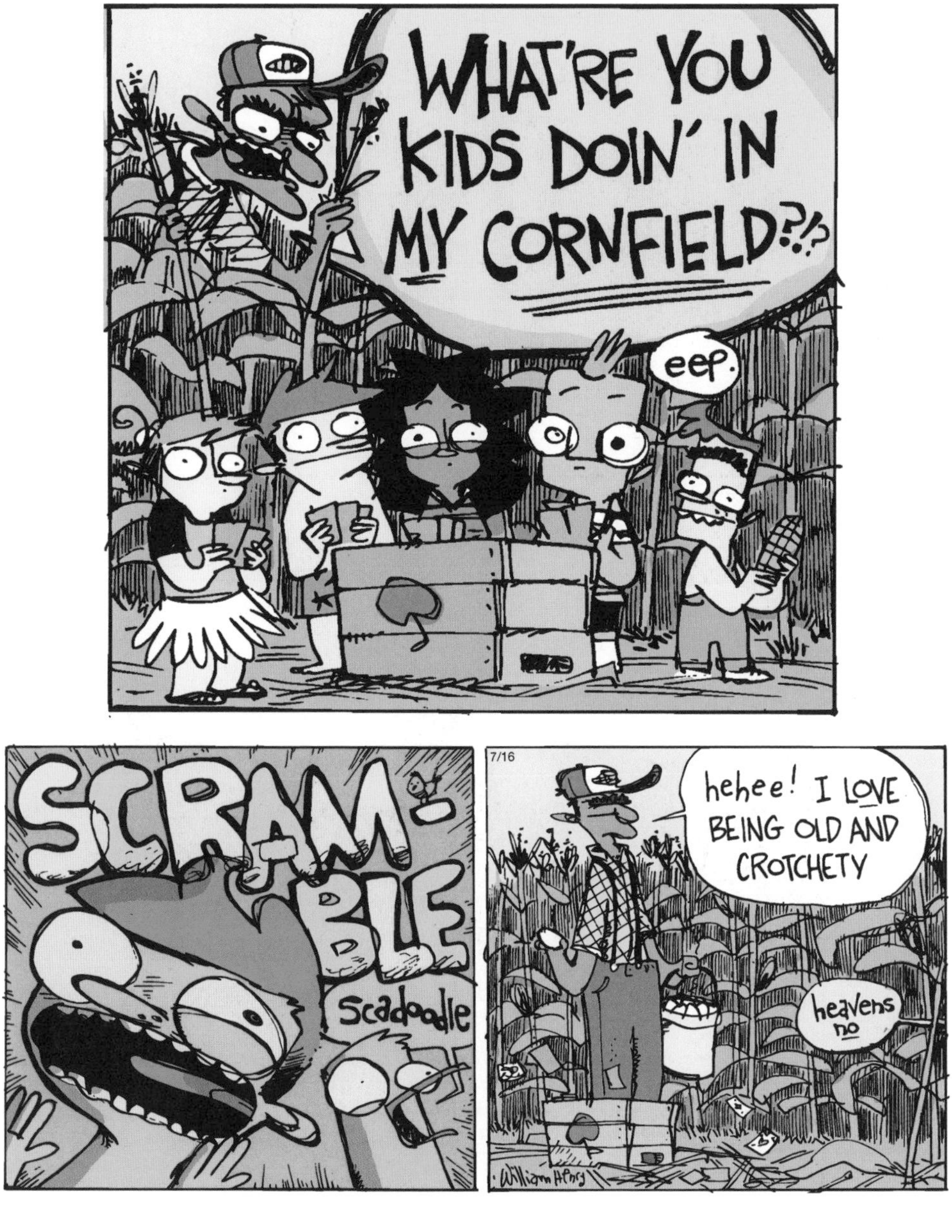
WHAT'RE YOU KIDS DOIN' IN MY CORNFIELD?!?
eep.
SCRAM-BLE
scadoodle
7/16
hehee! I LOVE BEING OLD AND CROTCHETY
heavens no
William Henry

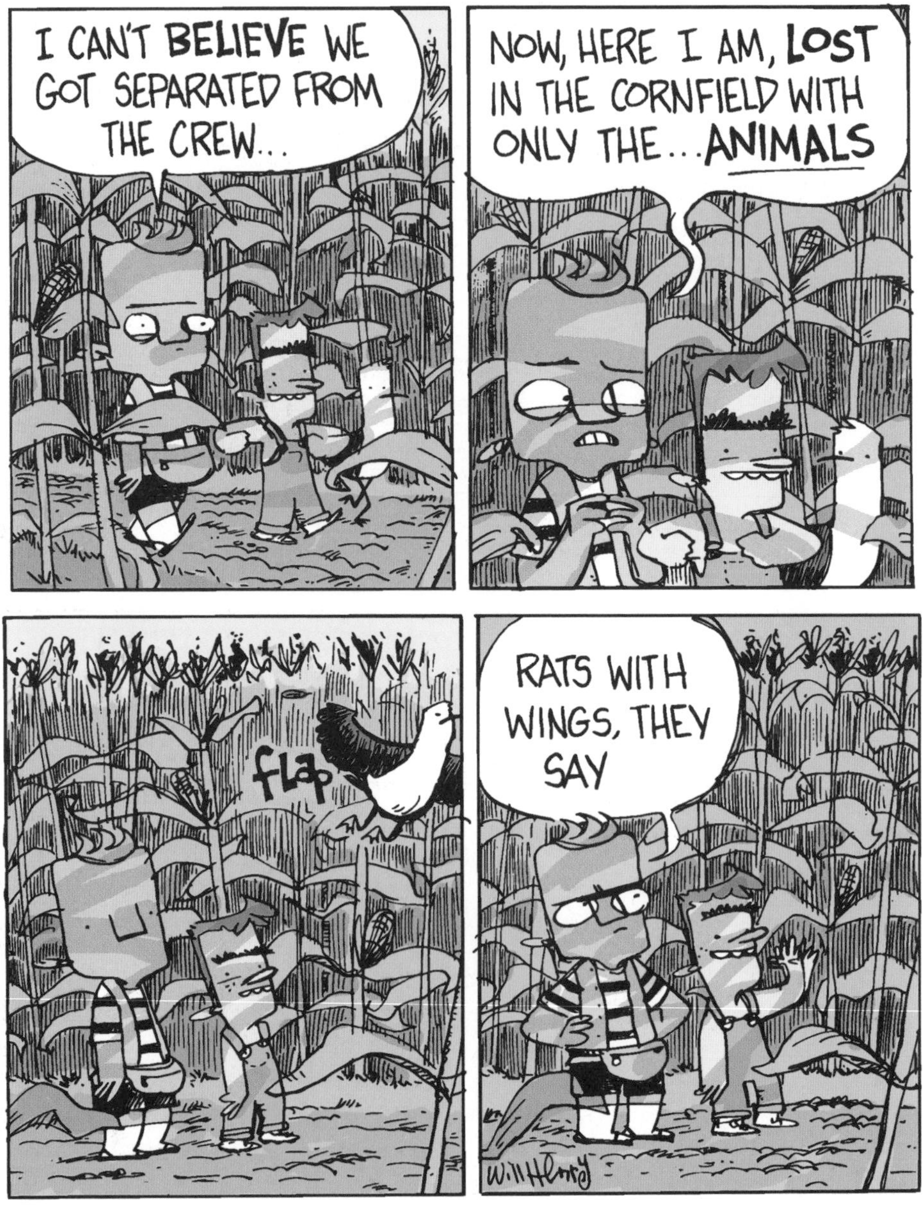
I CAN'T BELIEVE WE GOT SEPARATED FROM THE CREW...
NOW, HERE I AM, LOST IN THE CORNFIELD WITH ONLY THE... ANIMALS
FLAP
RATS WITH WINGS, THEY SAY
Will Henry

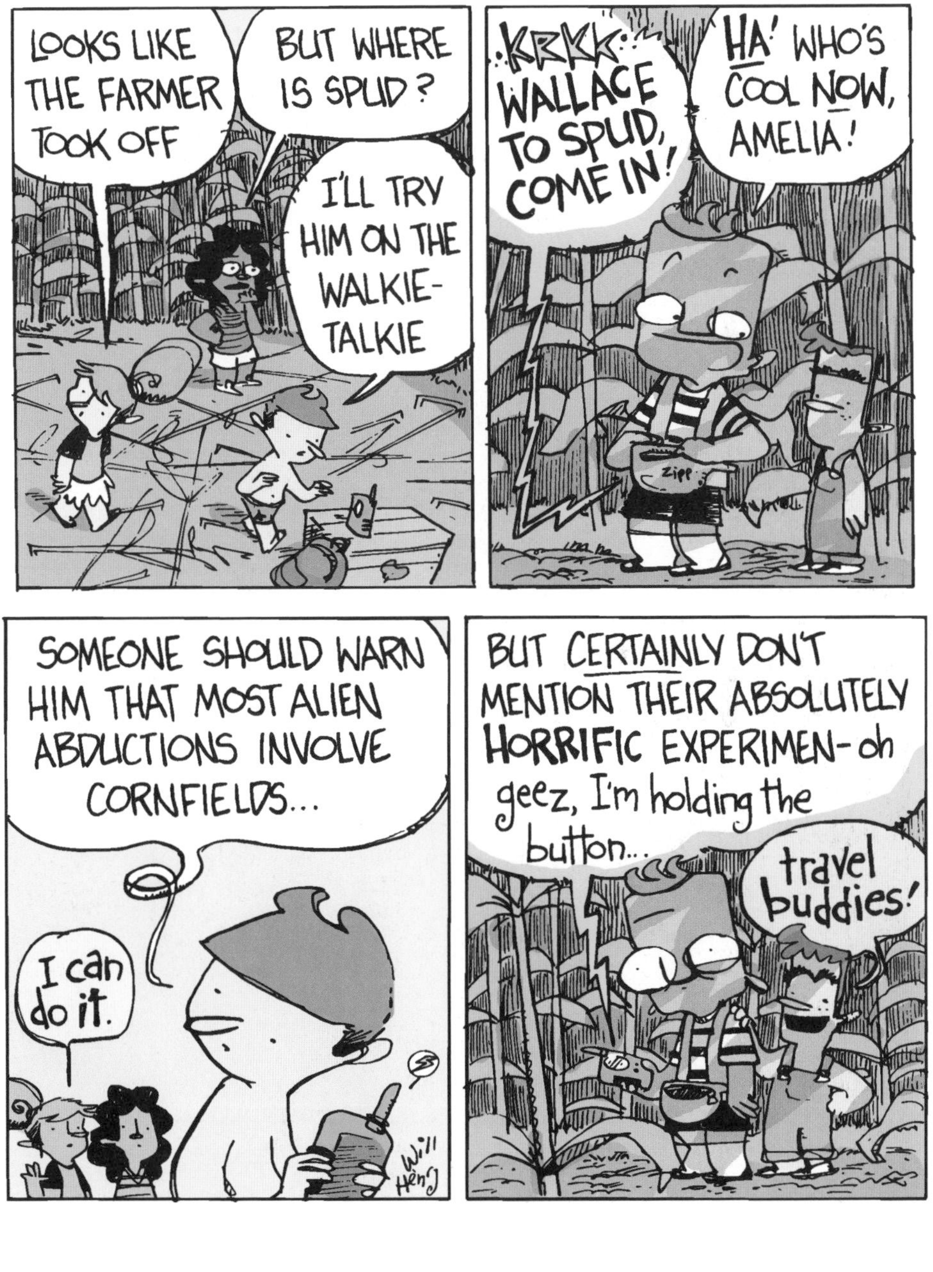
LOOKS LIKE THE FARMER TOOK OFF
BUT WHERE IS SPUD?
I'LL TRY HIM ON THE WALKIE-TALKIE
KRKK WALLACE TO SPUD, COME IN!
HA! WHO'S COOL NOW, AMELIA!
ZIPP
SOMEONE SHOULD WARN HIM THAT MOST ALIEN ABDUCTIONS INVOLVE CORNFIELDS...
I can do it.
Will Henry
BUT CERTAINLY DON'T MENTION THEIR ABSOLUTELY HORRIFIC EXPERIMEN- oh geez, I'm holding the button...
travel buddies!

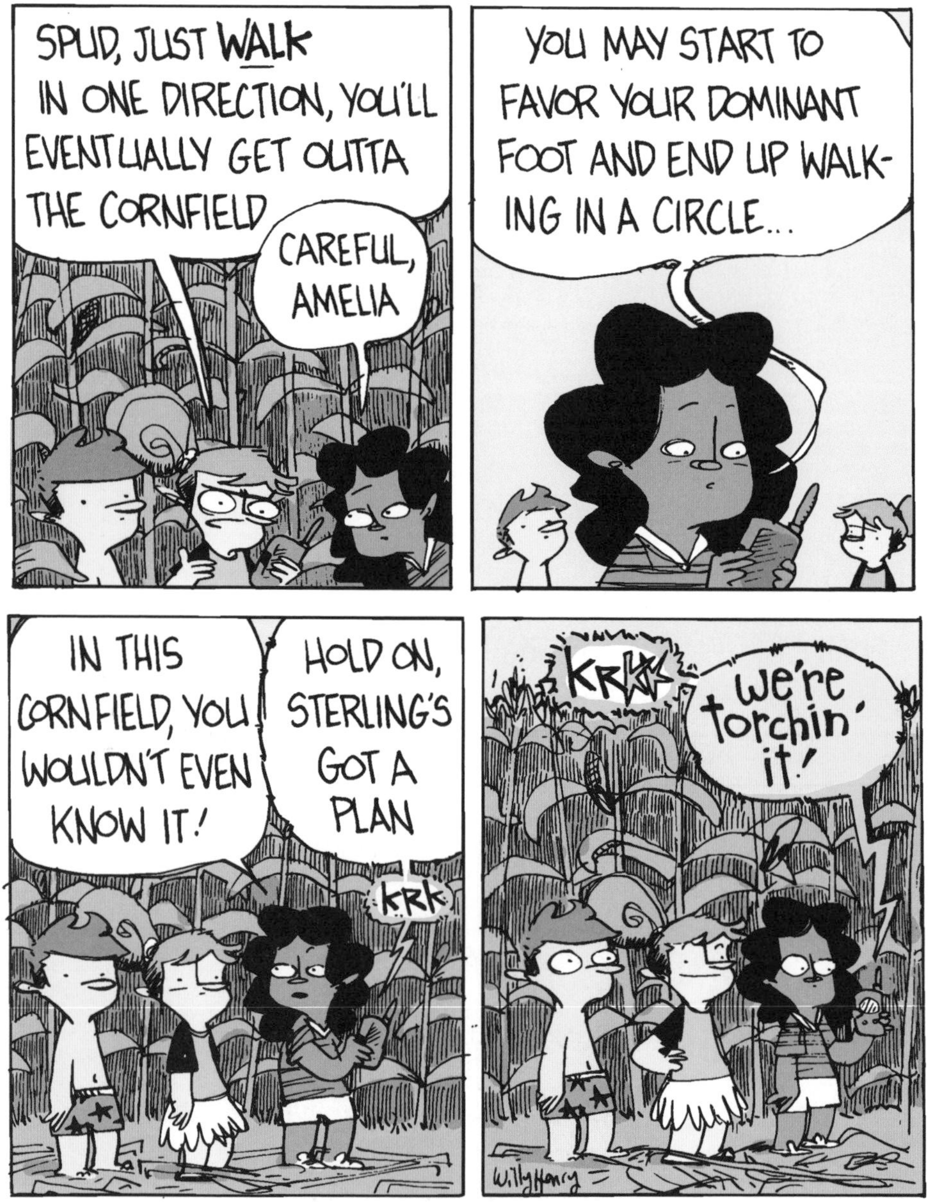
SPUD, JUST WALK IN ONE DIRECTION, YOU'LL EVENTUALLY GET OUTTA THE CORNFIELD
CAREFUL, AMELIA
YOU MAY START TO FAVOR YOUR DOMINANT FOOT AND END UP WALKING IN A CIRCLE...
IN THIS CORNFIELD, YOU WOULDN'T EVEN KNOW IT!
HOLD ON, STERLING'S GOT A PLAN
KRK
KRK
We're torchin' it!
WillyHenry

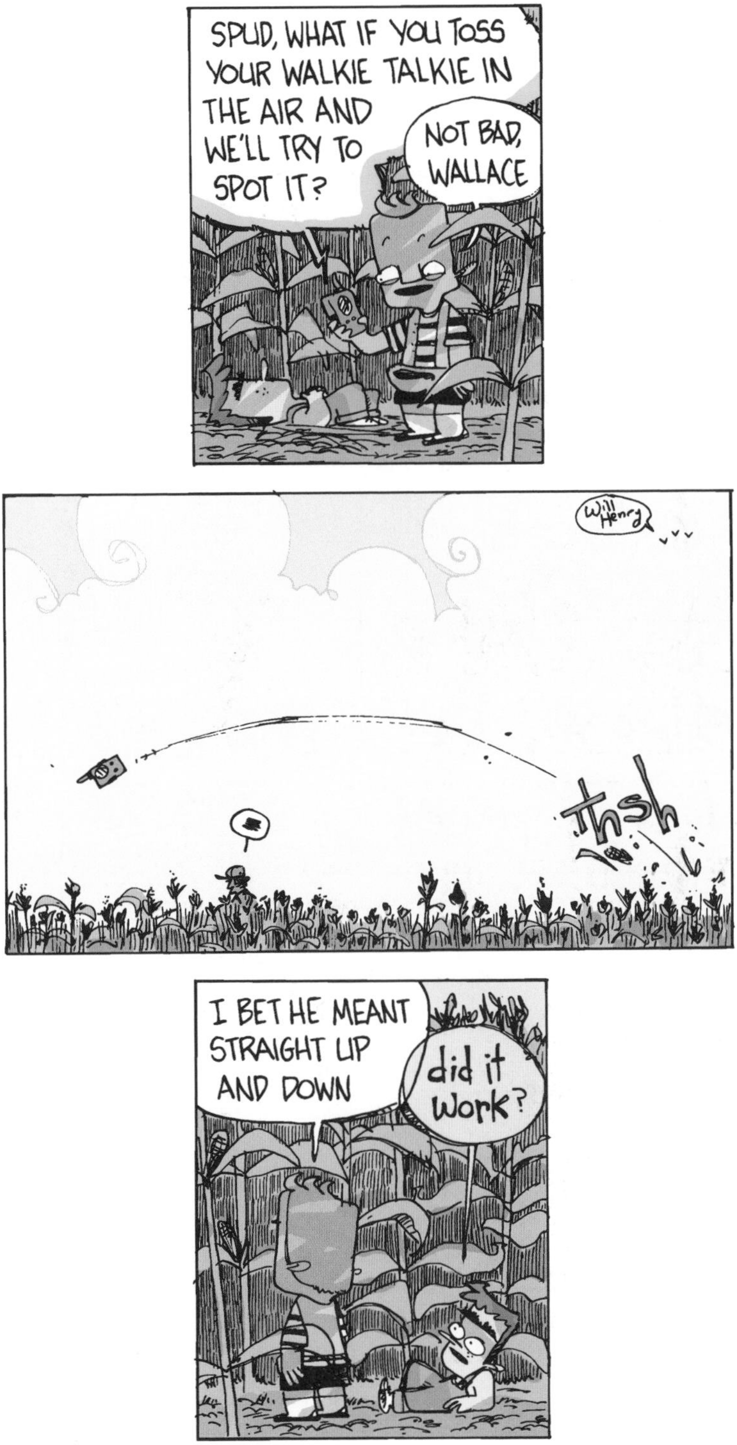
SPUD, WHAT IF YOU TOSS YOUR WALKIE TALKIE IN THE AIR AND WE'LL TRY TO SPOT IT?
NOT BAD, WALLACE
Will Henry
thsh
I BET HE MEANT STRAIGHT UP AND DOWN
did it work?

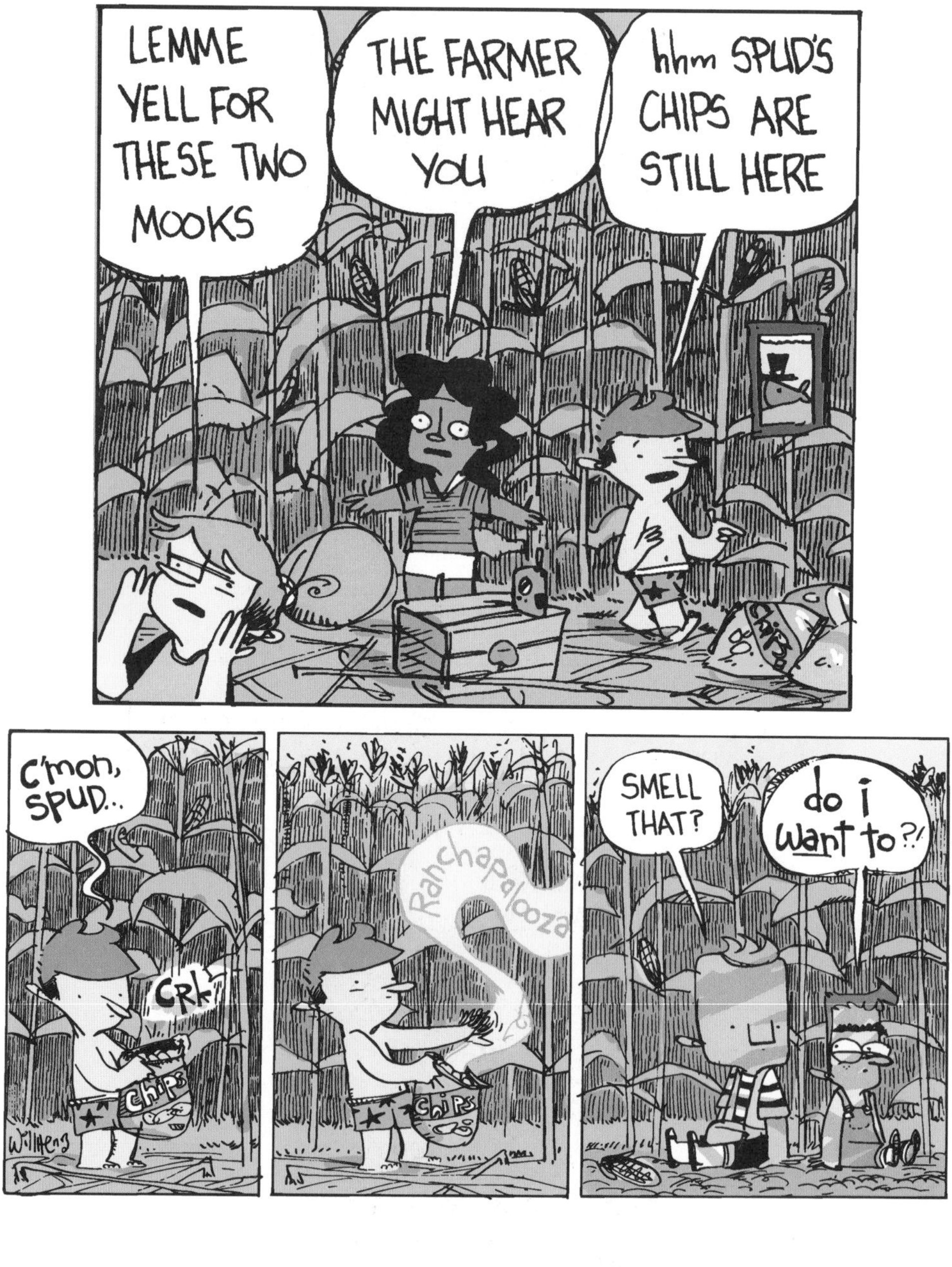
LEMME YELL FOR THESE TWO MOOKS
THE FARMER MIGHT HEAR YOU
hhm SPUD'S CHIPS ARE STILL HERE
CHIPS
C'mon, SPUD...
CRK
CHIPS
Ranchapalooza
CHIPS
SMELL THAT?
do i want to?!

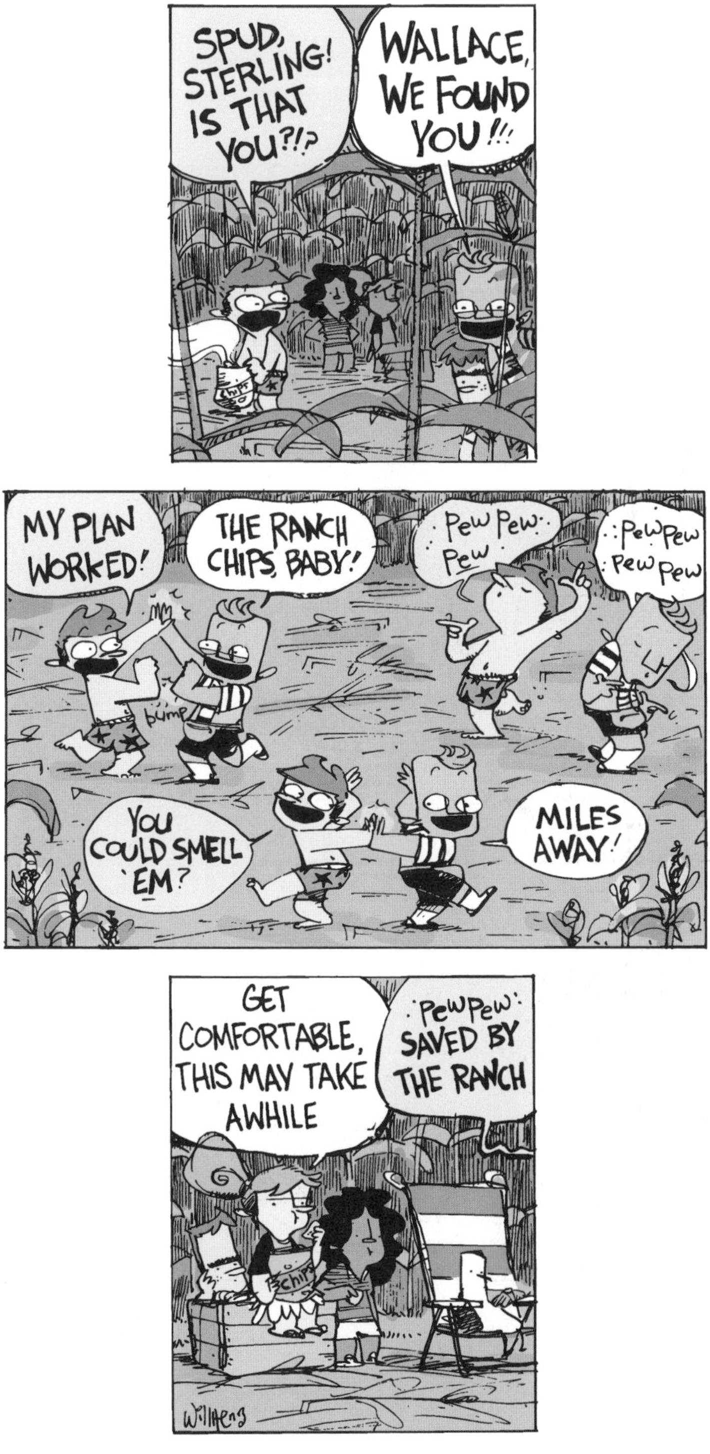
SPUD, STERLING! IS THAT YOU?!?
WALLACE, WE FOUND YOU!!!
MY PLAN WORKED!
THE RANCH CHIPS, BABY!
Pew Pew Pew
Pew Pew Pew Pew
bump
YOU COULD SMELL 'EM?
MILES AWAY!
GET COMFORTABLE, THIS MAY TAKE AWHILE
Pew Pew SAVED BY THE RANCH

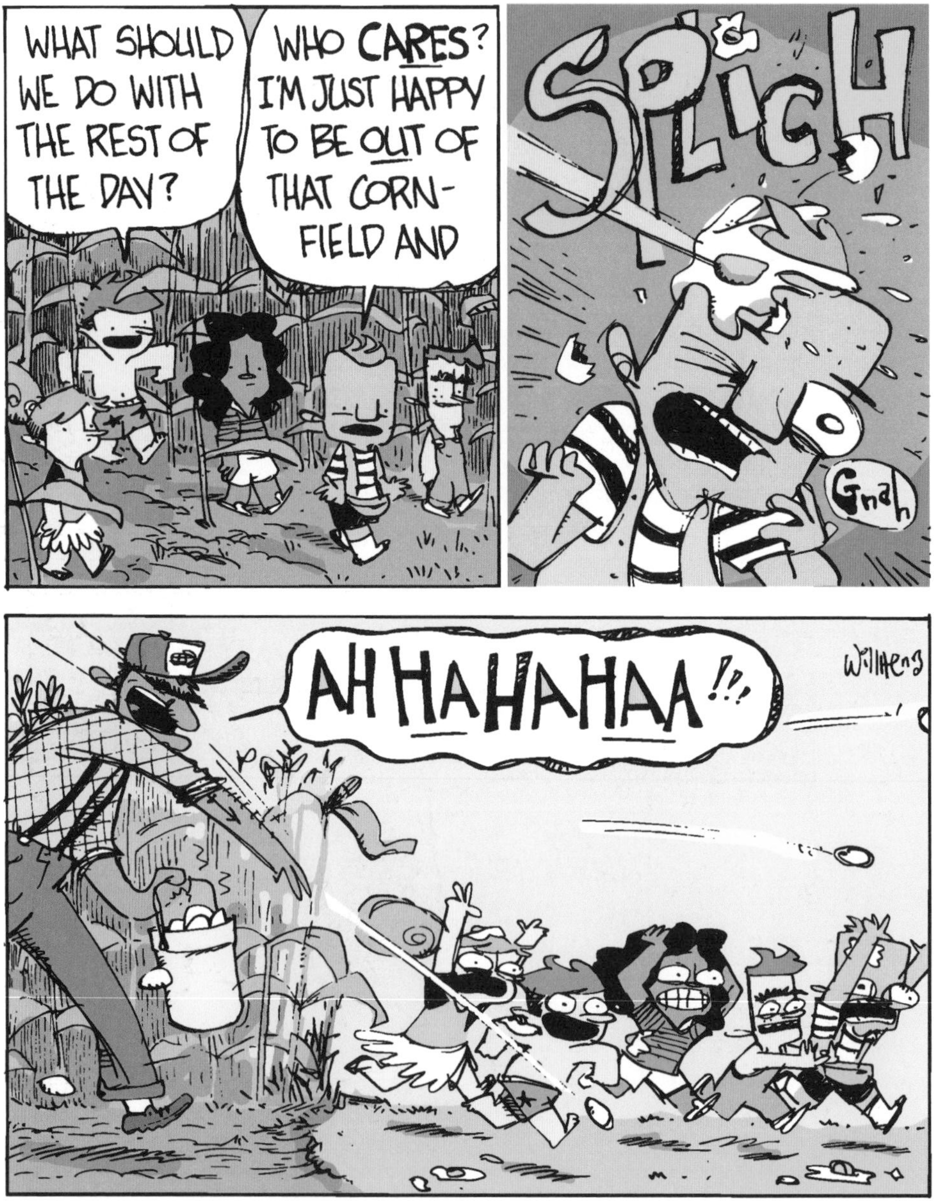
WHAT SHOULD WE DO WITH THE REST OF THE DAY?
WHO CARES? I'M JUST HAPPY TO BE OUT OF THAT CORN-FIELD AND
SPLICH
Gnah
AH HAHAHAA!!!

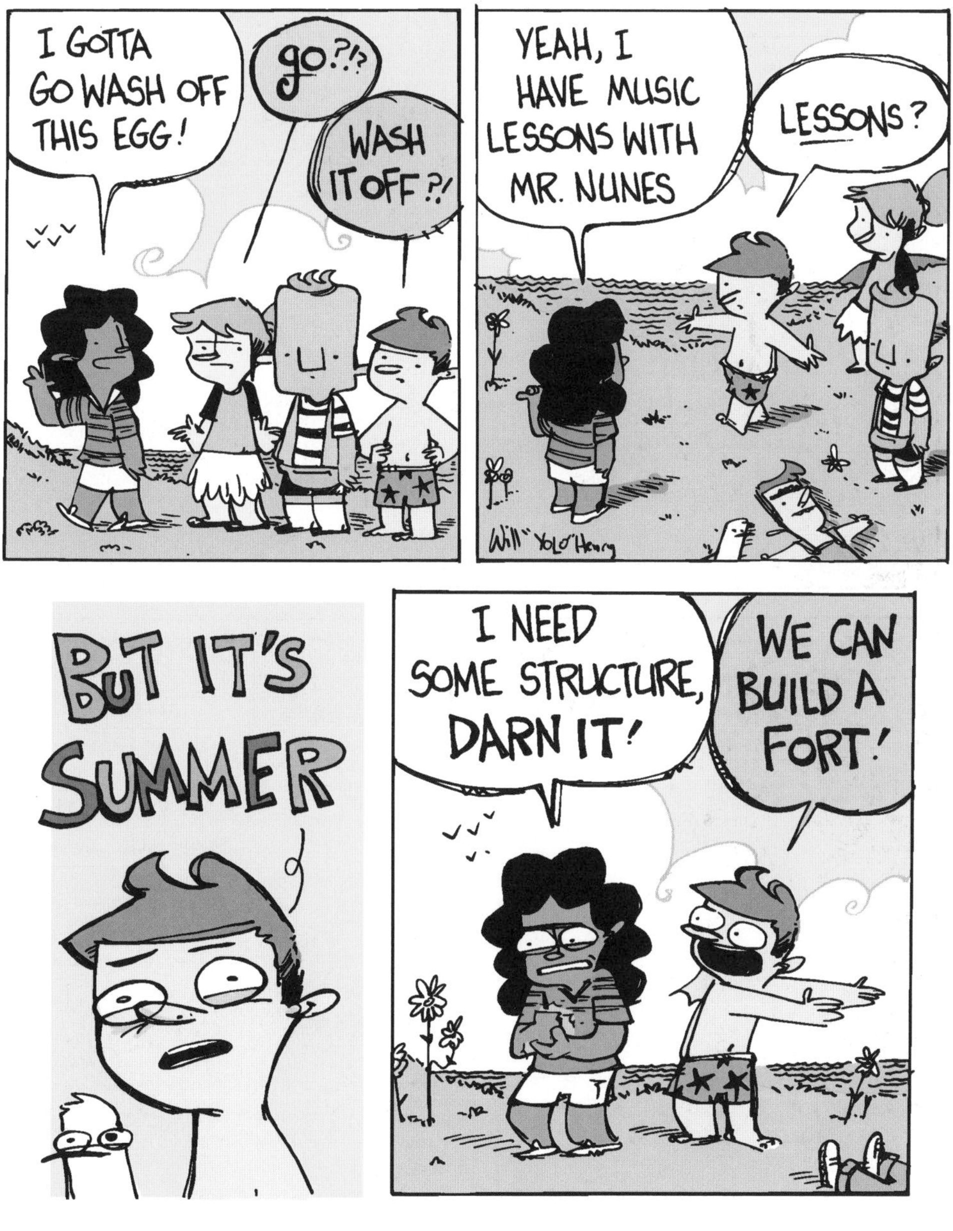
I GOTTA GO WASH OFF THIS EGG!
go?!?
WASH IT OFF?!
YEAH, I HAVE MUSIC LESSONS WITH MR. NUNES
LESSONS?
BUT IT'S SUMMER
I NEED SOME STRUCTURE, DARN IT!
WE CAN BUILD A FORT!

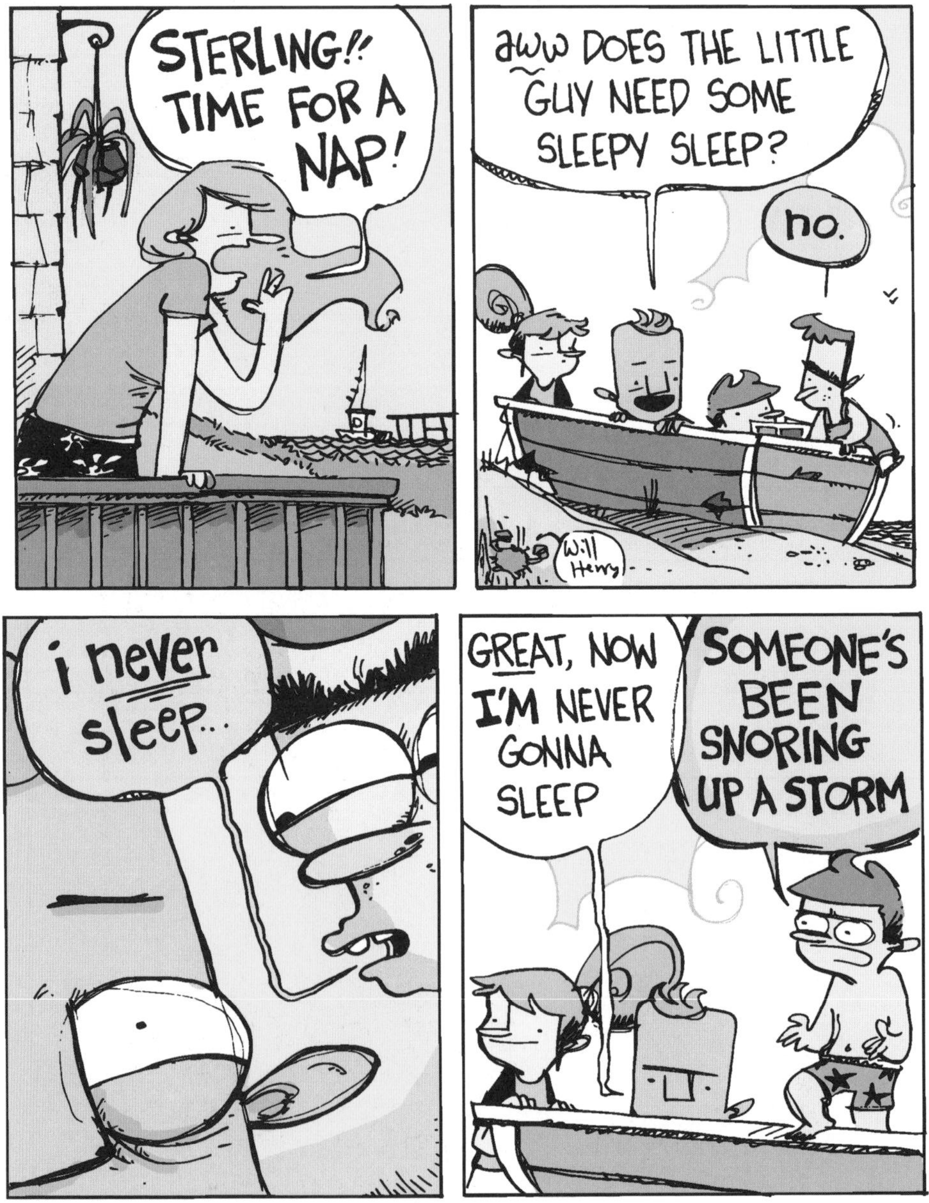

STERLING!! TIME FOR A NAP!
aww DOES THE LITTLE GUY NEED SOME SLEEPY SLEEP?
no.
Will Henry
i never sleep...
GREAT, NOW I'M NEVER GONNA SLEEP
SOMEONE'S BEEN SNORING UP A STORM

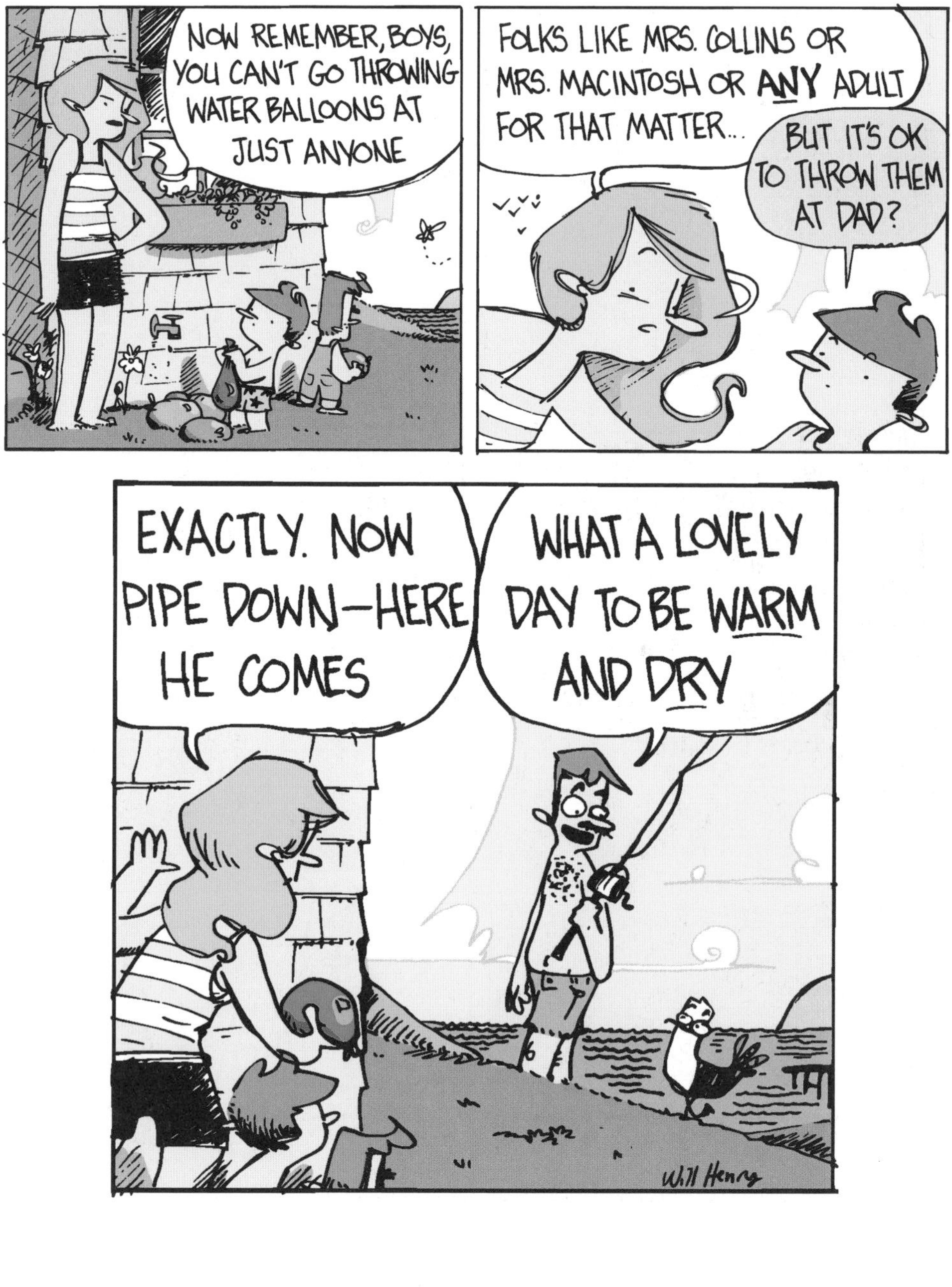
NOW REMEMBER, BOYS, YOU CAN'T GO THROWING WATER BALLOONS AT JUST ANYONE
FOLKS LIKE MRS. COLLINS OR MRS. MACINTOSH OR ANY ADULT FOR THAT MATTER...
BUT IT'S OK TO THROW THEM AT DAD?
EXACTLY. NOW PIPE DOWN—HERE HE COMES
WHAT A LOVELY DAY TO BE WARM AND DRY
Will Henry

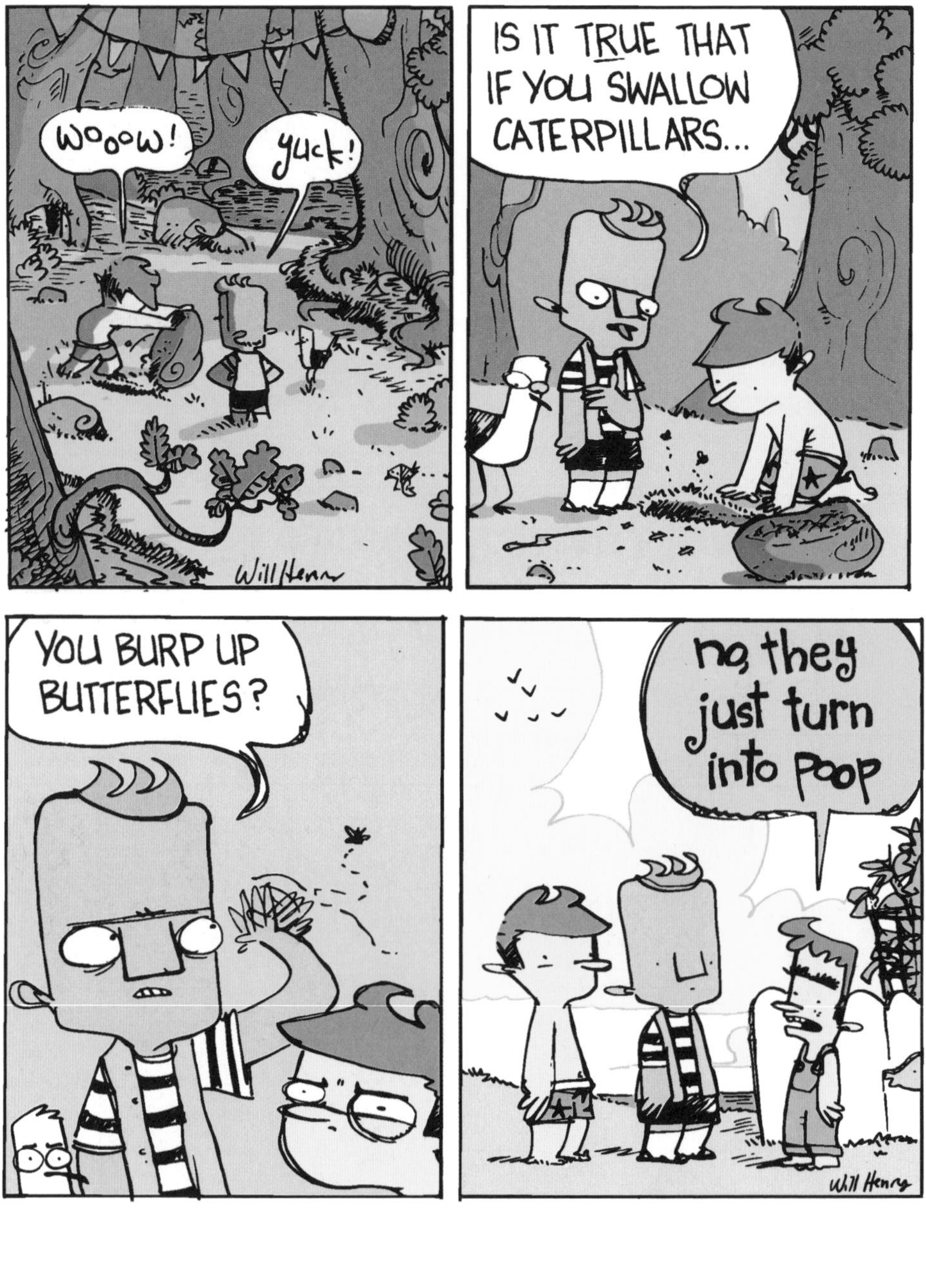
WOoOW!
yuck!
Will Henry
IS IT TRUE THAT IF YOU SWALLOW CATERPILLARS...
YOU BURP UP BUTTERFLIES?
no, they just turn into poop
Will Henry

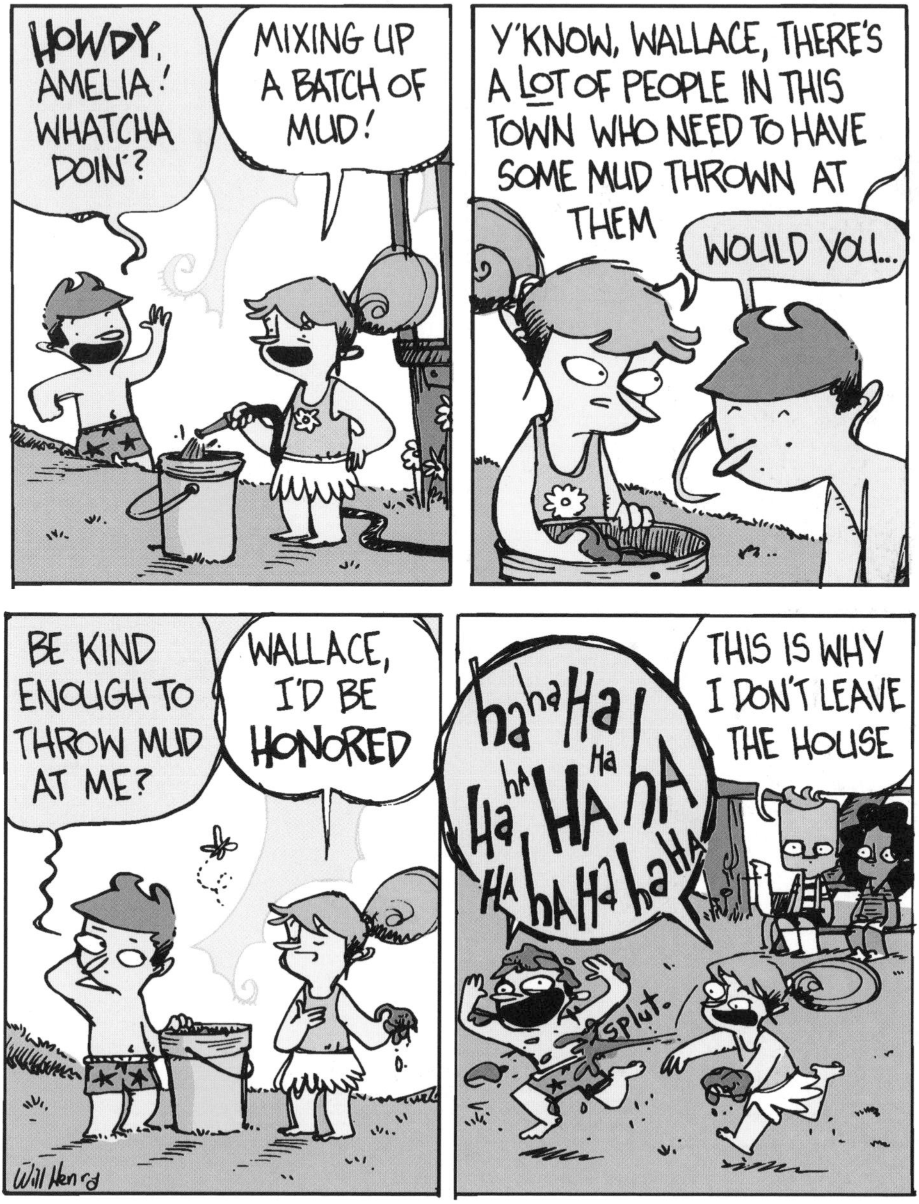
HOWDY, AMELIA! WHATCHA DOIN'?
MIXING UP A BATCH OF MUD!
Y'KNOW, WALLACE, THERE'S A LOT OF PEOPLE IN THIS TOWN WHO NEED TO HAVE SOME MUD THROWN AT THEM
WOULD YOU...
BE KIND ENOUGH TO THROW MUD AT ME?
WALLACE, I'D BE HONORED
haha Ha ha Ha ha Ha HA hA Ha haHa haHA
THIS IS WHY I DON'T LEAVE THE HOUSE
SPLUT.
Will Henry

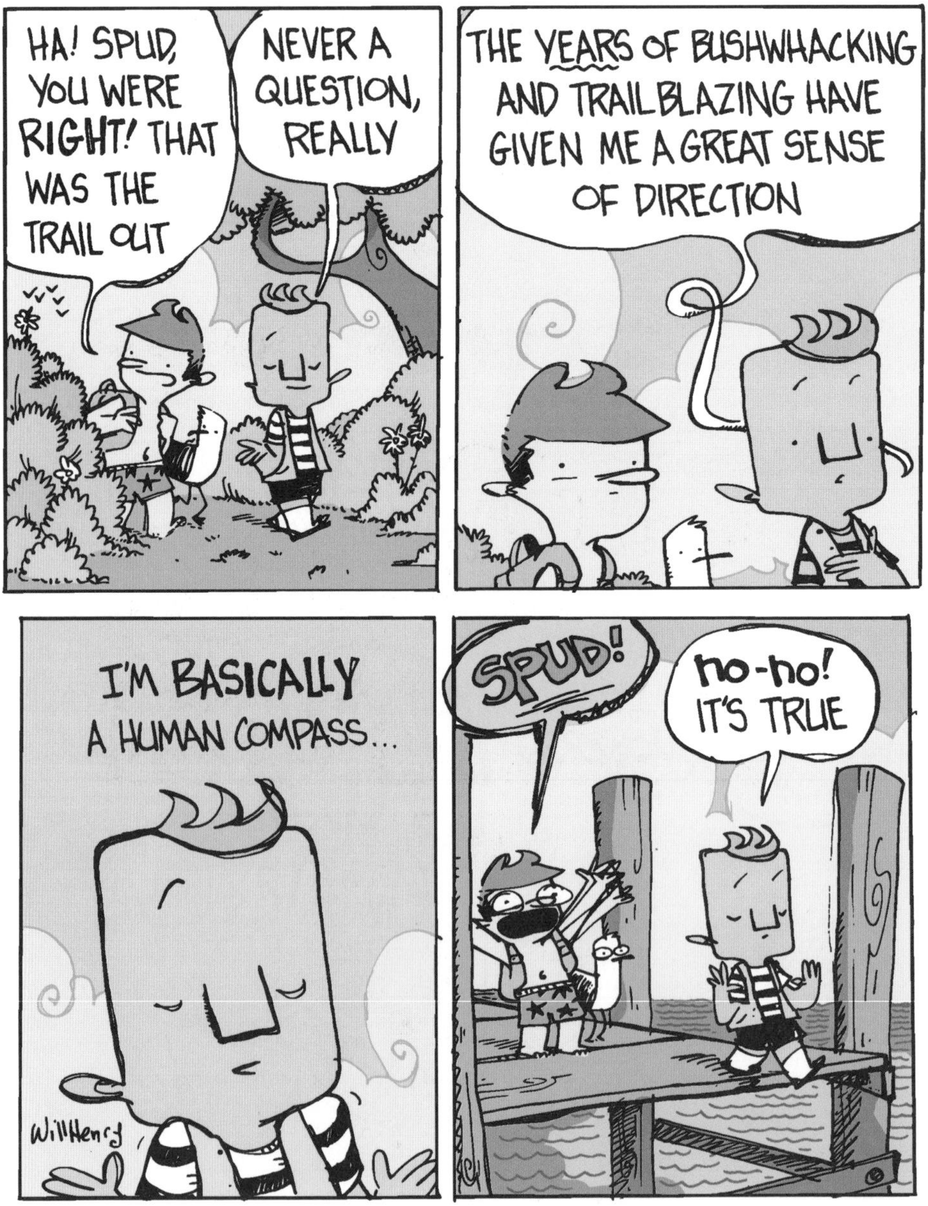
HA! SPUD, YOU WERE RIGHT! THAT WAS THE TRAIL OUT
NEVER A QUESTION, REALLY
THE YEARS OF BUSHWHACKING AND TRAILBLAZING HAVE GIVEN ME A GREAT SENSE OF DIRECTION
I'M BASICALLY A HUMAN COMPASS...
WillHenry
SPUD!
no-no! IT'S TRUE

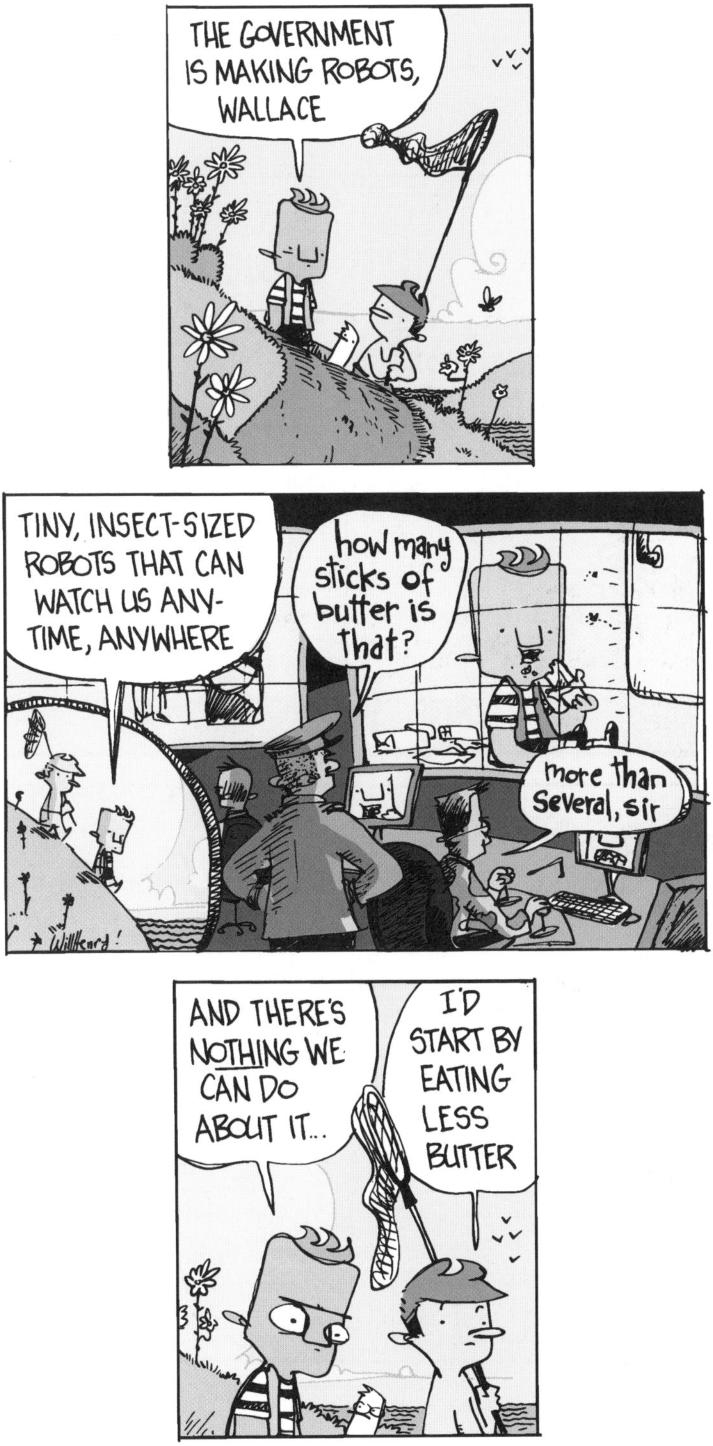
THE GOVERNMENT IS MAKING ROBOTS, WALLACE
TINY, INSECT-SIZED ROBOTS THAT CAN WATCH US ANY-TIME, ANYWHERE
how many sticks of butter is that?
more than several, sir
WillHenry!
AND THERE'S NOTHING WE CAN DO ABOUT IT...
I'D START BY EATING LESS BUTTER

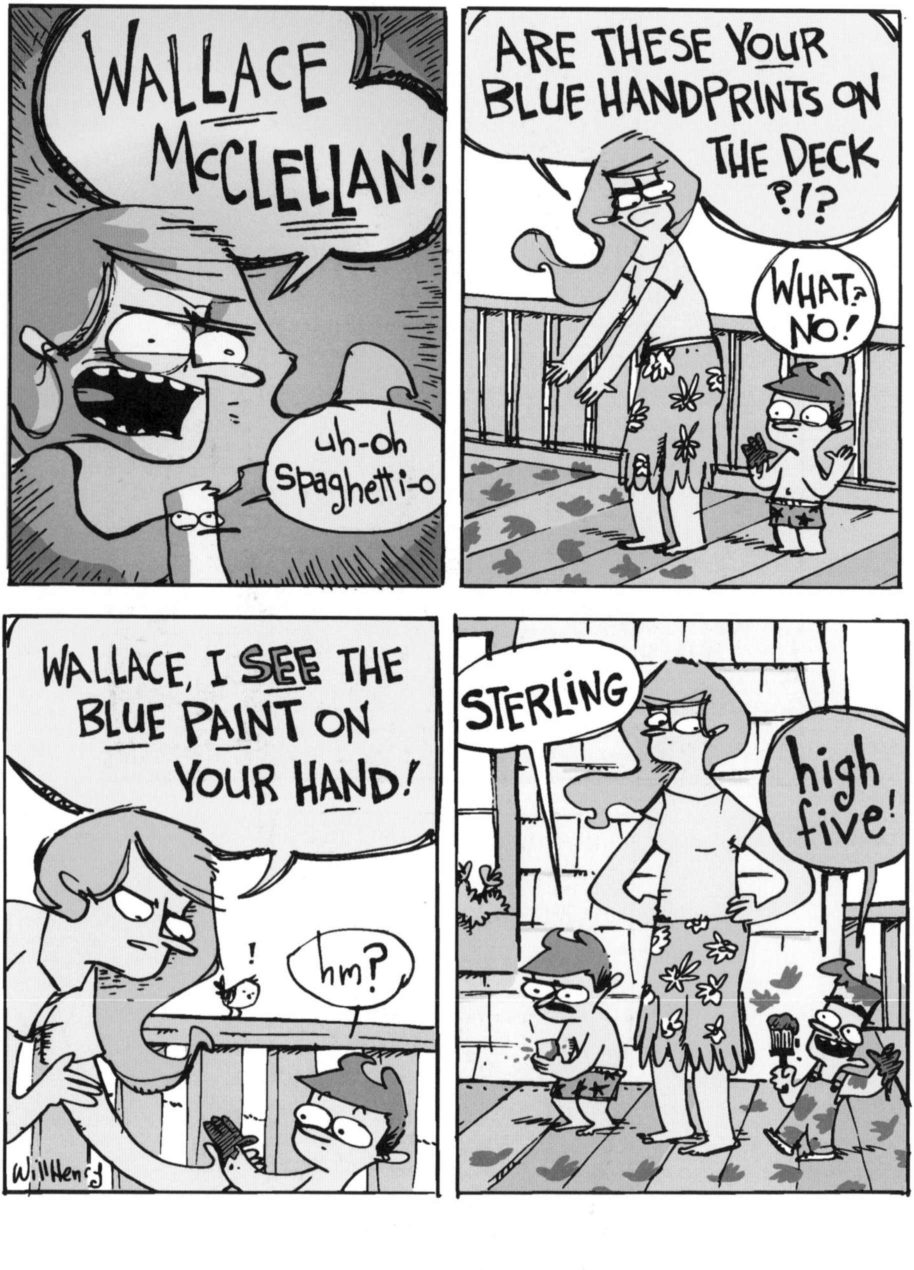
WALLACE McCLELLAN!
uh-oh spaghetti-o
ARE THESE YOUR BLUE HANDPRINTS ON THE DECK ?!?
WHAT? NO!
WALLACE, I SEE THE BLUE PAINT ON YOUR HAND!
!
hm?
WillHenry
STERLING
high five!

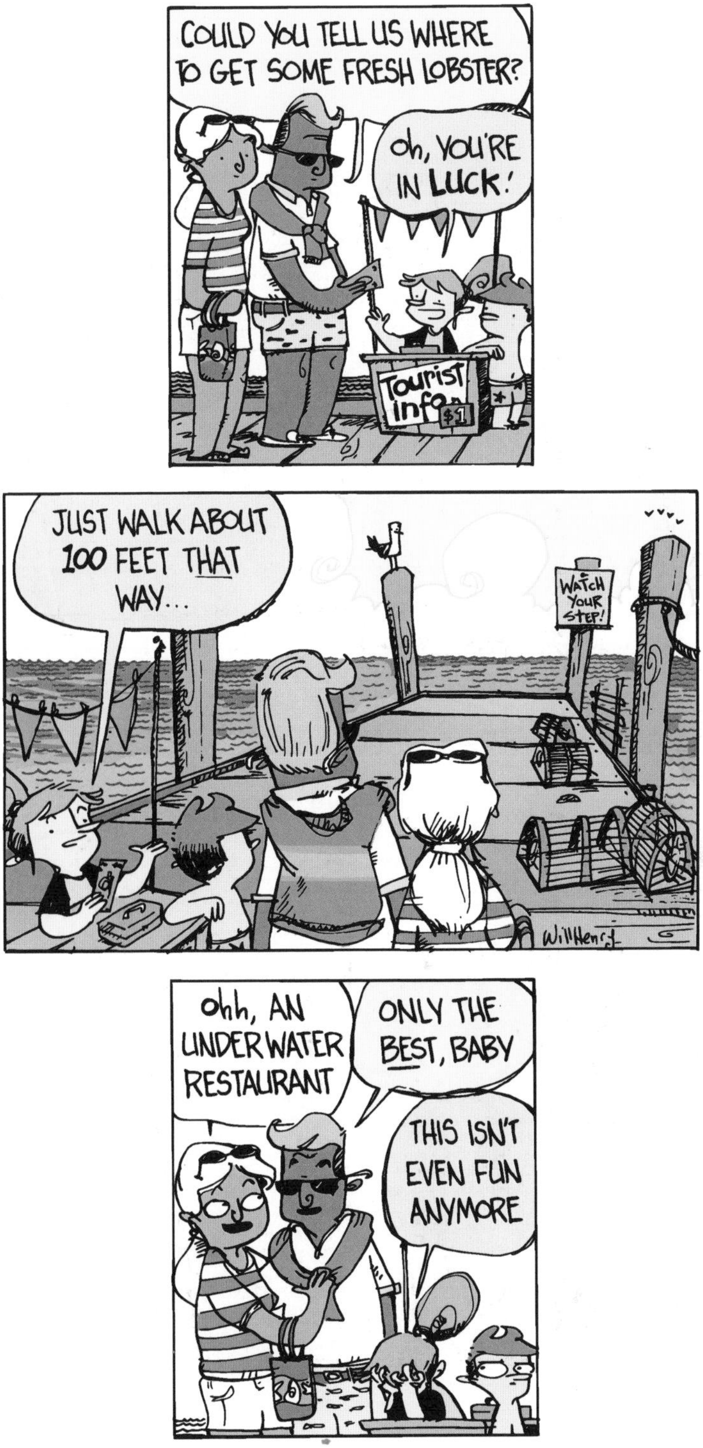
COULD YOU TELL US WHERE TO GET SOME FRESH LOBSTER?
oh, YOU'RE IN LUCK!
Tourist info
$1
JUST WALK ABOUT 100 FEET THAT WAY...
WATCH YOUR STEP!
Ohh, AN UNDERWATER RESTAURANT
ONLY THE BEST, BABY
THIS ISN'T EVEN FUN ANYMORE

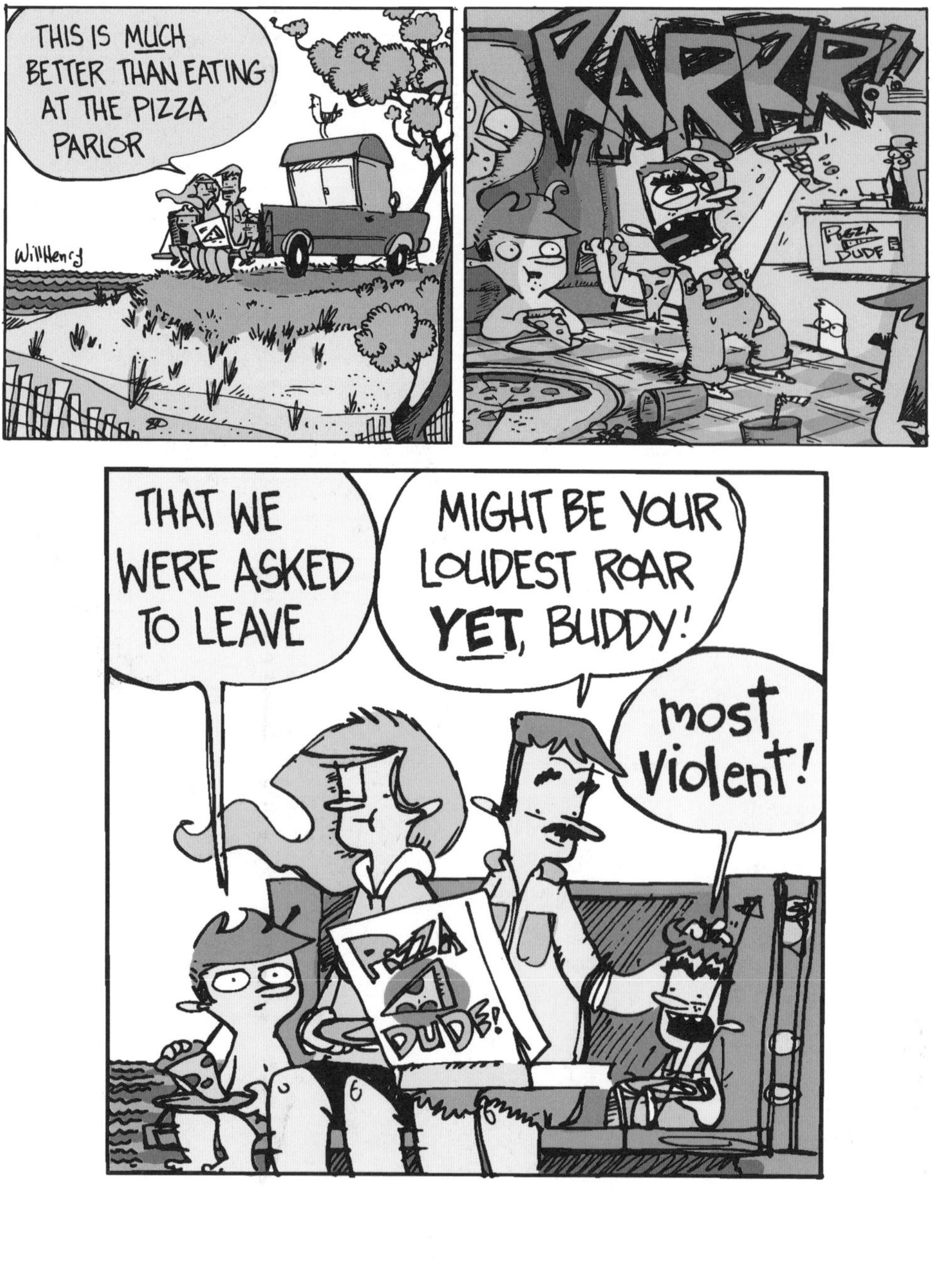

THIS IS MUCH BETTER THAN EATING AT THE PIZZA PARLOR
WillHenry
RARRR!!
PIZZA DUDE
THAT WE WERE ASKED TO LEAVE
MIGHT BE YOUR LOUDEST ROAR YET, BUDDY!
most violent!
PIZZA DUDE!

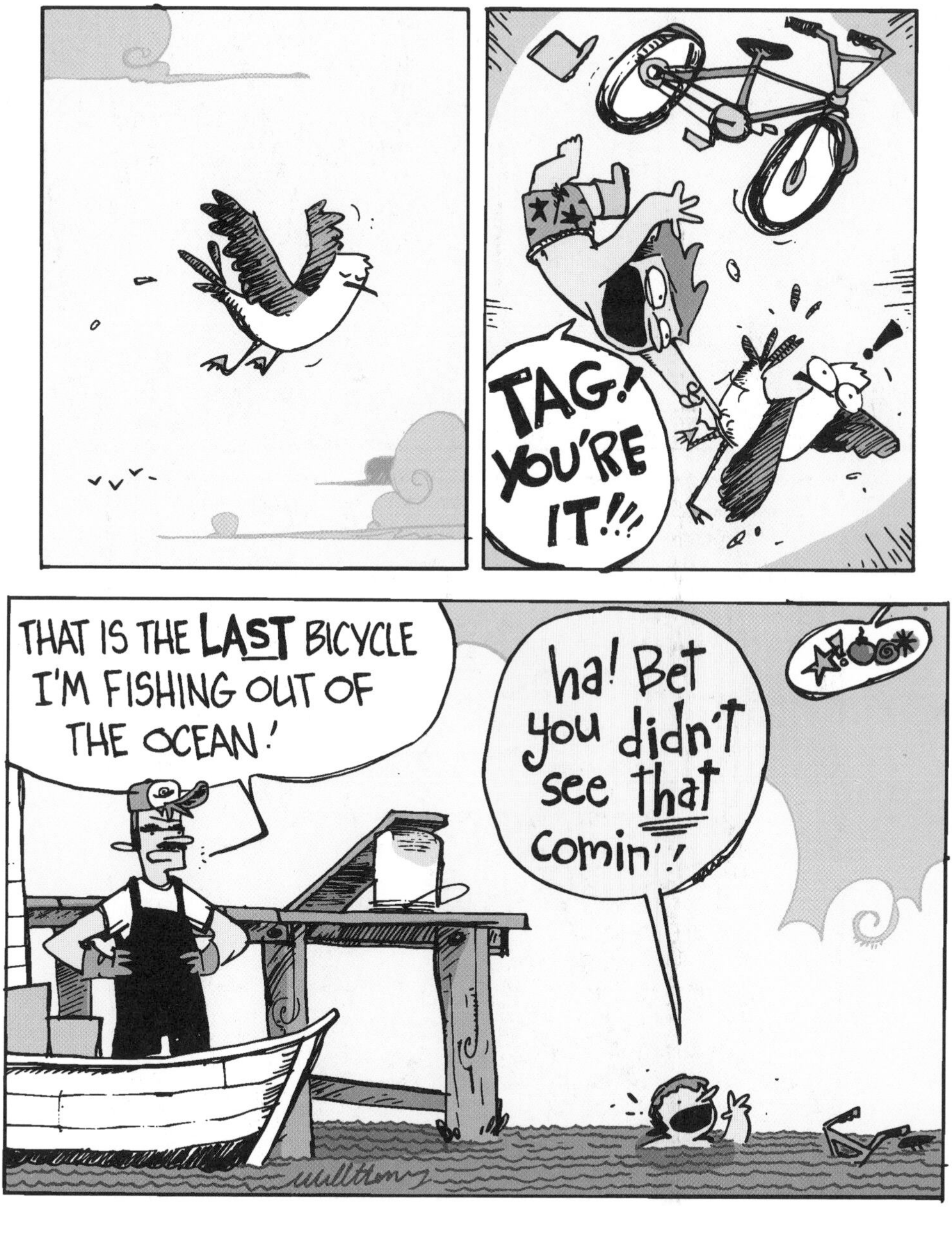
TAG! YOU'RE IT!!!
THAT IS THE LAST BICYCLE I'M FISHING OUT OF THE OCEAN!
ha! Bet you didn't see that comin'!

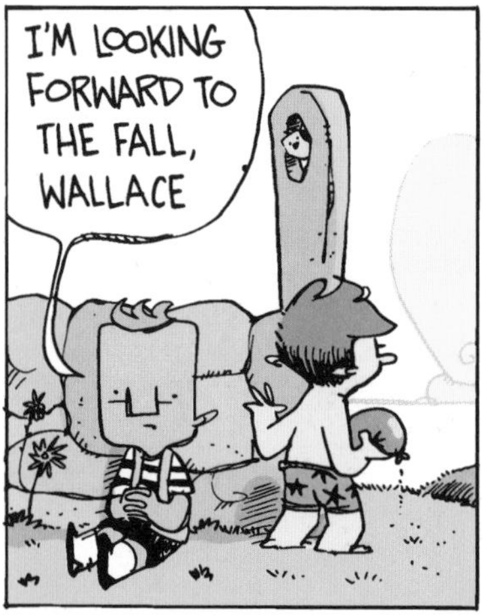
I'M LOOKING FORWARD TO THE FALL, WALLACE

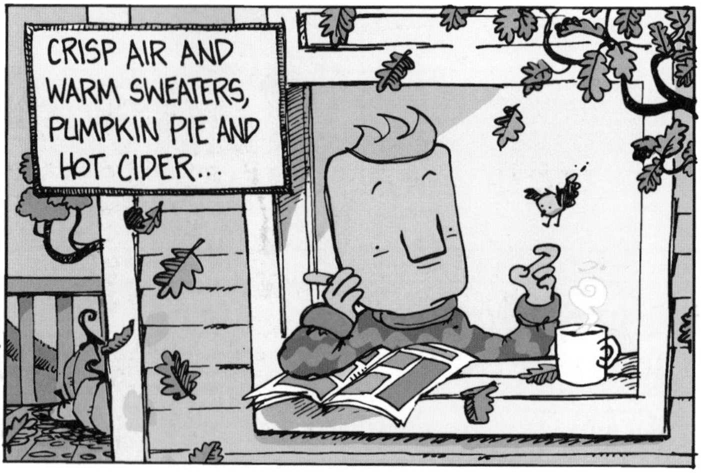
CRISP AIR AND WARM SWEATERS, PUMPKIN PIE AND HOT CIDER...

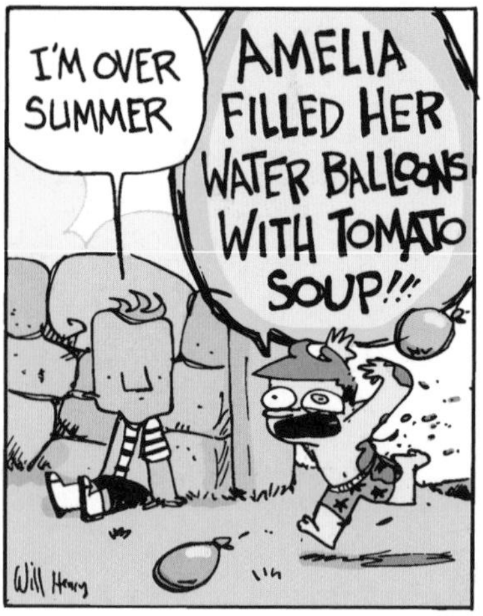
I'M OVER SUMMER
AMELIA FILLED HER WATER BALLOONS WITH TOMATO SOUP!!!
Will Henry

Will Henry
WHAT HAPPENED TO THE PICTURES OF OUR FAMILY?
WE SEE THOSE MUGS EVERY DAY

Seed Bombs

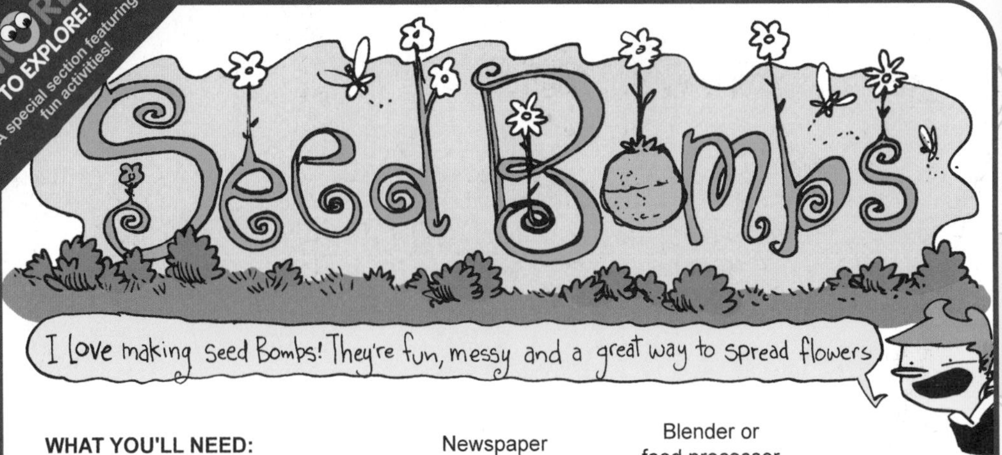
Seed Bombs
I love making Seed Bombs! They're fun, messy and a great way to spread flowers

WHAT YOU'LL NEED:

Flower seeds

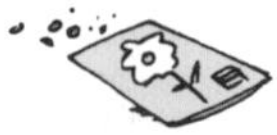

Soil

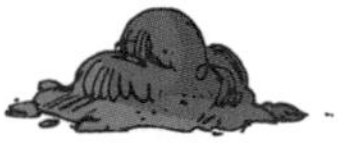

Newspaper or construction paper

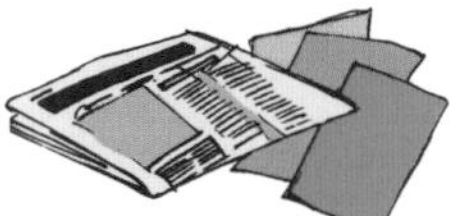

Blender or food processor

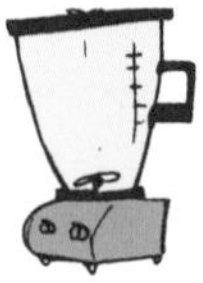

Strainer

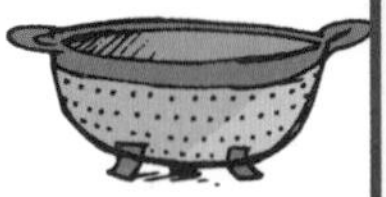

Tear up the paper into little pieces and put into a bowl.

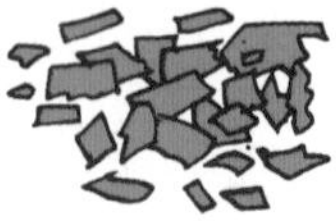

Fill the bowl with water until the paper is covered and let sit for 15 minutes.

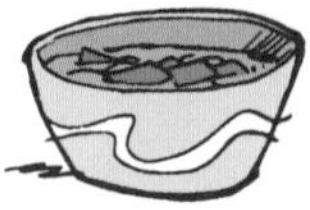

Pour paper and water into a blender or food processor and blend until it's a pulp.

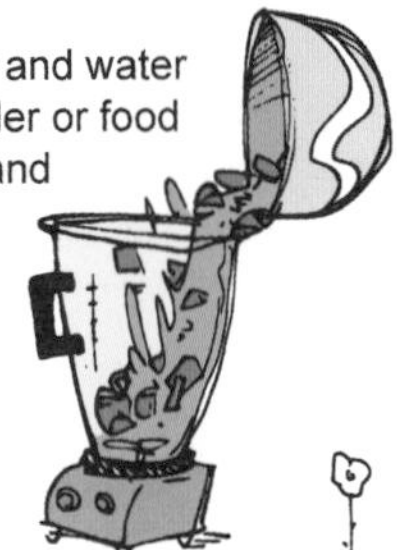

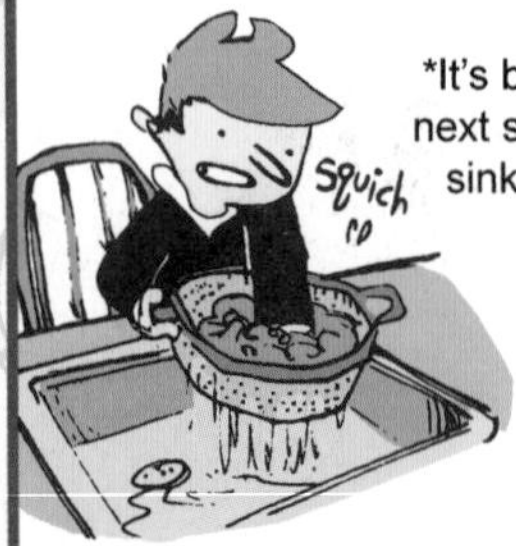
Squich

It's best to do the next steps over the sink or outside

Pour the pulp into a strainer and squeeze out as much water as you can.

Take a small scoop of pulp and press it into your hand to make a cup shape.

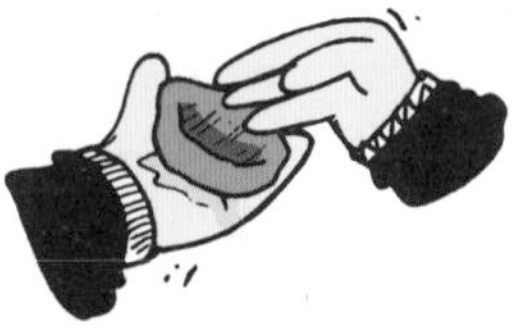

Add some soil to the cup and sprinkle the flower seeds on top.

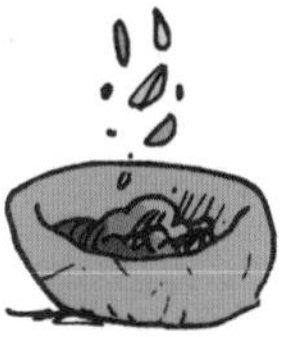

Add more pulp to the top of the soil and press into place, squeezing out as much water as you can.

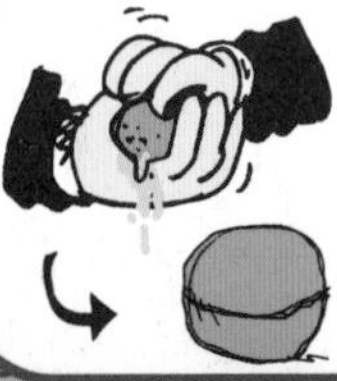

Let your Seed Bombs dry for 24 hours.

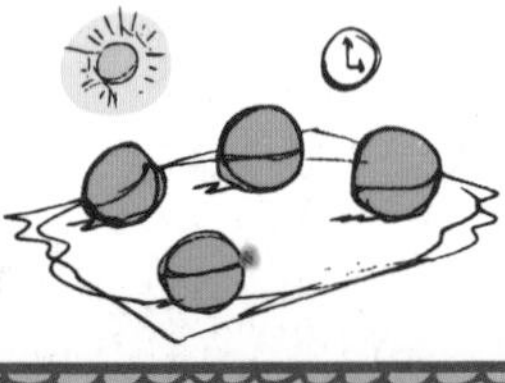

Once your Seed Bombs are dry, you can toss them wherever you want a flower to grow!

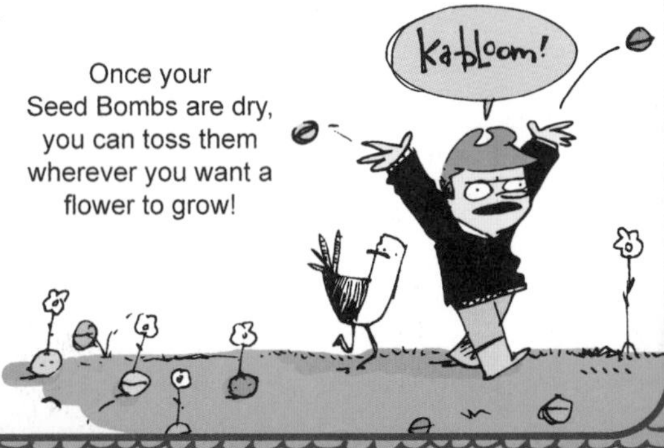
Kabloom!

MAKE YOUR OWN ROCK CANDY

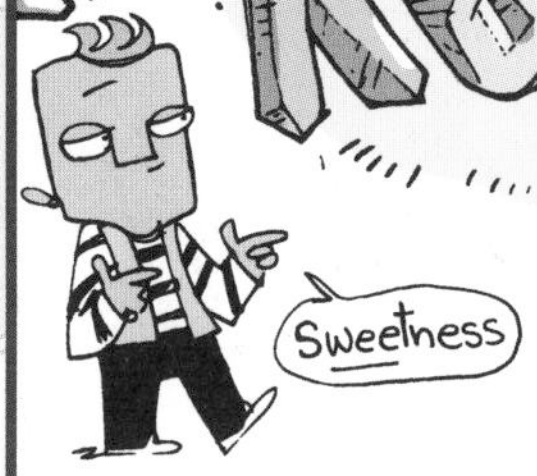
Sweetness

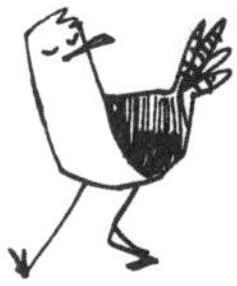

WHAT YOU'LL NEED:

Wooden skewers

Sugar

Water

Mason jars or similar size containers

Clothespins

Food coloring

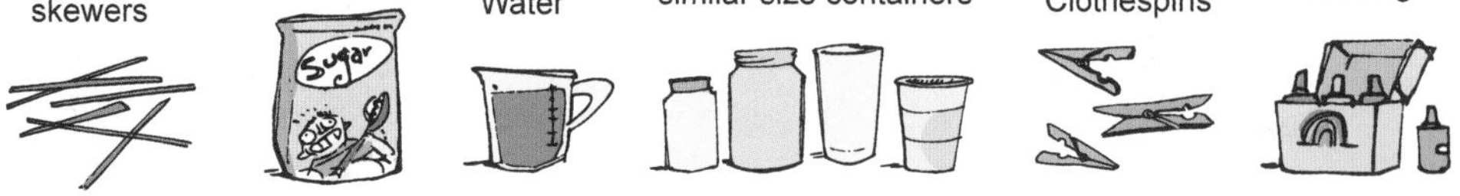
Sugar

With a parent's supervision, bring two cups of water to a boil.

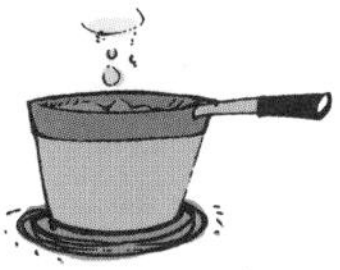

Slowly stir in four cups of sugar until dissolved, then remove from heat.

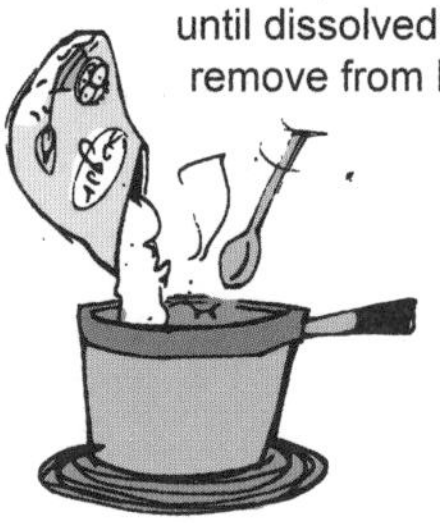

While waiting for the solution to cool (15–20 min), wet the skewers and roll them in sugar.

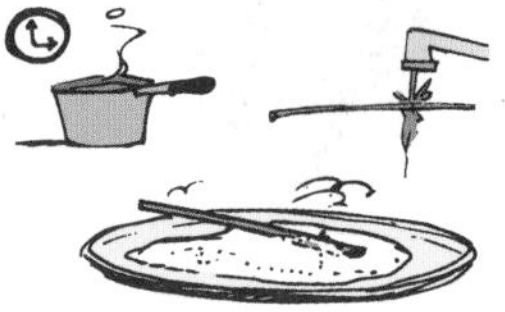

Set skewers aside and let dry. This will be the base for your crystals to grow. You will need one skewer per jar.

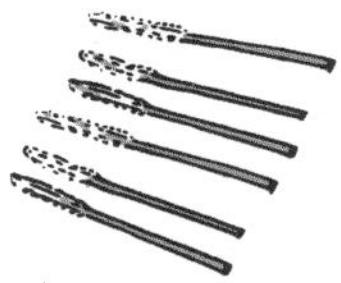

Once the sugar solution is cooled, carefully pour into jars. You can add food coloring to the jars if you'd like.

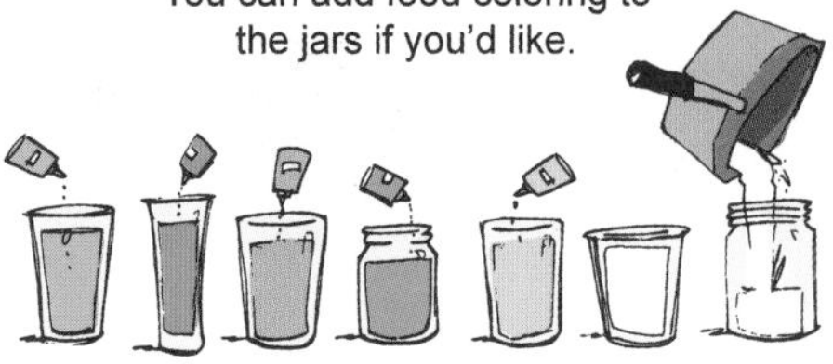

Dunk the skewers into the sugar solution, making sure not to touch the sides of the jar, and secure with a clothespin.

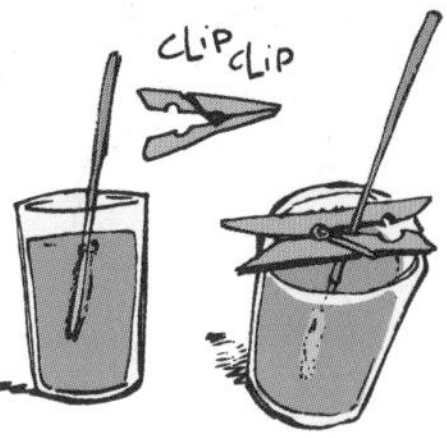
CLIP CLIP

Let the skewers sit in the jars for one week.

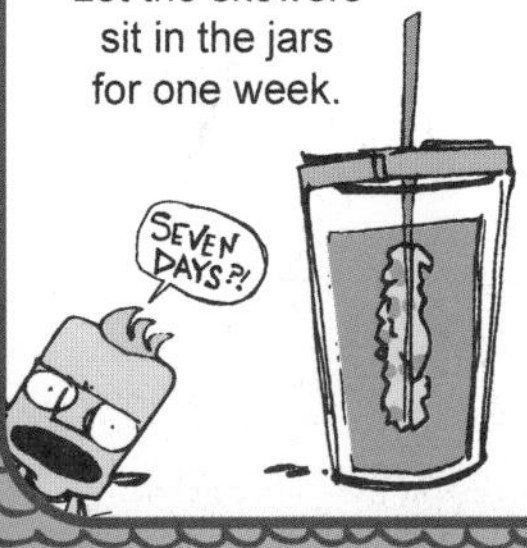
SEVEN DAYS?!

Once the crystals have formed, you can take the skewers out and enjoy your rock candy.

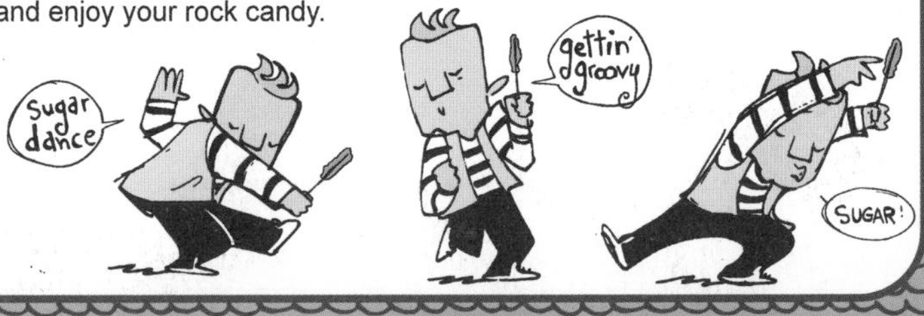
Sugar dance
gettin' groovy
SUGAR!

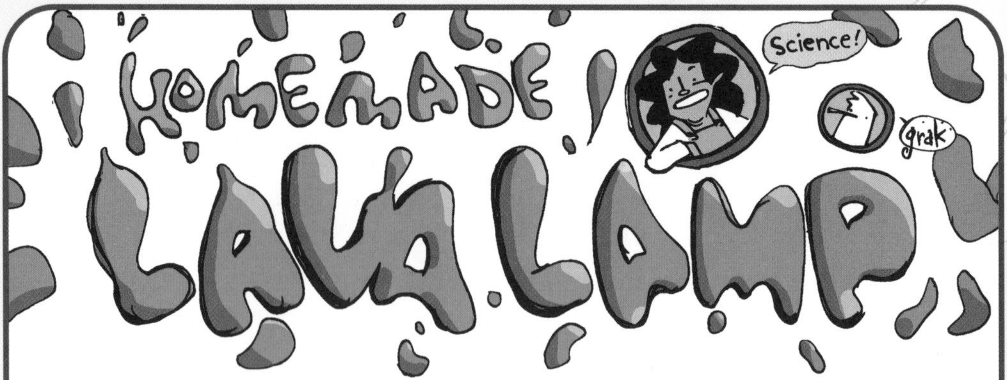
HOMEMADE
LAVA LAMP
Science!
grak

WHAT YOU'LL NEED:

Water

Alka-Seltzer

Vegetable oil

Food coloring

A large, clear bottle or jar (preferably with a cap)

Positive attitude

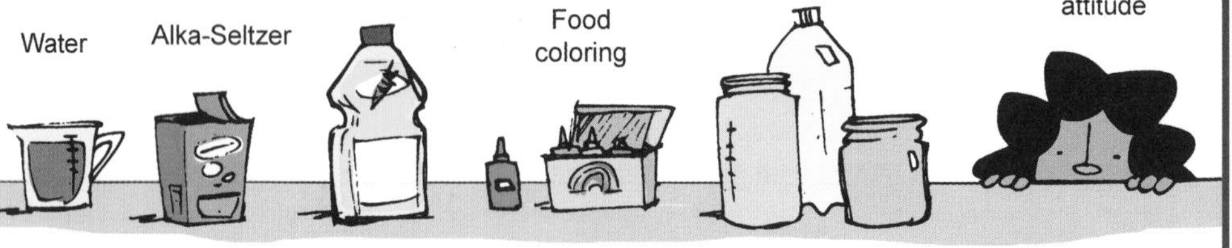

Fill 3/4 of the jar with the vegetable oil.

Fill the remaining space of the jar with water. Let sit until the water settles on the bottom.

Add a few drops of food coloring. The little blobs of coloring will drop to the bottom of the jar.

Break an Alka-Seltzer tablet into small pieces, and drop them into the jar one at a time.

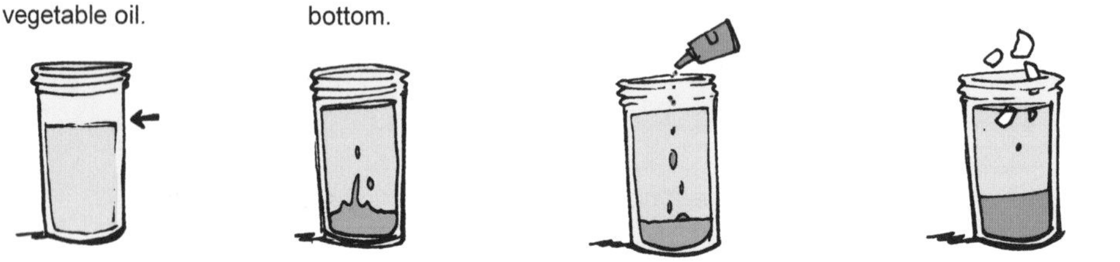

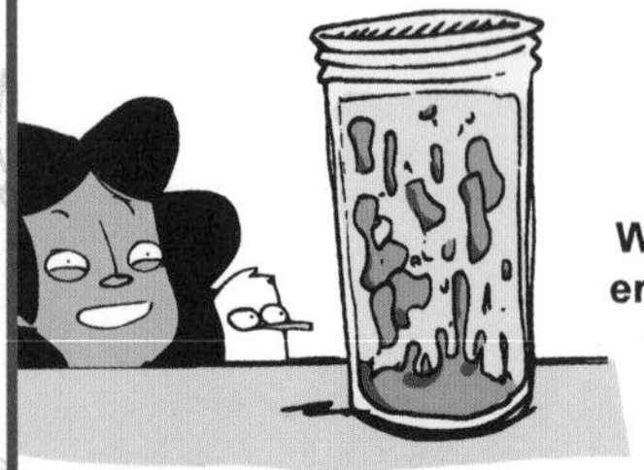

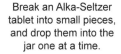

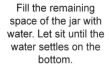

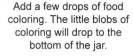

Watch the colors erupt in your lava lamp!

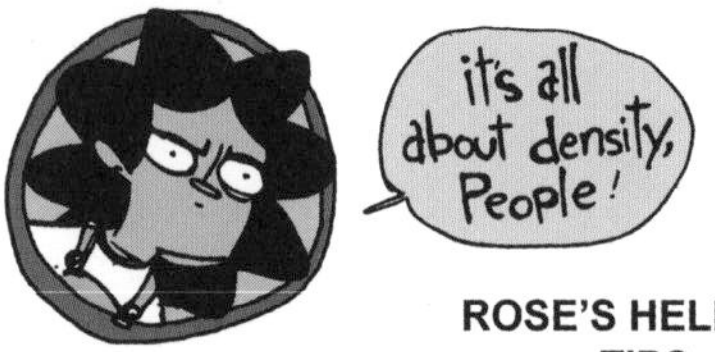
it's all about density, People!

ROSE'S HELPFUL TIPS

It's really neat to shine a flashlight through your lava lamp, especially in the dark.

When your lava lamp is done reacting, put a cap on the jar and save it for later.

Whenever your lava lamp loses its fizz, add more pieces of Alka-Seltzer.

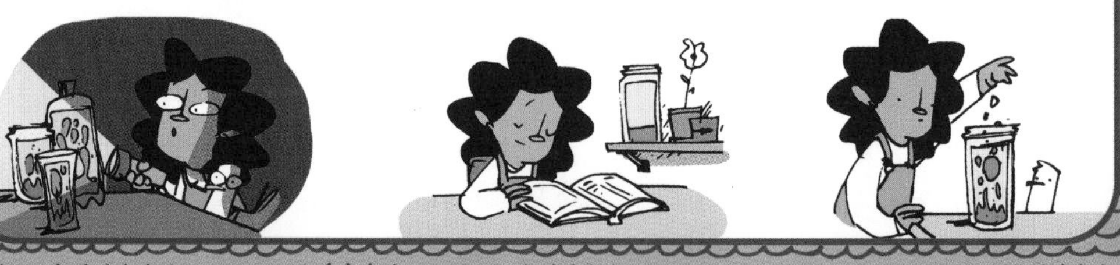

Wallace the Brave is distributed internationally by Andrews McMeel Syndication.

Andrews McMeel Publishing
a division of Andrews McMeel Universal
1130 Walnut Street, Kansas City, Missouri 64106

www.andrewsmcmeel.com

23 24 25 26 27 SDB 10 9 8 7 6 5 4 3 2 1

ISBN: 978-1-5248-8647-9

Library of Congress Control Number: 2023933233

Made by:
RR Donnelley (Guangdong) Printing Solutions Company Ltd
Address and location of manufacturer:
No. 2, Minzhu Road, Daning, Humen Town,
Dongguan City, Guangdong Province, China 523930
1st Printing—5/29/23

Look for these books!

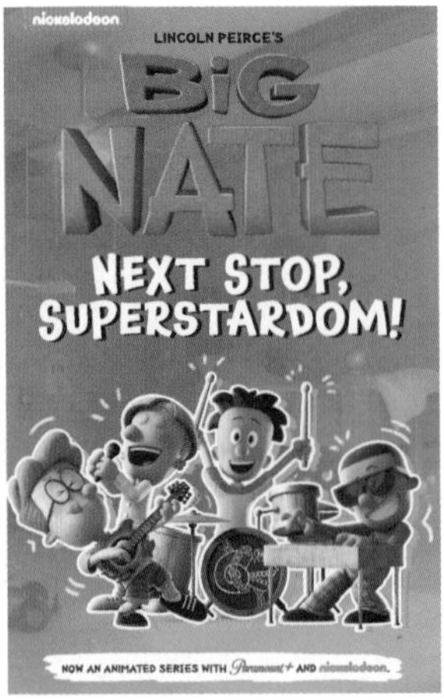
nickelodeon
LINCOLN PEIRCE'S
BIG NATE
NEXT STOP, SUPERSTARDOM!
NOW AN ANIMATED SERIES WITH Paramount+ AND nickelodeon.

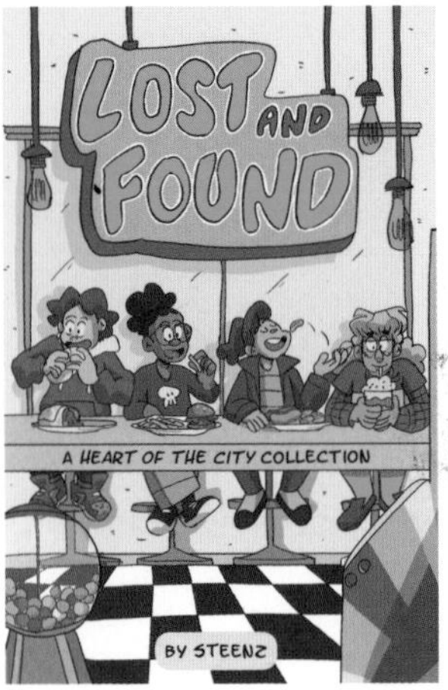
LOST AND FOUND
A HEART OF THE CITY COLLECTION
BY STEENZ

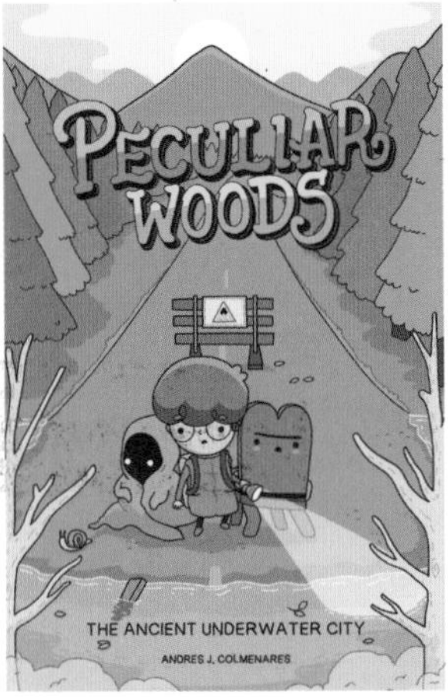
PECULIAR WOODS
THE ANCIENT UNDERWATER CITY
ANDRES J. COLMENARES

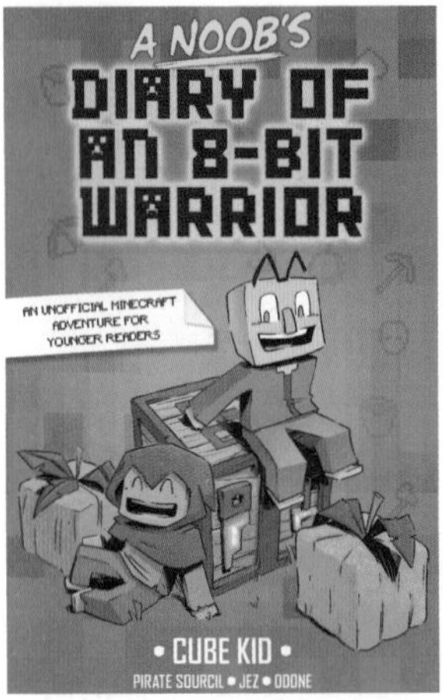
A NOOB'S
DIARY OF AN 8-BIT WARRIOR
AN UNOFFICIAL MINECRAFT ADVENTURE FOR YOUNGER READERS
• CUBE KID •
PIRATE SOURCIL • JEZ • ODONE

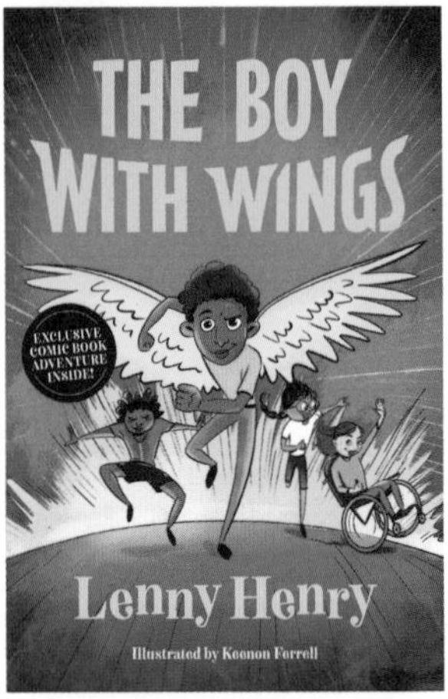
THE BOY WITH WINGS
EXCLUSIVE COMIC BOOK ADVENTURE INSIDE!
Lenny Henry
Illustrated by Keenon Ferrell

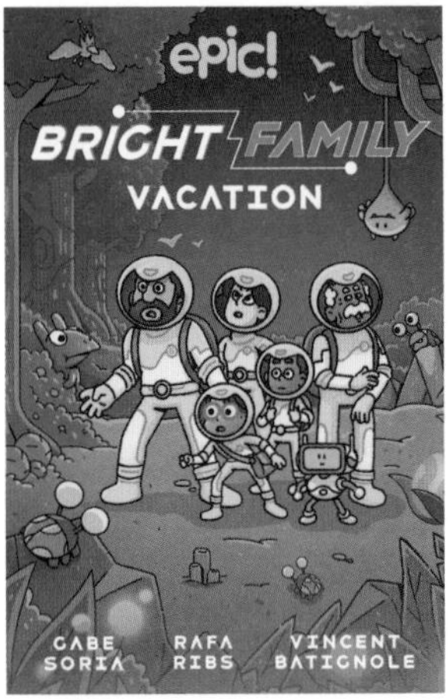
epic!
BRIGHT FAMILY
VACATION
GABE SORIA
RAFA RIBS
VINCENT BATIGNOLE

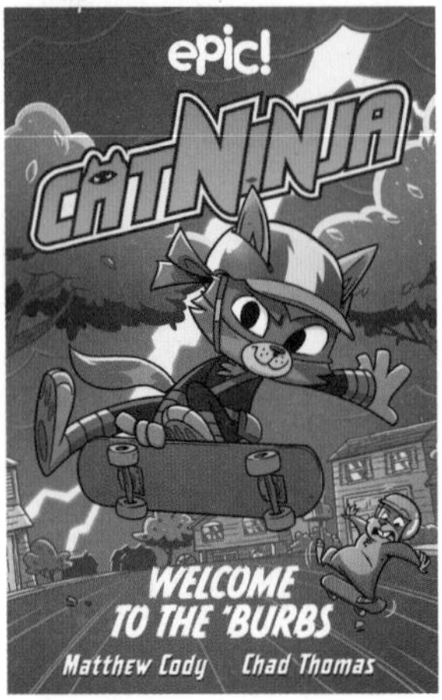
epic!
CATNINJA
WELCOME TO THE 'BURBS
Matthew Cody
Chad Thomas

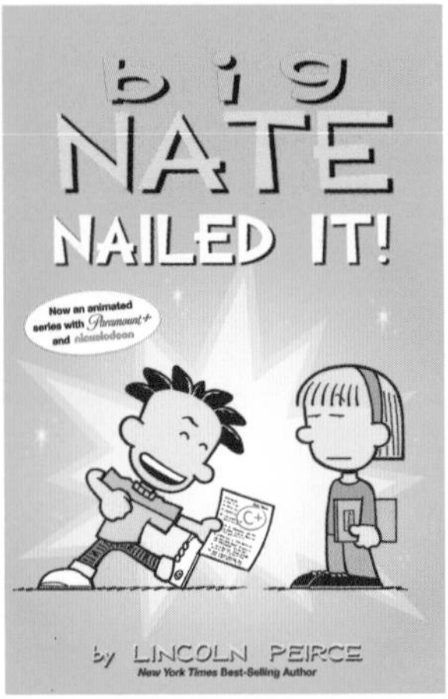
big NATE
NAILED IT!
Now an animated series with Paramount+ and nickelodeon
by LINCOLN PEIRCE
New York Times Best-Selling Author

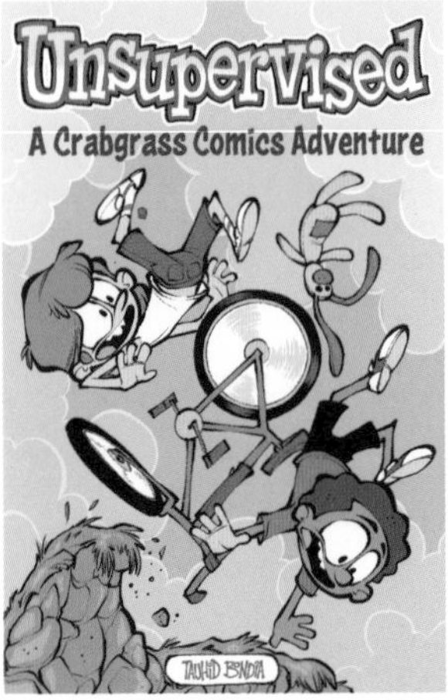
Unsupervised
A Crabgrass Comics Adventure
TAUHID BONDIA